EVERYMAN, I will go with thee,
and be thy guide,
In thy most need to go by thy side

SAKI ⟨H. H. MUNRO⟩

Born at Akyab, Burma, on 18 December 1870.
From 1902 to 1908 was foreign correspondent of
the *Morning Post*. Served as a private in the Royal
Fusiliers during the First World War, and died at
Beaumont-Hamel on 14 November 1916.

SAKI

Short Stories

Chosen by Emlyn Williams

Dent: London and Melbourne
EVERYMAN'S LIBRARY

© Preface and selection
J. M. Dent & Sons Ltd, 1978
All rights reserved
Made in Great Britain by
Guernsey Press Co. Ltd, Guernsey, C.I. for
J. M. Dent & Sons Ltd
Aldine House, 33 Welbeck Street, London W1M 8LX
First published in Everyman's Library in 1978
Reprinted 1980, 1982, 1985

British Library Cataloguing in Publication Data

Saki
    Saki: short stories
    I. Williams, Emlyn, b.1905
    823'.9'1FS   PR6025.U675

    ISBN 0–460–11105–1

CONTENTS

Preface	11
The Romancers	15
A Holiday Task	18
The Unkindest Blow	23
The Unrest-Cure	27
The Remoulding of Groby Lington	32
The Seven Cream Jugs	39
The Hounds of Fate	44
A Bread and Butter Miss	50
Fur	55
The Philanthropist and the Happy Cat	59
The Easter Egg	63
Morlvera	66
The Occasional Garden	70
The Secret Sin of Septimus Brope	74
The Blind Spot	81
The Reticence of Lady Anne	85
Tobermory	88
The Match-Maker	95
The Yarkand Manner	97
The Byzantine Omelette	101
Gabriel-Ernest	105
The Quince Tree	112
Excepting Mrs Pentherby	115

Laura	120
The Seventh Pullet	124
Tea	129
The Lumber-Room	133
The Treasure-Ship	138
The Background	142
The Stalled Ox	145
The Disappearance of Crispina Umberleigh	149
The Interlopers	153
Mrs Packletide's Tiger	159
The Way to the Dairy	162
The Gala Programme	168
The Schartz-Metterklume Method	171
Quail Seed	176
The Open Window	181
Louise	184
The Dreamer	187
Dusk	191
The Hedgehog	195
The Image of the Lost Soul	200
The Threat	202
The Sex that Doesn't Shop	206
Sredni Vashtar	208
The Chaplet	212
The Story of St Vespaluus	216
The Cupboard of the Yesterdays	223
The Phantom Luncheon	226

The Lull 230

The Story-Teller 234

Birds on the Western Front 239

The Mappined Life 242

A Defensive Diamond 246

PREFACE

In 1930, when I was an actor-playwright seeking a foothold in London, I was persuaded to sample the Saki stories by an older friend who – like thousands of other young people before the First World War – had eagerly awaited them as they came out in the *Westminster Gazette* and was later to re-treasure them in the trenches where the author was to lose his life.

I was immediately captivated by the gentle bite of the humour (just gentle enough not to draw blood), by the stylish wit, by the off-hand unexpected absurdities – by the sheer *fun* of the thing. A second reaction was to realize how much the stories had influenced Noël Coward, whose *Private Lives* had just opened. ('Whose yacht is that?' 'The Duke of Westminster's, it always is . . .' '. . . Certain women should be struck regularly. Like gongs . . .') On top of the fun, I was particularly drawn to the brilliant simplicity of *The Open Window*, and even toyed with the idea of making a one-act play of it; but the genre was out of fashion, and I moved on.

Forty-five years later, in 1975, my son presented me with a new issue of Saki. Refreshing my memory, I found myself looking at the stories with a new startled eye. For some time I had been presenting in the theatre, at intervals, pieces from Dickens and Dylan Thomas, adapted for solo performance; with this behind me, I was conditioned to realize that Saki was equally rich material for the spoken word. The qualities which I had long before appreciated, came to life with almost more spontaneity than on the printed page.

What was more (and as important), I found the comedy counterpointed by the 'dark' stories, in which sly urbanity runs – side by side, and uniquely – with the grimmest fantasy. Such a piece as *Sredni Vashtar* would provide the perfect, and essential, contrast to the frivolities.

I straightaway embarked on the two-year task of preparing *The Playboy of the Week-End World, a Solo Entertainment from the stories of Saki*. And since this started with weeks of reading everything he wrote (including the plays, *The Baker's Dozen*, *The Death-Trap*, *The Watched Pot*, which are a disappointment), I am relieved to feel that there is no danger of a reader of this book writing in with 'I do think you might have bothered to examine that rare gem which is my favourite, only to be found in the edition of . . .' I've examined them all.

Mind you, I am still faced with the spiky question to which any anthologist must be resigned. 'Why have you included "X" which I've never thought first-rate, and left out "Y" which is the best of all?'

The reproach is particularly to be expected in the case of our author. When engaged in performing the 'entertainment', I have found audiences divided into two categories, which must perforce be paralleled in a reading public. The first consists of people who have only known Saki vaguely by name, some even guessing him to be an exotic Oriental poet: and since they are legion, it is my pleasant duty, in the theatre, to get them acquainted with him, to their delight.

An ironical point about this category: even the ones who have settled for the Oriental poet, are invariably astonished to learn the source of one quotation with which they have been familiar for years — 'you mean *Saki* wrote that?' The quotation being, of course: 'The cook was a good cook, as cooks go; and as cooks go she went.' (It is so well-known, in fact, that I decided to use it only by transference. In a prologue, the author — through his mouthpiece the actor — explains his adoption of the *nom de plume*.

'I made a quick decision, asking nobody's consent:
    I thought "*H. H. Munro?*
    A good name, as names go" —
    And as names go . . . it went!'
And was replaced by *Saki*. Why *Saki*? It is the name of the wine-bearer in *The Rubáiyát* of Omar Khayyám ('Chosen, I think, because the wistful philosophy of Fitzgerald appealed to him and he took the name from that fine poet's verses,' said his friend Rothay Reynolds years later).

My second audience-category, a comparative minority but an important one, is formed of readers so devoted as to merit the title of 'Sakiologists'. 'You're doing *The Interlopers*, aren't you? And *The Unrest Cure*? And that choice line "Discipline, to be effective, must be optional"? And "A cat may have nine lives, but only one liver"?' Since Saki published 135 stories, and in the theatre I have used only 16, I have — more often than not — to give a disappointing answer. To which I always hasten to add that items which are effective on the printed page can fail to come to life in the theatre. During my long preliminary journey through the stories, over and over again I found myself frustrated: *The Philanthropist, The Schwartz-*

Metterklume Method, Morlvera – one after the other, they stubbornly refused to light up.

A baffling example of this was one of the best-known pieces, *Tobermory*, which I am happy to include in this selection. It is the inspired account of the panic caused at a house-party by a cat which has learnt to speak English as fluently and loftily as a man-about-town. I found that while the idea could be hilarious as a film cartoon synchronized with the right human voice, on the stage it simly could not work.

Conversely, I found that pieces which had, at first glance, looked unpromising for the theatre, came thrillingly to life before an audience: *Gabriel-Ernest, The Open Window* – and one particular one, very little known, which enables the performance to end on a new and poignant facet of Saki's talent. In *Birds on the Western Front*, he takes an entirely individual look at War: a Flanders private, an ornithologist, describes the nightmare around him as it affects the bird-life, also around him. A Bird's Eye View, literally. I felt it essential to include this rare piece in the present collection.

I have not found it easy to make my choices – 55 stories out of 135! And among the 55, few which one could confidently eliminate as near-misses; it was a relief to get to one which I could be sure wasn't good enough. It is hardly necessary to mention that I have kept in mind the essential aim to present both sides of the Saki coin, the 'witty' and the 'weird'; including, in both, his ambivalent love-fear attitude towards animals and children.

I have also tried to cater for methodical readers who prefer to progress systematically through a succession of stories. For such a menu, I have avoided too long a section of light courses (the 'witty') by interpolating, at intervals, a more substantial dish (the 'weird'). If the collection leads new readers to venture further, into the richness among the remaining 81 stories, and in the novel *The Unbearable Bassington*, I'll have done what I wanted. Noël Coward wrote that Saki had been one of the most significant influences on his career. What was good enough for him is good enough for me. And (I feel you'll agree) good enough for you too.

EMLYN WILLIAMS

THE ROMANCERS

It was autumn in London, that blessed season between the harshness of winter and the insincerities of summer; a trustful season when one buys bulbs and sees in the registration of one's vote, believing perpetually in spring and a change of Government.

Morton Crosby sat on a bench in a secluded corner of Hyde Park, lazily enjoying a cigarette and watching the slow grazing promenade of a pair of snow-geese, the male looking rather like an albino edition of the russet-hued female. Out of the corner of his eye Crosby also noted with some interest the hesitating hoverings of a human figure, which had passed and repassed his seat two or three times at shortening intervals, like a wary crow about to alight near some possibly edible morsel. Inevitably the figure came to an anchorage on the bench, within easy talking distance of its original occupant. The uncared-for clothes, the aggressive, grizzled beard, and the furtive, evasive eye of the new-comer bespoke the professional cadger, the man who would undergo hours of humiliating tale-spinning and rebuff rather than adventure on half a day's decent work.

For a while the new-comer fixed his eyes straight in front of him in a strenuous, unseeing gaze; then his voice broke out with the insinuating inflection of one who has a story to retail well worthy any loiterer's while to listen to.

'It's a strange world,' he said.

As the statement met with no response he altered it to the form of a question.

'I dare say you've found it to be a strange world, mister?'

'As far as I am concerned,' said Crosby, the strangeness has worn off in the course of thirty-six years.'

'Ah,' said the greybeard, 'I could tell you things that you'd hardly believe. Marvellous things that have really happened to me.'

Nowadays there is not demand for marvellous things that have really happened,' said Crosby discouragingly; 'the professional writers of fiction turn these things out so much better. For instance, my neighbours tell me wonderful, incredible things that their Aberdeens and chows and borzois have done; I never listen to them. On the other hand, I have read *The Hound of the Baskervilles* three times.'

The greybeard moved uneasily in his seat; then he opened up new country.

'I take it that you are a professing Christian,' he observed.

'I am a prominent and I think I may say an influential member of the Mussulman community of Eastern Persia,' said Crosby, making an excursion himself into the realms of fiction.

The greybeard was obviously disconcerted at this new check of introductory conversation, but the defeat was only momentary.

'Persia. I should never have taken you for a Persian,' he remarked, with a somewhat aggrieved air.

'I am not,' said Crosby; 'my father was an Afghan.'

'An Afghan!' said the other, smitten into bewildered silence for a moment. Then he recovered himself and renewed his attack.

'Afghanistan. Ah! We've had some wars with that country; now, I dare say, instead of fighting it we might have learned something from it. A very wealthy country, I believe. No real poverty there.'

He raised his voice on the word 'poverty' with a suggestion of intense feeling. Crosby saw the opening and avoided it.

'It possesses, nevertheless, a number of highly talented and ingenious beggars,' he said; 'if I had not spoken so disparagingly of marvellous things that have really happened I would tell you the story of Ibrahim and the eleven camel-loads of blotting-paper. Also I have forgotten exactly how it ended.'

'My own life-story is a curious one,' said the stranger, apparently stifling all desire to hear the history of Ibrahim; 'I was not always as you see me now.'

'We are supposed to undergo complete change in the course of every seven years,' said Crosby, as an explanation of the foregoing announcement.

'I mean I was not always in such distressing circumstances as I am at present,' pursued the stranger doggedly.

'That sounds rather rude,' said Crosby stiffly, considering that you are at present talking to a man reputed to be one of the most gifted conversationalists of the Afghan border.'

'I don't mean in that way,' said the greybeard hastily; 'I've been very much interested in your conversation. I was alluding to my unfortunate financial situation. You mayn't hardly believe it, but at the present moment I am absolutely without a farthing. Don't see any prospect of getting any money, either, for the next few days. I don't suppose you've ever found yourself in such a position,' he added.

'In the town of Yom,' said Crosby, 'which is in Southern Afghanistan, and which also happens to be my birthplace, there was a Chinese philosopher who used to say that one of the three chief human blessings was to be absolutely without money. I forget what the other two were.'

'Ah, I dare say,' said the stranger, in a tone that betrayed no enthusiasm for the philosopher's memory, 'and did he practise what he preached? That's the test.'

'He lived happily with very little money or resources,' said Crosby.

'Then I expect he had friends who would help him liberally whenever he was in difficulties, such as I am in at present.'

'In Yom,' said Crosby, 'it is not necessary to have friends in order to obtain help. Any citizen of Yom would help a stranger as a matter of course.'

The greybeard was now genuinely interested. The conversation had at last taken a favourable turn.

'If some one, like me, for instance, who was in undeserved difficulties, asked a citizen of that town you speak of for a small loan to tide over a few days' impecuniosity – five shillings, or perhaps a rather larger sum – would it be given to him as a matter of course?'

'There would be a certain preliminary,' said Crosby; 'one would take him to a wine-shop and treat him to a measure of wine, and then after a little high-flown conversation, one would put the desired sum in his hand and wish him good-day. It is a roundabout way of performing a simple transaction, but in the East all ways are roundabout.'

The listener's eyes were glittering.

'Ah,' he exclaimed, with a thin sneer ringing meaningly through his words, 'I suppose you've given up all those generous customs since you left your town. Don't practise them now, I expect.'

'No one who has lived in Yom,' said Crosby fervently, 'and remembers its green hills covered with apricot and almond trees, and the cold water that rushes down like a caress from the upland snows and dashes under the little wooden bridges, no one who remembers these things and treasures the memory of them would ever give up a single one of its unwritten laws and customs. To me they are as binding as though I still lived in that hallowed home of my youth.'

'Then if I was to ask you for a small loan – ' began the grey-

beard fawningly, edging nearer on the seat and hurriedly
wondering how large he might safely make his request, 'if I
was to ask you for, say – '

'At any other time, certainly,' said Crosby; 'in the months of
November and December, however, it is absolutely forbidden
for any one of our race to give or receive loans or gifts; in fact,
one does not willingly speak of them. It is considered unlucky.
We will therefore close this discussion.'

'But it is still October!' exclaimed the adventurer with an eager,
angry whine, as Crosby rose from his seat; 'wants eight days to
the end of the month!'

'The Afghan November began yesterday,' said Crosby severely,
and in another moment he was striding across the Park, leaving
his recent companion scowling and muttering furiously on the
seat.

'I don't believe a word of his story,' he chattered to himself;
'pack of nasty lies from beginning to end. Wish I'd told him so
to his face. Calling himself an Afghan.'

The snorts and snarls that escaped from him for the next
quarter of an hour went far to support the truth of the old saying
that two of a trade never agree.

A HOLIDAY TASK

Kenelm Jerton entered the dining-hall of the Golden Galleon
Hotel in the full crush of the luncheon hour. Nearly every seat
was occupied, and small additional tables had been brought in,
where floor space permitted, to accommodate late-comers, with
the result that many of the tables were almost touching each
other. Jerton was beckoned by a waiter to the only vacant table
that was discernible, and took his seat with the uncomfortable
and wholly groundless idea that nearly every one in the room
was staring at him. He was a youngish man of ordinary appearance, quiet of dress and unobtrusive of manner, and he could
never wholly rid himself of the idea that a fierce light of public
scrutiny beat on him as though he had been a notability or a
super-nut. After he had ordered his lunch there came the unavoidable interval of waiting, with nothing to do but to stare at
the flower-vase on his table and to be stared at (in imagination)
by several flappers, some maturer beings of the same sex, and a

satirical-looking Jew. In order to carry off the situation with some appearance of unconcern he became spuriously interested in the contents of the flower-vase.

'What is the name of those roses, d'you know?' he asked the waiter. The waiter was ready at all times to conceal his ignorance concerning items of the wine-list or *menu*; he was frankly ignorant as to the specific name of the roses.

'*Amy Silvester Partington,*' said a voice at Jerton's elbow.

The voice came from a pleasant-faced, well-dressed young woman who was sitting at a table that almost touched Jerton's. He thanked her hurriedly and nervously for the information and made some inconsequent remark about the flowers.

'It is a curious thing,' said the young woman, that I should be able to tell you the name of those roses without an effort of memory, because if you were to ask me my name I should be utterly unable to give it to you.'

Jerton had not harboured the least intention of extending his thirst for name-labels to his neighbour. After her rather remarkable announcement, however, he was obliged to say something in the way of polite inquiry.

'Yes,' answered the lady, 'I suppose it is a case of partial loss of memory. I was in the train coming down here; my ticket told me that I had come from Victoria and was bound for this place. I had a couple of five-pound notes and a sovereign on me, no visiting cards or any other means of identification, and no idea as to who I am. I can hazily recollect that I have a title; I am Lady Somebody – beyond that my mind is blank.'

'Hadn't you any luggage with you?' asked Jerton.

'That is what I didn't know. I knew the name of this hotel and made up my mind to come here, and when the hotel porter who meets the trains asked if I had any luggage I had to invent a dressing-bag and dress-basket; I could always pretend that they had gone astray. I gave him the name of Smith, and presently he emerged from a confused pile of luggage and passengers with a dressing-bag and dress-basket labelled Kestrel-Smith. I had to take them; I don't see what else I could have done.'

Jerton said nothing, but he rather wondered what the lawful owner of the baggage would do.

'Of course it was dreadful arriving at a strange hotel with the name of Kestrel-Smith, but it would have been worse to have arrived without luggage. Anyhow, I hate causing trouble.'

Jerton had visions of harassed railway officials and distraught

Kestrel-Smiths, but he made no attempt to clothe his mental picture in words. The lady continued her story.

'Naturally, none of my keys would fit the things, but I told an intelligent page-boy that I had lost my key-ring, and he had the locks forced in a twinkling. Rather too intelligent that boy; he will probably end in Dartmoor. The Kestrel-Smith toilet tools aren't up to much, but they are better than nothing.'

'If you feel sure that you have a title,' said Jerton, 'why not get hold of a peerage and go right through it?'

'I tried that. I skimmed through the list of the House of Lords in "Whitaker," but a mere printed string of names conveys awfully little to one, you know. If you were an army officer and had lost your identity you might pore over the Army List for months without finding out who you were. I'm going on another tack. I'm trying to find out by various little tests who I am *not* – that will narrow the range of uncertainty down a bit. You may have noticed, for instance, that I'm lunching principally off lobster Newburg.'

Jerton had not ventured to notice anything of the sort.

'It's an extravagance, because it's one of the most expensive dishes on the *menu,* but at any rate it proves that I'm not Lady Starping; she never touches shell-fish, and poor Lady Braddleshrub has no digestion at all; if I am *her* I shall certainly die in agony in the course of the afternoon, and the duty of finding out who I am will devolve on the press and the police and those sort of people; I shall be past caring. Lady Knewford doesn't know one rose from another and she hates men, so she wouldn't have spoken to you in any case; and Lady Mousehilton flirts with every man she meets – I haven't flirted with you, have I?'

Jerton hastily gave the required assurance.

'Well, you see,' continued the lady, 'that knocks four off the list at once.'

'It'll be rather a lengthy process bringing the list down to one,' said Jerton.

'Oh, but, of course, there are heaps of them that I couldn't possibly be – women who've got grandchildren or sons old enough to have celebrated their coming of age. I've only got to consider the ones about my own age. I tell you how you might help me this afternoon, if you don't mind; go through any of the back numbers of *Country Life* and those sort of papers that you can find in the smoking-room, and see if you come across my portrait with infant son or anything of that sort. It won't take you ten minutes. I'll meet you in the lounge about tea-time. Thanks awfully.'

And the Fair Unknown, having graciously pressed Jerton into the search for her lost identity, rose and left the room. As she passed the young man's table she halted for a moment and whispered:

'Did you notice that I tipped the waiter a shilling? We can cross Lady Ulwight off the list; she would have died rather than do that.'

At five o'clock Jerton made his way to the hotel lounge; he had spent a diligent but fruitless quarter of an hour among the illustrated weeklies in the smoking-room. His new acquaintance was seated at a small tea-table, with a waiter hovering in attendance.

'China tea or Indian?' she asked as Jerton came up.

'China, please, and nothing to eat. Have you discovered anything?'

'Only negative information. I'm not Lady Befnal. She disapproves dreadfully at any form of gambling, so when I recognized a well-known bookmaker in the hotel lobby I went and put a tenner on an unnamed filly by William the Third out of Mitrovitza for the three-fifteen race. I suppose the fact of the animal being nameless was what attracted me.'

'Did it win?' asked Jerton.

'No, came in fourth, the most irritating thing a horse can do when you've backed it win or place. Anyhow, I know now that I'm not Lady Befnal.'

'It seems to me that the knowledge was rather dearly bought,' commented Jerton.

'Well, yes, it has rather cleared me out,' admitted the identity-seeker; 'a florin is about all I've got left on me. The lobster Newburg made my lunch rather an expensive one, and, of course, I had to tip that boy for what he did to the Kestrel-Smith locks. I've got rather a useful idea, though. I feel certain that I belong to the Pivot Club; I'll go back to town and ask the hall porter if there are any letters for me. He knows all the members by sight, and if there are any letters or telephone messages waiting for me, of course that will solve the problem. If he says there aren't any, I shall say: "You know who I am don't you?" so I'll find out anyway.'

The plan seemed a sound one; a difficulty in its execution suggested itself to Jerton.

'Of course,' said the lady, when he hinted at the obstacle, 'there's my fare back to town, and my bill here and cabs and things. If you lend me three pounds that ought to see me through comfortably. Thanks ever so. Then there is the question of that luggage: I don't want to be saddled with that for the rest of my life. I'll have it brought down to the hall and you can pretend to mount guard over it while I'm writing a letter. Then I shall just slip away to the station, and you can wander off to the smoking-room, and they can do what they like with the things. They'll advertise them after a bit and the owner can claim them.'

Jerton acquiesced in the manoeuvre, and duly mounted guard over the luggage while its temporary owner slipped unobtrusively out of the hotel. Her departure was not, however, altogether unnoticed. Two gentlemen were strolling past Jerton, and one of them remarked to the other:

'Did you see that tall young woman in grey who went out just now? She is the Lady—'

His promenade carried him out of earshot at the critical moment when he was about to disclose the elusive identity. The Lady Who? Jerton could scarcely run after a total stranger, break into his conversation, and ask him for information concerning a chance passer-by. Besides, it was desirable that he should keep up the appearance of looking after the luggage. In a minute or two, however, the important personage, the man who knew, came strolling back alone. Jerton summoned up all his courage and waylaid him.

'I think I heard you say you knew the lady who went out of the hotel a few minutes ago, a tall lady dressed in grey. Excuse me for asking if you could tell me her name; I've been talking to her for half an hour; she – er – she knows all my people and seems to know me, so I suppose I've met her somewhere before, but I'm blest if I can put a name to her. Could you – ?'

'Certainly. She's a Mrs Stroppe.'

'*Mrs*?' queried Jerton.

'Yes, she's the Lady Champion at golf in my part of the world. An awful good sort, and goes about a good deal in Society, but she has an awkward habit of losing her memory every now and then, and gets into all sorts of fixes. She's furious, too, if you make any illusion to it afterwards. Good day, sir.'

The stranger passed on his way, and before Jerton had had time to assimilate his information he found his whole attention centred on an angry-looking lady who was making loud and fretful-seeming inquiries of the hotel clerks.

'Has any luggage been brought here from the station by mistake, a dress-basket and dressing-case, with the name Kestrel-Smith? It can't be traced anywhere. I saw it put in at Victoria, that I'll swear. Why – there *is* my luggage! and the locks have been tampered with!'

Jerton heard no more. He fled down to the Turkish bath, and stayed there for hours.

THE UNKINDEST BLOW

The season of strikes seemed to have run itself to a standstill. Almost every trade and industry and calling in which a dislocation could possibly be engineered had indulged in that luxury. The last and least successful convulsion had been the strike of the World's Union of Zoological Garden attendants, who, pending the settlement of certain demands, refused to minister further to the wants of the animals committed to their charge or to allow any other keepers to take their place. In this case the threat of the Zoological Gardens authorities that if the men 'came out' the animals should come out also had intensified and precipitated the crisis. This imminent prospect of the larger carnivores, to say nothing of rhinoceroses and bull bison, roaming at large and unfed in the heart of London, was not one which permitted of prolonged conferences. The Government of the day, which from its tendency to be a few hours behind the course of events had been nicknamed the Government of the afternoon, was obliged to intervene with promptitude and decision. A strong force of Blue-jackets was despatched to Regent's Park to take over the temporarily abandoned duties of the strikers. Blue-jackets were chosen in preference to land forces, partly on account of the traditional readiness of the British Navy to go anywhere and do anything, partly by reason of the familiarity of the average sailor with monkeys, parrots, and other tropical fauna, but chiefly at the urgent request of the First Lord of the Admiralty, who was keenly desirous of an opportunity for performing some personal act of unobtrusive public service within the province of his department.

'If he insists on feeding the infant jaguar himself, in defiance of its mother's wishes, there may be another by-election in the north,' said one of his colleagues, with a hopeful inflection in his voice. 'By-elections are not very desirable at present, but we must not be selfish.'

As a matter of fact the strike collapsed peacefully without any outside intervention. The majority of the keepers had become so attached to their charges that they returned to work of their own accord.

And then the nation and the newspapers turned with a sense of relief to happier things. It seemed as if a new era of contentment was about to dawn. Everybody had struck who could possibly want to strike or who could possibly be cajoled or bullied into striking, whether they wanted to or not. The lighter and brighter side of life might now claim some attention. And conspicuous among the other topics that sprang into sudden prominence was the pending Falvertoon divorce suit.

The Duke of Falvertoon was one of thost human *hors d'oeuvres* that stimulate the public appetite for sensation without giving it much to feed on. As a mere child he had been precociously brilliant; he had declined the editorship of the *Anglian Review* at an age when most boys are content to have declined *mensa*, a table, and though he could not claim to have originated the Futurist movement in literature, his 'Letters to a Possible Grandson,' written at the age of fourteen, had attracted considerable notice. In later days his brilliancy had been less conspicuously displayed. During a debate in the House of Lords on affairs in Morocco, at a moment when that country, for the fifth time in seven years, had brought half Europe to the verge of war, he had interpolated the remark 'a little Moor and how much it is,' but in spite of the encouraging reception accorded to this one political utterance he was never tempted to a further display in that direction. It began to be generally understood that he did not intend to supplement his numerous town and country residences by living overmuch in the public eye.

And then had come the unlooked-for tidings of the imminent proceedings for divorce. And such a divorce! There were cross-suits and allegations and counter-allegations, charges of cruelty and desertion, everything in fact that was necessary to make the case one of the most complicated and sensational of its kind. And the number of distinguished people involved or cited as witnesses not only embraced both political parties in the realm and several Colonial governors, but included an exotic contingent from France,

Hungary, the United States of North America, and the Grand Duchy of Baden. Hotel accommodation of the more expensive sort began to experience a strain on its resources. 'It will be quite like the Durbar without the elephants,' exclaimed an enthusiastic lady who, to do her justice, had never seen a Durbar. The general feeling was one of thankfulness that the last of the strikes had been got over before the date fixed for the hearing of the great suit.

As a reaction from the season of gloom and industrial strife that had just passed away the agencies that purvey and stage-manage sensations laid themselves out to do their level best on this momentous occasion. Men who had made their reputations as special descriptive writers were mobilized from distant corners of Europe and the further side of the Atlantic in order to enrich with their pens the daily printed records of the case; one word-painter, who specialized in descriptions of how witnesses turn pale under cross-examination, was summoned hurriedly back from a famous and prolonged murder trial in Sicily, where indeed his talents were being decidedly wasted. Thumb-nail artists and expert kodak manipulators were retained at extravagant salaries, and special dress reporters were in high demand. An enterprising Paris firm of costume builders presented the defendant Duchess with three special creations, to be worn, marked, learned, and extensively reported at various critical stages of the trial; and as for the cinematograph agents, their industry and persistence was untiring. Films representing the Duke saying good-bye to his favourite canary on the eve of the trial were in readiness weeks before the event was due to take place; other films depicted the Duchess holding imaginary consultations with fictitious lawyers or making a light repast off specially advertised vegetarian sandwiches during a supposed luncheon interval. As far as human foresight and human enterprise could go nothing was lacking to make the trial a success.

Two days before the case was down for hearing the advance reporter of an important syndicate obtained an interview with the Duke for the purpose of gleaning some final grains of information concerning his Grace's personal arrangements during the trial.

'I suppose I may say this will be one of the biggest affairs of its kind during the lifetime of a generation,' began the reporter as an excuse for the unsparing minuteness of detail that he was about to make quest for.

'I suppose so – if it comes off,' said the Duke lazily.

'If?' queried the reporter, in a voice that was something between a gasp and a scream.

'The Duchess and I are both thinking of going on strike,' said the Duke.

'Strike!'

The baleful word flashed out in all its old hideous familiarity. Was there to be no end to its recurrence?

'Do you mean,' faltered the reporter, 'that you are contemplating a mutual withdrawal of the charges?'

'Precisely,' said the Duke.

'But think of the arrangements that have been made, the special reporting, the cinematographs, the catering for the distinguished foreign witnesses, the prepared music-hall allusions; think of all the money that has been sunk –'

'Exactly,' said the Duke coldly, 'the Duchess and I have realized that it is we who provide the material out of which this great far-reaching industry has been built up. Widespread employment will be given and enormous profits made during the duration of the case, and we, on whom all the stress and racket falls, will get – what? An unenviable notoriety and the privilege of paying heavy legal expenses whichever way the verdict goes. Hence our decision to strike. We don't wish to be reconciled; we fully realize that it is a grave step to take, but unless we get some reasonable consideration out of this vast stream of wealth and industry that we have called into being we intend coming out of Court and staying out. Good afternoon.'

The news of this latest strike spread universal dismay. Its inaccessibility to the ordinary methods of persuasion made it peculiarly formidable. If the Duke and Duchess persisted in being reconciled the Government could hardly be called on to interfere. Public opinion in the shape of social ostracism might be brought to bear on them, but that was as far as coercive measures could go. There was nothing for it but a conference, with powers to propose liberal terms. As it was, several of the foreign witnesses had already departed and others had telegraphed cancelling their hotel arrangements.

The conference, protracted, uncomfortable, and occasionally acrimonious, succeeded at last in arranging for a resumption of litigation, but it was a fruitless victory. The Duke, with a touch of his earlier precocity, died of premature decay, a fortnight before the date fixed for the new trial.

THE UNREST-CURE

On the rack in the railway carriage immediately opposite Clovis was a solidly wrought travelling bag, with a carefully written label, on which was inscribed, 'J. P. Huddle, The Warren, Tilfield, near Slowborough.' Immediately below the rack sat the human embodiment of the label, a solid, sedate individual, sedately dressed, sedately conversational. Even without his conversation (which was addressed to a friend seated by his side, and touched chiefly on such topics as the backwardness of Roman hyacinths and the prevalence of measles at the Rectory), one could have gauged fairly accurately the temperament and mental outlook of the travelling bag's owner. But he seemed unwilling to leave anything to the imagination of a casual observer, and his talk grew presently personal and introspective.

'I don't know how it is,' he told his friend, 'I'm not much over forty, but I seem to have settled down into a deep groove of elderly middle-age. My sister shows the same tendency. We like everything to be exactly in its accustomed place; we like things to happen exactly at their appointed times; we like everything to be usual, orderly, punctual, methodical, to a hair's breadth, to a minute. It distresses and upsets us if it is not so. For instance, to take a very trifling matter, a thrush has built its nest year after year in the catkin-tree on the lawn; this year, for no obvious reason, it is building in the ivy on the garden wall. We have said very little about it, but I think we both feel that the change is unnecessary, and just a little irritating.'

'Perhaps,' said the friend, 'it is a different thrush.'

'We have suspected that,' said J. P. Huddle, 'and I think it gives us even more cause for annoyance. We don't feel that we want a change of thrush at our time of life! and yet, as I have said, we have scarcely reached an age when these things should make themselves seriously felt.'

'What you want,' said the friend,' is an Unrest-cure.'

'An Unrest-Cure? I've never heard of such a thing.'

'You've heard of Rest-cures for people who've broken down under stress of too much worry and strenuous living; well, you're suffering from overmuch repose and placidity, and you need the opposite kind of treatment.'

'But where would one go for such a thing?'

'Well, you might stand as an Orange candidate for Kilkenny, or do a course of district visiting in one of the Apache quarters of Paris, or give lectures in Berlin to prove that most of Wagner's music was written by Gambetta; and there's always the interior of Morocco to travel in. But, to be really effective, the Unrest-cure ought to be tried in the home. How you would do it I haven't the faintest idea.'

It was at this point in the conversation that Clovis became galvanized into alert attention. After all, his two days' visit to an elderly relative at Slowborough did not promise much excitement. Before the train had stopped he had decorated his sinister shirt-cuff with the inscription, 'J. P. Huddle, The Warren, Tilfield near Slowborough.'

Two mornings later Mr Huddle broke in on his sister's privacy as she sat reading *Country Life* in the morning room. It was her day and hour and place for reading *Country Life,* and the intrusion was absolutely irregular; but he bore in his hand a telegram, and in that household telegrams were recognized as happening by the hand of God. This particular telegram partook of the nature of a thunderbolt. 'Bishop examining confirmation class in neighbourhood unable stay rectory on account measles invokes your hospitality sending secretary arrange.'

'I scarcely know the Bishop; I've only spoken to him once,' exclaimed J. P. Huddle, with the exculpating air of one who realizes too late the indiscretion of speaking to strange Bishops. Miss Huddle was the first to rally; she disliked thunderbolts as fervently as her brother did, but the womanly instinct in her told her that thunderbolts must be fed.

'We can curry the cold duck,' she said. It was not the appointed day for curry, but the little orange envelope involved a certain departure from rule and custom. Her brother said nothing, but his eyes thanked her for being brave.

'A gentleman to see you,' announced the parlour-maid.

'The secretary!' murmured the Huddles in unison; they instantly stiffened into a demeanour which proclaimed that, though they held all strangers to be guilty, they were willing to hear anything they might have to say in their defence. The young gentleman, who came into the room with a certain elegant haughtiness, was not at all Huddle's idea of a bishop's secretary; he had not supposed that the episcopal establishment could have afforded such an expensively upholstered article when there were so many other claims on its resources. The face was fleetingly familiar; if he had bestowed more attention on the fellow-traveller sitting opposite him in the railway carriage two days before he might have recognized Clovis in his present visitor.

'You are the Bishop's secretary?' asked Huddle, becoming consciously deferential.

'His confidential secretary,' answered Clovis. 'You may call me Stanislaus; my other name doesn't matter. The Bishop and Colonel Alberti may be here to lunch. I shall be here in any case.'

It sounded rather like the programme of a Royal visit.

'The Bishop is examining a confirmation class in the neighbourhood, isn't he?' asked Miss Huddle.

'Ostensibly,' was the dark reply, followed by a request for a large-scale map of the locality.

Clovis was still immersed in a seemingly profound study of the map when another telegram arrived. It was addressed to 'Prince Stanislaus, care of Huddle, The Warren, etc.' Clovis glanced at the contents and announced: 'The Bishop and Alberti won't be here till late in the afternoon.' Then he returned to his scrutiny of the map.

The luncheon was not a very festive function. The princely secretary ate and drank with fair appetite, but severely discouraged conversation. At the finish of the meal he broke suddenly into a radiant smile, thanked his hostess for a charming repast, and kissed her hand with deferential rapture. Miss Huddle was unable to decide in her mind whether the action savoured of Louis Quatorzian courtliness or the reprehensible Roman attitude towards the Sabine women. It was not her day for having a headache, but she felt that the circumstances excused her, and retired to her room to have as much headache as was possible before the Bishop's arrival. Clovis, having asked the way to the nearest telegraph office, disappeared presently down the carriage drive. Mr Huddle met him in the hall some two hours later, and asked when the Bishop would arrive.

'He is in the library with Alberti,' was the reply.

'But why wasn't I told? I never knew he had come!' exclaimed Huddle.

'No one knows he is here,' said Clovis; 'the quieter we can keep matters the better. And on no account disturb him in the library. Those are his orders.'

'But what is all this mystery about? And who is Alberti? And isn't the Bishop going to have tea?'

'The Bishop is out for blood, not tea.'

'Blood!' gasped Huddle, who did not find that the thunderbolt improved on acquaintance.

'Tonight is going to be a great night in the history of Christendom,' said Clovis. 'We are going to massacre every Jew in the neighbourhood.'

'To massacre the Jews!' said Huddle indignantly. 'Do you mean to tell me there's a general rising against them?'

'No, it's the Bishop's own idea. He's in there arranging all the details now.'

'But – the Bishop is such a tolerant, humane man.'

'This is precisely what will heighten the effect of his action. The sensation will be enormous.'

That at least Huddle could believe.

'He will be hanged!' he exclaimed with conviction.

'A motor is waiting to carry him to the coast, where a steam yacht is in readiness.'

'But there aren't thirty Jews in the whole neighbourhood,' protested Huddle, whose brain, under the repeated shocks of the day, was operating with the uncertainty of a telegraph wire during earthquake disturbances.

'We have twenty-six on our list, said Clovis, referring to a bundle of notes. 'We shall be able to deal with them all the more thoroughly.'

'Do you mean to tell me that you are meditating violence against a man like Sir Leon Birberry,' stammered Huddle, 'he's one of the most respected men in the country.'

'He's down on our list,' said Clovis carelessly; 'after all, we've got men we can trust to do our job, so we shan't have to rely on local assistance. And we've got some Boy-scouts helping us as auxiliaries.'

'Boy-scouts!'

'Yes; when they understood there was real killing to be done they were even keener than the men.'

'This thing will be a blot on the Twentieth Century!'

'And your house will be the blotting-pad. Have you realized that half the papers of Europe and the United States will publish pictures of it? By the way, I've sent some photographs of you and your sister, that I found in the library, to the *Matin* and *Die*

Woche; I hope you don't mind. Also a sketch of the staircase; most of the killing will probably be done on the staircase.'

The emotions that were surging in J. P. Huddle's brain were almost too intense to be disclosed in speech, but he managed to gasp out : 'There aren't any Jews in this house.'

'Not at present,' said Clovis.

'I shall go to the police,' shouted Huddle with sudden energy.

'In the shrubbery,' said Clovis, 'are posted ten men, who have orders to fire on any one who leaves the house without my signal of permission. Another armed picquet is in ambush near the front gate. The Boy-scouts watch the back premises.'

At this moment the cheerful hoot of a motor-horn was heard from the drive. Huddle rushed to the hall door with the feeling of a man half-awakened from a nightmare, and beheld Sir Leon Birberry, who had driven himself over in his car. 'I got your telegram,' he said ; what's up?'

Telegram? It seemed to be a day of telegrams.

'Come here at once. Urgent. James Huddle, was the purport of the message displayed before Huddle's bewildered eyes.

'I see it all!' he exclaimed suddenly in a voice shaken with agitation, and with a look of agony in the direction of the shrubbery he hauled the astonished Birberry into the house. Tea had just been laid in the hall, but the now thoroughly panic-stricken Huddle dragged his protesting guest upstairs, and in a few minutes' time the entire household had been summoned to that region of momentary safety. Clovis alone graced the tea-table with his presence; the fanatics in the library were evidently too immersed in their monstrous machinations to dally with the solace of teacup and hot toast. Once the youth rose, in answer to the summons of the front-door bell, and admitted Mr Paul Isaacs, shoemaker and parish councillor, who had also received a pressing invitation to The Warren. With an atrocious assumption of courtesy, which a Borgia could hardly have outdone, the secretary escorted this new captive of his net to the head of the stairway, where his involuntary host awaited him.

And then ensued a long ghastly vigil of watching and waiting. Once or twice Clovis left the house to stroll across to the shrubbery, returning always to the library, for the purpose evidently of making a brief report. Once he took in the letters from the evening postman, and brought them to the top of the stairs with punctilious politeness. After his next absence he came half-way up the stairs to make an announcement.

'The Boy-scouts mistook my signal, and have killed the post-man. I've had very little practice in this sort of thing, you see. Another time I shall do better.'

The housemaid, who was engaged to be married to the evening postman, gave way to clamorous grief.

'Remember that your mistress has a headache,' said J. P. Huddle. (Miss Huddle's headache was worse).

Clovis hastened downstairs, and after a short visit to the library returned with another message:

'The Bishop is sorry to hear that Miss Huddle has a headache. He is issuing orders that as far as possible no firearms shall be used near the house; any killing that is necessary on the premises will be done with cold steel. The Bishop does not see why a man should not be a gentleman as well as a Christian.'

That was the last they saw of Clovis; it was nearly seven o'clock, and his elderly relative liked him to dress for dinner. But, though he had left them for ever, the lurking suggestion of his presence haunted the lower regions of the house during the long hours of the wakeful night, and every creak of the stairway, every rustle of wind through the shrubbery, was fraught with horrible meaning. At about seven next morning the gardener's boy and the early postman finally convinced the watchers that the Twentieth Century was still unblotted.

'I don't suppose,' mused Clovis, as an early train bore him townwards, 'that they will be in the least grateful for the Unrest-cure.'

THE REMOULDING OF
GROBY LINGTON

'A man is known by the company he keeps.'

In the morning-room of his sister-in-law's house Groby Lington fidgeted away the passing minutes with the demure restlessness of advanced middle age. About a quarter of an hour would have to elapse before it would be time to say his good-byes and make his way across the village green to the station, with a selected escort of nephews and nieces. He was a good-natured, kindly disposi-tioned man, and in theory he was delighted to pay periodical visits to the wife and children of his dead brother William; in practice, he infinitely preferred the comfort and seclusion of his own house and garden, and the companionship of his books and his parrot to these rather meaningless and tiresome incursions into a family circle with which he had little in common. It was not so much the spur of his own conscience that drove him to make the occasional short journey by rail to visit his relatives, as an obedient concession to the more insistent but vicarious conscience of his brother, Colonel John, who was apt to accuse him of neglecting poor old William's family. Groby usually forgot or ignored the existence of his neighbour kinsfolk until such time as he was threatened with a visit from the Colonel, when he would put matters straight by a hurried pilgrimage across the few miles of intervening country to renew his acquaintance with the young people and assume a kindly if rather forced interest in the well-being of his sister-in-law. On this occasion he had cut matters so fine between the timing of his exculpatory visit and the coming of Colonel John, that he would scarcely be home before the latter was due to arrive. Anyhow, Groby had got it over, and six or seven months might decently elapse before he need again sacrifice his comforts and inclinations on the altar of family sociability. He was inclined to be distinctly cheerful as he hopped about the room, picking up first one object, then another, and subjecting each to a brief bird-like scrutiny.

Presently his cheerful listlessness changed sharply to an attitude of vexed attention. In a scrap-book of drawings and caricatures belonging to one of his nephews he had come across an unkindly clever sketch of himself and his parrot, solemnly confronting each other in postures of ridiculous gravity and repose, and bearing a likeness to one another that the artist had done his utmost to accentuate. After the first flush of annoyance had passed away, Groby laughed good-naturedly and admitted to himself the cleverness of the drawing. Then the feeling of resentment repossessed him, resentment not against the caricaturist who had embodied the idea in pen and ink, but against the possible truth that the idea represented. Was it really the case that people grew in time to resemble the animals they kept as pets, and had he unconsciously become more and more like the comically solemn bird that was his constant companion? Groby was unusually silent as he walked to the train with his escort of chattering nephews and nieces, and during the short railway journey his mind was more and more possessed with an introspective conviction that he had gradually settled down into a sort of parrot-like existence. What, after all, did his daily routine amount to but a sedate meandering and pecking and perching, in his garden, among his fruit trees, in his wicker chair on the lawn, or by the fireside in his library? And what was the sum total of his conversation with chance-encountered neighbours? 'Quite a spring day, isn't it?' 'It looks as though we should have some rain.' 'Glad to see you about again; you must take care of yourself.' 'How the young folk shoot up, don't they?' Strings of stupid, inevitable perfunctory remarks came to his mind, remarks that were certainly not the mental exchange of human intelligences, but mere empty parrot-talk. One might really just as well salute one's acquaintances with 'Pretty Polly. Puss, puss, miaw!' Groby began to fume against the picture of himself as a foolish feathered fowl which his nephew's sketch had first suggested, and which his own accusing imagination was filling in with such unflattering detail.

'I'll give the beastly bird away,' he said resentfully; though he knew at the same time that he would do no such thing. It would look so absurd after all the years that he had kept the parrott and made much of it suddenly to try and find it a new home.

'Has my brother arrived?' he asked of the stable-boy, who had come with the pony-carriage to meet him.

'Yessir, came down by the two-fifteen. Your parrot's dead.' The boy made the latter announcement with the relish which his class finds in proclaiming a catastrophe.

'My parrot dead?' said Groby. 'What caused its death?'

'The ipe,' said the boy briefly.

'The ipe?' queried Groby. 'Whatever's that?'

'The ipe what the Colonel brought down with him,' came the rather alarming answer.

'Do you mean to say my brother is ill?' asked Groby. 'Is it something infectious?'

'Th' Colonel's so well as ever he was,' said the boy; and as no further explanation was forthcoming Groby had to possess himself in mystified patience till he reached home. His brother was wait-ing for him at the hall door.

'Have you heard about the parrot?' he asked at once. ' 'Pon my soul I'm awfully sorry. The moment he saw the monkey I'd brought down as a surprise for you he squawked out, "Rats to you, sir!" and the blessed monkey made one spring at him, got him by the neck and whirled him round like a rattle. He was as dead as mutton by the time I'd got him out of the little beggar's paws. Always been such a friendly little beast, the monkey has, should never have thought he'd got it in him to see red like that. Can't tell you how sorry I feel about it, and now of course you'll hate the sight of the monkey.'

'Not at all,' said Groby sincerely. A few hours earlier the tragic end which had befallen his parrot would have presented itself to him as a calamity; now it arrived almost as a polite attention on the part of the Fates.

'The bird was getting old, you know,' he went on, in explanation of his obvious lack of decent regret at the loss of his pet. 'I was really beginning to wonder if it was an unmixed kindness to let him go on living till he succumbed to old age. What a charming little monkey!' he added, when he was introduced to the culprit.

The new-comer was a small, long-tailed monkey from the Western Hemisphere, with a gentle, half-shy, half-trusting manner that instantly captured Groby's confidence; a student of simian character might have seen in the fitful red light in its eyes some indication of the underlying temper which the parrot had so rashly put to the test with such dramatic consequences for itself. The servants, who had come to regard the defunct bird as a regular member of the household, and one who gave really very little trouble, were scandalized to find his bloodthirsty aggressor installed in his place as an honoured domestic pet.

'A nasty heathen ipe what don't never say nothing sensible and cheerful, same as poor Polly did,' was the unfavourable verdict of the kitchen quarters.

One Sunday morning, some twelve or fourteen months after the visit of Colonel John and the parrot tragedy, Miss Wepley sat decorously in her pew in the parish church, immediately in front of that occupied by Groby Lington. She was, comparatively speaking, a newcomer in the neighbourhood, and was not personally acquainted with her fellow-worshipper in the seat behind, but for the past two years the Sunday morning service had brought them regularly within each other's sphere of consciousness. Without having paid particular attention to the subject, she could probably have given a correct rendering of the way in which he pronounced certain words occurring in the responses, while he was well aware of the trivial fact that, in addition to her prayer-book and handkerchief, a small paper packet of throat lozenges always reposed on the seat beside her. Miss Wepley rarely had recourse to her lozenges, but in case she should be taken with a fit of coughing she wished to have the emergency duly provided for. On this particular Sunday the lozenges occasioned an unusual diversion in the even tenor of her devotions, far more disturbing to her personally than a prolonged attack of coughing would have been. As she rose to take part in the singing of the first hymn, she fancied that she saw the hand of her neighbour, who was alone in the pew behind her, make a furtive downward grab at the packet lying on the seat; on turning sharply round she found that the packet had certainly disappeared, but Mr Lington was to all outward seeming serenely intent on his hymn-book. No amount of interrogatory glaring on the part of the despoiled lady could bring the least shade of conscious guilt to his face.

'Worse was to follow,' as she remarked afterwards to a scandalized audience of friends and acquaintances. 'I had scarcely knelt in prayer when a lozenge, one of *my* lozenges, came whizzing into the pew, just under my nose. I turned round and stared, but Mr Lington had his eyes closed and his lips moving as though engaged in prayer. The moment I resumed my devotions another lozenge came rattling in, and then another. I took no notice for a while, and then turned round suddenly just as the dreadful man was about to flip another one at me. He hastily pretended to be turning over the leaves of his book, but I was not to be taken in at that time. He saw that he had been discovered and no more lozenges came. Of course I have changed my pew.'

'No gentleman would have acted in such a disgraceful manner,' said one of her listeners; 'and yet Mr Lington used to be so respected by everybody. He seems to have behaved like a little ill-bred schoolboy.'

'He behaved like a monkey,' said Miss Wepley.

Her unfavourable verdict was echoed in other quarters about the same time. Groby Lington had never been a hero in the eyes of his personal retainers, but he had shared the approval accorded to his defunct parrot as a cheerful, well-dispositioned body, who gave no particular trouble. Of late months, however, this character would hardly have been endorsed by the members of his domestic establishment. The stolid stableboy, who had first announced to him the tragic end of his feathered pet, was one of the first to give voice to the murmurs of disapproval which became rampant and general in the servants' quarters, and he had fairly substantial grounds for his disaffection. In a burst of hot summer weather he had obtained permission to bathe in a modest-sized pond in the orchard, and thither one afternoon Groby had bent his steps, attracted by loud imprecations of anger mingled with the shriller chattering of monkey-language. He beheld his plump diminutive servitor, clad only in a waistcoat and a pair of socks, storming ineffectually at the monkey which was seated on a low branch of an apple tree, abstractedly fingering the remainder of the boy's outfit, which he had removed just out of his reach.

'The ipe's been an' took my clothes,' whined the boy, with the passion of his kind for explaining the obvious. His incomplete toilet effect rather embarrassed him, but he hailed the arrival of Groby with relief, as promising moral and material support in his efforts to get back his raided garments. The monkey had ceased its defiant jabbering, and doubtless with a little coaxing from its master it would hand back the plunder.

'If I lift you up,' suggested Groby, 'you will just be able to reach the clothes.'

The boy agreed, and Groby clutched him firmly by the waistcoat, which was about all there was to catch hold of, and lifted him clear of the ground. Then, with a deft swing he sent him crashing into a clump of tall nettles, which closed receptively round him. The victim had not been brought up in a school which teaches one to repress one's emotions – if a fox had attempted to gnaw at his vitals he would have flown to complain to the nearest hunt committee rather than have affected an attitude of stoical indifference. On this occasion the volume of sound which he produced under the stimulus of pain and rage and astonishment was generous and sustained, but above his bellowings he could disinctly hear the triumphant chattering of his enemy in the tree, and a peal of shrill laughter from Groby.

When the boy had finished an improvised St Vitus caracole, which would have brought him fame on the boards of the Coliseum, and which indeed met with ready appreciation and applause from the retreating figure of Groby Lington, he found that the monkey had also discreetly retired, while his clothes were scattered on the grass at the foot of the tree.

'They'm two ipes, that's what they be,' he muttered angrily, and if his judgment was severe, at least he spoke under the sting of considerable provocation.

It was a week or two later that the parlour-maid gave notice, having been terrified almost to tears by an outbreak of sudden temper on the part of the master anent some under-done cutlets. ''E knashed 'is teeth at me, 'e did reely,' she informed a sympathetic kitchen audience.

'I'd like to see 'im talk like that to me, I would,' said the cook
defiantly, but her cooking from that moment showed a marked
improvement.

It was seldom that Groby Lington so far detached himself from
his accustomed habits as to go and form one of a house-party,
and he was not a little piqued that Mrs Glenduff should have
stowed him away in the musty old Georgian wing of the house,
in the next room, moreover, to Leonard Spabbink, the eminent
pianist.

'He plays Liszt like an angel,' had been the hostess's enthusiastic testimonial.

'He may play him like a trout for all I care,' had been Groby's
mental comment, 'but I wouldn't mind betting that he snores.
He's just the sort and shape that would. And if I hear him snoring
through those ridiculous thin-panelled walls, there'll be trouble.'

He did, and there was.

Groby stood it for about two and a quarter minutes, and then
made his way through the corridor into Spabbink's room. Under
Groby's vigorous measures the musician's flabby, redundant
figure sat up in bewildered semi-consciousness like an ice-cream
that has been taught to beg. Groby prodded him into complete
wakefulness, and then the pettish self-satisfied pianist fairly lost
his temper and slapped his domineering visitant on the hand. In
another moment Spabbink was being nearly stifled and very effectually gagged by a pillow-case tightly bound round his head, while
his plump pyjama'd limbs were hauled out of bed and smacked,
pinched, kicked, and bumped in a catch-as-catch-can progress
across the floor, towards the flat shallow bath in whose utterly
inadequate depths Groby perseveringly strove to drown him. For
a few moments the room was almost in darkness: Groby's candle
had overturned in an early stage of the scuffle, and its flicker
scarcely reached to the spot where splashings, smacks, muffled
cries, and splutterings, and a chatter of ape-like rage told of the
struggle that was being waged round the shores of the bath. A
few instants later the one-sided combat was brightly lit up by the
flare of blazing curtains and rapidly kindling panelling.

When the hastily aroused members of the house-party stampeded
out on to the lawn, the Georgian wing was well alight and belch-
ing forth masses of smoke, but some moments elapsed before
Groby appeared with the half-drowned pianist in his arms, having
just bethought him of the superior drowning facilities offered by
the pond at the bottom of the lawn. The cool night air sobered

his rage, and when he found that he was innocently acclaimed as the heroic rescuer of poor Leonard Spabbink, and loudly commended for his presence of mind in tying a wet cloth round his head to protect him from smoke suffocation, he accepted the situation, and subsequently gave a graphic account of his finding the musician asleep with an overturned candle by his side and the conflagration well started. Spabbink gave his version some days later, when he had partially recovered from the shock of his midnight castigation and immersion, but the gentle pitying smiles and evasive comments with which his story was greeted warned him that the public ear was not at his disposal. He refused however, to attend the ceremonial presentation of the Royal Humane Society's life-saving medal.

It was about this time that Groby's pet monkey fell a victim to the disease which attacks so many of its kind when brought under the influence of a northern climate. Its master appeared to be profoundly affected by its loss, and never quite recovered the level of spirits that he had recently attained. In company with the tortoise, which Colonel John presented to him on his last visit, he potters about his lawn and kitchen garden, with none of his erstwhile sprightliness; and his nephews and nieces are fairly well justified in alluding to him as 'Old Uncle Groby.'

THE SEVEN CREAM JUGS

'I suppose we shall never see Wilfrid Pigeoncote here now that he has become heir to the baronetcy and to a lot of money,' observed Mrs Peter Pigeoncote regretfully to her husband.

'Well, we can hardly expect to,' he replied, 'seeing that we always choked him off from coming to see us when he was a prospective nobody. I don't think I've set eyes on him since he was a boy of twelve.'

'There was a reason for not wanting to encourage his acquaintanceship,' said Mrs Peter. 'With that notorious failing of his he was not the sort of person one wanted in one's house.'

'Well, the failing still exists, doesn't it?' said her husband; 'or do you suppose a reform of character is entailed along with the estate?'

'Oh, of course, there is still that drawback,' admitted the wife, 'but one would like to make the acquaintance of the future head of the family, if only out of mere curiosity. Besides, cynicism apart, his being rich *will* make a difference in the way people will look at his failing. When a man is absolutely wealthy, not merely well-to-do, all suspicion of sordid motive naturally disappears; the thing becomes merely a tiresome malady.'

Wilfrid Pigeoncote had suddenly become heir to his uncle, Sir Wilfrid Pigeoncote, on the death of his cousin, Major Wilfrid Pigeoncote, who had succumbed to the after-effects of a polo accident. (A Wilfred Pigeoncote had covered himself with honours in the course of Marlborough's campaigns, and the name Wilfrid had been a baptismal weakness in the family ever since.) The new heir to the family dignity and estates was a young man of about five-and-twenty, who was known more by reputation than by person to a wide circle of cousins and kinsfolk. And the reputation was an unpleasant one. The numerous other Wilfrids in the family were distinguished one from another chiefly by the names of their residences or professions, as Wilfrid of Hubbledown, and young Wilfrid the Gunner, but this particular scion was known by the ignominious and expressive label of Wilfrid the Snatcher. From his late schooldays onward he had been possessed by an acute and obstinate form of kleptomania; he had the acquisitive instinct of the collector without any of the collector's discrimination. Anything that was smaller and more portable than a sideboard and above the value of ninepence, had an irresistible attraction for him, provided that it fulfilled the necessary condition of belonging to someone else. On the rare occasions when he was included in a country-house party, it was usual and almost necessary for his host, or some member of the family, to make a friendly inquisition through his baggage on the eve of his departure, to see if he had packed up 'by mistake' anyone else's property. The search usually produced a large and varied yield.

'This is funny,' said Peter Pigeoncote to his wife, some half-hour after their conversation; 'here's a telegram from Wilfrid saying he's passing through here in his motor, and would like to stop and pay us his respects. Can stay for the night if it doesn't inconvenience us. Signed "Wilfrid Pigeoncote". Must be the Snatcher; none of the others have a motor. I suppose he's bringing us a present for the silver wedding.'

'Good gracious!' said Mrs Peter, as a thought struck her; 'this is rather an awkward time to have a person with his failing in the house. All those silver presents set out in the drawing-room, and others coming by every post; I hardly know what we've got and what are still to come. We can't lock them all up; he's sure to want to see them.'

'We must keep a sharp look-out, that's all,' said Peter reassuringly.

'But these practised kleptomaniacs are so clever,' said his wife apprehensively, 'and it will be so awkward if he suspects that we are watching him.'

Awkwardness was indeed the prevailing note that evening when the passing traveller was being entertained. The talk flitted nervously and hurriedly from one impersonal topic to another. The guest had none of the furtive, half-apologetic air that his cousins had rather expected to find; he was polite, well-assured, and, perhaps, just a little inclined to 'put on side.' His hosts, on the other hand, wore an uneasy manner that might have been the hallmark of conscious depravity. In the drawing-room, after dinner, their nervousness and awkwardness increased.

'Oh, we haven't shown you the silver-wedding presents,' said Mrs Peter suddenly, as though struck by a brilliant idea for entertaining the guest; 'here they all are. Such nice, useful gifts. A few duplicates, of course.'

'Seven cream jugs,' put in Peter.

'Yes, isn't it annoying,' went on Mrs Peter; 'seven of them. We feel that we must live on cream for the rest of our lives. Of course, some of them can be changed.'

Wilfrid occupied himself chiefly with such of the gifts as were of antique interest, carrying one or two of them over to the lamp to examine their marks. The anxiety of his hosts at these moments resembled the solicitude of a cat whose newly-born kittens are being handed round for inspection.

'Let me see; did you give me back the mustard-pot? This is its place here,' piped Mrs Peter.

'Sorry. I put it down by the claret-jug,' said Wilfrid, busy with another object.

'Oh, just let me have that sugar-sifter again,' asked Mrs Peter, dogged determination showing through her nervousness. 'I must label it who it comes from before I forget.'

Vigilance was not completely crowned with a sense of victory. After they had said 'Good night' to their visitor, Mrs Peter expressed her conviction that he had taken something.

'I fancy, by his manner, that there was something up,' corroborated her husband. 'Do you miss anything?'

'I can only make it thirty-four, and I think it should be thirty-five,' she announced. 'I can't remember if thirty-five includes the Archdeacon's cruet-stand that hasn't arrived yet.'

'How on earth are we to know?' said Peter. 'The mean pig hasn't brought us a present, and I'm hanged if he shall carry one off.'

'Tomorrow, when he's having his bath,' said Mrs Peter excitedly, 'he's sure to leave his keys somewhere, and we can go through his portmanteau. It's the only thing to do.'

On the morrow an alert watch was kept by the conspirators behind half-closed doors, and when Wilfrid, clad in a gorgeous bath-robe, had made his way to the bathroom, there was a swift and furtive rush by two excited individuals towards the principal guest-chamber. Mrs Peter kept guard outside, while her husband first made a hurried and successful search for the keys, and then plunged at the portmanteau with the air of a disagreeably conscientious Customs official. The quest was a brief one; a silver cream jug lay embedded in the folds of some zephyr shirts.

'The cunning brute,' said Mrs Peter; 'he took a cream jug because there were so many; he thought one wouldn't be missed. Quick, fly down with it and put it back among the others.'

Wilfrid was late in coming down to breakfast, and his manner showed plainly that something was amiss.

'It's an unpleasant thing to have to say,' he blurted out presently, 'but I'm afraid you must have a thief among your servants. Something's been taken out of my portmanteau. It was a little present from my mother and myself for your silver wedding. I should have given it to you last night after dinner, only it happened to be a cream jug, and you seemed annoyed at having so many duplicates, so I felt rather awkward about giving you another. I thought I'd get it changed for something else, and now it's gone.'

'Did you say it was from your *mother* and yourself?' asked Mr and Mrs Peter almost in unison. The Snatcher had been an orphan these many years.

'Yes, my mother's at Cairo just now, and she wrote to me at Dresden to try and get you something quaint and pretty in the old silver line, and I pitched on this cream jug.'

Both the Pigeoncotes had turned deadly pale. The mention of Dresden had thrown a sudden light on the situation. It was Wilfrid the Attaché, a very superior young man, who rarely came within their social horizon, whom they had been entertaining unawares in the supposed character of Wilfrid the Snatcher.

Lady Ernestine Pigeoncote, his mother, moved in circles which were entirely beyond their compass of ambitions, and the son would probably one day be an Ambassador. And they had rifled and despoiled his portmanteau! Husband and wife looked blankly and desperately at one another. It was Mrs Peter who arrived first at an inspiration.

'How dreadful to think there are thieves in the house! We keep the drawing-room locked up at night, of course, but anything might be carried off while we are at breakfast.'

She rose and went out hurriedly, as though to assure herself that the drawing-room was not being stripped of its silverware, and returned a moment later, bearing a cream jug in her hands.

'There are eight cream jugs now, instead of seven,' she cried; 'this one wasn't there before. What a curious trick of memory, Mr Wilfrid! You must have slipped downstairs with it last night and put it there before we locked up, and forgotten all about having done it in the morning.'

'One's mind often plays one little tricks like that,' said Mr Peter, with desperate heartiness. 'Only the other day I went into the town to pay a bill, and went in again next day, having clean forgotten that I'd –'

'It is certainly the jug that I brought for you,' said Wilfrid, looking closely at it; 'it was in my portmanteau when I got my bath-robe out this morning, before going to my bath, and it was not there when I unlocked the portmanteau on my return. Someone had taken it while I was away from the room.'

The Pigeoncotes had turned paler than ever. Mrs Peter had a final inspiration.

'Get me my smelling-salts, dear,' she said to her husband; 'I think they're in the dressing-room.'

Peter dashed out of the room with glad relief; he had lived so long during the last few minutes that a golden wedding seemed within measurable distance.

Mrs Peter turned to her guest with confidential coyness.

'A diplomat like you will know how to treat this as if it hadn't happened. Peter's little weakness; it runs in the family.'

'Good Lord! Do you mean to say he's a kleptomaniac, like Cousin Snatcher?'

'Oh, not exactly,' said Mrs Peter, anxious to whitewash her husband a little greyer than she was painting him. 'He would never touch anything he found lying about, but he can't resist making a raid on things that are locked up. The doctors have a special name for it. He must have pounced on your portmanteau the moment you went to your bath, and taken the first thing he came across. Of course, he had no motive for taking a cream jug; we've already got *seven*, as you know – not, of course, that we don't value the kind gift you and your mother – Hush, here's Peter coming.'

Mrs Peter broke off in some confusion, and tripped out to meet her husband in the hall.

'It's all right,' she whispered to him; I've explained everything. Don't say anything more about it.'

'Brave little woman,' said Peter, with a gasp of relief; 'I could never have done it.'

Diplomatic reticence does not necessarily extend to family affairs. Peter Pigeoncote was never able to understand why Mrs Consuelo van Bullyon, who stayed with them in the spring, always carried two very obvious jewel-cases with her to the bathroom, explaining them to any one she chanced to meet in the corridor as her manicure and face-massage set.

THE HOUNDS OF FATE

In the fading light of a close dull autumn afternoon Martin Stoner plodded his way along muddy lanes and rut-seamed cart tracks that led he knew not exactly whither. Somewhere in front of him, he fancied, lay the sea, and towards the sea his footsteps seemed persistently turning; why he was struggling wearily forward to that goal he could scarcely have explained, unless he was possessed by the same instinct that turns a hard-pressed stag cliffward in its last extremity. In his case the hounds of Fate were certainly pressing him with unrelentless insistence; hunger, fatigue, and despairing hopelessness had numbed his brain, and he could scarcely summon sufficient energy to wonder what underlying impulse was driving him onward. Stoner was one of those unfortunate individuals who seem to have tried everything; a natural slothfulness and improvidence had always intervened to blight any chance of even moderate success, and now he was at the end of his tether, and there was nothing more to try. Desperation had not awakened in him any dormant reserve of energy; on the contrary, a mental torpor grew up round the crisis of his fortunes.

With the clothes he stood up in, a halfpenny in his pocket, and no single friend or acquaintance to turn to, with no prospect either of a bed for the night or a meal for the morrow, Martin Stoner trudged stolidly forward, between moist hedgerows and beneath dripping trees, his mind almost a blank, except that he was subconsciously aware that somewhere in front of him lay the sea. Another consciousness obtruded itself now and then — the knowledge that he was miserably hungry. Presently he came to a halt by an open gateway that led into a spacious and rather neglected farm-garden; there was little sign of life about, and the farm-house at the further end of the garden looked chill and inhospitable. A drizzling rain, however, was setting in, and Stoner thought that here perhaps he might obtain a few minutes' shelter and buy a glass of milk with his last remaining coin. He turned slowly and wearily into the garden and followed a narrow, flagged part up to a side door. Before he had time to knock the door opened and a bent, withered-looking old man stood aside in the doorway as though to let him pass in.

'Come in, Mister Tom. I knew you would come back one of these days.'

Stoner lurched across the threshold and stood staring uncomprehendingly at the other.

'Sit down while I put you out a bit of supper,' said the old man with quavering eagerness. Stoner's legs gave way from very weariness, and he sank inertly into the armchair that had been pushed up to him. In another minute he was devouring the cold meat, cheese, and bread, that had been placed on the table at his side.

'You'm little changed these four years,' went on the old man, in a voice that sounded to Stoner as something in a dream, far away and inconsequent; 'but you'll find us a deal changed, you will. There's no one about the place same as when you left; nought but me and your old Aunt. I'll go and tell her that you'm come; she won't be seeing you, but she'll let you stay right enough. She always did say if you was to come back you should stay, but she'd never set eyes on you or speak to you again.'

The old man placed a mug of beer on the table in front of Stoner and then hobbled away down a long passage. The drizzle of rain had changed to a furious lashing downpour, which beat violently against door and windows. The wanderer thought with a shudder of what the sea-shore must look like under this drenching rainfall, with night beating down on all sides. He finished the

food and beer and sat numbly waiting for the return of his strange
host. As the minutes ticked by on the grandfather clock in the
corner a new hope began to flicker and grow in the young man's
mind; it was merely the expansion of his former craving for food
and a few minutes' rest into a longing to find a night's shelter
under this seemingly hospitable roof. A clattering of footsteps
down the passage heralded the old farm servant's return.

'The old missus won't see you, Master Tom, but she says you
are to stay. 'Tis right enough, seeing the farm will be yours when
she be put under earth. I've had a fire lit in your room, Master
Tom, and the maid has put fresh sheets on to the bed. You'll
find nought changed up there. Maybe you'm tired and would
like to go there now.'

Without a word Martin Stoner rose heavily to his feet and
followed his ministering angel along a passage, up a short creak-
ing stair, along another passage, and into a large room lit with a
cheerfully blazing fire. There was but little furniture, plain, old-
fashioned, and good of its kind; a stuffed squirrel in a case and
a wall calendar of four years ago were about the only symptoms
of decoration. But Stoner had eyes for little else than the bed, and
could scarce wait to tear his clothes off him before rolling in a
luxury of weariness into its comfortable depths. The hounds of
Fate seemed to have checked for a brief moment.

In the cold light of morning Stoner laughed mirthlessly as he
slowly realized the position in which he found himself. Perhaps
he might snatch a bit of breakfast on the strength of his likeness
to this other missing ne'er-do-well, and get safely away before
anyone discovered the fraud that had been thrust on him. In the
room downstairs he found the bent old man ready with a dish of
bacon and fried eggs for 'Master Tom's' breakfast, while a hard-
faced elderly maid brought in a teapot and poured him out a cup
of tea. As he sat at the table a small spaniel came up and made
friendly advances.

''Tis old Bowker's pup,' explained the old man, whom the
hard-faced maid had addressed as George. 'She was main fond
of you; never seemed the same after you went away to Australee.
She died 'bout a year agone. 'Tis her pup.'

Stoner found it difficult to regret her decease; as a witness for
identification she would have left something to be desired.

'You'll go for a ride, Master Tom?' was the next startling pro-
position that came from the old man. 'We've a nice little roan
cob that goes well in saddle. Old Biddy is getting a bit up in

years, though 'er goes well still, but I'll have the little roan saddled and brought round to door.'

'I've got no riding things,' stammered the castaway, almost laughing as he looked down at his one suit of well-worn clothes.

'Master Tom,' said the old man earnestly, almost with an offended air, 'all your things is just as you left them. A bit of airing before the fire an' they'll be all right. 'Twill be a bit of a distraction like, a little riding and wild-fowling now and agen. You'll find the folk around here has hard and bitter minds towards you. They hasn't forgotten nor forgiven. No one'll come nigh you, so you'd best get what distractions you can with horse and dog. They'm good company, too.'

Old George hobbled away to give his orders, and Stoner, feeling more than ever like one in a dream, went upstairs to inspect 'Master Tom's' wardrobe. A ride was one of the pleasures dearest to his heart, and there was some protection against immediate discovery of his imposture in the thought that none of Tom's aforetime companions were likely to favour him with a close inspection. As the interloper thrust himself into tolerably well-fitting riding cords he wondered vaguely what manner of misdeed the genuine Tom had committed to set the whole countryside against him. The thud of quick, eager hoofs on damp earth cut short his speculations. The roan cob had been brought up to the side door.

'Talk of beggars on horseback,' thought Stoner to himself, as he trotted rapidly along the muddy lanes where he had tramped yesterday as a down-at-heel outcast; and then he flung reflection indolently aside and gave himself up to the pleasure of a smart canter along the turf-grown side of a level stretch of road. At an open gateway he checked his pace to allow two carts to turn into a field. The lads driving the carts found time to give him a prolonged stare, and as he passed on he heard an excited voice call out, 'Tis Tom Prike! I knowed him at once; showing hisself here agen, is he?'

Evidently the likeness which had imposed at close quarters on a doddering old man was good enough to mislead younger eyes at a short distance.

In the course of his ride he met with ample evidence to confirm the statement that local folk had neither forgotten nor forgiven the bygone crime which had come to him as a legacy from the absent Tom. Scowling looks, mutterings, and nudgings greeted him whenever he chanced upon human beings; 'Bowker's pup,' trotting placidly by his side, seemed the one element of friendliness in a hostile world.

As he dismounted at the side door he caught a fleeting glimpse of a gaunt, elderly woman peering at him from behind the curtain of an upper window. Evidently this was his aunt by adoption.

Over the ample midday meal that stood in readiness for him Stoner was able to review the possibilities of his extraordinary situation. The real Tom, after four years of absence might suddenly turn up at the farm, or a letter might come from him at any moment. Again, in the character of heir to the farm, the false Tom might be called on to sign documents, which would be an embarrassing predicament. Or a relative might arrive who would not imitate the aunt's attitude of aloofness. All these things would mean ignominious exposure. On the other hand, the alternative was the open sky and the muddy lanes that led down to the sea. The farm offered him, at any rate, a temporary refuge from destitution; farming was one of the many things he had 'tried', and he would be able to do a certain amount of work in return for the hospitality to which he was so little entitled.

'Will you have cold pork for your supper,' asked the hard-faced maid, as she cleared the table, 'or will you have it hotted up?'

'Hot, with onions,' said Stoner. It was the only time in his life that he made a rapid decision. And as he gave the order he knew that he meant to stay.

Stoner kept rigidly to those portions of the house which seemed to have been allotted to him by a tacit treaty of delimitation. When he took part in the farm-work it was as one who worked under orders and never initiated them. Old George, the roan cob, and Bowker's pup were his sole companions in a world that was otherwise frostily silent and hostile. Of the mistress of the farm he saw nothing. Once, when he knew she had gone forth to church, he made a furtive visit to the farm parlour in an endeavour to glean some fragmentary knowledge of the young man whose place he had usurped, and whose ill-repute he had fastened on himself. There were many photographs hung on the walls, or stuck in prim frames, but the likeness he sought for was not among them. At last, in an album thrust out of sight, he came across what he wanted. There was a whole series, labelled 'Tom', a podgy child of three, in a fantastic frock, an awkward boy of about twelve, holding a cricket bat as though he loathed it, a rather good-looking youth of eighteen with very smooth, evenly parted hair, and, finally, a young man with a somewhat surly dare-devil expression. At this last portrait Stoner looked with particular interest; the likeness to himself was unmistakable.

From the lips of old George, who was garrulous enough on most subjects, he tried again and again to learn something of the nature of the offence which shut him off as a creature to be shunned and hated by his fellow-men.

'What do folk around here say about me?' he asked one day as they were walking home from an outlying field.

The old man shook his head.

'They be bitter agen you, mortal bitter. Ay, 'tis a sad business, a sad business.'

And never could he be got to say anything more enlightening.

On a clear frosty evening, a few days before the festival of Christmas, Stoner stood in a corner of the orchard which commanded a wide view of the countryside. Here and there he could see the twinkling dots of lamp or candle glow which told of human homes where the goodwill and jollity of the season held their sway. Behind him lay the grim, silent farmhouse, where no one ever laughed, where even a quarrel would have seemed cheerful. As he turned to look at the long grey front of the gloom-shadowed building, a door opened and old George came hurriedly forth. Stoner heard his adopted name called in a tone of strained anxiety. Instantly he knew that something untoward had happened, and with a quick revulsion of outlook his sanctuary became in his eyes a place of peace and contentment, from which he dreaded to be driven.

'Master Tom,' said the old man in a hoarse whisper, 'you must slip away quiet from here for a few days. Michael Ley is back in the village, an' he swears to shoot you if he can come across you. He'll do it, too, there's murder in the look of him. Get away under cover of night, 'tis only for a week or so, he won't be here longer.'

'But where am I to go?' stammered Stoner, who had caught the infection of the old man's obvious terror.

'Go right away along the coast to Punchford and keep hid there. When Michael's safe gone I'll ride the roan over to the Green Dragon at Punchford; when you see the cob stabled at the Green Dragon 'tis a sign you may come back agen.'

'But –' began Stoner hesitatingly.

''Tis all right for money,' said the other; 'the old Missus agrees you'd best do as I say, and she's given me this.'

The old man produced three sovereigns and some odd silver. Stoner felt more of a cheat than ever as he stole away that night from the back gate of the farm with the old woman's money in his pocket. Old George and Bowker's pup stood watching him a silent farewell from the yard. He could scarcely fancy that he would ever come back, and he felt a throb of compunction for those two humble friends who would wait wistfully for his return. Some day perhaps the real Tom would come back, and there would be wild wonderment among those simple farm folks as to the identity of the shadowy guest they had harboured under their roof. For his own fate he felt no immediate anxiety; three pounds goes but little way in the world when there is nothing behind it, but to a man who has counted his exchequer in pennies it seems a good starting-point. Fortune had done him a whimsically kind turn when last he trod these lanes as a hopeless adventurer, and there might yet be a chance of his finding some work and making a fresh start; as he got further from the farm his spirits rose higher. There was a sense of relief in regaining once more his lost identity and ceasing to be the uneasy ghost of another. He scarcely bothered to speculate about the implacable enemy who had dropped from nowhere into his life; since that life was now behind him one unreal item the more made little difference. For the first time for many months he began to hum a careless light-hearted refrain. Then there stepped out from the shadow of an overhanging oak tree a man with a gun. There was no need to wonder who he might be; the moonlight falling on his white set face revealed a glare of human hate such as Stoner in the ups and downs of his wanderings had never seen before. He sprang aside in a wild effort to break through the hedge that bordered the lane, but the tough branches held him fast. The hounds of Fate had waited for him in those narrow lanes, and this time they were not to be denied.

A BREAD AND BUTTER MISS

'Starling Chatter and Oakhill have both dropped back in the betting,' said Bertie van Tahn, throwing the morning paper across the breakfast table.

'That leaves Nursery Tea practically favourite,' said Odo Finsberry.

'Nursery Tea and Pipeclay are at the top of the betting at present,' said Bertie, 'but that French horse, Le Five O'Clock, seems to be fancied as much as anything. Then there is White-bait, and the Polish horse with a name like someone trying to stifle a sneeze in church; they both seem to have a lot of support.'

'It's the most open Derby there's been for years,' said Odo.

'It's simply no good trying to pick the winner on form,' said Bertie; 'one must just trust to luck and inspiration.'

'The question is whether to trust to one's own inspiration, or somebody else's. *Sporting Swank* gives Count Palatine to win, and Le Five O'Clock for a place.'

'Count Palatine – that adds another to our list of perplexities. Good morning, Sir Lulworth; have you a fancy for the Derby by any chance?'

'I don't usually take much interest in turf matters,' said Sir Lulworth, who had just made his appearance, 'but I always like to have a bet on the Guineas and the Derby. This year, I confess, it's rather difficult to pick out anything that seems markedly better than anything else. What do you think of Snow Bunting?'

'Snow Bunting?' said Odo, with a groan, 'there's another of them. Surely, Snow Bunting has no earthly chance?'

'My housekeeper's nephew, who is a shoeing-smith in the mounted section of the Church Lad's Brigade, and an authority on horseflesh, expects him to be among the first three.'

'The nephews of housekeepers are invariably optimists,' said Bertie; 'it's a kind of natural reaction against the professional pessimism of their aunts.'

'We don't seem to get much further in our search for the probable winner,' said Mrs de Claux; 'the more I listen to you experts the more hopelessly befogged I get.'

'It's all very well to blame us,' said Bertie to his hostess; '*you* haven't produced anything in the way of an inspiration.'

'My inspiration consisted in asking you down for Derby week,' retorted Mrs de Claux; 'I thought you and Odo between you might throw some light on *the* question of the moment.'

Further recriminations were cut short by the arrival of Lola Pevensey, who floated into the room with an air of gracious apology.

'So sorry to be so late,' she observed, making a rapid tour of inspection of the breakfast dishes.

'Did you have a good night?' asked her hostess with perfunctory solicitude.

'Quite, thank you,' said Lola; 'I dreamt a most remarkable dream.'

A flutter, indicative of general boredom, went round the table. Other people's dreams are about as universally interesting as accounts of other people's gardens, or chickens, or children.

'I dreamt about the winner of the Derby,' said Lola.

A swift reaction of attentive interest set in.

'Do tell us what you dreamt,' came in a chorus.

'The really remarkable thing about it is that I've dreamt it two nights running,' said Lola, finally deciding between the allurements of sausages and kedgeree; 'that is why I thought it worth mentioning. You know, when I dream things two or three nights in succession, it always means something; I have special powers in that way. For instance, I once dreamed three times that a winged lion was flying through the sky and one of his wings dropped off, and he came to the ground with a crash; just afterwards the Campanile at Venice fell down. The winged lion is the symbol of Venice, you know,' she added for the enlightenment of those who might not be versed in Italian heraldry. 'Then,' she continued, 'just before the murder of the King and Queen of Servia I had a vivid dream of two crowned figures walking into a slaughter-house by the banks of a big river, which I took to be the Danube; and only the other day –'

'Do tell us what you've dreamt about the Derby,' interrupted Odo impatiently.

'Well, I saw the finish of the race as clearly as anything; and one horse won easily, almost in a canter, and everybody cried out "Bread and Butter wins! Good old Bread and Butter." I heard the name distinctly, and I've had the same dream two nights running.'

'Bread and Butter,' said Mrs de Claux, 'now whatever horse can that point to? Why – of course, Nursery Tea!'

She looked round with the triumphant smile of a successful unraveller of mystery.

'How about Le Five O'Clock?' interposed Sir Lulworth.

'It would fit either of them equally well,' said Odo! 'can you remember any details about the jockey's colours? That might help us.'

'I seem to remember a glimpse of lemon sleeves or cap, but I can't be sure,' said Lola, after due reflection.

'There isn't a lemon jacket or cap in the race,' said Bertie, referring to a list of starters and jockeys; 'can't you remember anything about the appearance of the horse? If it were a thick-set animal, thick bread and butter would typify Nursery Tea; and if it were thin, of course, it would mean Le Five O'Clock.'

'That seems sound enough,' said Mrs de Claux; 'do think, Lola dear, whether the horse in your dream was thin or stoutly built.'

'I can't remember that it was one or the other,' said Lola; 'one wouldn't notice such a detail in the excitement of a finish.'

'But this is a symbolic animal,' said Sir Lulworth; 'if it were to typify thick or thin bread and butter, surely it ought to have been either as bulky and tubby as a shire cart-horse, or as thin as a heraldic leopard.'

'I'm afraid you are rather a careless dreamer,' said Bertie resentfully.

'Of course, at the moment of dreaming I thought I was witnessing a real race, not the portent of one,' said Lola; 'otherwise I should have particularly noticed all helpful details.'

'The Derby isn't run till tomorrow,' said Mrs de Claux; 'do you think you are likely to have the same dream again tonight? If so, you can fix your attention on the important detail of the animal's appearance.'

'I'm afraid I shan't sleep at all tonight,' said Lola pathetically; 'every fifth night I suffer from insomnia, and it's due tonight.'

'It's most provoking,' said Bertie; 'of course, we can back both horses, but it would be much more satisfactory to have all our money on the winner. Can't you take a sleeping-draught, or something?'

'Oakleaves, soaked in warm water and put under the bed, are recommended by some,' said Mrs de Claux.

'A glass of Benedictine, with a drop of eau-de-Cologne –' said Sir Lulworth.

'I have tried every known remedy,' said Lola, with dignity; 'I've been a martyr to insomnia for years.'

'But now we are being martyrs to it,' said Odo sulkily; 'I particularly want to land a big coup over this race.'

'I don't have insomnia for my own amusement,' snapped Lola.

'Let us hope for the best,' said Mrs de Claux soothingly; 'tonight may prove an exception to the fifth-night rule.'

But when breakfast time came round again Lola reported a blank night as far as visions were concerned.

'I don't suppose I had as much as ten minutes' sleep, and, certainly, no dreams.'

'I'm so sorry, for your sake in the first place, and ours as well,' said her hostess; 'do you think you could induce a short nap after breakfast? It would be so good for you – and you *might* dream something. There would still be time for us to get our bets on.'

'I'll try if you like,' said Lola; 'it sounds rather like a small child being sent to bed in disgrace.'

'I'll come and read the *Encyclopædia Britannica* to you if you think it will make you sleep any sooner,' said Bertie obligingly.

Rain was falling too steadily to permit of outdoor amusement, and the party suffered considerably during the next two hours from the absolute quiet that was enforced all over the house in order to give Lola every chance of achieving slumber. Even the click of billiard balls was considered a possible factor of disturbance, and the canaries were carried down to the gardener's lodge, while the cuckoo clock in the hall was muffled under several layers of rugs. A notice, 'Please do not Knock or Ring,' was posted on the front door at Bertie's suggestion, and guests and servants spoke in tragic whispers as though the dread presence of death or sickness had invaded the house. The precautions proved of no avail: Lola added a sleepless morning to a wakeful night, and the bets of the party had to be impartially divided between Nursery Tea and the French Colt.

'So provoking to have to split our bets,' said Mrs de Claux as her guests gathered in the hall later in the day, waiting for the result of the race.

'I did my best for you,' said Lola, feeling that she was not getting her due share of gratitude; 'I told you what I had seen in my dreams, a brown horse, called Bread and Butter, winning easily from all the rest.'

'What?' screamed Bertie, jumping up from his seat, 'a *brown* horse! Miserable woman, you never said a word about it's being a brown horse.'

'Didn't I,' faltered Lola. 'I thought I told you it was a brown horse. It was certainly brown in both dreams. But I don't see what colour has got to do with it. Nursery Tea and Le Five O'Clock are both chestnuts.'

'Merciful Heaven! Doesn't brown bread and butter with a sprinkling of lemon in the colours suggest anything to you?' raged Bertie.

A slow, cumulative groan broke from the assembly as the meaning of his words gradually dawned on his hearers.

For the second time that day Lola retired to the seclusion of her room; she could not face the universal looks of reproach directed at her when Whitebait was announced winner at the comfortable price of fourteen to one.

FUR

'You look worried, dear,' said Eleanor.

'I am worried,' admitted Suzanne; 'not worried exactly, but anxious. You see, my birthday happens *next* week—

'You lucky person,' interrupted Eleanor; 'my birthday doesn't come till the end of March.'

'Well, old Bertram Kneyght is over in England just now from the Argentine. He's a kind of distant cousin of my mother's, and so enormously rich that we've never let the relationship drop out of sight. Even if we don't see him or hear from him for years he is always Cousin Bertram when he does turn up. I can't say he's ever been of much solid use to us, but yesterday the subject of my birthday cropped up, and he asked me to let him know what I wanted for a present.'

'Now, I understand the anxiety,' observed Eleanor.

'As a rule when one is confronted with a problem like that,' said Suzanne, 'all one's ideas vanish; one doesn't seem to have a desire in the world. Now it so happens that I have been very keen on a little Dresden figure that I saw somewhere in Kensington; about thirty-six shillings, quite beyond my means. I was very nearly describing the figure, and giving Bertram the address of the shop. And then it suddenly struck me that thirty-six shillings was such a ridiculously inadequate sum for a man of his immense wealth to spend on a birthday present. He could give thirty-six pounds as easily as you or I could buy a bunch of violets. I don't want to be greedy, of course, but I don't like being wasteful.'

'The question is,' said Eleanor, 'what are his ideas as to present-giving? Some of the wealthiest people have curiously cramped views on that subject. When people grow gradually rich their requirements and standard of living expand in proportion, while their present-giving instincts often remain in the undeveloped condition of their earlier days. Something showy and not-too-expensive in a shop is their only conception of the ideal gift. That is why even quite good shops have their counters and windows crowded with things worth about four shillings that look as if they might be worth seven-and-six, and are priced at ten shillings and labelled "seasonable gifts".'

'I know,' said Suzanne; 'that is why it is so risky to be vague when one is giving indications of one's wants. Now if I say to him: "I am going out to Davos this winter, so anything in the travelling line would be acceptable," he *might* give me a dressing-bag with gold-mounted fittings, but, on the other hand, he might give me Baedeker's *Switzerland,* or *Ski-ing without Tears,* or something of that sort.'

'He would be more likely to say: "She'll be going to lots of dances, a fan will be sure to be useful".'

'Yes, and I've got tons of fans, so you see where the danger and anxiety lies. Now if there is one thing more than another that I urgently want it is furs. I simply haven't any. I'm told that Davos is full of Russians, and they are sure to wear the most lovely sables and things. To be among people who are smothered in furs when one hasn't any oneself makes one want to break most of the Commandments.'

'If it's furs that you're out for,' said Eleanor, 'you will have to superintend the choice of them in person. You can't be sure that your cousin knows the difference between silver-fox and ordinary squirrel.'

'There are some heavenly silver-fox stoles at Goliath and Mastodon's,' said Suzanne, with a sigh; 'if I could only inveigle Bertram into their building and take him for a stroll through the fur department!'

'He lives somewhere near there, doesn't he?' said Eleanor. 'Do you know what his habits are? Does he take a walk at any particular time of day?'

'He usually walks down to his club about three o'clock, if it's a fine day. That takes him right past Goliath and Mastodon's.'

'Let us two meet him accidentally at the street corner tomorrow,' said Eleanor; 'we can walk a little way with him, and with luck we ought to be able to side-track him into the shop. You can say you want to get a hair-net or something. When we're safely there I can say: "I wish you'd tell me what you want for your birthday." Then you'll have everything ready to hand – the rich cousin, the fur department, and the topic of birthday presents.'

'It's a great idea,' said Suzanne; 'you really are a brick. Come round tomorrow at twenty to three; don't be late, we must carry out our ambush to the minute.'

At a few minutes to three the next afternoon the fur-trappers walked warily towards the selected corner. In the near distance rose the colossal pile of Messrs Goliath and Mastodon's famed establishment. The afternoon was brilliantly fine, exactly the sort of weather to tempt a gentleman of advancing years into the discreet exercise of a leisurely walk.

'I say, dear, I wish you'd do something for me this evening,' said Eleanor to her companion; 'just drop in after dinner on some pretext or other, and stay on to make a fourth at bridge with Adela and the aunts. Otherwise I shall have to play, and Harry Scarisbrooke is going to come in unexpectedly about nine-fifteen, and I particularly wanted to be free to talk to him while the others are playing.'

'Sorry, my dear, no can do,' said Suzanne; 'ordinary bridge at threepence a hundred, with such dreadfully slow players as your aunts, bores me to tears. I nearly go to sleep over it.'

'But I most particularly want an opportunity to talk with Harry,' urged Eleanor, an angry glint coming into her eyes.

'Sorry, anything to oblige, but not that,' said Suzanne cheerfully; the sacrifices of friendship were beautiful in her eyes as long as she was not asked to make them.

Eleanor said nothing further on the subject but the corners of her mouth rearranged themselves.

'There's our man!' exclaimed Suzanne suddenly; 'hurry!'

Mr Bertram Kneyght greeted his cousin and her friend with genuine heartiness, and readily accepted their invitation to explore the crowded mart that stood temptingly at their elbow. The plate-glass doors swung open and the trio plunged bravely into the jostling throng of buyers and loiterers.

'Is it always as full as this?' asked Bertram of Eleanor.

'More or less, and autumn sales are on just now,' she replied.

Suzanne, in her anxiety to pilot her cousin to the desired haven of the fur department, was usually a few paces ahead of the others, coming back to them now and then if they lingered for a moment at some attractive counter, with the nervous solicitude of a parent rook encouraging its young ones on their first flying expedition.

'It's Suzanne's birthday on Wednesday next,' confided Eleanor to Bertram Kneyght at a moment when Suzanne had left them unusually far behind; 'my birthday comes the day before, so we are both on the look-out for something to give each other.'

'Ah,' said Bertram. 'Now, perhaps you can advise me on that very point. I want to give Suzanne something, and I haven't the least idea what she wants.'

'She's rather a problem,' said Eleanor. 'She seems to have everything one can think of, lucky girl. A fan is always useful; she'll be going to a lot of dances at Davos this winter. Yes, I should think a fan would please her more than anything. After our birthdays are over we inspect each other's muster of presents, and I always feel dreadfully humble. She gets such nice things, and I never have anything worth showing. You see, none of my relations or any of the people who give me presents are at all well off, so I can't expect them to do anything more than just remember the day with some little trifle. Two years ago an uncle on my mother's side of the family, who had come into a small legacy, promised me a silver-fox stole for my birthday. I can't tell you how excited I was about it, and I pictured myself showing it off to all my friends and enemies. Then just at that moment his wife died, and, of course, poor man, he could not be expected to think of birthday presents at such a time. He has lived abroad ever since, and I never got my fur. Do you know, to this day I can scarcely look at a silver-fox pelt in a shop window or round anyone's neck without feeling ready to burst into tears. I suppose if I hadn't had the prospect of getting one I shouldn't feel that way. Look, there is the fan counter, on your left; you can easily slip away into the crowd. Get her as nice a one as you can see – she is such a dear, dear girl.'

'Hullo, I thought I had lost you,' said Suzanne, making her way through an obstructive knot of shoppers. 'Where is Bertram?'

'I got separated from him long ago. I thought he was on ahead with you,' said Eleanor. 'We shall never find him in this crush.'

Which turned out to be a true prediction.

'All our trouble and forethought thrown away,' said Suzanne sulkily, when they had pushed their way fruitlessly through half a dozen departments.

'I can't think why you didn't grab him by the arm,' said Eleanor; 'I would have if I'd known him longer, but I'd only just been introduced. It's nearly four now, we'd better have tea.'

Some days later Suzanne rang Eleanor up on the telephone.

'Thank you very much for the photograph frame. It was just what I wanted. Very good of you. I say, do you know what that Kneyght person has given me? Just what you said he would –a wretched fan. What? Oh, yes, quite a good enough fan in its way, but still . . .'

'You must come and see what he's given me,' came in Eleanor's voice over the 'phone.

'You! Why should he give you anything?'

'Your cousin appears to be one of those rare people of wealth who take a pleasure in giving good presents,' came the reply.

'I wondered why he was so anxious to know where she lived,' snapped Suzanne to herself as she rang off.

A cloud has arisen between the friendships of the two young women; as far as Eleanor is concerned the cloud has a silver-fox lining.

THE PHILANTHROPIST AND THE HAPPY CAT

Jocantha Bessbury was in the mood to be serenely and graciously happy. Her world was a pleasant place, and it was wearing one of its pleasantest aspects. Gregory had managed to get home for a hurried lunch and a smoke afterwards in the little snuggery; the lunch had been a good one, and there was just time to do justice to the coffee and cigarettes. Both were excellent in their way, and Gregory was, in his way, an excellent husband. Jocantha rather suspected herself of making him a very charming wife, and more than suspected herself of having a first-rate dress-maker.

'I don't suppose a more thoroughly contented personality is to be found in all Chelsea,' observed Jocantha in allusion to herself; 'except perhaps Attab,' she continued, glancing towards the large tabby-marked cat that lay in considerable ease in a corner of the divan. 'He lies there, purring and dreaming, shifting his limbs now and then in an ecstasy of cushioned comfort. He seems the incarnation of everything soft and silky and velvety, without a sharp edge in his composition, a dreamer whose philosophy is sleep and let sleep; and then, as evening draws on, he goes out into the garden with a red glint in his eyes and slays a drowsy sparrow.'

'As every pair of sparrows hatches out ten or more young ones in a year, while their food supply remains stationary, it is just as well that the Attabs of the community should have that idea of how to pass an amusing afternoon,' said Gregory. Having delivered himself of this sage comment he lit another cigarette, bade Jocantha a playfully affectionate good-bye, and departed into the outer world.

'Remember, dinner's a wee bit earlier tonight, as we're going to the Haymarket,' she called after him.

Left to herself, Jocantha continued the process of looking at

her life with placid, introspective eyes. If she had not everything
she wanted in this world, at least she was very well pleased with
what she had got. She was very well pleased, for instance, with
the snuggery, which contrived somehow to be cozy and dainty
and expensive all at once. The porcelain was rare and beautiful,
the Chinese enamels took on wonderful tints in the firelight, the
rugs and hangings led the éye through sumptuous harmonies
of colouring. It was a room in which one might have suitably
entertained an ambassador or an archbishop, but it was also a
room in which one could cut out pictures for a scrap-book without
feeling that one was scandalizing the deities of the place with
one's litter. And as with the snuggery, so with the rest of the
house, and as with the house, so with the other departments of
Jocantha's life; she really had good reason for being one of the
most contented women in Chelsea.

From being in a mood of simmering satisfaction with her lot
she passed to the phase of being generously commiserating for
those thousands around her whose lives and circumstances were
dull, cheap, pleasureless, and empty. Work girls, shop assistants
and so forth, the class that have neither the happy-go-lucky freedom of the poor nor the leisured freedom of the rich, came
specially within the range of her sympathy. It was sad to think
that there were young people who, after a long day's work, had
to sit alone in chill, dreary bedrooms because they could not afford
the price of a cup of coffee and a sandwich in a restaurant, still
less a shilling for a theatre gallery.

Jocantha's mind was still dwelling on this theme when she
started forth on an afternoon campaign of desultory shopping;
it would be rather a comforting thing, she told herself, if she
could do something, on the spur of the moment, to bring a
gleam of pleasure and interest into the life of even one or two
wistful-hearted, empty-pocketed workers; it would add a good
deal to her sense of enjoyment at the theatre that night. She would
get two upper circle tickets for a popular play, make her way
into some cheap tea-shop, and present the tickets to the first couple
of interesting work girls with whom she could casually drop into
conversation. She could explain matters by saying that she was
unable to use the tickets herself and did not want them to be
wasted, and, on the other hand, did not want the trouble of
sending them back. On further reflection she decided that it
might be better to get only one ticket and give it to some lonely-
looking girl sitting eating her frugal meal by herself; the girl

might scrape acquaintance with her next-seat neighbour at the theatre and lay the foundations of a lasting friendship.

With the Fairy Godmother impulse strong upon her, Jocantha marched into a ticket agency and selected with immense care an upper circle seat for the 'Yellow Peacock', a play that was attracting a considerable amount of discussion and criticism. Then she went forth in search of a tea-shop and philanthropic adventure, at about the same time that Attab sauntered into the garden with a mind attuned to sparrow stalking. In a corner of an A.B.C. shop she found an unoccupied table, whereat she promptly installed herself, impelled by the fact that at the next table was sitting a young girl, rather plain of feature, with tired, listless eyes and a general air of uncomplaining forlornness. Her dress was of poor material, but aimed at being in the fashion, her hair was pretty, and her complexion bad; she was finishing a modest meal of tea and scone, and she was not very different in her way from thousands of other girls who were finishing, or beginning, or continuing their teas in London tea-shops at that exact moment. The odds were enormously in favour of the supposition that she had never seen the 'Yellow Peacock'; obviously she supplied excellent material for Jocantha's first experiment in haphazard benefaction.

Jocantha ordered some tea and a muffin, and then turned a friendly scrutiny on her neighbour with a view to catching her eye. At that precise moment the girl's face lit up with sudden pleasure, her eyes sparkled, a flush came into her cheeks, and she looked almost pretty. A young man, whom she greeted with an affectionate 'Hullo, Bertie' came up to her table and took his seat in a chair facing her. Jocantha looked hard at the new-comer; he was in appearance a few years younger than herself, very much better looking than Gregory, rather better looking, in fact, than any of the young men of her set. She guessed him to be a well-mannered young clerk in some wholesale warehouse, existing and amusing himself as best he might on a tiny salary, and commanding a holiday of about two weeks in the year. He was aware, of course, of his good looks, but with the shy self-consciousness of the Anglo-Saxon, not the blatant complacency of the Latin or Semite. He was obviously on terms of friendly intimacy with the girl he was talking to, probably they were drifting towards a formal engagement. Jocantha pictured the boy's home, in a rather narrow circle, with a tiresome mother who always wanted to know how and where he spent his evenings.

He would exchange that humdrum thraldom in due course for
a home of his own, dominated by a chronic scarcity of pounds,
shillings, and pence, and a dearth of most of the things that made
life attractive or comfortable. Jocantha felt extremely sorry for
him. She wondered if he had seen the 'Yellow Peacock'; the odds
were enormously in favour of the supposition that he had not. The
girl had finished her tea, and would shortly be going back to her
work; when the boy was alone it would be quite easy for Jocantha
to say: 'My husband has made other arrangements for me this
evening; would you care to make use of this ticket, which would
otherwise be wasted?' Then she could come there again one afternoon for tea, and, if she saw him, ask him how he liked the play.
If he was a nice boy and improved on acquaintance he could be
given more theatre tickets and perhaps asked to come one Sunday
to tea at Chelsea. Jocantha made up her mind that he would
improve on acquaintance, and that Gregory would like him, and
that the Fairy Godmother would prove far more entertaining
than she had originally anticipated. The boy was distinctly pre-
sentable; he knew how to brush his hair, which was possibly
an imitative faculty; he knew what colour of tie suited him,
which might be intuition; he was exactly the type that Jocantha
admired, which of course was accident. Altogether she was rather
pleased when the girl looked at the clock and bade a friendly but
hurried farewell to her companion. Bertie nodded 'good-bye',
gulped down a mouthful of tea, and then produced from his
overcoat pocket a paper-covered book, bearing the title *Sepoy and
Sahib, a Tale of the Great Mutiny*.

The laws of tea-shop etiquette forbid that you should offer
theatre tickets to a stranger without having first caught the stranger's eye. It is even better if you can ask to have a sugar basin passed
to you, having previously concealed the fact that you have a
large and well-filled sugar basin on your own table; this is not
difficult to manage, as the printed menu is generally nearly as
large as the table, and can be made to stand on end. Jocantha set
to work hopefully; she had a long and rather high-pitched discussion with the waitress concerning alleged defects in an altogether blameless muffin, she made loud and plaintive inquiries
about the tube service to some impossibly remote suburb, she
talked with brilliant insincerity to the tea-shop kitten, and as a
last resort she upset a milk-jug and swore at it daintily. Altogether
she attracted a good deal of attention, but never for a moment did
she attract the attention of the boy with the beautifully brushed

hair, who was some thousands of miles away in the baking plains of Hindostan, amid deserted bungalows, seething bazaars, and riotous barrack squares, listening to the throbbing of tom-toms and the distant rattle of musketry.

Jocantha went back to her house in Chelsea, which struck her for the first time as looking dull and over-furnished. She had a resentful conviction that Gregory would be uninteresting at dinner, and that the play would be stupid after dinner. On the whole her frame of mind showed a marked divergence from the purring complacency of Attab, who was again curled up in his corner of the divan with a great peace radiating from every curve of his body.

But then he had killed his sparrow.

THE EASTER EGG

It was distinctly hard lines for Lady Barbara, who came of good fighting stock, and was one of the bravest women of her genera-tion, that her son should be so undisguisedly a coward. Whatever good qualities Lester Slaggby may have possessed, and he was in some respects charming, courage could certainly never be imputed to him. As a child he had suffered from childish timidity, as a boy from unboyish funk, and as a youth he had exchanged un-reasoning fears for others which were more formidable from the fact of having a carefully thought-out basis. He was frankly afraid of animals, nervous with firearms, and never crossed the Channel without mentally comparing the numerical proportion of lifebelts to passengers. On horseback he seemed to require as many hands as a Hindu god, at least four for clutching the reins, and two more for patting the horse soothingly on the neck. Lady Barbara no longer pretended not to see her son's prevailing weak-ness; with her usual courage she faced the knowledge of it squarely, and, motherlike, loved him none the less.

Continental travel, anywhere away from the great tourist tracks, was a favoured hobby with Lady Barbara, and Lester joined her as often as possible. Eastertide usually found her at Knobaltheim, an upland township in one of those small princedoms that make freckles on the map of Central Europe.

A long-standing acquaintanceship with the reigning family made her a personage of due importance in the eyes of her old friend the Burgomaster, and she was anxiously consulted by that worthy on the momentous occasion when the Prince made known his intention of coming in person to open a sanatorium outside the town. All the usual items in a programme of welcome, some of them fatuous and commonplace, others quaint and charming, had been arranged for, but the Burgomaster hoped that the resourceful English lady might have something new and tasteful to suggest in the way of loyal greeting. The Prince was known to the outside world, if at all, as an old-fashioned reactionary, combating modern progress, as it were, with a wooden sword; to his own people he was known as a kindly old gentleman with a certain endearing stateliness which had nothing of standoffishness about it. Knobaltheim was anxious to do its best. Lady Barbara discussed the matter with Lester and one or two acquaintances in her little hotel, but ideas were difficult to come by.

'Might I suggest something to the gnädige Frau?' asked a sallow high-cheek-boned lady to whom the Englishwoman had spoken once or twice, and whom she had set down in her mind as probably a Southern Slav.

'Might I suggest something for the Reception Fest?' she went on, with a certain shy eagerness. 'Our little child here, our baby, we will dress him in a little white coat, with small wings, as an Easter angel, and he will carry a large white Easter egg, and inside shall be a basket of plover eggs, of which the Prince is so fond, and he shall give it to his Highness as Easter offering. It is so pretty an idea; we have seen it done once in Styria.'

Lady Barbara looked dubiously at the proposed Easter angel, a fair, wooden-faced child of about four years old. She had noticed it the day before in the hotel, and wondered rather how such a tow-headed child could belong to such a dark-visaged couple as the woman and her husband; probably, she thought, an adopted baby, especially as the couple were not young.

'Of course Gnädige Frau will escort the little child up to the Prince,' pursued the woman; 'but he will be quite good, and do as he is told.'

'We haf some pluffers' eggs shall come fresh from Wien,' said the husband.

The small child and Lady Barbara seemed equally unenthusiastic about the pretty idea; Lester was openly discouraging, but when the Burgomaster heard of it he was enchanted. The combination of sentiment and plovers' eggs appealed strongly to his Teutonic mind.

On the eventful day the Easter angel, really quite prettily and quaintly dressed, was a centre of kindly interest to the gala crowd marshalled to receive his Highness. The mother was unobtrusive and less fussy than most parents would have been under the circumstances, merely stipulating that she should place the Easter egg herself in the arms that had been carefully schooled how to hold the precious burden. Then Lady Barbara moved forward, the child marching stolidly and with grim determination at her side. It had been promised cakes and sweeties galore if it gave the egg well and truly to the kind old gentleman who was waiting to receive it. Lester had tried to convey to it privately that horrible smackings would attend any failure in its share of the proceedings, but it is doubtful if his German caused more than an immediate distress. Lady Barbara had thoughtfully provided herself with an emergency supply of chocolate sweetmeats; children may sometimes be time-servers, but they do not encourage long accounts. As they approached nearer to the princely daïs Lady Barbara stood discreetly aside, and the stolid-faced infant walked forward alone, with staggering but steadfast gait, encouraged by a murmur of elderly approval. Lester, standing in the front row of the onlookers, turned to scan the crowd for the beaming faces of the happy parents. In a side-road which led to the railway station he saw a cab; entering the cab with every appearance of furtive haste were the dark-visaged couple who had been so plausibly eager for the 'pretty idea.' The sharpened instinct of cowardice lit up the situation to him in one swift flash. The blood roared and surged to his head as though thousands of floodgates had been opened in his veins and arteries, and his brain was the common sluice in which all the torrents met. He saw nothing but a blur around him. Then the blood ebbed away in quick waves, till his very heart seemed drained and empty, and he stood nervously, helplessly, dumbly watching the child, bearing its accursed burden with slow, relentless steps nearer and nearer to the group that waited sheep-like to receive him. A fascinated curiosity compelled Lester to turn his head towards the fugitives; the cab had started at hot pace in the direction of the station.

The next moment Lester was running, running faster than any of those present had ever seen a man run, and – he was not running away. For that stray fraction of his life some unwonted impulse beset him, some hint of the stock he came from, and he ran unflinchingly towards danger. He stooped and clutched at the Easter egg as one tries to scoop up the ball in Rugby football. What he meant to do with it he had not considered, the thing was to get it. But the child had been promised cakes and sweetmeats if it safely gave the egg into the hands of the kindly old gentleman; it uttered no scream, but it held to its charge with limpet grip. Lester sank to his knees, tugging savagely at the tightly clasped burden, and angry cries rose from the scandalized onlookers. A questioning, threatening ring formed round him, then shrank back in recoil as he shrieked out one hideous word. Lady Barbara heard the word and saw the crowd race away like scattered sheep, saw the Prince forcibly hustled away by his attendants; also she saw her son lying prone in any agony of overmastering terror, his spasm of daring shattered by the child's unexpected resistance, still clutching frantically, as though for safety, at that white-satin gew-gaw, unable to crawl even from its deadly neighbourhood, able only to scream and scream and scream. In her brain she was dimly conscious of balancing, or striving to balance, the abject shame which had him now in thrall against the one compelling act of courage which had flung him grandly and madly on to the point of danger. It was only for the fraction of a minute that she stood watching the two entangled figures, the infant with its woodenly obstinate face and body tense with dogged resistance, and the boy limp and already nearly dead with a terror that almost stifled his screams; and over them the long gala streamers flapping gaily in the sunshine. She never forgot the scene; but then, it was the last she ever saw.

Lady Barbara carries her scarred face with its sightless eyes as bravely as ever in the world, but at Eastertide her friends are careful to keep from her ears any mention of the children's Easter symbol.

MORLVERA

The Olympic Toy Emporium occupied a conspicuous frontage in an important West End street. It was happily named Toy Emporium, because one would never have dreamed of according it the familiar and yet pulse-quickening name of toyshop. There was an air of cold splendour and elaborate failure about the wares that were set out in its ample windows; they were the sort of toys that a tired shop-assistant displays and explains at Christmastime to exclamatory parents and bored, silent children. The animal toys looked more like natural history models than the comfortable, sympathetic companions that one would wish, at a certain age, to take to bed with one, and to smuggle into the bathroom. The mechanical toys incessantly did things that no one could want a toy to do more than half a dozen times in its lifetime; it was a merciful reflection that in any right-minded nursery the lifetime would certainly be short.

Prominent among the elegantly dressed dolls that filled an entire section of the window frontage was a large hobble-skirted lady in a confection of peach-coloured velvet, elaborately set off with leopard skin accessories, if one may use such a conveniently comprehensive word in describing an intricate feminine toilette. She lacked nothing that is to be found in a carefully detailed fashion-plate – in fact, she might be said to have something more than the average fashion-plate female possesses; in place of a vacant, expressionless stare she had character in her face. It must be admitted that it was bad character, cold, hostile, inquisitorial, with a sinister lowering of one eyebrow and a merciless hardness about the corners of the mouth. One might have imagined histories about her by the hour, histories in which unworthy ambition, the desire for money, and an entire absence of all decent feeling would play a conspicuous part.

As a matter of fact, she was not without her judges and biographers, even in this shop-window stage of her career. Emmeline, aged ten, and Bert, aged seven, had halted on the way from their obscure back street to the minnow-stocked water of St James's Park, and were critically examining the hobble-skirted doll, and dissecting her character in no very tolerant spirit. There is probably a latent enmity between the necessarily under-clad and the unnecessarily over-dressed, but a little kindness and good-fellowship on the part of the latter will often change the sentiment to admiring devotion; if the lady in peach-coloured velvet and leopard skin had worn a pleasant expression in addition to her other elaborate furnishings, Emmeline at least might have respected and even loved her. As it was, she gave her a horrible reputation, based chiefly on a second-hand knowledge of gilded depravity derived from the conversation of those who were skilled in the art of novelette reading. Bert filled in a few damaging details from his own limited imagination.

'She is a bad lot, that one is,' declared Emmeline, after a long unfriendly stare; ''er 'usband 'ates 'er.'

''E knocks 'er abart,' said Bert with enthusiasm.

'No, 'e don't, cos 'e's dead; she poisoned 'im slow and gradual, so that nobody didn't know. Now she wants to marry a lord, with 'eaps and 'eaps of money. 'E's got a wife already, but she's going to poison 'er, too.'

'She's a bad lot, said Bert with growing hostility.

''Er mother 'ates 'er, and she's afraid of 'er, too, cos she's got a serkestic tongue; always talking serkesms, she is. She's greedy too; if there's fish going, she eats 'er own share and 'er little girl's as well, though the little girl is dellikit.'

'She 'ad a little boy once,' said Bert, 'but she pushed 'im into the water when nobody wasn't looking.'

'No, she didn't,' said Emmeline, 'she sent 'im away to be kep' by poor people, so 'er husbind wouldn't know where 'e was. They ill-treat 'im somethink cruel.'

'Wot's 'er nime?' asked Bert, thinking that it was time that so interesting a personality should be labelled.

''Er nime?' said Emmeline, thinking hard, ''er nime's Morl-vera.' It was as near as she could get to the name of an adventur-ess who figured prominently in a cinema drama. There was silence for a moment while the possibilities of the name were turned over in the children's minds.

'Those clothes she's got on ain't paid for, and never won't be,' said Emmeline; 'she thinks she'll get the rich lord to pay for 'em, but 'e wont. 'E's given 'er jools, 'underds of pounds' worth.'

''E won't pay for the clothes,' said Bert with conviction. Evidently there was some limit to the weak good nature of wealthy lords.

At that moment a motor carriage with liveried servants drew up at the emporium entrance; a large lady, with a penetrating and rather hurried manner of talking, stepped out, followed slowly and sulkily by a small boy, who had a very black scowl on his face and a very white sailor suit over the rest of him. The lady was continuing an argument which had probably commenced in Portman Square.

'Now, Victor, you are to come in and buy a nice doll for your cousin Bertha. She gave you a beautiful box of soldiers on your birthday, and you must give her a present on hers.'

'Bertha is a fat little fool,' said Victor, in a voice that was as loud as his mother's and had more assurance in it.

'Victor, you are not to say such things. Bertha is not a fool, and she is not in the least fat. You are to come in and choose a doll for her.'

The couple passed into the shop, out of view and hearing of the two back-street children.

'My, he is in a wicked temper,' exclaimed Emmeline, but both she and Bert were inclined to side with him against the absent Bertha, who was doubtless as fat and foolish as he had described her to be.

'I want to see some dolls,' said the mother of Victor to the nearest assistant; 'it's for a little girl of eleven.'

'A fat little girl of eleven,' added Victor by way of supplementary information.

'Victor, if you say such rude things about your cousin, you shall go to bed the moment we get home, without any tea.'

'This is one of the newest things we have in dolls,' said the assistant, removing a hobble-skirted figure in peach-coloured velvet from the window; 'leopard-skin toque and stole, the latest fashion. You won't get anything newer than that anywhere. It's an exclusive design.'

'Look!' whispered Emmeline outside; 'they've bin and took Morlvera.'

There was a mingling of excitement and a certain sense of bereavement in her mind; she would have liked to gaze at that embodiment of overdressed depravity for just a little longer.

'I 'spect she's going away in a kerridge to marry the rich lord,' hazarded Bert.

'She's up to no good,' said Emmeline vaguely.

Inside the shop the purchase of the doll had been decided on.

'It's a beautiful doll, and Bertha will be delighted with it,' asserted the mother of Victor loudly.

'Oh, very well,' said Victor sulkily; 'you needn't have it stuck into a box and wait an hour while it's being done up into a parcel. I'll take it as it is, and we can go round to Manchester Square and give it to Bertha, and get the thing done with. That will save me the trouble of writing. "For dear Bertha, with Victor's love", on a bit of paper.'

'Very well,' said his mother, 'we can go to Manchester Square on our way home. You must wish her many happy returns of tomorrow, and give her the doll.'

'I won't let the little beast kiss me,' stipulated Victor.

His mother said nothing; Victor had not been half as troublesome as she had anticipated. When he chose he could really be dreadfully naughty.

Emmeline and Bert were just moving away from the window

when Morlvera made her exit from the shop, very carefully held in Victor's arms. A look of sinister triumph seemed to glow in her hard, inquisitorial face. As for Victor, a certain scornful serenity had replaced the earlier scowls he had evidently accepted defeat with a contemptuous good grace.

The tall lady gave a direction to the footman and settled herself in the carriage. The little figure in the white sailor suit clambered in beside her, still carefully holding the elegantly garbed doll.

The car had to be backed a few yards in the process of turning. Very stealthily, very gently, very mercilessly Victor sent Morlvera flying over his shoulder, so that she fell into the road just behind the retrogressing wheel. With a soft, pleasant-sounding scrunch the car went over the prostrate form, then it moved forward again with another scrunch. The carriage moved off and left Bert and Emmeline gazing in scared delight at a sorry mess of petrol-smeared velvet, sawdust, and leopard skin, which was all that remained of the hateful Morlvera. They gave a shrill cheer, and then raced away shuddering from the scene of so much rapidly enacted tragedy.

Later that afternoon, when they were engaged in the pursuit of minnows by the waterside in St James's Park, Emmeline said in a solemn undertone to Bert –

'I've been finking. Do you know oo 'e was? 'E was 'er little boy wot she'd sent away to live wiv poor folks. 'E come back and done that.'

THE OCCASIONAL GARDEN

'Don't talk to me about town gardens,' said Elinor Rapsley; 'which means, of course, that I want you to listen to me for an hour or so while I talk about nothing else. "What a nice-sized garden you've got," people said to us when we first moved here. What I suppose they meant to say was what a nice-sized site for a garden we'd got. As a matter of fact, the size is all against it; it's too large to be ignored altogether and treated as a yard, and it's too small to keep giraffes in. You see, if we could keep giraffes or reindeer or some other species of browsing animal there we could explain the general absence of vegetation by a reference to the fauna of the garden: "You can't have wapiti *and* Darwin tulips, you know, so we didn't put down any bulbs last year." As it is, we haven't got the wapiti, and the Darwin tulips haven't survived the fact that most of the cats of the neighbourhood hold a parliament in the centre of the tulip bed; that rather forlorn-looking strip that we intended to be a border of alternating geranium and spiræa has been utilized by the cat-parliament as a division lobby. Snap divisions seem to have been rather frequent of late, far more frequent that the geranium blooms are likely to be. I shouldn't object so much to ordinary cats, but I do complain of having a congress of vegetarian cats in my garden; they must be vegetarians, my dear, because, whatever ravages they may commit among the sweet-pea seedlings, they never seem to touch the sparrows; there are always just as many adult sparrows in the garden on Saturday as there were on Monday, not to mention newly fledged additions. There seems to have been an irreconcilable difference of opinions between sparrows and Providence since the beginning of time as to whether a crocus looks best standing upright with its roots in the earth or in a recumbent posture with its stem neatly severed; the sparrows always have the last word in the matter, at least in our garden they do. I fancy that Providence must have originally intended to bring in an amending Act, or whatever it's called, providing either for a less destructive sparrow or a more indestructible crocus. The one consoling point about our garden is that it's not visible from the drawing-room or the smoking-room, so unless people are dining or lunching with us they can't spy out the nakedness of the land. That is why I am so furious with Gwenda Pottingdon, who has practically forced herself on me for lunch on Wednesday next; she heard me offer the Paulcote girl lunch if she was up shopping on that day, and, of course, she asked if she might come too. She is only coming to gloat over my bedraggled and flowerless borders and to sing the praises of her own detestably over-cultivated garden. I'm sick of being told that it's the envy of the neighbourhood; it's like everything else that belongs to her – her car, her dinner-parties, even her headaches, they are all superlative; no one else ever had anything like them. When her eldest child was confirmed it was such a sensational event, according to her account of it, that one almost expected questions to be asked about it in the House of Commons and now she's coming on purpose to stare at my few miserable pansies and the gaps in my sweet-pea border, and to give me a glowing full-length description of the rare and sumptuous blooms in her rose-garden.'

'My dear Elinor,' said the Baroness, 'you would save yourself

all this heart-burning and a lot of gardener's bills, not to mention
sparrow anxieties, simply by paying an annual subscription to the
O.O.S.A.'

'Never heard of it,' said Elinor; 'what is it?'

'The Occasional-Oasis Supply Association,' said the Baroness;
'it exists to meet cases exactly like yours, cases of backyards that
are of no practical use for gardening purposes, but are required
to blossom into decorative scenic backgrounds at stated intervals,
when a luncheon or dinner-party is contemplated. Supposing, for
instance, you have people coming to lunch at one-thirty; you just
ring up the Association at about ten o'clock the same morning,
and say, "Lunch garden." That is all the trouble you have to take.
By twelve forty-five your yard is carpeted with a strip of velvety
turf, with a hedge of lilac or red may, or whatever happens to be
in season, as a background, one or two cherry trees in blossom,
and clumps of heavily flowered rhododendrons filling in the odd
corners; in the foreground you have a blaze of carnations or Shir-
ley poppies, or tiger lilies in full bloom. As soon as the lunch is
over and your guests have departed the garden departs also, and
all the cats in Christendom can sit in council in your yard without
causing you a moment's anxiety. If you have a bishop or an anti-
quary or something of that sort coming to lunch you just mention
the fact when you are ordering the garden, and you get an old-
world pleasaunce, with clipped yew hedges and a sun-dial and
hollyhocks, and perhaps a mulberry tree, and borders of sweet-
williams and Canterbury bells, and an old-fashioned beehive or
two tucked away in a corner. Those are the ordinary lines of
supply that the Oasis Association undertakes, but by paying a
few guineas a year extra you are entitled to its emergency E.O.N.
service.'

'What on earth is an E.O.N. service?'

'It's just like a conventional signal to indicate special cases like
the incursion of Gwenda Pottingdon. It means you've got someone coming to lunch or dinner whose garden is alleged to be 'the
envy of the neighbourhood.'

'Yes,' exclaimed Elinor, with some excitement, 'and what happens then?'

'Something that sounds like a miracle out of the Arabian Nights.
Your backyard becomes voluptuous with pomegranate and almond
trees, lemon groves, and hedges of flowering cactus, dazzling
banks of azaleas, marble-basined fountains, in which chestnut-and-
white pond-herons step daintily amid exotic water-lilies, while

golden pheasants strut about on alabaster terraces. The whole effect rather suggests the idea that Providence and Norman Wilkinson have dropped mutual jealousies and collaborated to produce a background for an open-air Russian Ballet; in point of fact, it is merely the background to your luncheon party. If there is any kick left in Gwenda Pottingdon, or whoever your E.O.N. guest of the moment may be, just mention carelessly that your climbing putella is the only one in England, since the one at Chatsworth died last winter. There isn't such a thing as a climbing putella, but Gwenda Pottingdon and her kind don't usually know one flower from another without prompting.'

'Quick,' said Elinor, 'the address of the Association.'

Gwenda Pottingdon did not enjoy her lunch. It was a simple yet elegant meal, excellently cooked and daintily served, but the picquant sauce of her own conversation was notably lacking. She had prepared a long succession of eulogistic comments on the wonders of her town garden, with its unrivalled effects of horticultural magnificence, and, behold, her theme was shut in on every side by the luxuriant hedge of Siberian berberis that formed a glowing background to Elinor's bewildering fragment of fairyland. The pomegranate and lemon trees, the terraced fountain, where golden carp slithered and wriggled amid the roots of gorgeous-hued irises, the banked masses of exotic blooms, the pagoda-like enclosure, where Japanese sand-badgers disported themselves, all these contributed to take away Gwenda's appetite and moderate her desire to talk about gardening matters.

'I can't say I admire the climbing putella,' she observed shortly, 'and anyway it's not the only one of its kind in England; I happen to know of one in Hampshire. How gardening is going out of fashion, I suppose people haven't the time for it nowadays.'

Altogether it was quite one of Elinor's most successful luncheon parties.

It was distinctly an unforeseen catastrophe that Gwenda should have burst in on the household four days later at lunchtime and made her way unbidden into the dining-room.

'I thought I must tell you that my Elaine has had a water-colour sketch accepted by the Latent Talent Art Guild; it's to be exhibited at their summer exhibition at the Hackney Gallery. It will be the sensation of the moment in the art world— Hallo, what on earth has happened to your garden? It's not there!'

'Suffragettes,' said Elinor promptly; 'didn't you hear about it? They broke in and made hay of the whole thing in about ten minutes. I was so heartbroken at the havoc that I had the whole place cleared out; I shall have it laid out again on rather more elaborate lines.

'That,' she said to the Baroness afterwards, 'is what I call having an emergency brain.'

THE SECRET SIN OF SEPTIMUS BROPE

'Who and what is Mr Brope?' demanded the aunt of Clovis suddenly.

Mrs Riversedge, who had been snipping off the heads of defunct roses, and thinking of nothing in particular, sprang hurriedly to mental attention. She was one of those old-fashioned hostesses who consider that one ought to know something about one's guests, and that the something ought to be to their credit.

'I believe he comes from Leighton Buzzard,' she observed by way of preliminary explanation.

'In these days of rapid and convenient travel,' said Clovis, who was dispersing a colony of green-fly with visitations of cigarette smoke, 'to come from Leighton Buzzard does not necessarily denote any great strength of character. It might only mean mere restlessness. Now if he had left it under a cloud, or as a 'protest against the incurable and heartless frivolity of its inhabitants, that would tell us something about the man and his mission in life.'

'What does he do?' pursued Mrs Troyle magisterially.

'He edits the *Cathedral Monthly*,' said her hostess, 'and he's enormously learned about memorial brasses and transepts and the influence of Byzantine worship on modern liturgy, and all those sort of things. Perhaps he is just a little bit heavy and immersed in one range of subjects, but it takes all sorts to make a good house-party, you know. You don't find him *too* dull, do you?'

'Dullness I could overlook,' said the aunt of Clovis: 'what I cannot forgive is his making love to my maid.'

'My dear Mrs Troyle,' gasped the hostess, 'what an extraordinary idea! I assure you Mr Brope would not dream of doing such a thing.'

'His dreams are a matter of indifference to me; for all I care his slumbers may be one long indiscretion of unsuitable erotic advances, in which the entire servants' hall may be involved. But in his waking hours he shall not make love to my maid. It's no use arguing about it, I'm firm on the point.'

'But you must be mistaken,' persisted Mrs Riversedge; 'Mr Brope would be the last person to do such a thing.'

'He is the first person to do such a thing, as far as my information goes, and if I have any voice in the matter he certainly shall be the last. Of course, I am not referring to respectably-intentioned lovers.'

'I simply cannot think that a man who writes so charmingly and informingly about transepts and Byzantine influences would behave in such an unprincipled manner,' said Mrs Riversedge; 'what evidence have you that he's doing anything of the sort? I don't want to doubt your word, of course, but we mustn't be too ready to condemn him unheard, must we?'

'Whether we condemn him or not, he has certainly not been unheard. He has the room next to my dressing-room, and on two occasions, when I daresay he thought I was absent, I have plainly heard him announcing through the wall, "I love you, Florrie." Those partition walls upstairs are very thin; one can almost hear a watch ticking in the next room.'

'Is your maid called Florence?'

'Her name is Florinda.'

'What an extraordinary name to give a maid!'

'I did not give it to her; she arrived in my service already christened.'

'What I mean is,' said Mrs Riversedge, 'that when I get maids with unsuitable names I call them Jane; they soon get used to it.'

'An excellent plan,' said the aunt of Clovis coldly, 'unfortunately I have got used to being called Jane myself. It happens to be my name.'

She cut short Mrs Riversedge's flood of apologies by abruptly remarking:

'The question is not whether I'm to call my maid Florinda, but whether Mr Brope is to be permitted to call her Florrie. I am strongly of opinion that he shall not.'

'He may have been repeating the words of some song,' said Mrs Riversedge hopefully; 'there are lots of those sorts of silly refrains with girls' names,' she continued, turning to Clovis as a possible authority on the subject. "You mustn't call me Mary —"

'I shouldn't think of doing so,' Clovis assured her; 'in the first place, I've always understood that your name was Henrietta; and then I hardly know you well enough to take such a liberty.'

'I mean there's a *song* with that refrain,' hurriedly explained Mrs Riversedge, 'and there's "Rhoda, Rhoda kept a pagoda," and "Maisie is a daisy," and heaps of others. Certainly it doesn't sound like Mr Brope to be singing such songs, but I think we ought to give him the benefit of the doubt.'

'I had already done so,' said Mrs Troyle, 'until further evidence came my way.'

She shut her lips with the resolute finality of one who enjoys the blessed certainty of being implored to open them again.

'Further evidence!' exclaimed her hostess; 'do tell me!'

'As I was coming upstairs after breakfast Mr Brope was just passing my room. In the most natural way in the world a piece of paper dropped out of a packet that he held in his hand and fluttered to the ground just at my door. I was going to call out to him "You've dropped something," and then for some reason I held back and didn't show myself till he was safely in his room. You see it occurred to me that I was very seldom in my room just at that hour, and that Florinda was almost always there tidying up things about that time. So I picked up that innocent-looking piece of paper.'

Mrs Troyle paused again, with the self-applauding air of one who has detected an asp lurking in an apple-charlotte.

Mrs Riversedge snipped vigorously at the nearest rose bush, incidentally decapitating a Viscountess Folkestone that was just coming into bloom.

'What was on the paper?' she asked .

'Just the words in pencil, "I love you, Florrie," and then underneath, crossed out with a faint line, but perfectly plain to read, "Meet me in the garden by the yew." '

'There *is* a yew tree at the bottom of the garden,' admitted Mrs Riversedge.

'At any rate he appears to be truthful,' commented Clovis.

'To think that a scandal of this sort should be going on under my roof!' said Mrs Riversedge indignantly.

'I wonder why it is that scandal seems so much worse under a roof,' observed Clovis; 'I've always regarded it as a proof of the superior delicacy of the cat tribe that it conducts most of its scandals above the slates.'

'Now I come to think of it,' resumed Mrs Riversedge, 'there are things about Mr Brope that I've never been able to account for. His income, for instance: he only gets two hundred a year as editor of the *Cathedral Monthly,* and I know that his people are quite poor, and he hasn't any private means. Yet he manages to afford a flat somewhere in Westminster, and he goes abroad to Bruges and those sorts of places every year, and always dresses well, and gives quite nice luncheon-parties in the season. You can't do all that on two hundred a year, can you?'

'Does he write for any other papers?' queried Mrs Troyle.

'No, you see he specializes so entirely on liturgy and ecclesiastical architecture that his field is rather restricted. He once tried the *Sporting and Dramatic* with an article on church edifices in famous fox-hunting centres, but it wasn't considered of sufficient general interest to be accepted. No, I don't see how he can support himself in his present style merely by what he writes.'

'Perhaps he sells spurious transepts to American enthusiasts,' suggested Clovis.

'How could you sell a transept?' said Mrs Riversedge; such a thing would be impossible. '

'Whatever he may do to eke out his income,' interrupted Mrs Troyle, 'he is certainly not going to fill in his leisure moments by making love to my maid.'

'Of course not,' agreed her hostess; 'that must be put a stop to at once. But I don't quite know what we ought to do.'

'You might put a barbed wire entanglement round the yew tree as a precautionary measure,' said Clovis.

'I don't think that the disagreeable situation that has arisen is improved by flippancy,' said Mrs Riversedge; 'a good maid is a treasure –'

'I am sure I don't know what I should do without Florinda,' admitted Mrs Troyle; 'she understands my hair. I've long ago given up trying to do anything with it myself. I regard one's hair as I regard husbands: as long as one is seen together in public one's private divergences don't matter. Surely that was the luncheon gong.'

Septimus Brope and Clovis had the smoking-room to themselves after lunch. The former seemed restless and preoccupied, the latter quietly observant.

'What is a lorry?' asked Septimus suddenly; 'I don't mean

the thing on wheels, of course I know what that is, but isn't there a bird with a name like that, the larger form of a lorikeet?'

'I fancy it's a lorry, with one "r," ' said Clovis lazily, 'in which case it's no good to you.'

Septimus Brope stared in some astonishment.

'How do you mean, no good to me?' he asked, with more than a trace of uneasiness in his voice.

'Won't rhyme with Florrie,' explained Clovis briefly.

Septimus sat upright in his chair, with unmistakable alarm on his face.

'How did you find out? I mean, how did you know I was trying to get a rhyme to Florrie?' he asked sharply.

'I didn't know,' said Clovis, 'I only guessed. When you wanted to turn the prosaic lorry of commerce into a feathered poem flitting through the verdure of a tropical forest, I knew you must be working up a sonnet, and Florrie was the only female name that suggested itself as rhyming with lorry.'

Septimus still looked uneasy.

'I believe you know more,' he said.

Clovis laughed quietly, but said nothing.

'How much do you know?' Septimus asked desperately.

'The yew tree in the garden,' said Clovis.

'There! I felt certain I'd dropped it somewhere. But you must have guessed something before. Look here, you have surprised my secret. You won't give me away, will you? It is nothing to be ashamed of, but it wouldn't do for the editor of the *Cathedral Monthly* to go in openly for that sort of thing, would it?'

'Well, I suppose not,' admitted Clovis.

'You see,' continued Septimus, 'I get quite a decent lot of money out of it. I could never live in the style I do on what I get as editor of the *Cathedral Monthly*.'

Clovis was even more startled than Septimus had been earlier in the conversation, but he was better skilled in repressing surprise.

'Do you mean to say you get money out of – Florrie?' he asked.

'Not out of Florrie, as yet,' said Septimus; 'in fact, I don't mind saying that I'm having a good deal of trouble over Florrie. But there are a lot of others.'

Clovis's cigarette went out.

'This is *very* interesting,' he said slowly. And then, with Septimus Brope's next words, illumination dawned on him.

'There are heaps of others; for instance:

> "Cora with the lips of coral,
> You and I will never quarrel."

That was one of my earliest successes, and it still brings me in royalties. And then there is – "Esmeralda, when I first beheld her," and "Fair Teresa, how I love to please her," both of those have been fairly popular. And there is one rather dreadful one,' continued Septimus, flushing deep carmine, 'which has brought me in more money than any of the others:

> "Lively little Lucie
> With her naughty nez retrousse."

Of course, I loathe the whole lot of them; in fact, I'm rapidly becoming something of a woman-hater under their influence, but I can't afford to disregard the financial aspect of the matter. And at the same time you can understand that my position as an authority on ecclesiastical architecture and liturgical subjects would be weakened, if not altogether ruined, if it once got about that I was the author of "Cora with the lips of coral" and all the rest of them.'

Clovis had recovered sufficiently to ask in a sympathetic if rather unsteady, voice what was the special trouble with 'Florrie.'

'I can't get her into lyric shape, try as I will,' said Septimus mournfully. 'You see, one has to work in a lot of sentimental, sugary compliment with a catchy rhyme, and a certain amount of personal biography or prophecy. They've all of them got to have a long string of past successes recorded about them, or else you've got to foretell blissful things about them and yourself in the future. For instance, there is:

> "Dainty little girlie Mavis,
> She is such a rara avis,
> All the money I can save is
> All to be for Mavis mine."

It goes to a sickening namby-pamby waltz tune, and for months nothing else was sung and hummed in Blackpool and other popular centres.'

This time Clovis's self-control broke down badly.

'Please excuse me,' he gurgled, 'but I can't help it when I remember the awful solemnity of that article of yours that you so kindly read us last night, on the Coptic Church in its relation to early Christian worship.'

Septimus groaned.

'You see how it would be,' he said; 'as soon as people knew me to be the author of that miserable sentimental twaddle, all respect for the serious labours of my life would be gone. I dare say I know more about memorial brasses than anyone living, in fact I hope one day to publish a monograph on the subject, but I should be pointed out everywhere as the man whose ditties were in the mouths of nigger minstrels along the entire coast-line of our Island home. Can you wonder that I positively hate Florrie all the time that I'm trying to grind out sugar-coated rhapsodies about her?'

'Why not give free play to your emotions and be brutally abusive? An uncomplimentary refrain would have an instant success as a novelty if you were sufficiently outspoken.'

'I've never thought of that,' said Septimus, 'and I'm afraid I couldn't break away from the habit of fulsome adulation and suddenly change my style.'

'You needn't change your style in the least,' said Clovis; 'merely reverse the sentiment and keep to the inane phraseology of the thing. If you'll do the body of the song I'll knock off the refrain, which is the thing that principally matters, I believe. I shall charge half-shares in the royalties, and throw in my silence as to your guilty secret. In the eyes of the world you shall still be the man who has devoted his life to the study of transepts and Byzantine ritual; only sometimes, in the long winter evenings, when the wind howls drearily down the chimney and the rain beats against the windows, I shall think of you as the author of "Cora with the lips of coral." Of course, if in sheer gratitude at my silence you like to take me for a much-needed holiday to the Adriatic or somewhere equally interesting, paying all expenses, I shouldn't dream of refusing.'

Later in the afternoon Clovis found his aunt and Mrs River-sedge indulging in gentle exercise in the Jacobean garden.

'I've spoken to Mr Brope about F.,' he announced.

'How splendid of you! What did he say?' came in a quick chorus from the two ladies.

'He was quite frank and straightforward with me when he saw that I knew his secret,' said Clovis, 'and it seems that his intentions were quite serious, if slightly unsuitable. I tried to show him the impracticability of the course that he was follow-ing. He said he wanted to be understood, and he seemed to think that Florinda would excel in that requirement, but I pointed out that there were probably dozens of delicately nurtured, pure-hearted young English girls who would be capable of understanding him, while Florinda was the only person in the world who understood my aunt's hair. That rather weighed with him, for he's not really a selfish animal, if you take him in the right way, and when I appealed to the memory of his happy childish days, spent amid the daisied fields of Leighton Buzzard (I suppose daisies do grow there), he was obviously affected. Anyhow, he gave me his word that he would put Florinda absolutely out of his mind, and he has agreed to go for a short trip abroad as the best distraction for his thoughts. I am going with him as far as Ragusa. If my aunt should wish to give me a really nice scarf-pin (to be chosen by myself), as a small recognition of the very considerable service I have done her, I shouldn't dream of refusing. I'm not one of those who think that because one is abroad one can go about dressed anyhow.'

A few weeks later in Blackpool and places where they sing, the following refrain held undisputed sway:

> "How you bore me, Florrie,
>   With those eyes of vacant blue;
> You'll be very sorry, Florrie,
>   If I marry you.
> Though I'm easy-goin', Florrie,
>   This I swear is true,
> I'll throw you down a quarry, Florrie,
>   If I marry you."

THE BLIND SPOT

'You've just come back from Adelaide's funeral, haven't you?' said Sir Lulworth to his nephew; 'I suppose it was very like most other funerals?'

'I'll tell you about it at lunch,' said Egbert.

'You'll do nothing of the sort. It wouldn't be respectful either to your great-aunt's memory or to the lunch. We begin with Spanish olives, then a borsch, then more olives and a bird of some kind, and a rather enticing Rhenish wine, not at all expensive as wines go in this country, but still quite laudable in its way. Now there's absolutely nothing in that menu that harmonizes in the least with the subject of your great-aunt Adelaide or her funeral. She was a charming woman, and quite as intelligent as she had any need to be, but somehow she always reminded me of an English cook's idea of a Madras curry.'

'She used to say you were frivolous,' said Egbert. Something in his tone suggested that he rather endorsed the verdict.

'I believe I once considerably scandalized her by declaring that clear soup was a more important factor in life than a clear conscience. She had very little sense of proportion. By the way, she made you her principal heir, didn't she?'

'Yes,' said Egbert, 'and executor as well. It's in that connection that I particularly want to speak to you.'

'Business is not my strong point at any time,' said Sir Lulworth, 'and certainly not when we're on the immediate threshold of lunch.'

'It isn't exactly business,' explained Egbert, as he followed his uncle into the dining-room. 'It's something rather serious. Very serious.'

'Then we can't possibly speak about it now,' said Sir Lulworth; 'no one could talk seriously, during a borsch. A beautifully constructed borsch, such as you are going to experience presently, ought not only to banish conversation but almost to annihilate thought. Later on, when we arrive at the second stage of olives, I shall be quite ready to discuss that new book on Borrow, or, if you prefer it, the present situation in the Grand Duchy of Luxemburg. But I absolutely decline to talk anything approaching business till we have finished with the bird.'

For the greater part of the meal Egbert sat in an abstracted silence, the silence of a man whose mind is focussed on one topic. When the coffee stage had been reached he launched himself suddenly athwart his uncle's reminiscences of the Court of Luxemburg.

'I think I told you that great-aunt Adelaide had made me her executor. There wasn't very much to be done in the way of legal matters, but I had to go through her papers.'

'That would be a fairly heavy task. I should imagine there were reams of family letters.'

'Stacks of them, and most of them highly uninteresting. There was one packet, however, which I thought might repay a careful perusal. It was a bundle of correspondence from her brother Peter.'

'The Canon of tragic memory,' said Lulworth.

'Exactly, of tragic memory, as you say; a tragedy that has never been fathomed.'

'Probably the simplest explanation was the correct one,' said Sir Lulworth; 'he slipped on the stone staircase and fractured his skull in falling.'

Egbert shook his head. 'The medical evidence all went to prove that the blow on the head was struck by some one coming up behind him. A wound caused by violent contact with the steps could not possibly have been inflicted at that angle of the skull. They experimented with a dummy figure falling in every conceivable position.'

'But the motive?' exclaimed Sir Lulworth; 'no one had any interest in doing away with him, and the number of people who destroy Canons of the Established Church for the mere fun of killing must be extremely limited. Of course there are individuals of weak mental balance who do that sort of thing, but they seldom conceal their handiwork; they are more generally inclined to parade it.'

'His cook was under suspicion,' said Egbert shortly.

'I know he was,' said Sir Lulworth, 'simply because he was about the only person on the premises at the time of the tragedy. But could anything be sillier than trying to fasten a charge of murder on to Sebastien? He had nothing to gain, in fact, a good deal to lose, from the death of his employer. The Canon was paying him quite as good wages as I was able to offer him when I took him over into my service. I have since raised them to something a little more in accordance with his real worth, but at the time he was glad to find a new place without troubling about an increase of wages. People were fighting rather shy of him, and he had no friends in this country. No; if any one in the world was interested in the prolonged life and unimpaired digestion of the Canon it would certainly be Sebastien.'

'People don't always weigh the consequences of their rash acts,' said Egbert, 'otherwise there would be very few murders committed. Sebastien is a man of hot temper.'

'He is a Southerner,' admitted Sir Lulworth; 'to be geographically exact, I believe he hails from the French slopes of the Pyrennees. I took that into consideration when he nearly killed the gardener's boy the other day for bringing him a spurious substitute for sorrel. One must always make allowances for origin and locality and early environment; "Tell me your longitude and I'll know what latitude to allow you," is my motto.'

'There, you see,' said Egbert, 'he nearly killed the gardener's boy.'

'My dear Egbert, between nearly killing a gardener's boy and altogether killing a Canon there is a wide difference. No doubt you have often felt a temporary desire to kill a gardener's boy; you have never given way to it, and I respect you for your self-control. But I don't suppose you have ever wanted to kill an octogenerian Canon. Besides, as far as we know, there had never been any quarrel or disagreement between the two men. The evidence at the inquest brought that out very clearly.'

'Ah!' said Egbert, with the air of a man coming at last into a deferred inheritance of conversational importance, 'that is precisely what I want to speak to you about.'

He pushed away his coffee cup and drew a pocket-book from his inner breast-pocket. From the depths of the pocket-book he produced an envelope, and from the envelope he extracted a letter, closely written in a small, neat handwriting.

'One of the Canon's numerous letters to Aunt Adelaide,' he explained, 'written a few days before his death. Her memory was already failing when she received it, and I dare say she forgot the contents as soon as she had read it; otherwise, in the light of what subsequently happened, we should have heard something of this letter before now. If it had been produced at the inquest I fancy it would have made some difference in the course of affairs. The evidence, as you remarked just now, choked off suspicion against Sebastien by disclosing an utter absence of anything that could be considered a motive or provocation for the crime, if crime there was.'

'Oh, read the letter,' said Sir Lulworth impatiently.

'It's a long rambling affair, like most of his letters in his later years,' said Egbert. 'I'll read the part that bears immediately on the mystery.'

'"I very much fear I shall have to get rid of Sebastien. He cooks divinely, but he has the temper of a fiend or an anthropoid ape, and I am really in bodily fear of him. We had a dispute the other day as to the correct sort of lunch to be served on Ash Wednesday, and I got so irritated and annoyed at his conceit and obstinacy that at last I threw a cupful of coffee in his face and called him at the same time an impudent jackanapes. Very little of the coffee went actually in his face, but I have never seen a human being show such deplorable lack of self-control. I laughed at the threat of killing me that he spluttered out in his rage, and thought the whole thing would blow over, but I have several times since caught him scowling and muttering in a highly unpleasant fashion, and lately I have fancied that he was dogging my foot-steps about the grounds, particularly when I walk of an evening in the Italian Garden."

'It was on the steps in the Italian Garden that the body was found,' commented Egbert, and resumed reading.

'"I dare say the danger is imaginary; but I shall feel more at ease when he has quitted my service".'

Egbert paused for a moment at the conclusion of the extract; then, as his uncle made no remark, he added: 'If lack of motive was the only factor that saved Sebastien from prosecution, I fancy this letter will put a different complexion on matters.'

'Have you shown it to anyone else?' asked Sir Lulworth, reaching out his hand for the incriminating piece of paper.

'No,' said Egbert, handing it across the table, 'I thought I would tell you about it first. Heavens, what are you doing?'

Egbert's voice rose almost to a scream. Sir Lulworth had flung the paper well and truly into the glowing centre of the grate. The small, neat handwriting shivelled into black flaky nothingness.

'What on earth did you do that for?' gasped Egbert. 'That letter was our one piece of evidence to connect Sebastien with the crime!'

'That is why I destroyed it,' said Sir Lulworth.

'But why should you want to shield him?' cried Egbert; 'the man is a common murderer.'

'A common murderer, possibly, but a very uncommon cook.'

THE RETICENCE OF LADY ANNE

Egbert came into the large, dimly lit drawing-room with the air of a man who is not certain whether he is entering a dovecote or a bomb factory, and is prepared for either eventuality. The little domestic quarrel over the luncheon-table had not been fought to a definite finish, and the question was how far Lady Anne was in a mood to renew or forego hostilities. Her pose in the arm-chair by the tea-table was rather elaborately rigid; in the gloom of a December afternoon Egbert's pince-nez did not materially help him to discern the expression of her face.

By way of breaking whatever ice might be floating on the surface he made a remark about a dim religious light. He or

Lady Anne were accustomed to make that remark between
4-30 and 6 on winter and late autumn evenings; it was a part of
their married life. There was no recognized rejoinder to it, and
Lady Anne made none.

Don Tarquinio lay astretch on the Persian rug, basking in the
firelight with superb indifference to the possible ill-humour of
Lady Anne. His pedigree was as flawlessly Persian as the rug,
and his ruff was coming into the glory of its second winter. The
page-boy, who had Renaissance tendencies, had christened him
Don Tarquinio. Left to themselves, Egbert and Lady Anne would
unfailingly have called him Fluff, but they were not obstinate.

Egbert poured himself out some tea. As the silence gave no
sign of breaking on Lady Anne's initiative, he braced himself
for another Yermak effort.

'My remark at lunch had a purely academic application,' he
announced 'you seem to put an unnecessarily personal significance
into it.'

Lady Anne maintained her defensive barrier of silence. The
bullfinch lazily filled in the interval with an air from *Iphigénie en
Tauride*. Egbert recognized it immediately, because it was the
only air the bullfinch whistled, and he had come to them with
the reputation for whistling it. Both Egbert and Lady Anne
would have preferred something from *The Yeoman of the Guard*,
which was their favourite opera. In matters artistic they had a
similarity of taste. They leaned towards the honest and explicit
in art, a picture, for instance, that told its own story, with
generous assistance from its title. A riderless warhorse with
harness in obvious disarray, staggering into a courtyard full of
pale swooning women, and marginally noted 'Bad News', suggested to their minds a distinct interpretation of some military
catastrophe. They could see what it was meant to convey, and
explain it to friends of duller intelligence.

The silence continued. As a rule Lady Anne's displeasure
became articulate and markedly voluble after four minutes of
introductory muteness. Egbert seized the milk-jug and poured
some of its contents into Don Tarquinio's saucer; as the saucer
was already full to the brim an unsightly overflow was the result.
Don Tarquinio looked on with a surprised interest that evansced
into elaborate unconsciousness when he was appealed to by Egbert
to come and drink up some of the spilt matter. Don Tarquinio
was prepared to play many rôles in life, but a vacuum carpet-cleaner
was not one of them.

'Don't you think we're being rather foolish?' said Egbert cheerfully.

If Lady Anne thought so she didn't say so.

'I daresay the fault has been partly on my side,' continued Egbert, with evaporating cheerfulness. 'After all, I'm only human, you know. You seem to forget that I'm only human.'

He insisted on the point, as if there had been unfounded suggestions that he was built on Satyr lines, with goat continuations where the human left off.

The bullfinch recommenced its air from *Iphigénie en Tauride*. Egbert began to feel depressed. Lady Anne was not drinking her tea. Perhaps she was feeling unwell. But when Lady Anne felt unwell she was not wont to be reticent on the subject. 'No one knows what I suffer from indigestion,' was one of her favourite statements; but the lack of knowledge can only have been caused by defective listening; the amount of information available on the subject would have supplied material for a monograph.

Evidently Lady Anne was not feeling unwell.

Egbert began to think he was being unreasonably dealt with; naturally he began to make concessions.

'I daresay,' he observed, taking as central a position on the hearth-rug as Don Tarquinio could be persuaded to concede him, 'I may have been to blame. I am willing, if I can thereby restore things to a happier standpoint, to undertake to lead a better life.'

He wondered vaguely how it would be possible. Temptations came to him, in middle age, tentatively and without insistence, like a neglected butcher-boy who asks for a Christmas box in February for no more hopeful reason than that he didn't get one in December. He had no more idea of succumbing to them than he had of purchasing the fish-knives and fur boas that ladies are impelled to sacrifice through the medium of advertisement columns during twelve months of the year. Still, there was something impressive in this unasked for renunciation of possibly latent enormities.

Lady Anne showed no sign of being impressed.

Egbert looked at her nervously through his glasses. To get the worst of an argument with her was no new experience. To get the worst of a monologue was a humiliating novelty.

'I shall go and dress for dinner,' he announced in a voice into which he intended some shade of sternness to creep.

At the door a final access of weakness impelled him to make a further appeal.

'Aren't we being very silly?'

'A fool,' was Don Tarquin's mental comment as the door closed on Egbert's retreat. Then he lifted his velvet forepaws in the air and leapt lightly on to a bookshelf immediately under the bull-finch's cage. It was the first time he had seemed to notice the bird's existence, but he was carrying out a long-formed theory of action with the precision of mature deliberation. The bullfinch, who had fancied himself something of a despot, depressed himself of a sudden into a third of his normal displacement; then he fell to a helpless wing-beating and shrill cheeping. He had cost twenty-seven shillings without the cage, but Lady Anne made no sign of interfering. She had been dead for two hours.

TOBERMORY

It was a chill, rain-washed afternoon of a late August day, that indefinite season when partridges are still in security or cold storage, and there is nothing to hunt – unless one is bounded on the north by the Bristol Channel, in which case one may lawfully gallop after fat red stags. Lady Blemley's house-party was not bounded on the north by the Bristol Channel, hence there was a full gathering of her guests round the tea-table on this particular afternoon. And, in spite of the blankness of the season and the triteness of the occasion, there was no trace in the company of that fatigued restlessness which means a dread of the pianola and a subdued hankering for auction bridge. The undisguised open-mouthed attention of the entire party was fixed on the homely negative personality of Mr Cornelius Appin. Of all her guests, he was the one who had come to Lady Blemley with the vaguest reputation. Someone had said he was 'clever', and he had got his invitation in the moderate expectation, on the part of his hostess, that some portion at least of his cleverness would be contributed to the general entertainment. Until tea-time that day she had been unable to discover in what direction, if any, his cleverness lay. He was neither a wit nor a croquet champion, a hypnotic force nor a begetter of amateur theatricals. Neither did his exterior suggest a generous measure of mental deficiency. He had subsided into mere Mr Appin, and the Cornelius seemed a piece of transparent baptismal bluff. And now he was claiming to have launched on the world a discovery beside which the invention of gunpowder, of the printing-press, and of steam loco-motion were inconsiderable trifles. Science had made bewilder-ing strides in many directions during recent decades, but this thing seemed to belong to the domain of miracle rather than to scientific achievement.

'And do you really ask us to believe,' Sir Wilfrid was saying, 'that you have discovered a means for instructing animals in the art of human speech, and that dear old Tobermory has proved your first successful pupil?'

'It is a problem at which I have worked for the last seventeen years,' said Mr Appin, 'but only during the last eight or nine months have I been rewarded with glimmerings of success. Of course I have experimented with thousands of animals, but latterly only with cats, those wonderful creatures which have assimilated themselves so marvellously with our civilization while retaining all their highly developed feral instincts. Here and there among cats one comes across an outstanding superior intellect, just as one does among the ruck of human beings, and when I made the acquaintance of Tobermory a week ago I saw at once that I was in contact with a "Beyond-cat" of extraordinary intelligence. I had gone far along the road to success in recent experiments; with Tobermory, as you call him, I have reached the goal.'

Mr Appin concluded his remarkable statement in a voice which he strove to divest of a triumphant inflection. No one said 'Rats', though Clovis's lips moved in a monosyllabic contortion, which probably invoked those rodents of disbelief.

'And do you mean to say,' asked Miss Resker, after a slight pause, 'that you have taught Tobermory to say and understand easy sentences of one syllable?'

'My dear Miss Resker,' said the wonder-worker patiently, 'one teaches little children and savages and backward adults in that piecemeal fashion; when one has once solved the problem of making a beginning with an animal of highly developed intelli-gence one has no need for those halting methods. Tobermory can speak our language with perfect correctness.'

This time Clovis very distinctly said, 'Beyond-rats!' Sir Wilfrid was more polite, but equally sceptical.

'Hadn't we better have the cat in and judge for ourselves?' suggested Lady Blemley.

Sir Wilfrid went in search of the animal, and the company settled themselves down to the languid expectation of witnessing some more or less adroit drawing-room ventriloquism.

In a minute Sir Wilfrid was back in the room, his face white beneath its tan and his eyes dilated with excitement.

'By Gad, it's true!'

His agitiation was unmistakably genuine, and his hearers started forward in a thrill of awakened interest.

Collapsing into an armchair he continued breathlessly; 'I found him dozing in the smoking-room, and called out to him to come for his tea. He blinked at me in his usual way, and I said, 'Come on Toby; don't keep us waiting'; and, by Gad! he drawled out in a most horribly natural voice that he'd come when he dashed well pleased! I nearly jumped out of my skin!'

Appin had preached to absolutely incredulous hearers; Sir Wilfrid's statement carried instant conviction. A Babel-like chorus of startled exclamation arose, amid which the scientist sat mutely enjoying the first fruit of his stupendous discovery.

In the midst of the clamour Tobermory entered the room and made his way with velvet tread and studied unconcern across to the group seated round the tea-table.

A sudden hush of awkwardness and constraint fell on the company. Somehow there seemed an element of embarrassment in addressing on equal terms a domestic cat of acknowledged dental ability.

'Will you have some milk, Tobermory?' asked Lady Blemley in a rather strained voice.

'I don't mind if I do,' was the response, couched in a tone of even indifference. A shiver of suppressed excitement went through the listeners, and Lady Blemley might be excused for pouring out the saucerful of milk rather unsteadily.

'I'm afraid I've spilt a good deal of it,' she said apologetically.

'After all, it's not my Axminster,' was Tobermory's rejoinder.

Another silence fell on the group, and then Miss Resker, in her best district-visitor manner, asked if the human language had been difficult to learn. Tobermory looked squarely at her for a moment and then fixed his gaze serenely on the middle-distance. It was obvious that boring questions lay outside his scheme of life.

'What do you think of human intelligence?' asked Mavis Pellington lamely.

'Of whose intelligence in particular?' asked Tobermory coldly.

'Oh, well, mine for instance,' said Mavis, with a feeble laugh.

'You put me in an embarrassing position,' said Tobermory, whose tone and attitude certainly did not suggest a shred of embarrassment. 'When your inclusion in this house-party was suggested Sir Wilfrid protested that you were the most brainless woman of his acquaintance, and that there was a wide distinction between hospitality and the care of the feeble-minded. Lady Blemley replied that your lack of brain-power was the precise quality which had earned you your invitation, as you were the only person she could think of who might be idiotic enough to buy their old car. You know, the one they call "The Envy of Sisyphus", because it goes quite nicely up-hill if you push it.

Lady Blemley's protestations would have had greater effect if she had not casually suggested to Mavis only that morning that the car in question would be just the thing for her down at her Devonshire home.

Majod Barfield plunged in heavily to effect a diversion.

'How about your carrying-on with the tortoise-shell puss up at the stables, eh?'

The moment he had said it everyone realized the blunder.

'One does not usually discuss these matters in public,' said Tobermory frigidly. 'From a slight observation of your ways since you've been in this house I should imagine you'd find it inconvenient if I were to shift the conversation on to your own little affairs.'

The panic which ensued was not confined to the Major.

'Would you like to go and see if cook has got your dinner ready?' suggested Lady Blemley hurriedly, affecting to ignore the fact that it wanted at least two hours to Tobermory's dinner-time.

'Thanks,' said Tobermory, 'not quite so soon after my tea. I don't want to die of indigestion.'

'Cats have nine lives, you know,' said Sir Wilfrid heartily.

'Possibly,' answered Tobermory; 'but only one liver.'

'Adelaide!' said Mrs Cornett, 'do you mean to encourage that cat to go out and gossip about us in the servants' hall?'

The panic had indeed become general. A narrow ornamental balustrade ran in front of most of the bedroom windows at the Towers, and it was recalled with dismay that this had formed a favourite promenade for Tobermory at all hours, whence he could watch the pigeons – and heaven knew what else besides. If he intended to become reminiscent in his present outspoken strain the effect would be something more than disconcerting. Mrs Cornett, who spent much time at her toilet table, and whose complexion was reputed to be of a nomadic though punctual disposition, looked as ill at ease as the Major. Miss Scrawen, who wrote fiercely sensuous poetry and led a blameless life, merely displayed irritation; if you are methodical and virtuous in private you don't necessarily want every one to know it. Bertie van Tahn, who was so depraved at seventeen that he had long ago given up trying to be any worse, turned a dull shade of gardenia white, but he did not commit the error of dashing out of the room like Odo Finsberry, a young gentleman who was understood to be reading for the Church and who was possibly disturbed at the thought of scandals he might hear concerning other people. Clovis had the presence of mind to maintain a composed exterior; privately he was calculating how long it would take to procure a box of fancy mice through the agency of the *Exchange and Mart* as a species of hush-money.

Even in a delicate situation like the present, Agnes Resker could not endure to remain too long in the background.

'Why did I ever come down here?' she asked dramatically.

Tobermory immediately accepted the opening.

'Judging by what you said to Mrs Cornett on the croquet-lawn yesterday, you were out for food. You described the Blemleys as the dullest people to stay with that you knew, but said they were clever enough to employ a first-rate cook otherwise they'd find it difficult to get anyone to come down a second time.

'There's not a word of truth in it! I appeal to Mrs Cornett –' exclaimed the discomfited Agnes.

'Mrs Cornett repeated your remark afterwards to Bertie van Tahn,' continued Tobermory, 'and said "That woman is a regular Hunger Marcher; she'd go anywhere for four square meals a day,' and Bertie van Tahn said –'

At this point the chronicle mercifully ceased. Tobermory had caught a glimpse of the big yellow Tom from the Rectory working his way through the shrubbery towards the stable wing. In a flash he had vanished through the open French window.

With the disappearance of his too brilliant pupil Cornelius Appin found himself beset by a hurricane of bitter upbraiding, anxious inquiry, and frightened entreaty. The responsibility for the situation lay with him, and he must prevent matters from becoming worse. Could Tobermory impart his dangerous gift to other cats? was the first question he had to answer. It was possible, he replied, that he might have initiated his intimate friend the stable puss into his new accomplishment, but it was unlikely that his teaching could have taken a wider range as yet.

'Then,' said Mrs Cornett, 'Tobermory may be a valuable cat

and a great pet; but I'm sure you'll agree, Adelaide, that both he and the stable cat must be done away with without delay.'

'You don't suppose I've enjoyed the last quarter of an hour, do you?' said Lady Blemley bitterly. 'My husband and I are very fond of Tobermory – at least, we were before this horrible accomplishment was infused into him but now, of course, the only thing is to have him destroyed as soon as possible.'

'We can put some strychnine in the scraps he always gets at dinner-time,' said Sir Wilfrid, 'and I will go and drown the stable cat myself. The coachman will be very sore at losing his pet, but I'll say a very catching form of mange has broken out in cats and we're afraid of it spreading to the kennels.'

'But my great discovery!' expostulated Mr Appin; 'after all my years of experiment –'

'You can go and experiment on the short-horns at the farm, who are under proper control,' said Mrs Cornett, 'or the elephants at the Zoological Gardens. They're said to be highly intelligent, and they have this recommendation, that they don't come creeping about our bedrooms and under chairs, and so forth.'

An archangel ecstatically proclaiming the Millenium, and then finding that it clashed unpardonably with Henley and would have to be indefinitely postponed, could hardly have felt more crestfallen than Cornelius Appin at the reception of his wonderful achievement. Public opinion, however, was against him – in fact, had the general voice been consulted on the subject it is probable that a strong minority vote would have been in favour of including him in the strychnine diet.

Defective train arrangements and a nervous desire to see matters brought to a finish prevented an immediate dispersal of the party, but dinner that evening was not a social success. Sir Wilfrid had had rather a trying time with the stable cat and subsequently with the coachman. Agnes Resker ostentatiously limited her repast to a morsel of dry toast, which she bit as though it were a personal enemy; while Mavis Pellington maintained a vindictive silence throughout the meal. Lady Blemley kept up a flow of what she hoped was conversation, but her attention was fixed on the doorway. A plateful of carefully dosed fish scraps was in readiness on the sideboard, but sweets and savoury and dessert went their way, and no Tobermory appeared either in the dining-room or kitchen.

The sepulchral dinner was cheerful compared with the subsequent vigil in the smoking room. Eating and drinking had at least supplied a distraction and cloak to the prevailing embarrassment. Bridge was out of the question in the general tension of nerves and tempers, and after Odo Finsberry had given a lugubrious rendering of 'Mélisande in the Wood' to a frigid audience, music was tacitly avoided. At eleven the servants went to bed, announcing that the small window in the pantry had been left open as usual for Tobermory's private use. The guests read steadily through the current batch of magazines, and fell back gradually on the 'Badminton Library' and bound volumes of *Punch*. Lady Blemley made periodic visits to the pantry, returning each time with an expression of listless depression which forestalled questioning.

At two o'clock Clovis broke the dominating silence.

'He won't turn up tonight. He's probably in the local newspaper office at the present moment, dictating the first instalment of his reminiscences. Lady What's-her-name's book won't be in it. It will be the event of the day.'

Having made his contribution to the general cheerfulness, Clovis went to bed. At long intervals the various members of the house-party followed his example.

The servants taking round the early tea made a uniform announcement in reply to a uniform question. Tobermory had not returned.

Breakfast was, if anything, a more unpleasant function than dinner had been, but before its conclusion the situation was relieved. Tobermory's corpse was brought in from the shrubbery, where a gardener had just discovered it. From the bites on his throat and the yellow fur which coated his claws it was evident that he had fallen in unequal combat with the big Tom from the Rectory.

By midday most of the guests had quitted the Towers, and after lunch Lady Blemley had sufficiently recovered her spirits to write an extremely nasty letter to the Rectory about the loss of her valuable pet.

Tobermory had been Appin's one successful pupil, and he was destined to have no successor. A few weeks later an elephant in the Dresden Zoological Garden, which had shown no previous signs of irritability, broke loose and killed an Englishman who had apparently been teasing it. The victim's name was variously reported in the papers as Oppin and Eppelin, but his front name was faithfully rendered Cornelius.

'If he was trying German irregular verbs on the poor beast,' said Clovis, 'he deserved all he got.'

The grill-room clock struck eleven with the respectful unobtrusiveness of one whose mission in life is to be ignored. When the flight of time should really have rendered abstinence and migration imperative the lighting apparatus would signal the fact in the usual way.

Six minutes later Clovis approached the supper-table, in the blessed expectancy of one who has dined sketchily and long ago.

'I'm starving,' he announced, making an effort to sit down gracefully and read the menu at the same time.

'So I gathered,' said his host, 'from the fact that you were nearly punctual. I ought to have told you that I'm a Food Reformer. I've ordered two bowls of bread-and-milk and some health biscuits. I hope you don't mind.'

Clovis pretended afterwards that he didn't go white above the collar-line for the fraction of a second.

'All the same,' he said, 'you ought not to joke about such things. There really are such people. I've known people who've met them. To think of all the adorable things there are to eat in the world, and then to go through life munching sawdust and being proud of it.'

'They're like the Flagellants of the Middle Ages, who went about mortifying themselves.'

'They had some excuse,' said Clovis. 'They did it to save their immortal souls, didn't they? You needn't tell me that a man who doesn't love oysters and asparagus and good wines has got a soul, or a stomach either. He's simply got the instinct for being unhappy highly developed.'

Clovis relapsed for a few golden moments into tender intimacies with a succession of rapidly disappearing oysters.

'I think oysters are more beautiful than any religion,' he resumed presently. 'They not only forgive our unkindness to them; they justify it, they incite us to go on being perfectly horrid to them. Once they arrive at the supper-table they seem to enter thoroughly into the spirit of the thing. There's nothing in Christianity or Buddhism that quite matches the sympathetic unselfishness of an oyster. Do you like my new waistcoat? I'm wearing it for the first time to-night.'

'It looks like a great many others you've had lately, only worse. New dinner waistcoats are becoming a habit with you.'

'They say one always pays for the excesses of one's youth; mercifully that isn't true about one's clothes. My mother is thinking of getting married.'

'Again!'

'It's the first time.'

'Of course, you ought to know. I was under the impression that she'd been married once or twice at least.'

'Three times, to be mathematically exact. I meant that it was the first time she'd thought about getting married; the other times she did it without thinking. As a matter of fact, it's really I who am doing the thinking for her in this case. You see, it's quite two years since her last husband died.'

'You evidently think that brevity is the soul of widowhood.'

'Well, it struck me that she was getting moped, and beginning to settle down, which wouldn't suit her a bit. The first symptom that I noticed was when she began to complain that we were living beyond our income. All decent people live beyond their incomes nowadays, and those who aren't respectable live beyond other people's. A few gifted individuals manage to do both.'

'It's hardly so much a gift as an industry.'

'The crisis came,' returned Clovis, 'when she suddenly started the theory that late hours were bad for one, and wanted me to be in by one o'clock every night. Imagine that sort of thing for me, who was eighteen on my last birthday.'

'On your last two birthdays, to be mathematically exact.'

'Oh, well, that's not my fault. I'm not going to arrive at nineteen as long as my mother remains at thirty-seven. One must have some regard for appearances.'

'Perhaps your mother would age a little in the process of settling down.'

'That's the last thing she'd think of. Feminine reformations always start in on the failings of other people. That's why I was so keen on the husband idea.'

'Did you go as far as to select the gentleman, or did you merely throw out a general idea, and trust to the force of suggesion?'

'If one wants a thing done in a hurry one must see to it oneself. I found a military Johnny hanging round on a loose end at the club, and took him home to lunch once or twice. He'd spent most of his life on the Indian frontier, building roads, and relieving famines and minimizing earthquakes, and all that sort of thing that one does do on frontiers. He could talk sense to a peevish cobra in fifteen native languages, and probably knew what to do if you found a rogue elephant on your croquet-lawn; but he was shy and diffident with women. I told my mother privately that he was an absolute woman-hater; so, of course, she laid herself out to flirt all she knew, which isn't a little.'

'And was the gentleman responsive?'

'I hear he told some one at the club that he was looking out for a Colonial job, with plenty of hard work, for a young friend of his, so I gather that he has some idea of marrying into the family.'

'You seem destined to be the victim of the reformation, after all.'

Clovis wiped the trace of Turkish coffee and the beginnings of a smile from his lips, and slowly lowered his dexter eyelid. Which, being interpreted, probably meant; 'I *don't* think!'

THE YARKAND MANNER

Sir Lulworth Quayne was making a leisurely progress through the Zoological Society's Gardens in company with his nephew, recently returned from Mexico. The latter was interested in comparing and contrasting allied types of animals occurring in the North American and Old World fauna.

'One of the most remarkable things in the wanderings of species,' he observed, 'is the sudden impulse to trek and migrate that breaks out now and again, for no apparent reason, in communities of hitherto stay-at-home animals.'

'In human affairs the same phenomenon is occasionally noticeable,' said Sir Lulworth; 'perhaps the most striking instance of it occurred in this country while you were away in the wilds of Mexico. I mean the wander fever which suddenly displayed itself in the managing and editorial staffs of certain London newspapers. It began with the stampede of the entire staff of one of our most brilliant and enterprising weeklies to the banks of the Seine and the heights of Montmartre. The migration was a brief one, but it heralded an era of restlessness in the Press world which lent quite a new meaning to the phrase "newspaper

circulation." Other editorial staffs were not slow to imitate the
example that had been set them. Paris soon dropped out of fashion as being too near home; Nürnberg, Seville, and Salonica became more favoured as planting-out grounds for the personnel of
not only weekly but daily papers as well. The localities were
perhaps not always well chosen; the fact of a leading organ of
Evangelical thought being edited for two successive fortnights
from Trouville and Monte Carlo was generally admitted to have
been a mistake. And even when enterprising and adventurous
editors took themselves and their staffs further afield there were
some unavoidable clashings. For instance, the *Scrutator, Sporting
Bluff* and *The Damsels' Own Paper* all pitched on Khartoum for
the same week. It was, perhaps, a desire to outdistance all possible competition that influenced the management of the *Daily
Intelligencer*, one of the most solid and respected organs of Liberal opinion, in its decision to transfer its offices for three or four
weeks from Fleet Street to Eastern Turkestan, allowing, of
course, a necessary margin of time for the journey there and
back. This was, in many respects, the most remarkable of all the
Press stampedes that were experienced at this time. There was
no make-believe about the undertaking; proprietor, manager, editor, sub-editors, leader-writers, principal reporters, and so forth,
all took part in what was popularly alluded to as the *Drang nach
Osten;* an intelligent and efficient office-boy was all that was left
in the deserted hive of editorial industry.'

'That was doing things rather thoroughly, wasn't it?' said the
nephew.

'Well, you see,' said Sir Lulworth, the migration idea was
falling somewhat into disrepute from the half-hearted manner
in which it was occasionally carried out. You were not impressed by the information that such and such a paper was being
edited and brought out at Lisbon or Innsbruck if you chanced
to see the principal leader-writer or the art editor lunching as
usual at their accustomed restaurants. The *Daily Intelligencer*
was determined to give no loophole for cavil at the genuineness
of its pilgrimage, and it must be admitted that to a certain extent
the arrangements made for transmitting copy and carrying on
the usual features of the paper during the long outward journey
worked smoothly and well. The series of articles which commenced at Baku on "What Cobdenism might do for the camel
industry" ranks among the best of the recent contributions to
Free Trade literature, while the views on foreign policy enunci-

ated "from a roof in Yarkand" showed at least as much grasp of the international situation as those that had germinated within half a mile of Downing Street. Quite in keeping, too, with the older and better traditions of British journalism was the manner of the home-coming; no bombast, no personal advertisement, no flamboyant interviews. Even a complimentary luncheon at the Voyagers' Club was courteously declined. Indeed, it began to be felt that the self-effacement of the returned pressmen was being carried to a pedantic length. Foreman compositors, advertisement clerks, and other members of the non-editorial staff, who had, of course, taken no part in the great trek, found it as impossible to get into direct communication with the editor and his satellites now that they had returned as when they had been excusably inaccessible in Central Asia. The sulky, overworked office-boy, who was the one connecting link between the editorial brain and the business departments of the paper, sardonically explained the new aloofness as the "Yarkand manner." Most of the reporters and sub-editors seemed to have been dismissed in autocratic fashion since their return and new ones engaged by letter; to these the editor and his immediate associates remained an unseen presence, issuing its instructions solely through the medium of curt type-written notes. Something mystic and Tibetan and forbidden had replaced the human bustle and democratic simplicity of pre-migration days, and the same experience was encountered by those who made social overtures to the returned wanderers. The most brilliant hostess of Twentieth Century London flung the pearl of her hospitality into the unresponsive trough of the editorial letterbox; it seemed as if nothing short of a Royal command would drag the hermit-souled *revenants* from their self-imposed seclusion. People began to talk unkindly of the effect of high altitudes and Eastern atmosphere on minds and temperaments unused to such luxuries. The Yarkand manner was not popular.'

'And the contents of the paper,' said the nephew, 'did they show the influence of the new style?'

'Ah!' said Sir Lulworth, 'that was the exciting thing. In home affairs, social questions, and the ordinary events of the day not much change was noticeable. A certain Oriental carelessness seemed to have crept into the editorial department, and perhaps a note of lassitude not unnatural in the work of men who had returned from what had been a fairly arduous journey. The aforetime standard of excellence was scarcely maintained, but at any

rate the general lines of policy and outlook were not departed
from. It was in the realm of foreign affairs that a startling change
took place. Blunt, forcible, outspoken articles appeared, couched
in language which nearly turned the autumn manoeuvres of six
important Powers into mobilizations. Whatever else the *Daily
Intelligencer* had learned in the East, it had not acquired the art
of diplomatic ambiguity. The man in the street enjoyed the
articles and bought the paper as he had never bought it before;
the men in Downing Street took a different view. The Foreign
Secretary, hitherto accounted a rather reticent man, became positively garrulous in the course of perpetually disavowing the senti-
ments expressed in the *Daily Intelligencer's* leaders; and then
one day the Government came to the conclusion that something
definite and drastic must be done. A deputation, consisting of the
Prime Minister, the Foreign Secretary, four leading financiers,
and a well-known Nonconformist divine, made its way to the
offices of the paper. At the door leading to the editorial department the way was barred by a nervous but defiant office-boy.

‘ "You can't see the editor nor any of the staff," he announced.

‘ "We insist on seeing the editor or some responsible person,’
said the Prime Minister, and the deputation forced its way in.
The boy had spoken truly; there was no one to be seen. In the
whole suite of rooms there was no sign of human life.

‘ "Where is the editor?" "Or the foreign editor?" "Or the
chief leader-writer?" "Or anybody?"

‘In answer to the shower of questions the boy unlocked a
drawer and produced a strange-looking envelope, which bore
a Khokand postmark, and a date of some seven or eight months
back. It contained a scrap of paper on which was written the
following message:

> "Entire party captured by brigand tribe on homeward jour-
> ney. Quarter of million demanded as ransom, but would
> probably take less. Inform Government, relations, and
> friends."

‘There followed the signatures of the principal members of the
party and instructions as to how and where the money was to
be paid.

‘The letter had been directed to the office-boy-in-charge, who
had quietly suppressed it. No one is a hero to one's own office-
boy, and he evidently considered that a quarter of a million was
an unwarrantable outlay for such a doubtfully advantageous ob-

ject as the repatriation of an errant newspaper staff. So he drew the editorial and other salaries, forged what signatures were necessary, engaged new reporters, did what sub-editing he could and made as much use as possible of the large accumulation of special articles that was held in reserve for emergencies. The articles on foreign affairs were entirely his own composition.

'Of course the whole thing had to be kept as quiet as possible; an interim staff, pledged to secrecy, was appointed to keep the paper going till the pining captives could be sought out, ransomed, and brought home, in twos and threes to escape notice, and gradually things were put back on their old footing. The articles on foreign affairs reverted to the wonted traditions of the paper.'

'But,' interposed the nephew, 'how on earth did the boy account to the relatives all those months for the non-appearance –'

'That,' said Sir Lulworth, 'was the most brilliant stroke of all. To the wife or nearest relative of each of the missing men he forwarded a letter, copying the handwriting of the supposed writer as well as he could, and making excuses about vile pens and ink; in each letter he told the same story, varying only the locality, to the effect that the writer, alone of the whole party, was unable to tear himself away from the wild liberty and allurements of Eastern life, and was going to spend several months roaming in some selected region. Many of the wives started off immediately in pursuit of their errant husbands, and it took the Government a considerable time and much trouble to reclaim them from their fruitless quests along the banks of the Oxus, the Gobi Desert, the Orenburg steppe, and other outlandish places. One of them, I believe, is still lost somewhere in the Tigris Valley.'

'And the boy?'

'Is still in journalism.'

THE BYZANTINE OMELETTE

Sophie Chattel-Monkheim was a Socialist by conviction and a Chattel-Monkheim by marriage. The particular member of that wealthy family whom she had married was rich, even as his relatives counted riches. Sophie had very advanced and decided views as to the distribution of money: it was a pleasing and fortunate circumstance that she also had the money. When she inveighed eloquently against the evils of capitalism at drawing-room meetings and Fabian conferences she was conscious of a comfortable feeling that the system, with all its inequalities and iniquities, would probably last her time. It is one of the consolations of middle-aged reformers that the good they inculcate must live after them if it is to live at all.

On a certain spring evening, somewhere towards the dinner-hour, Sophie sat tranquilly between her mirror and her maid, undergoing the process of having her hair built into an elaborate reflection of the prevailing fashion. She was hedged around with a great peace, the peace of one who has attained a desired end with much effort and perseverance, and who has found it still eminently desirable in its attainment. The Duke of Syria had consented to come beneath her roof as a guest, was even now installed beneath her roof, and would shortly be sitting at her dining-table. As a good Socialist, Sophie disapproved of social distinctions, and derided the idea of a princely caste, but if there were to be these artificial gradations of rank and dignity she was pleased and anxious to have an exalted specimen of an exalted order included in her house-party. She was broad-minded enough to love the sinner while hating the sin – not that she entertained any warm feeling of personal affection for the Duke of Syria, who was a comparative stranger, but still, as Duke of Syria, he was very, very welcome beneath her roof. She could not have explained why, but no one was likely to ask her for an explanation, and most hostesses envied her.

'You must surpass yourself tonight, Richardson,' she said complacently to her maid; 'I must be looking my very best. We must all surpass ourselves.'

The maid said nothing, but from the concentrated look in her eyes and the deft play of her fingers it was evident that she was beset with the ambition to surpass herself.

A knock came at the door, a quiet but peremptory knock, as of someone who would not be denied.

'Go and see who it is,' said Sophie; 'it may be something about the wine.'

Richardson held a hurried conference with an invisible messenger at the door; when she returned there was noticeable a curious listlessness in place of her hitherto alert manner.

'What is it?' asked Sophie.

'The household servants have "downed tools", madame,' said Richardson.

'Downed tools!' exclaimed Sophie; 'do you mean to say they've gone on strike?'

'Yes, madame,' said Richardson, adding the information: 'It's Gaspare that the trouble is about.'

'Gaspare?' said Sophie wonderingly; 'the emergency chef! The omelette specialist!'

'Yes, madame. Before he became an omelette specialist he was a valet, and he was one of the strike-breakers in the great strike at Lord Grimford's two years ago. As soon as the household staff here learned that you had engaged him they resolved to "down tools" as a protest. They haven't got any grievance against you personally, but they demand that Gaspare should be immediately dismissed.'

'But,' protested Sophie, 'he is the only man in England who understands how to make a Byzantine omelette. I engaged him specially for the Duke of Syria's visit, and it would be impossible to replace him at short notice. I should have to send to Paris, and the Duke loves Byzantine omelettes. It was the one thing we talked about coming from the station.'

'He was one of the strike-breakers at Lord Grimford's,' reiterated Richardson.

'This is too awful,' said Sophie; 'a strike of servants at a moment like this, with the Duke of Syria staying in the house. Something must be done immediately. Quick, finish my hair and I'll go and see what I can do to bring them round.'

'I can't finish your hair, madame,' said Richardson quietly, but with immense decision. 'I belong to the union and I can't do another half-minute's work till the strike is settled. I'm sorry to be disobliging.'

'But this is inhuman!' exclaimed Sophie tragically 'I've always been a model mistress and I've refused to employ any but union servants, and this is the result. I can't finish my hair myself; I don't know how to. What am I to do? It's wicked!'

'Wicked is the word,' said Richardson 'I'm a good Conservative, and I've no patience with this Socialist foolery, asking your pardon. It's tyranny, that's what it is, all along the line, but I've my living to make, same as other people, and I've got to belong to the union. I couldn't touch another hairpin without a strike permit, not if you was to double my wages.'

The door burst open and Catherine Malsom raged into the room.

'Here's a nice affair,' she screamed, 'a strike of household servants without a moment's warning, and I'm left like this! I can't appear in public in this condition.'

After a very hasty scrutiny Sophie assured her that she could not.

'Have they all struck?' she asked her maid.

'Not the kitchen staff,' said Richardson, 'they belong to a different union.'

'Dinner at least will be assured,' said Sophie, 'that is something to be thankful for.'

'Dinner!' snorted Catherine, 'what on earth is the good of dinner when none of us will be able to appear at it? Look at your hair – and look at me! or rather, don't.'

'I know it's difficult to manage without a maid; can't your husband be any help to you?' asked Sophie despairingly.

'Henry? He's in worse case than any of us. His man is the only person who really understands that ridiculous new-fangled Turkish bath that he insists on taking with him everywhere.'

'Surely he could do without a Turkish bath for one evening,' said Sophie; 'I can't appear without hair, but a Turkish bath is a luxury.'

'My good woman,' said Catherine, speaking with a fearful intensity, 'Henry was *in* the bath when the strike started. *In* it, do you understand? He's there now.'

'Can't he get out?'

'He doesn't know how to. Every time he pulls the lever marked "release" he only releases hot steam. There are two kinds of steam in the bath, "bearable" and "scarcely bearable"; he has released them both. By this time I'm probably a widow.'

'I simply can't send away Gaspare,' wailed Sophie; 'I should never be able to secure another omelette specialist.'

'Any difficulty that I may experience in securing another husband is of course a trifle beneath anyone's consideration,' said Catherine bitterly.

Sophie capitulated. 'Go,' she said to Richardson, 'and tell the Strike Committee, or whoever are directing this affair, that Gaspare is herewith dismissed. And ask Gaspare to see me presently in the library, when I will pay him what is due to him and make what excuses I can; and then fly back and finish my hair.'

Some half an hour later Sophie marshalled her guests in the Grand Salon preparatory to the formal march to the dining-room. Except that Henry Malsom was of the ripe raspberry tint that one sometimes sees at private theatricals representing the human complexion, there was little outward sign among those assembled of the crisis that had just been encountered and surmounted. But the tension had been too stupefying while it lasted not to leave some mental effects behind it. Sophie talked at random to her illustrious guest, and found her eyes straying with increasing frequency towards the great doors through which would presently come the blessed announcement that dinner was served. Now and again she glanced mirror-ward at the reflection of her wonderfully coiffed hair, as an insurance underwriter might gaze thankfully at an overdue vessel that had ridden safely into harbour in the wake of a devastating hurricane. Then the doors opened and the welcome figure of the butler entered the room. But he made no general announcement of the banquet in readiness, and the doors closed behind him; his message was for Sophie alone.

'There is no dinner, madame,' he said gravely; 'the kitchen staff have "downed tools". Gaspare belongs to the Union of Cooks and Kitchen Employés, and as soon as they heard of his summary dismissal at a moment's notice they struck work. They demand his instant reinstatement and an apology to the union. I may add, madame, that they are very firm; I've been obliged even to hand back the dinner rolls that were already on the table.'

After the lapse of eighteen months Sophie Chattel-Monkheim is beginning to go about again among her old haunts and associates, but she still has to be very careful. The doctors will not let her attend anything at all exciting, such as a drawing-room meeting or a Fabian conference; it is doubtful, indeed, whether she wants to.

GABRIEL-ERNEST

'There is a wild beast in your woods,' said the artist Cunningham, as he was being driven to the station. It was the only remark he had made during the drive, but as Van Cheele had talked incessantly his companion's silence had not been noticeable.

'A stray fox or two and some resident weasels. Nothing more formidable,' said Van Cheele. The artist said nothing.

'What did you mean about a wild beast?' said Van Cheele later, when they were on the platform.

'Nothing. My imagination. Here is the train,' said Cunningham.

That afternoon Van Cheele went for one of his frequent rambles through his woodland property. He had a stuffed bittern in his study, and knew the names of quite a number of wild flowers, so his aunt had possibly some justification in describing him as a great naturalist. At any rate, he was a great walker. It was his custom to take mental notes of everything he saw during his walks, not so much for the purpose of assisting contemporary science as to provide topics for conversation afterwards. When the bluebells began to show themselves in flower he made a point of informing everyone of the fact; the season of the year might have warned his hearers of the likelihood of such an occurrence, but at least they felt that he was being absolutely frank with them.

What Van Cheele saw on this particular afternoon was, however, something far removed from his ordinary range of experience. On a shelf of smooth stone overhanging a deep pool in the hollow of an oak coppice a boy of about sixteen lay asprawl, drying his wet brown limbs luxuriously in the sun. His wet hair, parted by a recent dive, lay close to his head, and his light-brown eyes, so light that there was an almost tigerish gleam in them, were turned towards Van Cheele with a certain lazy watchfulness. It was an unexpected apparition, and Van Cheele found himself engaged in the novel process of thinking before he spoke. Where on earth could this wild-looking boy hail from? The miller's wife had lost a child some two months ago, supposed to have been swept away by the mill-race, but that had been a mere baby, not a half-grown lad.

'What are you doing there?' he demanded.

'Obviously, sunning myself,' replied the boy.

'Where do you live?'

'Here, in these woods.'

'You can't live in the woods,' said Van Cheele.

'They are very nice woods,' said the boy, with a touch of patronage in his voice.

'But where do you sleep at night?'

'I don't sleep at night; that's my busiest time.'

Van Cheele began to have an irritated feeling that he was grappling with a problem that was eluding him.

'What do you feed on?' he asked.

'Flesh,' said the boy, and he pronounced the word with slow relish, as though he were tasting it.

'Flesh! What flesh?'

'Since it interests you, rabbits, wild-fowl, hares, poultry, lambs in their season, children when I can get any; they're usually too well locked in at night, when I do most of my hunting. It's quite two months since I tasted child-flesh.'

Ignoring the chaffing nature of the last remark, Van Cheele tried to draw the boy on the subject of possible poaching operations.

'You're talking rather through your hat when you speak of feeding on hares.' (Considering the nature of the boy's toilet, the simile was hardly an apt one.) 'Our hillside hares aren't easily caught.'

'At night I hunt on four feet,' was the somewhat cryptic response.

'I suppose you mean that you hunt with a dog?' hazarded Van Cheele.

The boy rolled slowly over on to his back, and laughed a weird low laugh, that was pleasantly like a chuckle, and disagreeably like a snarl.

'I don't fancy any dog would be very anxious for my company, especially at night.'

Van Cheele began to feel that there was something positively uncanny about the strange-eyed, strange-tongued youngster.

'I can't have you staying in these woods,' he declared authoritatively.

'I fancy you'd rather have me here than in your house,' said the boy.

The prospect of this wild, nude animal in Van Cheele's primly ordered house was certainly an alarming one.

'If you don't go I shall have to make you,' said Van Cheele.

The boy turned like a flash, plunged into the pool, and in a moment had flung his wet and glistening body half-way up the bank where Van Cheele was standing. In an otter the movement would not have been remarkable; in a boy Van Cheele found it sufficiently startling. His foot slipped as he made an involuntary backward movement, and he found himself almost prostrate on the slippery weed-grown bank, with those tigerish yellow eyes

not very far from his own. Almost instinctively he half-raised his
hand to his throat. The boy laughed again, a laugh in which the
snarl had nearly driven out the chuckle, and then, with another
of his astonishing lightning movements, plunged out of view
into a yielding tangle of weed and fern.

'What an extraordinary wild animal!' said Van Cheele as he
picked himself up. And then he recalled Cunningham's remark,
'There is a wild beast in your woods.'

Walking slowly homeward, Van Cheele began to turn over
in his mind various local occurrences which might be traceable
to the existence of this astonishing young savage.

Something had been thinning the game in the woods lately,
poultry had been missing from the farms, hares were growing
unaccountably scarcer, and complaints had reached him of lambs
being carried off bodily from the hills. Was it possible that this
wild boy was really hunting the countryside in company with
some clever poacher dog? He had spoken of hunting 'four-footed'
by night, but then, again, he had hinted strangely at no dog
caring to come near him, 'especially at night'. It was certainly
puzzling. And then, as Van Cheele ran his mind over the various
depredations that had been committed during the last month or
two, he came suddenly to a dead stop, alike in his walk and his
speculations. The child missing from the mill two months ago —
the accepted theory was that it had tumbled into the mill-race
and been swept away; but the mother had always declared she
had heard a shriek on the hill side of the house, in the opposite
direction from the water. It was unthinkable, of course, but he
wished that the boy had not made that uncanny remark about
child-flesh eaten two months ago. Such dreadful things should
not be said even in fun.

Van Cheele, contrary to his usual wont, did not feel disposed
to be communicative about his discovery in the wood. His position
as a parish councillor and justice of the peace seemed somehow
compromised by the fact that he was harbouring a personality of
such doubtful repute on his property; there was even a possibility
that a heavy bill for damages for raided lambs and poultry might
be laid at his door. At dinner that night he was quite unusually
silent.

'Where's your voice gone to?' said his aunt. 'One would
think you had seen a wolf.'

Van Cheele, who was not familiar with the old saying, thought
the remark rather foolish; if he *had* seen a wolf on his property

his tongue would have been extraordinarily busy with the subject.

At breakfast next morning Van Cheele was conscious that his feeling of uneasiness regarding yesterday's episode had not wholly disappeared, and he resolved to go by train to the neighbouring cathedral town, hunt up Cunningham, and learn from him what he had really seen that had prompted the remark about a wild beast in the woods. With this resolution taken, his usual cheerfulness partially returned, and he hummed a bright little melody as he sauntered to the morning-room for his customary cigarette. As he entered the room the melody made way abruptly for a pious invocation. Gracefully asprawl on the ottoman, in an attitude of almost exaggerated repose, was the boy of the woods. He was drier than when Van Cheele had last seen him, but no other alteration was noticeable in his toilet.

'How dare you come here?' asked Van Cheele furiously.

'You told me I was not to stay in the woods,' said the boy calmly.

'But not to come here. Supposing my aunt should see you!'

And with a view to minimizing that catastrophe Van Cheele hastily obscured as much of his unwelcome guest as possible under the folds of a *Morning Post*. At that moment his aunt entered the room.

'This is a poor boy who has lost his way – and lost his memory. He doesn't know who he is or where he comes from,' explained Van Cheele desperately, glancing apprehensively at the waif's face to see whether he was going to add inconvenient candour to his other savage propensities.

Miss Van Cheele was enormously interested.

'Perhaps his underlinen is marked,' she suggested.

'He seems to have lost most of that, too,' said Van Cheele, making frantic little grabs at the *Morning Post* to keep it in its place.

A naked homeless child appealed to Miss Van Cheele as warmly as a stray kitten or derelict puppy would have done.

'We must do all we can for him,' she decided, and in a very short time a messenger, dispatched to the rectory, where a page-boy was kept, had returned with a suit of pantry clothes, and the necessary accessories of shirt, shoes, collar, etc. Clothed, clean and groomed, the boy lost none of his uncanniness in Van Cheele's eyes, but his aunt found him sweet.

'We must call him something till we know who he really is,' she said. 'Gabriel-Ernest, I think; those are nice suitable names.'

Van Cheele agreed, but he privately doubted whether they

were being grafted on to a nice suitable child. His misgivings
were not diminished by the fact that his staid and elderly spaniel had bolted out of the house at the first incoming of the boy,
and now obstinately remained shivering and yapping at the
farther end of the orchard, while the canary, usually as vocally
industrious as Van Cheele himself, had put itself on an allow-
ance of frightened cheeps. More than ever he was resolved to
consult Cunningham without loss of time.

As he drove off to the station his aunt was arranging that
Gabriel-Ernest should help her to entertain the infant members
of her Sunday-school class at tea that afternoon.

Cunningham was not at first disposed to be communicative.

'My mother died of some brain trouble,' he explained, 'so you
will understand why I am averse to dwelling on anything of an
impossibly fantastic nature that I may see or think that I have
seen.'

'But what did you see?' persisted Van Cheele.

'What I thought I saw was something so extraordinary that
no really sane man could dignify it with the credit of having
actually happened. I was standing, the last evening I was with
you, half-hidden in the hedgegrowth by the orchard gate, watching the dying glow of the sunset. Suddenly I became aware of
a naked boy, a bather from some neighbouring pool, I took him
to be, who was standing out on the bare hillside also watching
the sunset. His pose was so suggestive of some wild faun of
Pagan myth that I instantly wanted to engage him as a model,
and in another moment I think I should have hailed him. But
just then the sun dipped out of view, and all the orange and
pink slid out of the landscape, leaving it cold and grey. And
at the same moment an astounding thing happened – the boy
vanished too!'

'What! vanished away into nothing?' asked Van Cheele excitedly.

'No; that is the dreadful part of it,' answered the artist; 'on
the open hillside where the boy had been standing a second ago,
stood a large wolf, blackish in colour, with gleaming fangs and
cruel, yellow eyes. You may think –'

But Van Cheele did not stop for anything as futile as thought.
Already he was tearing at top speed towards the station. He dismissed the idea of a telegram. 'Gabriel-Ernest is a werewolf' was
a hopelessly inadequate effort at conveying the situation, and his
aunt would think it was a code message to which he had omitted

to give her the key. His one hope was that he might reach home before sundown. The cab which he chartered at the other end of the railway journey bore him with what seemed exasperating slowness along the country roads, which were pink and mauve with the flush of the sinking sun. His aunt was putting away some unfinished jams and cake when he arrived.

'Where is Gabriel-Ernest?' he almost screamed.

'He is taking the little Toop child home,' said his aunt. 'It was getting so late, I thought it wasn't safe to let it go back alone. What a lovely sunset, isn't it?'

But Van Cheele, although not oblivious of the glow in the western sky, did not stay to discuss its beauties. At a speed for which he was scarcely geared he raced along the narrow lane that led to the home of the Toops. On one side ran the swift current of the mill-stream, on the other rose the stretch of bare hillside. A dwindling rim of red sun showed still on the sky-line, and the next turning must bring him in view of the ill-assorted couple he was pursuing. Then the colour went suddenly out of things, and a grey light settled itself with a quick shiver over the landscape. Van Cheele heard a shrill wail of fear, and stopped running.

Nothing was ever seen again of the Toop child or Gabriel-Ernest, but the latter's discarded garments were found lying in the road, so it was assumed that the child had fallen into the water, and that the boy had stripped and jumped in, in a vain endeavour to save it. Van Cheele and some workmen who were near by at the time testified to having heard a child scream loudly just near the spot where the clothes were found. Mrs Toop, who had eleven other children, was decently resigned to her bereavement, but Miss Van Cheele sincerely mourned her lost foundling. It was on her initiative that a memorial brass was put up in the parish church to 'Gabriel-Ernest, an unknown boy, who bravely sacrificed his life for another.'

Van Cheele gave way to his aunt in most things, but he flatly refused to subscribe to the Gabriel-Ernest memorial.

THE QUINCE TREE

'I've just been to see old Betsy Mullen,' announced Vera to her aunt, Mrs Bebberly Cumble; 'she seems in rather a bad way about her rent. She owes about fifteen weeks of it, and says she doesn't know where any of it is to come from.'

'Betsy Mullen always is in difficulties with her rent, and the more people help her with it the less she troubles about it,' said the aunt. 'I certainly am not going to assist her any more. The fact is, she will have to go into a smaller and cheaper cottage; there are several to be had at the other end of the village for half the rent that she is paying, or supposed to be paying, now. I told her a year ago that she ought to move.'

'But she wouldn't get such a nice garden anywhere else,' protested Vera, 'and there's such a jolly quince tree in the corner. I don't suppose there's another quince tree in the whole parish. And she never makes any quince jam; I think to have a quince tree and not to make quince jam shows such strength of character. Oh, she can't possibly move away from that garden.'

'When one is sixteen,' said Mrs Bebberly Cumble severely, 'one talks of things being impossible which are merely uncongenial. It is not only possible but it is desirable that Betsy Mullen should move into smaller quarters; she has scarcely enough furniture to fill that big cottage.'

'As far as value goes,' said Vera after a short pause, 'there is more in Betsy's cottage than in any other house for miles round.'

'Nonsense,' said the aunt; 'she parted with whatever old china ware she had long ago.'

'I'm not talking about anything that belongs to Betsy herself,' said Vera darkly; 'but of course, you don't know what I know, and I don't suppose I ought to tell you.'

'You must tell me at once,' exclaimed the aunt, her senses leaping into alertness like those of a terrier suddenly exchanging a bored drowsiness for the lively anticipation of an immediate rat hunt.

'I'm perfectly certain that I oughtn't to tell you anything about it,' said Vera, 'but, then, I often do things that I oughtn't to do.'

'I should be the last person to suggest that you should do anything that you ought not to do –' began Mrs Bebberly Cumble impressively.

'And I am always swayed by the last person who speaks to me,' admitted Vera, 'so I'll do what I ought not to do and tell you.'

Mrs Bebberly Cumble thrust a very pardonable sense of exasperation into the background of her mind and demanded impatiently:

'What is there in Betsy Mullen's cottage that you are making such a fuss about?'

'It's hardly fair to say that *I've* made a fuss about it,' said Vera; 'this is the first time I've mentioned the matter, but there's been no end of trouble and mystery and newspaper speculation about it. It's rather amusing to think of the columns of conjecture in the Press and the police and detectives hunting about everywhere at home and abroad, and all the while that innocent-looking little cottage has held the secret.'

'You don't mean to say it's the Louvre picture, La Something or other, the woman with the smile, that disappeared about two years ago?' exclaimed the aunt with rising excitement.

'Oh, no, not that,' said Vera, 'but something quite as important and just as mysterious – if anything, rather more scandalous.'

'Not the Dublin –?'

Vera nodded.

'The whole jolly lot of them.'

'In Betsy's cottage? Incredible!'

'Of course Betsy hasn't any idea as to what they are,' said Vera; 'she just knows that they are something valuable and that she must keep quiet about them. I found out quite by accident what they were and how they came to be there. You see, the people who had them were at their wits' end to know where to stow them away for safe keeping, and some one who was motoring through the village was struck by the snug loneliness of the cottage and thought it would be just the thing. Mrs Lamper arranged the matter with Betsy and smuggled the things in.'

'Mrs Lamper?'

'Yes, she does a lot of district visiting, you know.'

'I am quite aware that she takes soup and flannel and improving literature to the poorer cottages,' said Mrs Bebberly Cumble, 'but that is hardly the same sort of thing as disposing of stolen goods, and she must have known something about their history; any one who reads the papers, even casually, must have been aware of the theft, and I should think the things were not hard to recognize. Mrs Lamper has always had the reputation of being a very conscientious woman.'

'Of course she was screening some one else,' said Vera. 'A remarkable feature of the affair is the extraordinary number of quite respectable people who have involved themselves in its meshes by trying to shield others. You would be really astonished if you knew some of the names of the individuals mixed up in it, and I don't suppose a tithe of them knew who the original culprits were; and now I've got you entangled in the mess by letting you into the secret of the cottage.'

'You most certainly have not entangled me,' said Mrs Bebberly Cumble indignantly. 'I have no intention of shielding anybody. The police must know about it at once; a theft is a theft, whoever is involved. If respectable people choose to turn themselves into receivers and disposers of stolen goods, well, they've ceased to be respectable, that's all. I shall telephone immediately —'

'Oh, aunt,' said Vera reproachfully, 'it would break the poor Canon's heart if Cuthbert were to be involved in a scandal of this sort. You know it would.'

'Cuthbert involved! How can you say such things when you know how much we all think of him?'

'Of course I know you think a lot of him, and that he's engaged to marry Beatrice, and that it will be a frightfully good match, and that he's your ideal of what a son-in-law ought to be. All the same, it was Cuthbert's idea to stow the things away in the cottage, and it was his motor that brought them. He was only doing it to help his friend Pegginson, you know — the Quaker man, who is always agitating for a smaller Navy. I forget how he got involved in it. I warned you that there were lots of quite respectable people mixed up in it, didn't I? That's what I meant when I said it would be impossible for old Betsy to leave the cottage; the things take up a good bit of room, and she couldn't go carrying them about with her other goods and chattels without attracting notice. Of course if she were to fall ill and die it would be equally unfortunate. Her mother lived to be over ninety, she tells me, so with due care and an absence of worry she ought to last for another dozen years at least. By that time perhaps some other arrangements will have been made for disposing of the wretched things.'

'I shall speak to Cuthbert about it – after the wedding,' said Mrs Bebberly Cumble.

'The wedding isn't till next year,' said Vera, in recounting the story to her best girl friend, 'and meanwhile old Betsy is living rent free, with soup twice a week and my aunt's doctor to see her whenever she has a finger ache.'

'But how on earth did you get to know about it all?' asked her friend, in admiring wonder.

'It was a mystery –' said Vera.

'Of course it was a mystery, a mystery that baffled everybody. What beats me is how you found out –'

'Oh, about the jewels? I invented that part,' explained Vera; 'I mean the mystery was where old Betsy's arrears of rent were to come from; and she would have hated leaving that jolly quince tree.'

EXCEPTING MRS PENTHERBY

It was Reggie Bruttle's own idea for converting what had threatened to be an albino elephant into a beast of burden that should help him along the stony road of his finances. 'The Limes,' which had come to him by inheritance without any accompanying provision for its upkeep, was one of those pretentious, un-accommodating mansions which none but a man of wealth could afford to live in, and which not one wealthy man in a hundred would choose on its merits. It might easily languish in the estate market for years, set round with notice-boards proclaiming it, in the eyes of a sceptical world, to be an eminently desirable residence.

Reggie's scheme was to turn it into the headquarters of a prolonged country-house party, in session during the months from October till the end of March – a party consisting of young or youngish people of both sexes, too poor to be able to do much hunting or shooting on a serious scale, but keen on getting their fill of golf, bridge, dancing, and occasional theatre-going. No one was to be on the footing of a paying guest, but every one was to rank as a paying host; a committee would look after the catering and expenditure, and an informal sub-committee would make itself useful in helping forward the amusement side of the scheme.

As it was only an experiment, there was to be a general agreement on the part of those involved in it to be as lenient and mutually helpful to one another as possible. Already a promising nucleus, including one or two young married couples, had been got together, and the thing seemed to be fairly launched.

'With good management and a little unobtrusive hard work, I think the thing ought to be a success,' said Reggie, and Reggie was one of those people who are painstaking first and optimistic afterwards.

'There is one rock on which you will unfailingly come to grief, manage you never so wisely,' said Major Dagberry cheerfully; 'the women will quarrel. Mind you,' continued this prophet of disaster, 'I don't say that some of the men won't quarrel too, probably they will; but the women are bound to. You can't prevent it; it's in the nature of the sex. The hand that rocks the cradle rocks the world, in a volcanic sense. A woman will endure discomforts, and make sacrifices, and go without things to an heroic extent, but the one luxury she will not go without is her quarrels. No matter where she may be, or how transient her appearance on a scene, she will install her feminine feuds as assuredly as a Frenchman would concoct soup in the waste of the Arctic regions. At the commencement of a sea voyage, before the male traveller knows half a dozen of his fellow-passengers by sight, the average woman will have started a couple of enmities, and laid in material for one or two more – provided, of course, that there are sufficient women aboard to permit quarrelling in the plural. If there's no one else she will quarrel with the stewardess. This experiment of yours is to run for six months; in less than five weeks there will be war to the knife declaring itself in half a dozen different directions.'

'Oh, come, there are only eight women in the party; they won't all pick quarrels quite as soon as that,' protested Reggie.

'They won't all originate quarrels, perhaps,' conceded the Major, 'but they will all take sides, and just as Christmas is upon you, with its conventions of peace and good will, you will find yourself in for a glacial epoch of cold, unforgiving hostility, with an occasional Etna flare of open warfare. You can't help it, old boy; but, at any rate, you can't say you were not warned.'

The first five weeks of the venture falsified Major Dagberry's prediction and justified Reggie's optimism. There were, of course, occasional small bickerings, and the existence of certain jealousies might be detected below the surface of everyday intercourse; but, on the whole, the womenfolk got on remarkably well together. There was, however, a notable exception. It had not taken five weeks for Mrs Pentherby to get herself cordially disliked by the members of her own sex; five days had been amply sufficient. Most of the women declared that they had detested her the moment they set eyes on her; but that was probably an afterthought.

With the menfolk she got on well enough, without being of the type of woman who can only bask in male society; neither was she lacking in the general qualities which make an individual useful and desirable as a member of a co-operative community. She did not try to 'get the better of' her fellow-hosts by snatching little advantages or cleverly evading her just contributions; she was not inclined to be boring or snobbish in the way of personal reminiscence. She played a fair game of bridge, and her card-room manners were irreproachable. But wherever she came in contact with her own sex the light of battle kindled at once; her talent for arousing animosity seemed to border on positive genius.

Whether the object of her attentions was thick-skinned or sensitive, quick-tempered or good-natured, Mrs Pentherby managed to achieve the same effect. She exposed little weaknesses, she prodded sore places, she snubbed enthusiasms, she was generally right in a matter of argument, or, if wrong, she somehow contrived to make her adversary appear foolish and opinionated. She did, and said, horrible things in a matter-of-fact innocent way, and she did, and said, matter-of-fact innocent things in a horrible way. In short, the unanimous feminine verdict on her was that she was objectionable.

There was no question of taking sides, as the Major had anticipated; in fact, dislike of Mrs Pentherby was almost a bond of union between the other women, and more than one threatening disagreement had been rapidly dissipated by her obvious and malicious attempts to inflame and extend it; and the most irritating thing about her was her successful assumption of unruffled composure at moments when the tempers of her adversaries were with difficulty kept under control. She made her most scathing remarks in the tone of a tube conductor announcing that the next station is Brompton Road – the measured, listless tone of one who knows he is right, but is utterly indifferent to the fact that he proclaims.

On one occasion Mrs Val Gwepton, who was not blessed with the most reposeful of temperaments, fairly let herself go, and gave Mrs Pentherby a vivid and truthful *résumé* of her opinion of her. The object of this unpent storm of accumulated animosity waited patiently for a lull, and then remarked quietly to the angry little woman –

'And now, my dear Mrs Gwepton, let me tell you something that I've been wanting to say for the last two or three minutes, only you wouldn't give me a chance; you've got a hairpin dropping out on the left side. You thin-haired women always find it difficult to keep your hairpins in.'

'What can one do with a woman like that?' Mrs Val demanded afterwards of a sympathizing audience.

Of course, Reggie received numerous hints as to the unpopularity of this jarring personality. His sister-in-law openly tackled him on the subject of her many enormities. Reggie listened with the attenuated regret that one bestows on an earthquake disaster in Bolivia or a crop failure in Eastern Turkestan, events which seem so distant that one can almost persuade oneself they haven't happened.

'That woman has got some hold over him,' opined his sister-in-law darkly; 'either she is helping him to finance the show, and presumes on the fact, or else, which Heaven forbid, he's got some queer infatuation for her. Men do take the most extraordinary fancies.'

Matters never came exactly to a crisis. Mrs Pentherby, as a source of personal offence, spread herself over so wide an area that no one woman of the party felt impelled to rise up and declare that she absolutely refused to stay another week in the same house with her. What is everybody's tragedy is nobody's tragedy. There was even a certain consolation in comparing notes as to specific acts of offence. Reggie's sister-in-law had the added interest of trying to discover the secret bond which blunted his condemnation of Mrs Pentherby's long catalogue of misdeeds. There was little to go on from his manner towards her in public, but he remained obstinately unimpressed by anything that was said against her in private.

With the one exception of Mrs Pentherby's unpopularity, the house-party scheme was a success on its first trial, and there was no difficulty about reconstructing it on the same lines for another winter session. It so happened that most of the women of the party, and two or three of the men, would not be available on this occasion, but Reggie had laid his plans well ahead and booked plenty of 'fresh blood' for the new departure. It would be, if anything, rather a larger party than before.

'I'm so sorry I can't join this winter,' said Reggie's sister-in-law, 'but we must go to our cousins in Ireland; we've put them off so often. What a shame! You'll have none of the same women this time.'

'Excepting Mrs Pentherby,' said Reggie demurely.

'Mrs Pentherby! *Surely*, Reggie, you're not going to be so idiotic as to have that woman again! She'll set all the women's backs up just as she did this time. What *is* this mysterious hold she's got over you?'

'She's invaluable,' said Reggie; 'she's my official quarreller.'

'Your — what did you say?' gasped his sister-in-law.

'I introduced her into the house-party for the express purpose of concentrating the feuds and quarrelling that would otherwise have broken out in all directions among the women-kind. I didn't need the advice and warning of sundry friends to foresee that we shouldn't get through six months of close companionship without a certain amount of pecking and sparring, so I thought the best thing was to localize and sterilize it in one process. Of course, I made it well worth the lady's while, and she didn't know any of you from Adam, and as you don't even know her real name, she didn't mind getting herself disliked in a useful cause.'

'You mean to say she was in the know all the time?'

'Of course she was, and so were one or two of the men, so she was able to have a good laugh with us behind the scenes when she'd done anything particularly outrageous. And she really enjoyed herself. You see, she's in the position of poor relation in a rather pugnacious family, and her life has been largely spent in smoothing over other people's quarrels. You can imagine the welcome relief of being able to go about saying and doing perfectly exasperating things to a whole houseful of women — and all in the cause of peace.'

'I think you are the most odious person in the whole world,' said Reggie's sister-in-law. Which was not strictly true; more than anybody, more than ever she disliked Mrs Pentherby. It was impossible to calculate how many quarrels that woman had done her out of.

LAURA

'You are not really dying, are you?' asked Amanda.

'I have the doctor's permission to live till Tuesday,' said Laura.

'But today is Saturday; this is serious!' gasped Amanda.

'I don't know about it being serious; it is certainly Saturday,' said Laura.

'Death is always serious,' said Amanda.

'I never said I was going to die. I am presumably going to leave off being Laura, but I shall go on being something. An animal of some kind, I suppose. You see, when one hasn't been very good in the life one has just lived, one reincarnates in some lower organism. And I haven't been very good, when one comes to think of it. I've been petty and mean and vindictive and all that sort of thing when circumstances have seemed to warrant it.'

'Circumstances never warrant that sort of thing,' said Amanda hastily.

'If you don't mind my saying so,' observed Laura, 'Egbert is a circumstance that would warrant any amount of that sort of thing. You're married to him – that's different; you've sworn to love, honour and endure him: I haven't.'

'I don't see what's wrong with Egbert,' protested Amanda.

'Oh, I dare say the wrongness has been on my part,' admitted Laura dispassionately; 'he has merely been the extenuating circumstance. He made a thin, peevish kind of fuss, for instance, when I took the collie puppies from the farm out for a run the other day.'

'They chased his young broods of speckled Sussex and drove two sitting hens off their nests, besides running all over the flower beds. You know how devoted he is to his poultry and garden.'

'Anyhow, he needn't have gone on about it for the entire evening, and then have said, "Let's say no more about it" just when I was beginning to enjoy the discussion. That's where one of my petty vindictive revenges came in,' added Laura with an unrepentant chuckle. 'I turned the entire family of speckled Sussex into his seedling shed the day after the puppy episode.'

'How could you?' exclaimed Amanda.

'It came quite easy,' said Laura; 'two of the hens pretended to be laying at the time, but I was firm.'

'And we thought it was an accident!'

'You see,' resumed Laura, 'I really *have* some grounds for supposing that my next incarnation will be in a lower organism. I shall be an animal of some kind. On the other hand, I haven't been a bad sort in my way, so I think I may count on being a nice animal, something elegant and lively, with a love of fun. An otter, perhaps.'

'I can't imagine you as an otter,' said Amanda.

'Well, I don't suppose you can imagine me as an angel, if it comes to that,' said Laura.

Amanda was silent. She couldn't.

'Personally I think an otter life would be rather enjoyable,' continued Laura; 'salmon to eat all the year round, and the satisfaction of being able to catch the trout in their own homes without having to wait for hours till they condescend to rise to the fly you've been dangling before them; and an elegant svelte figure –'

'Think of the otter hounds,' interposed Amanda; 'how dreadful to be hunted and harried and finally worried to death!'

'Rather fun with half the neighbourhood looking on, and anyhow not worse than this Saturday-to-Tuesday business of dying by inches; and then I should go on into something else. If I had been a moderately good otter I suppose I should get back into human shape of some sort; probably something rather primitive – a little brown, unclothed Nubian boy, I should think.'

'I wish you would be serious,' sighed Amanda; 'you really ought to be if you're only going to live till Tuesday.'

As a matter of fact Laura died on Monday.

'So dreadfully upsetting,' Amanda complained to her uncle-in-law, Sir Lulworth Quayne. 'I've asked quite a lot of people down for golf and fishing, and the rhododendrons are just looking their best.'

'Laura always was inconsiderate,' said Sir Lulworth; 'she was born during Goodwood week, with an Ambassador staying in the house who hated babies.'

'She had the maddest kind of ideas,' said Amanda; 'do you know if there was any insanity in her family?'

'Insanity? No, I never heard of any. Her father lives in West Kensington, but I believe he's sane on all other subjects.'

'She had an idea that she was going to be reincarnated as an otter,' said Amanda.

'One meets with those ideas of reincarnation so frequently even in the West,' said Sir Lulworth, 'that one can hardly set them down as being mad. And Laura was such an unaccountable person in this life that I should not like to lay down definite rules as to what she might be doing in an after state.'

'You think she really might have passed into some animal form?' asked Amanda. She was one of those who shape their opinions rather readily from the standpoint of those around them.

Just then Egbert entered the breakfast-room, wearing an air of bereavement that Laura's demise would have been insufficient, in itself, to account for.

'Four of my speckled Sussex have been killed,' he exclaimed; 'the very four that were to go to the show on Friday. One of them was dragged away and eaten right in the middle of that new carnation bed that I've been to such trouble and expense over. My best flower bed and my best fowls singled out for destruction; it almost seems as if the brute that did the deed had special knowledge how to be as devastating as possible in a short space of time.'

'Was it a fox, do you think?' asked Amanda.

'Sounds more like a polecat,' said Sir Lulworth.

'No,' said Egbert, 'there were marks of webbed feet all over the place, and we followed the tracks down to the stream at the bottom of the garden; evidently an otter.'

Amanda looked quickly and furtively across at Sir Lulworth.

Egbert was too agitated to eat any breakfast, and went out to superintend the strengthening of the poultry yard defences.

'I think she might at least have waited till the funeral was over,' said Amanda in a scandalized voice.

'It's her own funeral, you know,' said Sir Lulworth; 'it's a nice point in etiquette how far one ought to show respect to one's own mortal remains.'

Disregard for mortuary convention was carried to further lengths next day; during the absence of the family at the funeral ceremony the remaining survivors of the speckled Sussex were massacred. The marauder's line of retreat seemed to have embraced most of the flower beds on the lawn, but the strawberry beds in the lower garden had also suffered.

'I shall get the otter hounds to come here at the earliest possible moment,' said Egbert savagely.

'On no account! You can't dream of such a thing!' exclaimed Amanda. 'I mean, it wouldn't do, so soon after a funeral in the house.'

'It's a case of necessity,' said Egbert; 'once an otter takes to that sort of thing it won't stop.'

'Perhaps it will go elsewhere now that there are no more fowls left,' suggested Amanda.

'One would think you wanted to shield the beast,' said Egbert.

'There's been so little water in the stream lately,' objected Amanda; 'it seems hardly sporting to hunt an animal when it has so little chance of taking refuge anywhere.'

'Good gracious!' fumed Egbert, 'I'm not thinking about sport. I want to have the animal killed as soon as possible.'

Even Amanda's opposition weakened when, during church time on the following Sunday, the otter made its way into the house, raided half a salmon from the larder and worried it into scaly fragments on the Persian rug in Egbert's studio.

'We shall have it hiding under our beds and biting pieces out of our feet before long,' said Egbert, and from what Amanda knew of this particular otter she felt that the possibility was not a remote one.

On the evening preceding the day fixed for the hunt Amanda spent a solitary hour walking by the banks of the stream, making what she imagined to be hound noises. It was charitably supposed by those who overheard her performance, that she was practising for farmyard imitations at the forthcoming village entertainment.

It was her friend and neighbour, Aurora Burret, who brought her news of the day's sport.

'Pity you weren't out; we had quite a good day. We found at once, in the pool just below your garden.'

'Did you – kill?' asked Amanda.

'Rather. A fine she-otter. Your husband got rather badly bitten in trying to "tail it". Poor beast, I felt quite sorry for it, it had such a human look in its eyes when it was killed. You'll call me silly, but do you know who the look reminded me of? My dear woman, what is the matter?'

When Amanda had recovered to a certain extent from her attack of nervous prostration Egbert took her to the Nile Valley to recuperate. Change of scene speedily brought about the desired recovery of health and mental balance. The escapades of an adventurous otter in search of a variation of diet were viewed in their proper light. Amanda's normally placid temperament reasserted itself. Even a hurricane of shouted curses, coming from her husband's dressing-room, in her husband's voice, but hardly in his usual vocabulary, failed to disturb her serenity as she made a leisurely toilet one evening in a Cairo hotel.

'What is the matter? What has happened?' she asked in amused curiosity.

'The little beast has thrown all my clean shirts into the bath! Wait till I catch you, you little –'

'What little beast?' asked Amanda, suppressing a desire to laugh; Egbert's language was so hopelessly inadequate to express his outraged feelings.

'A little beast of a naked brown Nubian boy,' spluttered Egbert.

And now Amanda is seriously ill.

THE SEVENTH PULLET

'It's not the daily grind that I complain of,' said Blenkinthrope resentfully; 'it's the dull grey sameness of my life outside of office hours. Nothing of interest comes my way, nothing remarkable or out of the common. Even the little things that I do try to find some interest in don't seem to interest other people. Things in my garden, for instance.'

'The potato that weighed just over two pounds,' said his friend Gorworth.

'Did I tell you about that?' said Blenkinthrope; 'I was telling the others in the train this morning. I forgot if I'd told you.'

'To be exact you told me that it weighed just under two pounds, but I took into account the fact that abnormal vegetables and freshwater fish have an after-life, in which growth is not arrested.'

'You're just like the others,' said Blenkinthrope sadly; 'you only make fun of it.'

'The fault is with the potato, not with us,' said Gorworth; 'we are not in the least interested in it because it is not in the least interesting. The men you go up in the train with every day are just in the same case as yourself; their lives are commonplace and not very interesting to themselves, and they certainly are not going to wax enthusiastic over the commonplace events in other men's lives. Tell them something startling, dramatic, piquant, that has happened to yourself or to someone in your family, and you will capture their interest at once. They will talk about you with a certain personal pride to all their acquaintances. "Man I know intimately, fellow called Blenkinthrope, lives down my way, had two of his fingers clawed clean off by a lobster he was carrying home to supper. Doctor says entire hand may have to come off." Now that is conversation of a very high order. But imagine walking into a tennis club with the remark : "I know a man who has grown a potato weighing two and a quarter pounds".'

'But hang it all, my dear fellow,' said Blenkinthrope impatiently, 'haven't I just told you that nothing of a remarkable nature ever happens to me ?'

'Invent something,' said Gorworth. Since winning a prize for excellence in Scriptural knowledge at a preparatory school he had felt licensed to be a little more unscrupulous than the circle he moved in. Much might surely be excused to one who in early life could give a list of seventeen trees mentioned in the Old Testament.

'What sort of thing?' asked Blenkinthrope, somewhat snappishly.

'A snake got into your hen-run yesterday morning and killed six out of seven pullets, first mesmerizing them with its eyes and then biting them as they stood helpless. The seventh pullet was one of that French sort, with feathers all over its eyes, so it escaped the mesmeric snare, and just flew at what it could see of the snake and pecked it to pieces.'

'Thank you,' said Blenkinthrope stiffly; 'it's a very clever invention. If such a thing had really happened in my poultry-run I admit I should have been proud and interested to tell people about it. But I'd rather stick to fact, even if it is plain fact.' All the same his mind dwelt wistfully on the story of the Seventh Pullet. He could picture himself telling it in the train amid the absorbed interest of his fellow-passengers. Unconsciously all sorts of little details and improvements began to suggest themselves.

Wistfulness was still his dominant mood when he took his seat in the railway carriage the next morning. Opposite him sat Stevenham, who had attained to a recognized brevet of importance through the fact of an uncle having dropped dead in the act of voting at a Parliamentary election. That had happened three years ago, but Stevenham was still deferred to on all questions of home and foreign politics.

'Hullo, how's the giant mushroom, or whatever it was?' was all the notice Blenkinthrope got from his fellow travellers.

Young Duckby, whom he mildly disliked, speedily monopolized the general attention by an account of a domestic bereavement.

'Had four young pigeons carried off last night by a whacking big rat. Oh, a monster he must have been; you could tell by the size of the hole he made breaking into the loft.'

No moderate-sized rat ever seemed to carry out any predatory operations in these regions; they were all enormous in their enormity.

'Pretty hard lines that,' continued Duckby, seeing that he had secured the attention and respect of the company; 'four squeakers carried off at one swoop. You'd find it rather hard to match that in the way of unlooked-for bad luck.'

'I had six pullets out of a pen of seven killed by a snake yesterday afternoon,' said Blenkinthrope, in a voice which he hardly recognized as his own.

'By a snake?' came in excited chorus.

'It fascinated them with its deadly, glittering eyes, one after the other, and struck them down while they stood helpless. A bedridden neighbour, who wasn't able to call for assistance, witnessed it all from her bedroom window.'

'Well, I never!' broke in the chorus, with variations.

'The interesting part of it is about the seventh pullet, the one that didn't get killed,' resumed Blenkinthrope, slowly lighting a cigarette. His diffidence had left him, and he was beginning to realize how safe and easy depravity can seem once one has the courage to begin. 'The six dead birds were Minorcas; the seventh was a Houdan with a mop of feathers all over its eyes. It could hardly see the snake at all, so of course it wasn't mesmerized like the others. It just could see something wriggling on the ground, and went for it and pecked it to death.'

'Well, I'm blessed!' exclaimed the chorus.

In the course of the next few days Blenkinthrope discovered how little the loss of one's self-respect affects one when one has gained the esteem of the world. His story found its way into one of the poultry papers, and was copied thence into a daily news-sheet as a matter of general interest. A lady wrote from the North of Scotland recounting a similar episode which she had witnessed as occurring between a stoat and a blind grouse. Somehow a lie seems so much less reprehensible when one can call it a lee.

For a while the adapter of the Seventh Pullet story enjoyed to the full his altered standing as a person of consequence, one who had had some share in the strange events of his times. Then he was thrust once again into the cold grey background by the sudden blossoming into importance of Smith-Paddon, a daily fellow traveller, whose little girl had been knocked down and nearly hurt by a car belonging to a musical-comedy actress. The actress was not in the car at the time, but she was in numerous photographs which appeared in the illustrated papers of Zoto Dobreen inquiring after the well-being of Maisie, daughter of Edmund Smith-Paddon, Esq. With this new human interest to absorb them the travelling companions were almost rude when Blenkinthrope tried to explain his contrivance for keeping vipers and peregrine falcons out of his chicken-run.

Gorworth, to whom he unburdened himself in private, gave him the same counsel as theretofore.

'Invent something.'

'Yes, but what?'

The ready affirmative coupled with the question betrayed a significant shifting of the ethical standpoint.

It was a few days later that Blenkinthrope revealed a chapter of family history to the customary gathering in the railway carriage.

'Curious thing happened to my aunt, the one who lives in Paris,' he began. He had several aunts, but they were all geographically distributed over Greater London.

'She was sitting on a seat in the Bois the other afternoon, after lunching at the Roumanian Legation.'

Whatever the story gained in picturesqueness for the dragging-in of diplomatic 'atmosphere', it ceased from that moment to command any acceptance as a record of current events. Gorworth had warned his neophyte that this would be the case, but the traditional enthusiasm of the neophyte had triumphed over discretion.

'She was feeling rather drowsy, the effect probably of the champagne, which she's not in the habit of taking in the middle of the day. '

A subdued murmur of admiration went round the company. Blenkinthrope's aunts were not used to taking champagne in the middle of the year, regarding it exclusively as a Christmas and New Year accessory.

'Presently a rather portly gentleman passed by her seat and paused an instant to light a cigar. At that moment a youngish man came up behind him, drew the blade from a swordstick, and stabbed him half a dozen times through and through. "Scoundrel," he cried to his victim, "you do not know me. My name is Henri Leturc." The elderman wiped away some of the blood that was spattering his clothes, turned to his assailant, and said: "And since when has an attempted assassination been considered an introduction?" Then he finished lighting his cigar and walked away. My aunt had intended screaming for the police, but seeing the indifference with which the principal in the affair treated the matter she felt that it would be an impertinence on her part to interfere. Of course I need hardly say she put the whole thing down to the effects of a warm, drowsy afternoon and the Legation champagne. Now comes the astonishing part of my story. A fortnight later a bank manager was stabbed to death with a swordstick in that very part of the Bois. His assassin was the son of a charwoman formerly working at the bank, who had been dismissed from his job by the manager on account of chronic intemperance. His name was Henri Leturc.'

From that moment Blenkinthrope was tacitly accepted as the Munchausen of the party. No effort was spared to draw him out from day to day in the exercise of testing their powers of credulity, and Blenkinthrope, in the false security of an assured and receptive audience, waxed industrious and ingenious in supplying the demand for marvels. Duckby's satirical story of a tame otter that had a tank in the garden to swim in, and whined restlessly whenever the water-rate was overdue, was scarcely an unfair parody of some of Blenkinthrope's wilder efforts. And then one day came Nemesis.

Returning to his villa one evening Blenkinthrope found his wife sitting in front of a pack of cards, which she was scrutinizing with unusual concentration.

'The same old patience-game?' he asked carelessly.

'No dear; this is the Death's Head patience, the most difficult of them all. I've never got it to work out, and somehow I should be rather frightened if I did. Mother only got it out once in her life; she was afraid of it, too. Her great-aunt had done it once and fallen dead from excitement the next moment, and mother always had a feeling that she would die if she ever got it out. She died the same night that she did it. She was in bad health at the time, certainly, but it was a strange coincidence.'

'Don't do it if it frightens you,' was Blenkinthrope's practical comment as he left the room. A few minutes later his wife called to him.

'John, it gave me such a turn, I nearly got it out. Only the five of diamonds held me up at the end. I really thought I'd done it.'

'Why, you can do it,' said Blenkinthrope, who had come back

to the room; 'if you shift the eight of clubs on to that open nine
the five can be moved on to the six.'

His wife made the suggested move with hasty, trembling
fingers, and piled the outstanding cards on to their respective
packs. Then she followed the example of her mother and great-
grand-aunt.

Blenkinthrope had been genuinely fond of his wife, but in the
midst of his bereavement one dominant thought obtruded itself.
Something sensational and real had at last come into his life; no
longer was it a grey, colourless record. The headlines which
might appropriately describe his domestic tragedy kept shaping
themselves in his brain. 'Inherited presentiment comes true.' 'The
Death's Head patience: Card-game that justified its sinister name
in three generations.' He wrote out a full story of the fatal
occurrence for the *Essex Vedette,* the editor of which was a friend
of his, and to another friend he gave a condensed account, to be
taken up to the office of one of the halfpenny dailies. But in both
cases his reputation as a romancer stood fatally in the way of the
fulfilment of his ambitions. 'Not the right thing to be Munchaus-
ening in a time of sorrow,' agreed his friends among themselves,
and a brief note of regret at the 'sudden death of the wife of our
respected neighbour, Mr John Blenkinthrope, from heart failure',
appearing in the news column of the local paper was the forlorn
outcome of his visions of widespread publicity.

Blenkinthrope shrank from the society of his erstwhile travelling companions and took to travelling townwards by an earlier
train. He sometimes tries to enlist the sympathy and attention
of a chance acquaintance in details of the whistling prowess of
his best canary or the dimensions of his largest beetroot; he
scarcely recognizes himself as the man who was once spoken
about and pointed out as the owner of the Seventh Pullet.

TEA

James Cushat-Prinkly was a young man who had always had a
settled conviction that one of these days he would marry; up to
the age of thirty-four he had done nothing to justify that conviction. He liked and admired a great many women collectively and
dispassionately without singling out one for especial matrimonial
consideration, just as one might admire the Alps without feeling

that one wanted any particular peak as one's own private property.

His lack of initiative in this matter aroused a certain amount of impatience among the sentimentally minded women-folk of his home circle; his mother, his sisters, an aunt-in-residence, and two or three intimate matronly friends, regarded his dilatory approach to the married state with a disapproval that was far from being inarticulate. His most innocent flirtations were watched with the straining eagerness which a group of unexercised terriers concentrates on the slightest movements of a human being who may be reasonably considered likely to take them for a walk. No decent-souled mortal can long resist the pleading of several pairs of walk-beseeching dog-eyes; James Cushat-Prinkly was not sufficiently obstinate or indifferent to home influences to disregard the obviously expressed wish of his family that he should become enamoured of some nice marriageable girl, and when his Uncle Jules departed this life and bequeathed him a comfortable little legacy it really seemed the correct thing to do to set about discovering someone to share it with him. The process of discovery was carried on more by the force of suggestion and the weight of public opinion than by any initiative of his own; a clear working majority of his female relatives and the aforesaid matronly friends had pitched on Joan Sebastable as the most suitable young woman in his range of acquaintance to whom he might propose marriage, and James became gradually accustomed to the idea that he and Joan would go together through the prescribed stages of congratulations, present-receiving, Norwegian or Mediterranean hotels, and eventual domesticity. It was necessary, however, to ask the lady what she thought about the matter; the family had so far conducted and directed the flirtation with ability and discretion, but the actual proposal would have to be an individual effort.

Cushat-Prinkly walked across the Park towards the Sebastable residence in a frame of mind that was moderately complacent. As the thing was going to be done he was glad to feel that he was going to get it settled and off his mind that afternoon. Proposing marriage, even to a nice girl like Joan, was a rather irksome business, but one could not have a honeymoon in Minorca and a subsequent life of married happiness without such preliminary. He wondered what Minorca was really like as a place to stop in; in his mind's eye it was an island in perpetual half-mourning, with black or white Minorca hens running all over it. Probably it would not be a bit like that when one came to examine it.

People who had been in Russia had told him that they did not remember having seen any Muscovy ducks there, so it was possible that there would be no Minorca fowls on the island.

His Mediterranean musings were interrupted by the sound of a clock striking the half-hour. Half-past four. A frown of dissatisfaction settled on his face. He would arrive at the Sebastable mansion just at the hour of afternoon tea. Joan would be seated at a low table, spread with an array of silver kettles and cream-jugs and delicate porcelain teacups, behind which her voice would tinkle pleasantly in a series of little friendly questions about weak or strong tea, how much, if any, sugar, milk, cream, and so forth. 'Is it one lump? I forgot. You do take milk, don't you? Would you like some more hot water, if it's too strong?'

Cushat-Prinkly had read of such things in scores of novels, and hundreds of actual experiences had told him that they were true to life. Thousands of women, at this solemn afternoon hour, were sitting behind dainty porcelain and silver fittings, with their voices tinkling pleasantly in a cascade of solicitous little questions. Cushat-Prinkly detested the whole system of afternoon tea. According to his theory of life a woman should lie on a divan or couch, talking with incomparable charm or looking unutterable thoughts, or merely silent as a thing to be looked on, and from behind a silken curtain a small Nubian page should silently, bring in a tray with cups and dainties, to be accepted silently, as a matter of course, without drawn-out chatter about cream and sugar and hot water. If one's soul was really enslaved at one's mistress's feet, how could one talk coherently about weakened tea? Cushat-Prinkly had never expounded his views on the subject to his mother; all her life she had been accustomed to tinkle pleasantly at tea-time behind dainty porcelain and silver, and if he had spoken to her about divans and Nubian pages she would have urged him to take a week's holiday at the seaside. Now, as he passed through a tangle of small streets that led indirectly to the elegant Mayfair terrace for which he was bound, a horror at the idea of confronting Joan Sebastable at her tea-table seized on him. A momentary deliverance presented itself; on one floor of a narrow little house at the noisier end of Esquimault Street lived Rhoda Ellam, a sort of remote cousin, who made a living by creating hats out of costly materials. The hats really looked as if they had come from Paris; the cheques she got for them unfortunately never looked as if they were going to Paris. However, Rhoda appeared to find life amusing and to have a fairly good time in spite of her straitened circumstances. Cushat-Prinkly decided to climb up to her floor and defer by half-an-hour or so the important business which lay before him; by spinning out his visit he could contrive to reach the Sebastable mansion after the last vestiges of dainty porcelain had been cleared away.

Rhoda welcomed him into a room that seemed to do duty as workshop, sitting-room, and kitchen combined, and to be wonderfully clean and comfortable at the same time.

'I'm having a picnic meal,' she announced. 'There's caviare in that jar at your elbow. Begin on that brown bread-and-butter while I cut some more. Find yourself a cup; the teapot is behind you. Now tell me about hundreds of things.'

She made no other allusion to food, but talked amusingly and made her visitor talk amusingly too. At the same time she cut the bread-and-butter with a masterly skill and produced red pepper and sliced lemon, where so many women would merely have produced reasons and regrets for not having any. Cushat-Prinkly found that he was enjoying an excellent tea without having to answer as many questions about it as a Minister for Agriculture might be called on to reply to during an outbreak of cattle plague.

'And now tell me why you have come to see me,' said Rhoda suddenly. 'You arouse not merely my curiosity but my business instincts. I hope you've come about hats. I heard that you had come into a legacy the other day, and, of course, it struck me that it would be a beautiful and desirable thing for you to celebrate the event by buying brilliantly expensive hats for all your sisters. They may not have said anything about it, but I feel sure the same idea has occurred to them. Of course, with Goodwood on us, I am rather rushed just now, but in my business we're accustomed to that; we live in a series of rushes – like the infant Moses.'

'I didn't come about hats,' said her visitor. 'In fact I don't think I really came about anything. I was passing and I just thought I'd look in and see you. Since I've been sitting talking to you, however, a rather important idea has occurred to me. If you'll forget Goodwood for a moment and listen to me, I'll tell you what it is.'

'Some forty minutes later James Cushat-Prinkly returned to the bosom of his family, bearing an important piece of news.

'I'm engaged to be married,' he announced.

A rapturous outbreak of congratulation and self-applause broke out.

'Ah, we knew! We saw it coming! We foretold it weeks ago!'

'I'll bet you didn't,' said Cushat-Prinkly. 'If anyone had told me at lunch-time today that I was going to ask Rhoda Ellam to marry me and that she was going to accept me, I would have laughed at the idea.'

The romantic suddenness of the affair in some measure compensated James's women-folk for the ruthless negation of all their patient effort and skilled diplomacy. It was rather trying to have to deflect their enthusiasm at a moment's notice from Joan Sebastable to Rhoda Ellam; but, after all, it was James's wife who was in question, and his tastes had some claim to be considered.

On a September afternoon of the same year, after the honeymoon in Minorca had ended, Cushat-Prinkly came into the drawing-room of his new house in Granchester Square. Rhoda was seated at a low table, behind a service of dainty porcelain and gleaming silver. There was a pleasant tinkling note in her voice as she handed him a cup.

'You like it weaker than that, don't you? Shall I put some more hot water to it? No?'

THE LUMBER-ROOM

The children were to be driven, as a special treat, to the sands at Jagborough. Nicholas was not to be one of the party; he was in disgrace. Only that morning he had refused to eat his wholesome bread-and-milk on the seemingly frivolous ground that there was a frog in it. Older and wiser and better people had told him that there could not possibly be a frog in his bread-and-milk and that he was not to talk nonsense; he continued, nevertheless, to talk what seemed the veriest nonsense, and described with much detail the colouration and markings of the alleged frog. The dramatic part of the incident was that there really was a frog in Nicholas' basin of bread-and-milk; he had put it there himself, so he felt entitled to know something about it. The sin of taking a frog from the garden and putting it into a bowl of wholesome bread-and-milk was enlarged on at great length, but the fact that stood out clearest in the whole affair, as it presented itself to the mind of Nicholas, was that the older, wiser, and better people had been proved to be profoundly in error in matters about which they had expressed the utmost assurance.

'You said there couldn't possibly be a frog in my bread-and-milk; there *was* a frog in my bread-and-milk,' he repeated, with the insistence of a skilled tactician who does not intend to shift from favourable ground.

So his boy-cousin and girl-cousin and his quite uninteresting younger brother were to be taken to Jagborough sands that afternoon and he was to stay at home. His cousins' aunt, who insisted, by an unwarranted stretch of imagination, in styling herself his aunt also, had hastily invented the Jagborough expedition in order to impress on Nicholas the delights that he had justly forfeited by his disgraceful conduct at the breakfast-table. It was her habit, whenever one of the children fell from grace, to improvise something of a festival nature from which the offender would be rigorously debarred; if all the children sinned collectively they were suddenly informed of a circus in the neighbouring town, a circus of unrivalled merit and uncounted elephants, to which, but for their depravity, they would have been taken that very day.

A few decent tears were looked for on the part of Nicholas when the moment for the departure of the expedition arrived. As a matter of fact, however, all the crying was done by his girl-cousin, who scraped her knee rather painfully against the step of the carriage as she was scrambling in.

'How she did howl,' said Nicholas cheerfully, as the party drove off without any of the elation of high spirits that should have characterized it.

'She'll soon get over that,' said the *soi-disant* aunt; 'it will be a glorious afternoon for racing about over those beautiful sands. How they will enjoy themselves!'

'Bobby won't enjoy himself much, and he won't race much either,' said Nicholas with a grim chuckle; 'his boots are hurting him. They're too tight.'

'Why didn't he tell me they were hurting?' asked the aunt with some asperity.

'He told you twice, but you weren't listening. You often don't listen when we tell you important things.'

'You are not to go into the gooseberry garden,' said the aunt, changing the subject.

'Why not?' demanded Nicholas.

'Because you are in disgrace,' said the aunt loftily.

Nicholas did not admit the flawlessness of the reasoning; he felt perfectly capable of being in disgrace and in a gooseberry garden at the same moment. His face took on an expression of considerable obstinacy. It was clear to his aunt that he was determined to get into the gooseberry garden, 'only,' as she remarked to herself, 'because I have told him he is not to.'

Now the gooseberry garden had two doors by which it might be entered, and once a small person like Nicholas could slip in there he could effectually disappear from view amid the masking growth of artichokes, raspberry canes, and fruit bushes. The aunt had many other things to do that afternoon, but she spent an hour or two in trivial gardening operations among flower beds and shrubberies, whence she could keep a watchful eye on the two doors that led to the forbidden paradise. She was a woman of few ideas, with immense powers of concentration.

Nicholas made one or two sorties into the front garden, wriggling his way with obvious stealth of purpose towards one or other of the doors, but never able for a moment to evade the aunt's watchful eye. As a matter of fact, he had no intention of trying to get into the gooseberry garden, but it was extremely convenient for him that his aunt should believe that he had; it was a belief that would keep her on self-imposed sentry-duty for the greater part of the afternoon. Having thoroughly confirmed and fortified her suspicions, Nicholas slipped back into the house and rapidly put into execution a plan of action that had long germinated in his brain. By standing on a chair in the library one could reach a shelf on which reposed a fat, important-looking key. The key was as important as it looked; it was the instrument which kept the mysteries of the lumber-room secure from unauthorized intrusion, which opened a way only for aunts and such-like privileged persons. Nicholas had not had much experience of the art of fitting keys into keyholes and turning locks, but for some days past he had practised with the key of the school-room door; he did not believe in trusting too much to luck and accident. The key turned stiffly in the lock, but it turned. The door opened, and Nicholas was in an unknown land, compared with which the gooseberry garden was a stale delight, a mere material pleasure.

Often and often Nicholas had pictured to himself what the lumber-room might be like, that region that was so carefully sealed from youthful eyes and concerning which no questions were ever answered. It came up to his expectations. In the first place it was large and dimly lit, one high window opening on to the forbidden garden being its only source of illumination. In the second place it was a storehouse of unimagined treasures. The aunt-by-assertion was one of those people who think that things spoil by use and consign them to dust and damp by way of preserving them. Such parts of the house as Nicholas knew best were rather bare and cheerless, but here there were wonderful things for the eye to feast on. First and foremost there was a piece of framed tapestry that was evidently meant to be a fire-screen. To Nicholas it was a living, breathing story; he sat down on a roll of Indian hangings, glowing in wonderful colours beneath a layer of dust, and took in all the details of the tapestry picture. A man, dressed in the hunting costume of some remote period, had just transfixed a stag with an arrow; it could not have been a difficult shot because the stag was only one or two paces away from him; in the thickly growing vegetation that the picture suggested it would not have been difficult to creep up to a feeding stag, and the two spotted dogs that were springing forward to join in the chase had evidently been trained to keep to heel till the arrow was discharged. That part of the picture was simple, if interesting, but did the huntsman see, what Nicholas saw, that four galloping wolves were coming in his direction through the wood? There might be more than four of them hidden behind the trees, and in any case would the man and his dogs be able to cope with the four wolves if they made an attack? The man had only two arrows left in his quiver, and he might miss with one or both of them; all one knew about his skill in shooting was that he could hit a large stag at a ridiculously short range. Nicholas sat for many golden minutes revolving the possibilities of the scene; he was inclined to think that there were more than four wolves and that the man and his dogs were in a tight corner.

But there were other objects of delight and interest claiming his instant attention; there were quaint twisted candlesticks in the shape of snakes, and a teapot fashioned like a china duck, out of whose open beak the tea was supposed to come. How dull and shapeless the nursery teapot seemed in comparison! And there was a carved sandal-wood box packed tight with aromatic cotton-wool, and between the layers of cotton-wool were little brass figures, hump-necked bulls, and peacocks and goblins, delightful to see and to handle. Less promising in appearance was a large square book with plain black covers; Nicholas peeped into it, and, behold, it was full of coloured pictures of birds. And such birds! In the garden, and in the lanes when he went for a walk, Nicholas came across a few birds, of which the largest were an occasional magpie or wood-pigeon; here were herons and bustards, kites, toucans, tiger-bitterns, brush turkeys, ibises, golden pheasants, a whole portrait gallery of undreamed-of creatures. And as he was admiring the colouring of the mandarin duck and assigning a life-history to it, the voice of his aunt in shrill vociferation of his name came from the gooseberry garden without. She had grown suspicious at his long disappearance, and had leapt to the conclusion that he had climbed over the wall behind the sheltering screen of the lilac bushes; she was now engaged in energetic and rather hopeless search for him among the artichokes and raspberry canes.

'Nicholas, Nicholas!' she screamed, 'you are to come out of this at once. It's no use trying to hide there; I can see you all the time.'

It was probably the first time for twenty years that anyone had smiled in that lumber-room.

Presently the angry repetitions of Nicholas' name gave way to a shriek, and a cry for somebody to come quickly. Nicholas shut the book, restored it carefully to its place in a corner, and shook some dust from a neighbouring pile of newspapers over it. Then he crept from the room, locked the door, and replaced the key exactly where he had found it. His aunt was still calling his name when he sauntered into the front garden.

'Who's calling?' he asked.

'Me,' came the answer from the other side of the wall; 'didn't you hear me? I've been looking for you in the gooseberry garden, and I've slipped into the rain-water tank. Luckily there's no water in it, but the sides are slippery and I can't get out. Fetch the little ladder from under the cherry tree –'

'I was told I wasn't to go into the gooseberry garden,' said Nicholas promptly.

'I told you not to, and now I tell you that you may,' came the voice from the rain-water tank, rather impatiently.

'Your voice doesn't sound like aunt's,' objected Nicholas; 'you may be the Evil One tempting me to be disobedient. Aunt often tells me that the Evil One tempts me and that I always yield. This time I'm not going to yield.'

'Don't talk nonsense,' said the prisoner in the tank; 'go and fetch the ladder.'

'Will there be strawberry jam for tea?' asked Nicholas innocently.

'Certainly there will be,' said the aunt, privately resolving that Nicholas should have none of it.

'Now I know that you are the Evil one and not aunt,' shouted Nicholas gleefully; 'when we asked aunt for strawberry jam yesterday she said there wasn't any. I know there are four jars of it in the store cupboard, because I looked, and of course you know it's there, but *she* doesn't, because she said there wasn't any. Oh, Devil, you *have* sold yourself!'

There was an unusual sense of luxury in being able to talk to an aunt as though one was talking to the Evil One, but Nicholas knew, with childish discernment, that such luxuries were not to be over-indulged in. He walked noisily away, and it was a kitchenmaid, in search of parsley, who eventually rescued the aunt from the rain-water tank.

Tea that evening was partaken of in a fearsome silence. The tide had been at its highest when the children had arrived at Jagborough Cove, so there had been no sands to play on — a circumstance that the aunt had overlooked in the haste of organizing her punitive expedition. The tightness of Bobby's boots had had disastrous effect on his temper the whole of the afternoon, and altogether the children could not have been said to have enjoyed themselves. The aunt maintained the frozen muteness of one who has suffered undignified and unmerited detention in a rain-water tank for thirty-five minutes. As for Nicholas, he, too, was silent, in the absorption of one who has much to think about; it was just possible, he considered, that the huntsman would escape with his hounds while the wolves feasted on the stricken stag.

THE TREASURE-SHIP

The great galleon lay in semi-retirement under the sand, weed and water of the northern bay where the fortune of war and weather had long ago ensconced it. Three and a quarter centuries had passed since the day when it had taken the high seas as an important unit of a fighting squadron — precisely which squadron the learned were not agreed. The galleon had brought nothing into the world, but it had, according to tradition and report, taken much out of it. But how much? There again the learned were in disagreement. Some were as generous in their estimate as an income-tax assessor, others applied a species of higher criticism to the submerged treasure chests, and debased their contents to the currency of goblin gold. Of the former school was Lulu, Duchess of Dulverton.

The Duchess was not only a believer in the existence of a sunken treasure of alluring proportions; she also believed that she knew a method by which the said treasure might be precisely located and cheaply disembedded. An aunt on her mother's side of the family had been Maid of Honour at the Court of Monaco, and had taken a respectful interest in the deep-sea researches in which the Throne of that country, impatient, perhaps of its terrestrial restrictions, was wont to immerse itself. It was through the instrumentality of this relative that the Duchess learned of an invention, perfected and very nearly patented by a Monegaskan savant, by means of which the home-life of the Mediterranean sardine might be studied at a depth of many fathoms in a cold white light of more than ball-room brilliancy. Implicated in this invention (and, in the Duchess's eyes, the most attractive part of it) was an electric suction dredge, specially designed for dragging to the surface such objects of interest and value as might be found in the more accessible levels of the ocean-bed. The rights of the invention were to be acquired for a matter of eighteen hundred francs, and the apparatus for a few thousand more. The Duchess of Dulverton was rich, as the world counted wealth; she nursed the hope of being one day rich at her own computation. Companies had been formed and efforts had been made again and again during the course of three centuries to probe for the alleged treasures of the interesting galleon; with the aid of this invention she considered that she might go to work on the wreck privately and independently. After all, one of her ancestors on her mother's side was descended from Medina Sidonia, so she was of opinion that she had as much right to the treasure as anyone. She acquired the invention and bought the apparatus.

Among other family ties and encumbrances, Lulu possessed a nephew, Vasco Honiton, a young gentleman who was blessed with a small income and a large circle of relatives, and lived impartially and precariously on both. The name Vasco had been given him possibly in the hope that he might live up to its adventurous tradition, but he limited himself strictly to the home industry of adventurer, preferring to exploit the assured rather than to explore the unknown. Lulu's intercourse with him had been restricted of recent years to the negative processes of being out of town when he called on her, and short of money when he wrote to her. Now, however, she bethought herself of his eminent suitability for the direction of a treasure-seeking experiment; if anyone could extract gold from an unpromising situation it would certainly be Vasco — of course, under the necessary safeguards in the way of supervision. Where money was in question Vasco's conscience was liable to fits of obstinate silence.

Somewhere in the west coast of Ireland the Dulverton property included a few acres of shingle, rock, and heather, too barren to support even an agrarian outrage, but embracing a small and fairly deep bay where the lobster yield was good in most seasons. There was a bleak little house on the property, and for those who liked lobsters and solitude, and were able to accept an Irish cook's ideas as to what might be perpetrated in the name of mayonnaise, Innisgluther was a tolerable exile during the summer months. Lulu seldom went there herself, but she lent the house lavishly to friends and relations. She put it now at Vasco's disposal.

'It will be the very place to practise and experiment with the salvage apparatus,' she said; 'the bay is quite deep in places, and you will be able to test everything thoroughly before starting on the treasure hunt.'

In less than three weeks Vasco turned up in town to report progress.

'The apparatus works beautifully,' he informed his aunt; 'the deeper one got the clearer everything grew. We found something in the way of a sunken wreck to operate on, too!'

'A wreck in Innisgluther Bay!' exclaimed Lulu.

'A submerged motor-boat, the *Sub-Rosa*,' said Vasco.

'No! really?' said Lulu; 'poor Billy Yuttley's boat. I remember it went down somewhere off that coast some three years ago. His body was washed ashore at the Point. People said at the time that the boat was capsized intentionally — a case of suicide, you know. People always say that sort of thing when anything tragic happens.'

'In this case they were right,' said Vasco.

'What do you mean?' asked the Duchess hurriedly. 'What makes you think so?'

'I know,' said Vasco simply.

'Know? How can you know? How can anyone know? The thing happened three years ago.'

'In a locker of the *Sub-Rosa* I found a water-tight strong-box. It contained papers.' Vasco paused with dramatic effect and searched for a moment in the inner breast-pocket of his coat. He drew out a folded slip of paper. The Duchess snatched at it in almost indecent haste and moved appreciably nearer the fireplace.

'Was this in the *Sub-Rosa's* strong-box?' she asked.

'Oh, no,' said Vasco carelessly, 'that is a list of the well-known people who would be involved in a very disagreeable scandal if the *Sub-Rosa's* papers were made public. I've put you at the head of it, otherwise it follows alphabetical order.'

The Duchess gazed helplessly at the string of names, which seemed for the moment to include nearly everyone she knew. As a matter of fact, her own name at the head of the list exercised an almost paralysing effect on her thinking faculties.

'Of course you have destroyed the papers?' she asked, when she had somewhat recovered herself. She was conscious that she made the remark with an entire lack of conviction.

Vasco shook his head.

'But you should have,' said Lulu angrily; 'if, as you say, they are highly compromising –'

'Oh, they are, I assure you of that,' interposed the young man.

'Then you should put them out of harm's way at once. Supposing anything should leak out, think of all these poor unfortunate people who would be involved in the disclosures,' and Lulu tapped the list with an agitated gesture.

'Unfortunate, perhaps, but not poor,' corrected Vasco; 'if you read the list carefully you'll notice that I haven't troubled to include anyone whose financial standing isn't above question.'

Lulu glared at her nephew for some moments in silence. Then she asked hoarsely: 'What are you going to do?'

'Nothing – for the remainder of my life,' he answered meaningly. 'A little hunting, perhaps,' he continued, 'and I shall have a villa at Florence. The Villa Sub-Rosa would sound rather quaint and picturesque, don't you think, and quite a lot of people would be able to attach a meaning to the name. And I suppose I must have a hobby; I shall probably collect Raeburns.'

Lulu's relative, who lived at the Court of Monaco, got quite a snappish answer when she wrote recommending some further invention in the realm of marine research.

'That woman's art-jargon tires me,' said Clovis to his journalist friend. 'She's so fond of talking of certain pictures as "growing on one", as though they were a sort of fungus.'

'That reminds me,' said the journalist, 'of the story of Henri Deplis. Have I ever told it you?'

Clovis shook his head.

'Henri Deplis was by birth a native of the Grand Duchy of Luxembourg. On maturer reflection he became a commercial traveller. His business activities frequently took him beyond the limits of the Grand Duchy, and he was stopping in a small town of Northern Italy when news reached him from home that a legacy from a distant and deceased relative had fallen to his share.

'It was not a large legacy, even from the modest standpoint of Henri Deplis, but it impelled him towards some seemingly harmless extravagances. In particular it led him to patronize local art as represented by the tattoo-needles of Signor Andreas Pincini. Signor Pincini was, perhaps, the most brilliant master of tattoo craft that Italy had ever known, but his circumstances were decidedly impoverished, and for the sum of six hundred francs he gladly undertook to cover his client's back, from the collar-bone down to the waist-line, with a glowing representation of the Fall of Icarus. The design, when finally developed, was a slight disappointment to Monsieur Deplis, who had suspected Icarus of being a fortress taken by Yallenstein in the Thirty Years' War, but he was more than satisfied with the execution of the work, which was acclaimed by all who had the privilege of seeing it as Pincini's masterpiece.

'It was his greatest effort, and his last. Without even waiting to be paid, the illustrious craftsman departed this life, and was buried under an ornate tombstone, whose winged cherubs would have afforded singularly little scope for the exercise of his favourite art. There remained, however, the widow Pincini, to whom the six hundred francs were due. And thereupon arose the great crisis in the life of Henri Deplis, traveller of commerce. The legacy, under the stress of numerous little calls on its substance, had dwindled to very insignificant proportions, and when a pressing wine bill and sundry other current accounts had been paid, there remained little more than 430 francs to offer to the widow. The lady was properly indignant, not wholly, as she volubly explained, on account of the suggested writing-off of 170 francs, but also at the attempt to depreciate the value of her late husband's acknowledged masterpiece. In a week's time Deplis was obliged to reduce his offer to 405 francs, which circumstance fanned the widow's indignation into a fury. She cancelled the sale of the work of art, and a few days later Deplis learned with a sense of consternation that she had presented it to the municipality of Bergamo, which had gratefully accepted it. He left the neighbourhood as unobtrusively as possible, and was genuinely relieved when his business commands took him to Rome, where he hoped his identity and that of the famous picture might be lost sight of.

'But he bore on his back the burden of the dead man's genius. On presenting himself one day in the steaming corridor of a vapour bath, he was at once hustled back into his clothes by the proprietor, who was a North Italian, and who emphatically refused to allow the celebrated Fall of Icarus to be publicly on view without the permission of the municipality of Bergamo. Public interest and official vigilance increased as the matter became more widely known, and Deplis was unable to take a simple dip in the sea or river on the hottest afternoon unless clothed up to the collar-bone in a substantial bathing garment. Later on the authorities of Bergamo conceived the idea that salt water might be injurious to the masterpiece, and a perpetual injunction was obtained which debarred the muchly harassed commercial traveller from sea bathing under any circumstances. Altogether, he was fervently thankful when his employers found him a new range of activities in the neighbourhood of Bordeaux. His thankfulness, however, ceased abruptly at the Franco-Italian frontier. An imposing array of official force barred his departure, and he was sternly reminded of the stringent law which forbids the exportation of Italian works of art.

'A diplomatic parley ensued between the Luxemburgian and Italian Governments, and at one time the European situation became overcast with the possibilities of trouble. But the Italian Government stood firm; it declined to concern itself in the least with the fortunes or even the existence of Henri Deplis, commercial traveller, but was immovable in its decision that the Fall of Icarus (by the late Pincini, Andreas) at present the property of the municipality of Bergamo, should not leave the country.

'The excitement died down in time, but the unfortunate Deplis, who was of a constitutionally retiring disposition, found himself a few months later once more the storm-centre of a furious controversy. A certain German art expert, who had obtained from the municipality of Bergamo permission to inspect the famous masterpiece, declared it to be a spurious Pincini, probably the work of some pupil whom he had employed in his declining years. The evidence of Deplis on the subject was obviously worthless, as he had been under the influence of the customary narcotics during the long process of pricking in the design. The editor of an Italian art journal refuted the contentions of the German expert and undertook to prove that his private life did not conform to any modern standard of decency. The whole of Italy and Germany were drawn into the dispute, and the rest of Europe was soon involved in the quarrel. There were stormy scenes in the Spanish Parliament, and the University of Copenhagen bestowed a gold medal on the German expert (afterwards sending a commission to examine his proofs on the spot), while two Polish schoolboys in Paris committed suicide to show what *they* thought of the matter.

'Meanwhile, the unhappy human background fared no better than before, and it was not surprising that he drifted into the ranks of Italian anarchists. Four times at least he was escorted to the frontier as a dangerous and undesirable foreigner, but he always brought back as the Fall of Icarus (attributed to Pincini, Andreas, early Twentieth Century). And then one day, at an anarchist congress in Genoa, a fellow-worker, in the heat of debate, broke a phial full of corrosive liquid over his back. The red shirt that he was wearing mitigated the effects, but the Icarus was ruined beyond recognition. His assailant was severely reprimanded for assaulting a fellow-anarchist and received seven years' imprisonment for defacing a national art treasure. As soon as he was able to leave the hospital Henri Deplis was put across the frontier as an undesirable alien.

'In the quieter streets of Paris, especially in the neighbourhood of the Ministry of Fine Arts, you may sometimes meet a depressed, anxious-looking man, who, if you pass him the time of day, will answer you with a slight Luxemburgian accent. He nurses the illusion that he is one of the lost arms of the Venus de Milo, and hopes that the French Government may be persuaded to buy him. On all other subjects I believe he is tolerably sane.'

THE STALLED OX

Theophil Eshley was an artist by profession, a cattle painter by force of environment. It is not to be supposed that he lived on a ranch or a dairy farm, in an atmosphere pervaded with horn and hoof, milking-stool, and branding-iron. His home was in a park-like, villa-dotted district that only just escaped the reproach of being suburban. On one side of his garden there abutted a small, picturesque meadow, in which an enterprising neighbour pastured some small picturesque cows of the Channel Island persuasion. At noonday in summertime the cows stood knee-deep in tall meadow-grass under the shade of a group of walnut trees, with the sunlight falling in dappled patches on their mouse-sleek coats. Eshley had conceived and executed a dainty picture of two reposeful milch-cows in a setting of walnut tree and meadow-grass and filtered sunbeam, and the Royal Academy encourages orderly, methodical habits in its children. Eshley had painted a successful and acceptable picture of cattle drowsing picturesquely under walnut trees, and as he had begun, so, of necessity, he went on. His 'Noontide Peace,' a study of two dun cows under a walnut tree was followed by 'A Mid-day Sanctuary,' a study of a walnut tree, with two dun cows under it. In due succession there came 'Where the Gad-Flies Cease from Troubling,' 'The Haven of the Herd,' and 'A Dream in Dairyland,' studies of walnut trees and dun cows. His two attempts to break away from his own tradition were signal failures: 'Turtle Doves Alarmed by Sparrow-hawk' and 'Wolves on the Roman Campagna' came back to his studio in the guise of abominable heresies, and Eshley climbed back into grace and the public gaze with 'A Shaded Nook Where Drowsy Milkers Dream.'

On a fine afternoon in late autumn he was putting some finishing touches to a study of meadow weeds when his neighbour, Adela Pingsford, assailed the outer door of his studio with loud peremptory knockings.

'There is an ox in my garden,' she announced, in explanation of the tempestuous intrusion.

'An ox,' said Eshley blankly, and rather fatuously; 'what kind of ox?'

'Oh, I don't know what kind,' snapped the lady. 'A common

or garden ox, to use the slang expression. It is the garden part of it that I object to. My garden has just been put straight for the winter, and an ox roaming about in it won't improve matters. Besides, there are the chrysanthemums just coming into flower.'

'How did it get into the garden?' asked Eshley.

'I imagine it came in by the gate,' said the lady impatiently; 'it couldn't have climbed the walls, and I don't suppose anyone dropped it from an aeroplane as a Bovril advertisement. The immediately important question is not how it got in, but how to get it out.'

'Won't it go?' said Eshley.

'If it was anxious to go,' said Adela Pingsford rather angrily, 'I should not have come here to chat with you about it. I'm practically all alone; the housemaid is having her afternoon out and the cook is lying down with an attack of neuralgia. Anything that I may have learned at school or in after life about how to remove a large ox from a small garden seems to have escaped from my memory now. All I could think of was that you were a near neighbour and a cattle painter, presumably more or less familiar with the subjects that you painted, and that you might be of some slight assistance. Possibly I was mistaken.'

'I paint dairy cows, certainly,' admitted Eshley, 'but I cannot claim to have had any experience in rounding up stray oxen. I've seen it done on a cinema film, of course, but there were always horses and lots of other accessories; besides, one never knows how much of those pictures are faked.'

Adela Pingsford said nothing, but led the way to her garden. It was normally a fair-sized garden, but it looked small in comparison with the ox, a huge mottled brute, dull red about the head and shoulders, passing to dirty white on the flanks and hind-quarters, with shaggy ears and large blood-shot eyes. It bore about as much resemblance to the dainty paddock heifers that Eshley was accustomed to paint as the chief of a Kurdish nomad clan would to a Japanese tea-shop girl. Eshley stood very near the gate while he studied the animal's appearance and demeanour. Adela Pingsford continued to say nothing.

'It's eating a chrysanthemum,' said Eshley at last, when the silence had become unbearable.

'How observant you are,' said Adela bitterly. 'You seem to notice everything. As a matter of fact, it has got six chrysanthemums in its mouth at the present moment.'

The necessity for doing something was becoming imperative.

Eshley took a step or two in the direction of the animal, clapped hands, and made noises of the 'Hish' and 'Shoo' variety. If the ox heard them it gave no outward indication of the fact.

'If any hens should ever stray into my garden,' said Adela, 'I should certainly send for you to frighten them out. You "shoo" beautifully. Meanwhile, do you mind trying to drive that ox away? That is a *Mademoiselle Louise Bichot* that he's begun on now,' she added in icy calm, as a glowing orange head was crushed into the huge munching mouth.

'Since you have been so frank about the variety of the chrysanthemum,' said Eshley, 'I don't mind telling you that this is an Ayrshire ox.'

The icy calm broke down; Adela Pingsford used language that sent the artist instinctively a few feet nearer to the ox. He picked up a pea-stick and flung it with some determination against the animal's mottled flanks. The operation of mashing *Mademoiselle Louise Bichot* into a petal salad was suspended for a long moment, while the ox gazed with concentrated inquiry at the stick-thrower. Adela gazed with equal concentration and more obvious hostility at the same focus. As the beast neither lowered its head nor stamped its feet Eshley ventured on another javelin exercise with another pea-stick. The ox seemed to realize at once that it was to go; it gave a hurried final pluck at the bed where the chrysanthemums had been, and strode swiftly up the garden. Eshley ran to head it towards the gate, but only succeeded in quickening its pace from a walk to a lumbering trot. With an air of inquiry, but with no real hesitation, it crossed the tiny strip of turf that the charitable called the croquet lawn, and pushed its way through the open French window into the morning-room. Some chrysanthemums and other autumn herbage stood about the room in vases, and the animal resumed its browsing operations; all the same, Eshley fancied that the beginnings of a hunted look had come into its eyes, a look that counselled respect. He discontinued his attempt to interfere with its choice of surroundings.

'Mr Eshley,' said Adela in a shaking voice, 'I asked you to drive that beast out of my garden, but I did not ask you to drive it into my house. If I must have it anywhere on the premises, I prefer the garden to the morning-room.'

'Cattle drives are not in my line,' said Eshley; 'if I remember, I told you so at the outset.'

'I quite agree,' retorted the lady, 'painting pretty pictures of pretty little cows is what you're suited for. Perhaps you'd like to do a nice sketch of that ox making itself at home in my morning-room?'

This time it seemed as if the worm had turned; Eshley began striding away.

'Where are you going?' screamed Adela.

'To fetch implements,' was the answer.

'Implements? I won't have you use a lasso. The room will be wrecked if there's a struggle.'

But the artist marched out of the garden. In a couple of minutes he returned, laden with easel, sketching-stool, and painting materials.

'Do you mean to say that you're going to sit quietly down and paint that brute while it's destroying my morning-room?' gasped Adela.

'It was your suggestion,' said Eshley, setting his canvas in position.

'I forbid it; I absolutely forbid it!' stormed Adela.

'I don't see what standing you have in the matter,' said the artist; 'you can hardly pretend that it's your ox, even by adoption.'

'You seem to forget that it's in my morning-room, eating my flowers,' came the raging retort.

'You seem to forget that the cook has neuralgia,' said Eshley; 'she may be just dozing off into a merciful sleep and your outcry will waken her. Consideration for others should be the guiding principle of people in our station of life.'

'The man is mad!' exclaimed Adela tragically. A moment later it was Adela herself who appeared to go mad. The ox had finished the vase-flowers and the cover of *Israel Kalisch*, and appeared to be thinking of leaving its rather restricted quarters Eshley noticed its restlessness and promptly flung it some bunches of Virginia leaves as an inducement to continue the sitting.

'I forget how the proverb runs,' he observed; 'something about "better a dinner of herbs than a stalled ox where hate is." We seem to have all the ingredients for the proverb ready to hand.'

'I shall go to the Public Library and get them to telephone for the police,' announced Adela, and, raging audibly, she departed.

Some minutes later the ox, awakening probably to the suspicion that oil cake and chopped mangold was waiting for it in some appointed byre, stepped with much precaution out of the morning-room, stared with grave inquiry at the no longer obtrusive and pea-stick-throwing human, and then lumbered heavily but swiftly out of the garden. Eshley packed up his tools and followed the animal's example and 'Larkdene' was left to neuralgia and the cook.

The episode was the turning-point in Eshley's artistic career. His remarkable picture, 'Ox in a Morning-room, Late Autumn,' was one of the sensations and successes of the next Paris Salon, and when it was subsequently exhibited at Munich it was bought by the Bavarian Government, in the teeth of the spirited bidding of three meat-extract firms. From that moment his success was continuous and assured, and the Royal Academy was thankful, two years later, to give a conspicuous position on its walls to his large canvas 'Barbary Apes Wrecking a Boudoir.'

Ashley presented Adela Pingsford with a new copy of *Israel Kalisch*, and a couple of finely flowering plants of *Madame André Blusset*, but nothing in the nature of real reconciliation has taken place between them.

THE DISAPPEARANCE OF CRISPINA UMBERLEIGH

In a first-class carriage of a train speeding Balkanward across the flat, green Hungarian plain, two Britains sat in friendly, fitful converse. They had first foregathered in the cold grey dawn at the frontier line, where the presiding eagle takes on an extra head and Teuton lands pass from Hohenzollern to Habsburg keeping – and where a probing official beak requires to delve in a polite and perhaps perfunctory, but always tiresome, manner into the baggage of sleep-hungry passengers. After a day's break of their journey at Vienna the travellers had again foregathered at the trainside and paid one another the compliment of settling instinctively into the same carriage. The elder of the two had the appearance and manner of a diplomat; in point of fact he was the well-connected foster-brother of a wine business. The other was certainly a journalist. Neither man was talkative and each was grateful to the other for not being talkative. That is why from time to time they talked.

One topic of conversation naturally thrust itself forward in front of all others. In Vienna the previous day they had learned of the mysterious vanishing of a world-famous picture from the walls of the Louvre.

'A dramatic disappearance of that sort is sure to produce a crop of imitations,' said the Journalist.

'It has had a lot of anticipations, for the matter of that,' said the Wine-brother.

'Oh, of course there have been thefts from the Louvre before.'

'I was thinking of the spiriting away of human beings rather than pictures. In particular I was thinking of the case of my aunt, Crispina Umberleigh.'

'I remember hearing something of the affair,' said the Journalist, 'but I was away from England at the time. I never quite knew what was supposed to have happened.'

'You may hear what really happened if you will respect it as a confidence,' said the Wine Merchant. 'In the first place I may say that the disappearance of Mrs Umberleigh was not regarded by the family entirely as a bereavement. My uncle, Edward Umberleigh, was not by any means a weak-kneed individual, in fact in the world of politics he had to be reckoned with more or less as a strong man, but he was unmistakably dominated by Crispina; indeed I never met any human being who was not frozen into subjection when brought into prolonged contact with her. Some people are born to command; Crispina Mrs Umberleigh was born to legislate, codify, administrate, censor, license, ban, execute, and sit in judgment generally. If she was not born with that destiny she adopted it at an early age. From the kitchen regions upwards every one in the household came under her despotic sway and stayed there with the submissiveness of molluscs involved in a glacial epoch. As a nephew on a footing of only occasional visits she affected me merely as an epidemic, disagreeable while it lasted, but without any permanent effect; but her own sons and daughters stood in mortal awe of her; their studies, friendships, diet, amusements, religious observances, and way of doing their hair were all regulated and ordained according to the august lady's will and pleasure. This will help you to understand the sensation of stupefaction which was caused in the family when she unobtrusively and inexplicably vanished. It was as though St Paul's Cathedral or the Piccadilly Hotel had disappeared in the night, leaving nothing but an open space to mark where it had stood. As far as was known nothing was troubling her; in fact there was much before her to make life particularly well worth living. The youngest boy had come back from school with an unsatisfactory report, and she was to have sat in judgment on him the very afternoon of the day she disappeared – if it had been he who had vanished in a hurry one could have supplied the motive. Then she was in the middle of a newspaper correspondence with a rural dean in which she had already proved him guilty of heresy, inconsistency, and unworthy quibbling, and no ordinary consideration would have induced her to discontinue the controversy. Of course the matter was put in the hands of the police, but as far as possible it was kept out of the papers, and the generally accepted explanation of her withdrawal from her social circle was that she had gone into a nursing home.'

'And what was the immediate effect on the home circle?' asked the Journalist.

'All the girls bought themselves bicycles; the feminine cycling craze was still in existence, and Crispina had rigidly vetoed any participation in it among the members of her household. The youngest boy let himself go to such an extent during his next term that it had to be his last as far as that particular establishment was concerned. The elder boys propounded a theory that their mother might be wandering somewhere abroad, and searched for her assiduously, chiefly, it must be admitted, in a class of Montmartre resort where it was extremely improbable that she would be found.'

'And all this while couldn't your uncle get hold of the least clue?'

'As a matter of fact he had received some information, though of course I did not know of it at the time. He got a message one day telling him that his wife had been kidnapped and smuggled out of the country; she was said to be hidden away, in one of the islands off the coast of Norway I think it was, in comfortable surroundings and well cared for. And with the information came a demand for money; a lump sum was to be handed over to her kidnappers and a further sum of £2,000 was to be paid yearly. Failing this she would be immediately restored to her family.'

'It was certainly an inverted form of holding to ransom,' he said.

'If you had known my aunt,' said the Wine Merchant, 'you would have wondered that they didn't put the figure higher.'

'I realize the temptation. Did your uncle succumb to it?'

'Well, you see, he had to think of others as well as himself. For the family to have gone back into the Crispina thraldom after having tasted the delights of liberty would have been a tragedy, and there were even wider considerations to be taken into account. Since his bereavement he had unconsciously taken up a far bolder and more initiatory line in public affairs, and his popularity and influence had increased correspondingly. From being merely a strong man in the political world he began to be spoken of as *the* strong man. All this he knew would be jeopardized if he once more dropped into the social position of the husband of Mrs Umberleigh. He was a rich man, and the £2,000 a year, though not exactly a fleabite, did not seem an extravagant price to pay for the boarding-out of Crispina. Of course, he had severe qualms of conscience about the arrangement. Later on, when he took me into his confidence, he told me that in paying the ransom, or hush-money as I should have called it, he was partly influenced by the fear that if he refused it the kidnappers might have vented their rage and disappointment on their captive. It was better, he said, to think of her being well cared for as a highly valued paying-guest in one of the Lofoden Islands than to have her struggling miserably home in a maimed and mutilated condition. Anyway he paid the yearly instalment as punctually as one pays a fire insurance, and with equal promptitude there would come an acknowledgment of the money and a brief statement to the effect that Crispina was in good health and fairly cheerful spirits. One report even mentioned that she was busying herself with a scheme for proposed reforms in Church management to be pressed on the local pastorate. Another spoke of a rheumatic attack and a journey to a 'cure' on the mainland, and on that occasion an additional eighty pounds was demanded and conceded. Of course it was to the interest of the kidnappers to keep their charge in good health, but the secrecy with which they managed to shroud their arrangements argued a really wonderful organization. If my uncle was paying a rather high price, at least he could console himself with the reflection that he was paying specialists' fees.'

'Meanwhile had the police given up all attempts to track the missing lady?' asked the Journalist.

'Not entirely; they came to my uncle from time to time to report on clues which they thought might yield some elucidation as to her fate or whereabouts, but I think they had their suspicions that he was possessed of more information than he had put at their disposal. And then, after a disappearance of more than eight years, Crispina returned with dramatic suddenness to the home she had left so mysteriously.'

'She had given her captors the slip?'

'She had never been captured. Her wandering away had been caused by a sudden and complete loss of memory. She usually dressed rather in the style of a superior kind of charwoman, and it was not so very surprising that she should have imagined that she was one, and still less that people should accept her statement and help her to get work. She had wandered as far afield as Birmingham, and found fairly steady employment there, her energy and enthusiasm in putting people's rooms in order counter-balancing her obstinate and domineering characteristics. It was the shock of being patronizingly addressed as 'my good woman' by a curate, who was disputing with her where the stove should be placed in a parish concert hall, that led to the sudden restoration of her memory. "I think you forget who you are speaking to," she observed crushingly, which was rather unduly severe, considering she had only just remembered it herself.'

'But,' exclaimed the Journalist, 'the Lofoden Island people! Who had they got hold of?'

'A purely mythical prisoner. It was an attempt in the first place by some one who knew something of the domestic situation, probably a discharged valet, to bluff a lump sum out of Edward Umberleigh before the missing woman turned up; the subsequent yearly instalments were an unlooked-for increment to the original haul.

'Crispina found that the eight year's interregnum had materially weakened her ascendancy over her now grown-up offspring. Her husband, however, never accomplished anything great in the political world after her return; the strain of trying to account satisfactorily for an unspecified expenditure of sixteen-thousand pounds spread over eight years sufficiently occupied his mental energies. Here is Belgrade and another custom house.'

THE INTERLOPERS

In a forest of mixed growth somewhere on the eastern spurs of the Carpathians, a man stood one winter night watching and listening, as though he waited for some beast of the woods to come within the range of his vision, and, later, of his rifle. But the game for whose presence he kept so keen an outlook was none that figured in the sportsman's calendar as lawful and proper for the chase; Ulrich von Gradwitz patrolled the dark forest in quest of a human enemy.

The forest lands of Gradwitz were of wide extent and well stocked with game; the narrow strip of precipitous woodland that lay on its outskirts was not remarkable for the game it harboured or the shooting it afforded, but it was the most jealously guarded of all its owner's territorial possessions. A famous lawsuit, in the days of his grandfather, had wrested it from the illegal possession of a neighbouring family of petty landowners; the dispossessed party had never acquiesced in the judgment of the Courts, and a long series of poaching affrays and similar scandals had embittered the relationship between the families for three generations. The neighbour feud had grown into a personal one since Ulrich had come to be head of his family; if there was a man in the world whom he detested and wished ill to it was Georg Znaeym, the inheritor of the quarrel and the tireless game-snatcher and raider of the disputed border-forest. The feud might, perhaps, have died down or been compromised if the personal ill-will of the two men had not stood in the way; as boys they had thirsted for one another's blood, as men each prayed that misfortune might fall on the other, and this windscourged winter night Ulrich had banded together his foresters to watch the dark forest, not in quest of four-footed quarry, but to keep a look-out for the prowling thieves whom he suspected of being afoot from across the land boundary. The roebuck, which usually kept in the sheltered hollows during a stormwind, were running like driven things tonight, and there was movement and unrest among the creatures that were wont to sleep through the dark hours. Assuredly there was a disturbing element in the forest, and Ulrich could guess the quarter from whence it came.

He strayed away by himself from the watchers whom he had placed in ambush on the crest of the hill, and wandered far down the steep slopes amid the wild tangle of undergrowth, peering through the tree-trunks and listening through the whistling and skirling of the wind and the restless beating of the branches for sight or sound of the marauders. If only on this wild night, in this dark, lone spot, he might come across Georg Znaeym, man to man, with none to witness – that was the wish that was uppermost in his thoughts. And as he stepped round the trunk of a huge beech he came face to face with the man he sought.

The two enemies stood glaring at one another for a long silent moment. Each had a rifle in his hand, each had hate in his heart and murder uppermost in his mind. The chance had come to give full play to the passions of a lifetime. But a man who has been brought up under the code of a restraining civilization cannot easily nerve himself to shoot down his neighbour in cold blood and without word spoken, except for an offence against his heart and honour. And before the moment of hesitation had given way to action a deed of Nature's own violence overwhelmed them both. A fierce shriek of the storm had been answered by a splitting crash over their heads, and ere they could leap aside a mass of falling beech tree had thundered down on them. Ulrich von Gradwitz found himself stretched on the ground, one arm numb beneath him and the other held almost as helplessly in a tight tangle of forked branches, while both legs were pinned beneath the fallen mass. His heavy shooting-boots had saved his feet from being crushed to pieces, but if his fractures were not as serious as they might have been, at least it was evident that he could not move from his present position till some one came to release him. The descending twigs had slashed the skin of his face, and he had to wink away some drops of blood from his eyelashes before he could take in a general view of the disaster. At his side, so near that under ordinary circumstances he could almost have touched him, lay Georg Znaeym, alive and struggling, but obviously as helplessly pinned down as himself. All round them lay a thick-strewn wreckage of splintered branches and broken twigs.

Relief at being alive and exasperation at his captive plight brought a strange medley of pious thank-offerings and sharp curses to Ulrich's lips. Georg, who was nearly blinded with the blood which trickled across his eyes, stopped his struggling for a moment to listen, and then gave a short, snarling laugh.

'So you're not killed, as you ought to be,' but you're caught anyway,' he said; 'caught fast. Ho, what a jest, Ulrich von Gradwitz snarled in his stolen forest. There's real justice for you!'

And he laughed again, mockingly and savagely.

'I'm caught in my own forest-land,' retorted Ulrich. 'When my men come to release us you will wish, perhaps, that you were in a better plight than caught poaching on a neighbour's land, shame on you.'

Georg was silent for a moment; then he answered quietly.

'Are you sure that your men will find much to release? I have men, too, in the forest tonight, close behind me, and *they* will be here first and do the releasing. When they drag me out from under these damned branches it won't need much clumsiness on their part to roll this mass of trunk right over on the top of you. Your men will find you dead under a fallen beach tree. For form's sake I shall send my condolences to your family.'

'It is a useful hint,' said Ulrich fiercely. 'My men had orders to follow in ten minutes' time, seven of which must have gone by already, and when they get me out – I will remember the hint. Only as you will have met your death poaching on my lands, I don't think I can decently send any message of condolence to your family.'

'Good,' snarled Georg, 'good. We fight this quarrel out to the death, you and I and our foresters, with no cursed interlopers to come between us. Death and damnation to you, Ulrich von Gradwitz.'

'The same to you, Georg Znaeym, forest-thief, game-snatcher.'

Both men spoke with the bitterness of possible defeat before them, for each knew that it might be long before his men would seek him out or find him; it was a bare matter of chance which party would arrive first on the scene.

Both had now given up the useless struggle to free themselves from the mass of wood that held them down. Ulrich limited his endeavours to an effort to bring his one partially free arm near enough to his outer coat pocket to draw out his wine-flask. Even when he had accomplished that operation it was long before he could manage the unscrewing of the stopper or get any of the liquid down his throat. But what a Heaven-sent draught it seemed! It was an open winter, and little snow had fallen as yet, hence the captives suffered less from the cold than might have been the case at that season of the year; never-theless, the wine was warming and reviving to the wounded man, and he looked across with something like a throb of pity to where his enemy lay, just keeping the groans of pain and weariness from crossing his lips.

'Could you reach this flask if I threw it over to you?' asked Ulrich suddenly; 'there is good wine in it, and one may as well be as comfortable as one can. Let us drink, even if tonight one of us dies.'

'No, I can scarcely see anything; there is so much blood caked round my eyes,' said Georg, 'and in any case I don't drink wine with an enemy.'

Ulrich was silent for a few minutes, and lay listening to the weary screeching of the wind. An idea was slowly forming and growing in his brain, an idea that gained strength every time that he looked across at the man who was fighting so grimly against pain and exhaustion. In the pain and languor that Ulrich himself was feeling the old fierce hatred seemed to be dying down.

'Neighbour,' he said presently, 'do as you please if your men come first. It was a fair compact. But as for me, I've changed my mind. If my men are the first to come you shall be the first to be helped, as though you were my guest. We have quarrelled like devils all our lives over this stupid strip of forest, where the trees can't even stand upright in a breath of wind. Lying here tonight, thinking, I've come to think we've been rather fools; there are better things in life than getting the better of a boundary dispute. Neighbour, if you will help me to bury the old quarrel I – I will ask you to be my friend.'

Georg Znaeym was silent for so long that Ulrich thought, perhaps, he had fainted with the pain of his injuries. Then he spoke slowly and in jerks.

'How the whole region would stare and gabble if we rode into the market-square together. No one living can remember seeing a Znaeym and a von Gradwitz talking to one another in friendship. And what peace there would be among the forester folk if we ended our feud tonight. And if we choose to make peace among our people there is none other to interfere, no interlopers from outside . . . You would come and keep the Sylvester night beneath my roof, and I would come and feast on some high day at your castle . . . I would never fire a shot on your land, save when you invited me as a guest; and you should come and shoot with me down in the marshes where the wildfowl are. In all the country-side there are none that could hinder if we willed to make peace. I never thought to have wanted to do other than hate you all my life, but I think I have changed my mind about things too, this last half-hour. And you offered me your wine-flask . . . Ulrich von Gradwitz, I will be your friend.'

For a space both men were silent, turning over in their minds the wonderful changes that this dramatic reconciliation would bring about. In the cold, gloomy forest, with the wind tearing in fitful gusts through the naked branches and whistling round the tree-trunks, they lay and waited for the help that would now bring release and succour to both parties. And each prayed a private prayer that his men might be the first to arrive, so that he might be the first to show honourable attention to the enemy that had become a friend.

Presently, as the wind dropped for a moment, Ulrich broke silence.

'Let's shout for help,' he said; 'in this lull our voices may carry a little way.'

'They won't carry far through the trees and undergrowth,' said Georg, 'but we can try. Together, then.'

The two raised their voices in a prolonged hunting call.

'Together again,' said Ulrich a few minutes later, after listening in vain for an answering halloo.

'I heard something that time, I think,' said Ulrich.

'I heard nothing but the pestilential wind,' said Georg hoarsely.

There was silence again for some minutes, and then Ulrich gave a joyful cry.

'I can see figures coming through the wood. They are following in the way I came down the hillside.'

Both men raised their voices in as loud a shout as they could muster.

'They hear us! They've stopped. Now they see us. They're running down the hill towards us,' cried Ulrich.

'How many of them are there?' asked Georg.

'I can't see distinctly,' said Ulrich; 'nine or ten.'

'Then they are yours,' said Georg; 'I had only seven out with me.'

'They are making all the speed they can, brave lads,' said Ulrich gladly.

'Are they your men?' asked Georg. 'Are they your men?' he repeated impatiently as Ulrich did not answer.

'No,' said Ulrich with a laugh, the idiotic chattering laugh of a man unstrung with hideous fear.

'Who are they?' asked Georg quickly, straining his eyes to see what the other would gladly not have seen.

'*Wolves.*'

MRS PACKLETIDE'S TIGER

It was Mrs Packletide's pleasure and intention that she should shoot a tiger. Not that the lust to kill had suddenly descended on her, or that she felt that she would leave India safer and more wholesome than she had found it, with one fraction less of wild beast per million inhabitants. The compelling motive for her sudden deviation towards the footsteps of Nimrod was the fact that Loona Bimberton had recently been carried eleven miles in an aeroplane by an Algerian aviator, and talked of nothing else; only a personally procured tiger-skin and a heavy harvest of Press photographs could successfully counter that sort of thing. Mrs Packletide had already arranged in her mind the lunch she would give at her house in Curzon Street, ostensibly in Loona Bimberton's honour, with a tiger-skin rug occupying most of the foreground and all of the conversation. She had also already designed in her mind the tiger-claw brooch that she was going to give Loona Bimberton on her next birthday. In a world that is supposed to be chiefly swayed by hunger and by love, Mrs Packletide was an exception; her movements and motives were largely governed by dislike of Loona Bimberton.

Circumstances proved propitious. Mrs Packletide had offered a thousand rupees for the opportunity of shooting a tiger without overmuch risk or exertion, and it so happened that a neighbouring village could boast of being the favoured rendezvous of an animal of respectable antecedents, which had been driven by the increasing infirmities of age to abandon game-killing and confine its appetite to the smaller domestic animals. The prospect of earning the thousand rupees had stimulated the sporting and commercial instinct of the villagers; children were posted night and day on the outskirts of the local jungle to head the tiger back in the unlikely event of his attempting to roam away to fresh hunting-grounds, and the cheaper kinds of goats were left about with elaborate carelessness to keep him satisfied with his present quarters. The one great anxiety was lest he should die of old age before the date appointed for the memsahib's shoot. Mothers carrying their babies home through the jungle after the day's work in the fields hushed their singing lest they might curtail the restful sleep of the venerable herd-robber.

The great night duly arrived, moonlit and cloudless. A platform had been constructed in a comfortable and conveniently placed tree, and thereon crouched Mrs Packletide and her paid companion, Miss Mebbin. A goat, gifted with a particularly persistent bleat, such as even a partially deaf tiger might be reasonably expected to hear on a still night, was tethered at the correct distance. With an accurately sighted rifle and a thumb-nail pack of patience cards the sportswoman awaited the coming of the quarry.

'I suppose we are in some danger?' said Miss Mebbin.

She was not actually nervous about the wild beast, but she had a morbid dread of performing an atom more service than she had been paid for.

'Nonsense,' said Mrs Packletide; 'it's a very old tiger. It couldn't spring up here even if it wanted to.'

'If it's an old tiger I think you ought to get it cheaper. A thousand rupees is a lot of money.'

Louisa Mebbin adopted a protective elder-sister attitude towards money in general, irrespective of nationality or denomination. Her energetic intervention had saved many a rouble from dissipating itself in tips in some Moscow hotel, and francs and centimes clung to her instinctively under circumstances which would have driven them headlong from less sympathetic hands. Her speculations as to the market depreciation of tiger remnants were cut short by the appearance on the scene of the animal itself. As soon as it caught sight of the tethered goat it lay flat on the earth, seemingly less from a desire to take advantage of all available cover than for the purpose of snatching a short rest before commencing the grand attack.

'I believe it's ill,' said Louisa Mebbin, loudly in Hindustani, for the benefit of the village headman, who was in ambush in a neighbouring tree.

'Hush!' said Mrs Packletide, and at that moment the tiger commenced ambling towards his victim.

'Now, now!' urged Miss Mebbin with some excitement; 'if he doesn't touch the goat we needn't pay for it.' (The bait was an extra.)

The rifle flashed out with a loud report, and the great tawny beast sprang to one side and then rolled over in the stillness of death. In a moment a crowd of excited natives had swarmed on to the scene, and their shouting speedily carried the glad news to the village, where a thumping of tom-toms took up the chorus

of triumph. And their triumph and rejoicing found a ready echo
in the heart of Mrs Packletide; already that luncheon-party in
Curzon Street seemed immeasurably nearer.

It was Louisa Mebbin who drew attention to the fact that the
goat was in death-throes from a mortal bullet-wound, while no
trace of the rifle's deadly work could be found on the tiger.
Evidently the wrong animal had been hit, and the beast of prey
had succumbed to heart-failure, caused by the sudden report of
the rifle, accelerated by senile decay. Mrs Packletide was pardonably annoyed at the discovery; but, at any rate, she was the possessor of a dead tiger, and the villagers, anxious for their thousand
rupees, gladly connived at the fiction that she had shot the beast.
And Miss Mebbin was a paid companion. Therefore did Mrs
Packletide face the cameras with a light heart, and her pictured
fame reached from the pages of the *Texas Weekly Snapshot* to
the illustrated Monday supplement of the *Novoe Vremya*. As for
Loona Bimberton, she refused to look at an illustrated paper for
weeks, and her letter of thanks for the gift of a tiger-claw brooch
was a model of repressed emotions. The luncheon-party she
declined; there are limits beyond which repressed emotions
become dangerous.

From Curzon Street the tiger-skin rug travelled down to the
Manor House, and was duly inspected and admired by the county,
and it seemed a fitting and appropriate thing when Mrs Packletide went to the County Costume Ball in the character of Diana.
She refused to fall in, however, with Clovis's tempting suggestion
of a primeval dance party, at which every one should wear the
skins of beasts they had recently slain. 'I should be in rather a
Baby Bunting condition,' confessed Covis, 'with a miserable
rabbit-skin or two to wrap up in, but then,' he added, with a
rather malicious glance at Diana's proportions, 'my figure is quite
as good as that Russian dancing boy's.'

'How amused everyone would be if they knew what really happened,' said Louisa Mebbin a few days after the ball.

'What do you mean?' asked Mrs Packletide quickly.

'How you shot the goat and frightened the tiger to death,' said
Miss Mebbin, with her disagreeably pleasant laugh.

'No one would believe it,' said Mrs Packletide, her face changing colour as rapidly as though it were going through a book of
patterns before post-time.

'Loona Bimberton would,' said Miss Mebbin. Mrs Packletide's face settled on an unbecoming shade of greenish white.

'You surely wouldn't give me away?' she asked.

'I've seen a week-end cottage near Dorking that I should rather like to buy,' said Miss Mebbin with seeming irrelevance. 'Six hundred and eighty, freehold. Quite a bargain, only I don't happen to have the money.'

Louisa Mebbin's pretty week-end cottage, christened by her 'Les Fauves', and gay in summer-time with its garden borders of tiger-lilies, is the wonder and admiration of her friends.

'It is a marvel how Louisa manages to do it,' is the general verdict.

Mrs Packletide indulges in no more big-game shooting.

'The incidental expenses are so heavy,' she confides to inquiring friends.

THE WAY TO THE DAIRY

The Baroness and Clovis sat in a much-frequented corner of the Park exchanging biographical confidences about the long succession of passers-by.

'Who are those depressed-looking young women who have just gone by?' asked the Baroness; 'they have the air of people who have bowed to destiny and are not quite sure whether the salute will be returned.'

'Those,' said Clovis, 'are the Brimley Bomefields. I dare say you would look depressed if you had been through their experiences.

'I'm always having depressing experiences,' said the Baroness, 'but I never give them outward expression. It's as bad as looking one's age. Tell me about the Brimley Bomefields.'

'Well,' said Clovis, 'the beginning of their tragedy was that they found an aunt. The aunt had been there all the time, but they had very nearly forgotten her existence until a distant relative refreshed their memory by remembering her very distinctly in his will; it is wonderful what the force of example will accomplish. The aunt, who had been unobtrusively poor, became quite pleasantly rich, and the Brimley Bomefields grew suddenly concerned at the loneliness of her life and took her under their collective wings. She had as many wings around her at this time as one of those beast-things in Revelation.'

'So far I don't see any tragedy from the Brimley Bomefields' point of view,' said the Baroness.

'We haven't got to it yet,' said Clovis. 'The aunt had been used to living very simply, and had seen next to nothing of what we should consider life, and her nieces didn't encourage her to do much in the way of making a splash with her money. Quite a good deal of it would come to them at her death, and she was a fairly old woman, but there was one circumstance which cast a shadow of gloom over the satisfaction they felt in the discovery and acquisition of this desirable aunt: she openly acknowledged that a comfortable slice of her little fortune would go to a nephew on the other side of her family. He was rather a deplorable thing in rotters, and quite hopelessly top-hole in the way of getting through money, but he had been more or less decent to the old lady in her unremembered days, and she wouldn't hear anything against him. At least, she wouldn't pay any attention to what she did hear, but her nieces took care that she should have to listen to a good deal in that line. It seemed such a pity, they said among themselves, that good money should fall into such worthless hands. They habitually spoke of their aunt's money as "good money", as though other people's aunts dabbled for the most part in spurious currency.

'Regularly after the Derby, St Leger, and other notable racing events they indulged in audible speculations as to how much money Roger had squandered in unfortunate betting transactions.

'"His travelling expenses must come to a big sum," said the eldest Brimley Bomefield one day; "they say he attends every race-meeting in England, besides others abroad, I shouldn't wonder if he went all the way to India to see the race for the Calcutta Sweepstake that one hears so much about."

'"Travel enlarges the mind, my dear Christine," said her aunt.

'"Yes, dear aunt, travel undertaken in the right spirit," agreed Christine; "but travel pursued merely as a means towards gambling and extravagant living is more likely to contract the purse than to enlarge the mind. However, as long as Roger enjoys himself, I suppose he doesn't care how fast or unprofitably the money goes, or where he is to find more. It seems a pity, that's all."

'The aunt by that time had begun to talk of something else, and it was doubtful if Christine's moralizing had been even accorded a hearing. It was her remark, however – the aunt's remark, I mean – about travel enlarging the mind, that gave the youngest Brimley Bomefield her great idea for the showing-up of Roger.

'"If aunt could only be taken somewhere to see him gambling and throwing away money," she said, "it would open her eyes to his character more effectually than anything we can say."

'"My dear Veronique," said her sisters, "we can't go following him to race-meetings."

'"Certainly not to race-meetings," said Veronique, "but we might go to some place where one can look on at gambling without taking part in it."

'"Do you mean Monte Carlo?" they asked her, beginning to jump rather at the idea.

'"Monte Carlo is a long way off, and has a dreadful reputation," said Veronique; "I shouldn't like to tell our friends that we were going to Monte Carlo. But I believe Roger usually goes to Dieppe about this time of year, and some quite respectable English people go there, and the journey wouldn't be expensive. If aunt could stand the Channel crossing the change of scene might do her a lot of good."

'And that was how the fateful idea came to the Brimley Bomefields.

'From the very first set-off disaster hung over the expedition, as they afterwards remembered. To begin with, all the Brimley Bomefields were extremely unwell during the crossing, while the aunt enjoyed the sea air and made friends with all manner of strange travelling companions. Then although it was many years since she had been on the Continent, she had served a very practical apprenticeship there as a paid companion, and her knowledge of colloquial French beat theirs to a standstill. It became increasingly difficult to keep under their collective wings a person who knew what she wanted and was able to ask for it and to see that she got it. Also, as far as Roger was concerned, they drew Dieppe blank; it turned out that he was staying at Pourville, a little watering-place a mile or two further west. The Brimley Bomefields discovered that Dieppe was too crowded and frivolous, and persuaded the old lady to migrate to the comparative seclusion of Pourville.

' "You won't find it dull, you know," they assured her; "there is a little casino attached to the hotel, and you can watch the people dancing and throwing away their money at *petits chevaux*."

'It was just before *petits chevaux* had been supplanted by *boule*.

'Roger was not staying in the same hotel, but they knew that the casino would be certain of his patronage on most afternoons and evenings.

'On the first evening of their visit they wandered into the casino after a fairly early dinner, and hovered near the tables. Bertie van Tahn was staying there at the time, and he described the whole incident to me. The Brimley Bomefields kept a furtive watch on the doors as though they were expecting someone to turn up, and the aunt got more and more amused and interested watching the little horses whirl round and round the board.

' "Do you know, poor little number eight hasn't won for the last thirty-two times," she said to Christine; "I've been keeping count. I shall really have to put five francs on him to encourage him."

' "Come and watch the dancing, dear," said Christine nervously. It was scarcely a part of their strategy that Roger should come in and find the old lady backing her fancy at the *petits chevaux* table.

' "Just wait while I put five francs on number eight," said the aunt, and in another moment her money was lying on the table. The horses commenced to move round; it was a slow race this time, and number eight crept up at the finish like some crafty demon and placed his nose just a fraction in front of number three, who had seemed to be winning easily. Recourse had to be had to measurement, and the number eight was proclaimed the winner. The aunt picked up thirty-five francs. After that the Brimley Bomefields would have had to have used concerted force to get far away from the tables. When Roger appeared on the scene she was fifty-two francs to the good; her nieces were hovering forlornly in the background, like chickens that have been hatched out by a duck and are despairingly watching their parent disporting herself in a dangerous and uncongenial element. The supper-party which Roger insisted on standing that night in honour of his aunt and the three Miss Brimley Bomefields was remarkable for the unrestrained gaiety of two of the participants and the funereal mirthlessness of the remaining guests.

' "I do not think," Christine confided afterwards to a friend, who re-confided it to Bertie van Tahn, "that I shall ever be able to touch *pâté de foie gras* again. It would bring back memories of that awful evening."

'For the next two or three days the nieces made plans for returning to England or moving on to some other resort where there was no casino. The aunt was busy making a system for winning at *petits chevaux*. Number eight, her first love, had been running rather unkindly for her, and a series of plunges on number five had turned out even worse. .

'"Do you know, I dropped over seven hundred francs at the tables this afternoon," she announced cheerfully at dinner on the fourth evening of their visit.

'"Aunt! Twenty-eight pounds! And you were losing last night too."

'"Oh, I shall get it all back," she said optimistically; "but not here. These silly little horses are no good. I shall go somewhere where one can play comfortably at roulette. You needn't look so shocked. I've always felt that, given the opportunity, I should be an inveterate gambler, and now you darlings have put the opportunity in my way. I must drink your very good healths. Waiter, a bottle of *Pontet Canet*. Ah, it's number seven on the wine list; I shall plunge on number seven tonight. It won four times running this afternoon when I was backing that silly number five."

'Number seven was not in a winning mood that evening. The Brimley Bomefields, tired of watching disaster from a distance, drew near to the table where their aunt was now an honoured habituée, and gazed mournfully at the successive victories of one and five and eight and four, which swept "good money" out of the purse of seven's obstinate backer. The day's losses totalled something very near two thousand francs.

'"You incorrigible gamblers," said Roger chaffingly to them, when he found them at the tables.

'"We are not gambling," said Christine freezingly; 'we are looking on."

'"I don't think," said Roger knowingly; "of course you're a syndicate and aunt is putting the stakes on for all of you. Anyone can tell by your looks when the wrong horse wins that you've got a stake on."

'Aunt and nephew had supper alone that night, or at least they would have if Bertie hadn't joined them; all the Brimley Bomefields had headaches.

'The aunt carried them all off to Dieppe the next day and set cheerily about the task of winning back some of her losses. Her luck was variable; in fact, she had some fair streaks of good fortune, just enough to keep her thoroughly amused with her new distraction; but on the whole she was a loser. The Brimley Bomefields had a collective attack of nervous prostration on the day when she sold out a quantity of shares in Argentine rails. "Nothing will ever bring that money back," they remarked lugubriously to one another.

'Veronique at last could bear it no longer, and went home; you see, it had been her idea to bring the aunt on this disastrous expedition, and though the others did not cast the fact verbally in her face, there was certain lurking reproach in their eyes which was harder to meet than actual upbraidings. The other two remained behind, forlornly mounting guard over their aunt until such time as the waning of the Dieppe season should at last turn her in the direction of home and safety. They made anxious calculations as to how little "good money" might, with reasonable luck, be squandered in the meantime. Here, however, their reckoning went far astray; the close of the Dieppe season merely turned their aunt's thoughts in search of some other convenient gambling resort. "Show a cat the way to the dairy —" I forget how the proverb goes on, but it summed up the situation as far as the Brimley Bomefields' aunt was concerned. She had been introduced to unexplored pleasures, and found them greatly to her liking, and she was in no hurry to forego the fruits of her newly acquired knowledge. You see, for the first time in her life the old thing was thoroughly enjoying herself; she was losing money, but she had plenty of fun and excitement over the process, and she had enough left to do very comfortably on. Indeed, she was only just learning to understand the art of doing oneself well. She was a popular hostess, and in return her fellow-gamblers were always ready to entertain her to dinners and suppers when their luck was in. Her nieces, who still remained in attendance on her, with the pathetic unwillingness of a crew to leave a foundering treasure ship which might yet be steered into port, found little pleasure in these Bohemian festivities; to see "good money" lavished on good living for the entertainment of a nondescript circle of acquaintances who were not likely to be in any way socially useful to them, did not attune them to a spirit of revelry. They contrived, whenever possible, to excuse themselves from participation in their aunt's deplored gaieties; the Brimley Bomefield headaches became famous.

'And one day the nieces came to the conclusion that, as they would have expressed it, "no useful purpose would be served" by their continued attendance on a relative who had so thoroughly emancipated herself from the sheltering protection of their wings. The aunt bore the announcement of their departure with a cheerfulness that was almost disconcerting.

'"It's time you went home and had those headaches seen to by a specialist," was her comment on the situation.

'The homeward journey of the Brimley Bomefields was a veritable retreat from Moscow, and what made it the more bitter was the fact that the Moscow, in this case, was not overwhelmed with fire and ashes, but merely extravagantly over-illuminated.

'From mutual friends and acquaintances they sometimes get glimpses of their prodigal relative, who has settled down into a confirmed gambling maniac, living on such salvage of income as obliging moneylenders have left at her disposal.

'So you need not be surprised,' concluded Clovis, 'if they do wear a depressed look in public.'

'Which is Veronique?' asked the Baroness.

'The most depressed-looking of the three,' said Clovis.

THE GALA PROGRAMME
AN UNRECORDED EPISODE IN ROMAN HISTORY

It was an auspicious day in the Roman Calendar, the birthday of the popular and gifted young Emperor Placidus Superbus. Everyone in Rome was bent on keeping high festival, the weather was at its best, and naturally the Imperial Circus was crowded to its fullest capacity. A few minutes before the hour fixed for the commencement of the spectacle a loud fanfare of trumpets proclaimed the arrival of Caesar, and amid the vociferous acclamations of the multitude the Emperor took his seat in the Imperial Box. As the shouting of the crowd died away an even more thrilling salutation could be heard in the near distance, the angry, impatient roaring and howling of the beasts caged in the Imperial menagerie.

'Explain the programme to me,' commanded the Emperor, having beckoned the Master of the Ceremonies to his side.

That eminent official wore a troubled look.

'Gracious Caesar,' he announced, 'a most promising and entertaining programme has been devised and prepared for your august approval. In the first place there is to be a chariot contest of unusual brilliancy and interest; three teams that have never hitherto suffered defeat are to contend for the Herculaneum Trophy, together with the purse which your Imperial generosity has been pleased to add. The chances of the competing teams are accounted to be as nearly as possible equal, and there is much wagering among the populace. The black Thracians are perhaps the favourites –'

'I know, I know,' interrupted Caesar, who had listened to exhaustive talk on the same subject all the morning; 'what else is there on the programme?'

'The second part of the programme,' said the Imperial Official, 'consists of a grand combat of wild beasts, specially selected for their strength, ferocity, and fighting qualities. There will appear simultaneously in the arena fourteen Nubian lions and lionesses, five tigers, six Syrian bears, eight Persian panthers, and three North African ditto, a number of wolves and lynxes from the Teutonic forests, and seven gigantic wild bulls from the same region. There will also be wild swine of unexampled savageness, a rhinoceros from the Barbary coast, some ferocious man-apes, and a hyena, reputed to be mad.'

'It promises well, 'said the Emperor.

'It *promised* well, O Caesar,' said the official dolorously, 'it promised marvellously well; but between the promise and the performance a cloud has arisen.'

'A cloud? What cloud?' queried Caesar, with a frown.

'The Suffragettes,' explained the official; 'they threaten to interfere with the chariot race.'

'I'd like to see them do it !' exclaimed the Emperor indignantly.

'I fear your Imperial wish may be unpleasantly gratified,' said the Master of the Ceremonies; 'we are taking, of course, every possible precaution, and guarding all the entrances to the arena and the stables with a triple guard; but it is rumoured that at the signal for the entry of the chariots five hundred women will let themselves down with ropes from the public seats and swarm all over the course. Naturally no race could be run under such circumstances; the programme will be ruined.'

'On my birthday,' said Placidus Superbus, 'they would not dare to do such an outrageous thing.'

'The more august the occasion, the more desirous they will be to advertise themselves and their cause,' said the harassed official; 'they do not scruple to make riotous interference even with the ceremonies in the temples.'

'Who *are* these Suffragettes?' asked the Emperor. 'Since I came back from the Pannonian expedition I have heard of nothing else but their excesses and demonstrations.'

'They are a political sect of very recent origin, and their aim seems to be to get a big share of political authority into their hands. The means they are taking to convince us of their fitness to help in making and administering the laws consist of wild indulgence in tumult, destruction, and defiance of all authority. They have already damaged some of the most historically valuable of our public treasures, which can never be replaced.'

'Is it possible that the sex which we hold in such honour and for which we feel such admiration can produce such hordes of Furies?' asked the Emperor.

'It takes all sorts to make a sex,' observed the Master of the Ceremonies, who possessed a certain amount of worldly wisdom; 'also,' he continued anxiously, 'it takes very little to upset a gala programme.'

'Perhaps the disturbance that you anticipate will turn out to be an idle threat,' said the Emperor consolingly.

'But if they should carry out their intention,' said the official, 'the programme will be utterly ruined.'

The Emperor said nothing.

Five minutes later the trumpets rang out for the commencement of the entertainment. A hum of excited anticipation ran through the ranks of the spectators, and final bets on the issue of the great race were hurriedly shouted. The gates leading from the stables were slowly swung open, and a troop of mounted attendants rode round the track to ascertain that everything was clear for the momentous contest. Again the trumpets rang out, and then, before the foremost chariot had appeared, there arose a wild tumult of shouting, laughing, angry protests, and shrill screams of defiance. Hundreds of women were being lowered by their accomplices into the arena. A moment later they were running and dancing in frenzied troops across the track where the chariots were supposed to compete. No team of arena-trained horses would have faced such a frantic mob; the race was clearly an impossibility. Howls of disappointment and rage rose from the spectators, howls of triumph echoed back from the women in possession. The vain efforts of the circus attendants to drive out the invading horde merely added to the uproar and confusion; as fast as the Suffragettes were thrust away from one portion of the track they swarmed on to another.

The Master of the Ceremonies was nearly delirious from rage and mortification. Placidus Superbus, who remained calm and unruffled as ever, beckoned to him and spoke a word or two in his ear. For the first time that afternoon the sorely tried official was seen to smile.

A trumpet rang out from the Imperial Box; an instant hush fell over the excited throng. Perhaps the Emperor, as a last resort, was going to announce some concession to the Suffragettes.

'Close the stable gates,' commanded the Master of the Ceremonies, 'and open all the menagerie dens. It is the Imperial pleasure that the second portion of the programme be taken first.'

It turned out that the Master of the Ceremonies had in no wise exaggerated the probable brilliancy of this portion of the spectacle. The wild bulls were really wild, and the hyena reputed to be mad thoroughly lived up to its reputation.

THE SCHARTZ-METTERKLUME METHOD

Lady Carlotta stepped out on to the platform of the small wayside station and took a turn or two up and down its uninteresting length, to kill time till the train should be pleased to proceed on its way. Then, in the roadway beyond, she saw a horse struggling with a more than ample load, and a carter of the sort that seems to bear a sullen hatred against the animal that helps him to earn a living. Lady Carlotta promptly betook her to the roadway, and put rather a different complexion on the struggle. Certain of her acquaintances were wont to give her plentiful admonition as to the undesirability of interfering on behalf of a distressed animal, such interference being 'none of her business.' Only once had she put the doctrine of non-interference into practice, when one of its most eloquent exponents had been besieged for nearly three hours in a small and extremely uncomfortable may-tree by an angry boar-pig, while Lady Carlotta, on the other side of the fence, had proceeded with the water-colour sketch she was engaged on, and refused to interfere between the boar and his prisoner. It is to be feared that she lost the friendship of the ultimately rescued lady. On this occasion she merely lost the train, which gave way to the first sign of impatience it had shown throughout the journey, and steamed off without her. She bore the desertion with philosophical indifference; her friends and relations were thoroughly well used to the fact of her luggage arriving without her. She wired a vague non-committal message to her destination to say that she was coming on 'by another train.' Before she had time to think what her next move might be, she was confronted by an imposingly attired lady, who seemed to be taking a prolonged mental inventory of her clothes and looks.

'You must be Miss Hope, the governess I've come to meet,' said the apparition, in a tone that admitted of very little argument.

'Very well, if I must I must,' said Lady Carlotta to herself with dangerous meekness.

'I am Mrs Quabarl,' continued the lady; 'and where, pray, is your luggage?'

'It's gone astray,' said the alleged governess; falling in with the excellent rule of life that the absent are always to blame; the luggage had, in point of fact, behaved with perfect correctitude. 'I've just telegraphed about it,' she added, with a nearer approach to truth.

'How provoking,' said Mrs Quabarl; 'these railway companies are so careless. However, my maid can lend you things for the night,' and she led the way to her car.

During the drive to the Quabarl mansion Lady Carlotta was impressively introduced to the nature of the charge that had been thrust upon her; she learned that Claude and Wilfrid were delicate, sensitive young people, that Irene had the artistic temperament highly developed, and that Viola was something or other else of a mould equally commonplace among children of that class and type in the twentieth century.

'I wish them not only to be *taught*,' said Mrs Quabarl, 'but *interested* in what they learn. In their history lessons, for instance, you must try to make them feel that they are being introduced to the life-stories of men and women who really lived, not merely committing a mass of names and dates to memory. French, of course, I shall expect you to talk at meal-times several days in the week.'

'I shall talk French four days of the week and Russian in the remaining three.'

'Russian? My dear Miss Hope, no one in the house speaks or understands Russian.'

'That will not embarrass me in the least,' said Lady Carlotta coldly.

Mrs Quabarl, to use a colloquial expression, was knocked off her perch. She was one of those imperfectly self-assured individuals who are magnificent and autocratic as long as they are not seriously opposed. The least show of unexpected resistance goes a long way towards rendering them cowed and apologetic. When the new governess failed to express wondering admiration of the large newly purchased and expensive car, and lightly alluded to the superior advantages of one or two makes which had just been put on the market, the discomfiture of her patroness became almost abject. Her feelings were those which might have animated a general of ancient warfaring days, on beholding his heaviest battle-elephant ignominiously driven off the field by slingers and javelin throwers.

At dinner that evening, although reinforced by her husband, who usually duplicated her opinions and let her moral support generally, Mrs Quabarl regained none of her lost ground. The governess not only helped herself well and truly to wine, but held forth with considerable show of critical knowledge on various vintage matters, concerning which the Quabarls were in no wise able to pose as authorities. Previous governesses had limited their conversation in the wine topic to a respectful and doubtless sincere expression of a preference for water. When this one went as far as to recommend a wine firm in whose hands you could not go very far wrong Mrs Quabarl thought it time to turn the conversation into more usual channels.

'We got very satisfactory references about you from Canon Teep,' she observed; 'a very estimable man, I should think.'

'Drinks like a fish and beats his wife, otherwise a very lovable character,' said the governess imperturbably.

'My *dear* Miss Hope! I trust you are exaggerating,' exclaimed the Quabarls in unison.

'One must in justice admit that there is some provocation,' continued the romancer. 'Mrs Teep is quite the most irritating bridge-player that I have ever sat down with; her leads and declarations would condone a certain amount of brutality in her partner, but to souse her with the contents of the only soda-water syphon in the house on a Sunday afternoon, when one couldn't get another, argues an indifference to the comfort of others which I cannot altogether overlook. You may think me hasty in my judgments, but it was practically on account of the syphon incident that I left.'

'We will talk of this some other time,' said Mrs Quabarl hastily.

'I shall never allude to it again,' said the governess with decision.

Mr Quabarl made a welcome diversion by asking what studies the new instructress proposed to inaugurate on the morrow.

'History to begin with,' she informed him.

'Ah, history,' he observed sagely; 'now in teaching them history you must take care to interest them in what they learn. You must make them feel they are being introduced to the life-stories of men and women who really lived –'

'I've told her all that,' interposed Mrs Quabarl.

'I teach history on the Schartz-Metterklume method,' said the governess loftily.

'Ah, yes,' said her listeners, thinking it expedient to assume an acquaintance at least with the name.

'What are you children doing out here?' demanded Mrs Quabarl the next morning, on finding Irene sitting rather glumly at the head of the stairs, while her sister was perched in an attitude of depressed discomfort on the window-seat behind her, with a wolf-skin rug almost covering her.

'We are having a history lesson,' came the unexpected reply. 'I am supposed to be Rome, and Viola up there is the she-wolf; not a real wolf, but the figure of one that the Romans used to set store by – I forget why. Claude and Wilfrid have gone to fetch the shabby women.'

'The shabby women?'

'Yes, they've got to carry them off. They didn't want to, but Miss Hope got one of father's fives-bats and said she'd give them a number nine spanking if they didn't, so they've gone to do it.'

A loud, angry screaming from the direction of the lawn drew Mrs Quabarl thither in hot haste, fearful lest the threatened castigation might even now be in process of infliction. The outcry, however, came principally from the two small daughters of the lodge-keeper, who were being hauled and pushed towards the house by the panting and dishevelled Claude and Wilfrid, whose task was rendered even more arduous by the incessant, if not very effectual, attacks of the captured maidens' small brother. The governess, fives-bat in hand, sat negligently on the stone balustrade, presiding over the scene with the cold impartiality of a Goddess of Battles. A furious and repeated chorus of 'I'll tell muvver' rose from the lodge children, but the lodge-mother, who was hard of hearing, was for the moment immersed in the preoccupation of her washtub. After an apprehensive glance in the direction of the lodge (the good woman was gifted with the highly militant temper which is sometimes the privilege of deafness) Mrs Quabarl flew indignantly to the rescue of the struggling captives.

'Wilfrid! Claude! Let those children go at once. Miss Hope, what on earth is the meaning of this scene?'

'Early Roman history; the Sabine women, don't you know? It's the Schartz-Metterklume method to make children understand history by acting it themselves; fixes it in their memory, you know. Of course, if, thanks to your interference, your boys go through life thinking that the Sabine women ultimately escaped I really cannot be held responsible.'

'You may be very clever and modern, Miss Hope,' said Mrs Quabarl firmly, 'but I should like you to leave here by the next train. Your luggage will be sent after you as soon as it arrives.'

'I'm not certain exactly where I shall be for the next few days,' said the dismissed instructress of youth; 'you might keep my luggage till I wire my address. There are only a couple of trunks and some golf-clubs and a leopard cub.'

'A leopard cub!' gasped Mrs Quabarl. Even in her departure this extraordinary person seemed destined to leave a trail of embarrassment behind her.

'Well, it's rather left off being a cub; it's more than half-grown, you know. A fowl every day and a rabbit on Sundays is what it usually gets. Raw beef makes it too excitable. Don't trouble about getting the car for me, I'm rather inclined for a walk.'

And Lady Carlotta strode out of the Quabarl horizon.

The advent of the genuine Miss Hope, who had made a mistake as to the day on which she was due to arrive, caused a turmoil which that good lady was quite unused to inspiring. Obviously the Quabarl family had been woefully befooled, but a certain amount of relief came with the knowledge.

'How tiresome for you, dear Carlotta,' said her hostess, when the overdue guest ultimately arrived; 'how very tiresome losing your train and having to stop overnight in a strange place.'

'Oh, dear, no,' said Lady Carlotta; 'not at all tiresome — for me.'

QUAIL SEED

The outlook is not encouraging for us smaller businesses,' said Mr Scarrick to the artist and his sister, who had taken rooms over his suburban grocery store. 'These big concerns are offering all sorts of attractions to the shopping public which we couldn't afford to imitate, even on a small scale – reading-rooms and play-rooms and gramophones and Heaven knows what. People don't care to buy half a pound of sugar nowadays unless they can listen to Harry Lauder and have the latest Australian cricket scores ticked off before their eyes. With the big Christmas stock we've got in we ought to keep half a dozen assistants hard at work, but as it is my nephew Jimmy and myself can pretty well attend to it ourselves. It's a nice stock of goods, too, if I could only run it off in a few weeks' time, but there's no chance of that – not unless the London line was to get snowed up for a fortnight before Christmas. I did have a sort of idea of engaging Miss Luffcombe to give recitations during afternoons; she made a great hit at the Post Office entertainments with her rendering of "Little Beatrice's Resolve." '

'Anything less likely to make your shop a fashionable shopping centre I can't imagine,' said the artist, with a very genuine shudder; 'if I were trying to decide between the merits of Carlsbad plums and confected figs as a winter dessert it would infuriate me to have my train of thought entangled with little Beatrice's resolve to be an Angel of Light or a girl scout. No,' he continued, 'the desire to get something thrown in for nothing is a ruling passion with the feminine shopper, but you can't afford to pander effectively to it. Why not appeal to another instinct, which dominates not only the woman shopper but the male shopper – in fact, the entire human race?'

'What is that instinct, sir?' said the grocer.

Mrs Greyes and Miss Fritten had missed the 2.18 to Town, and as there was not another train till 3.12 they thought that they might as well make their grocery purchases at Scarrick's. It would not be sensational, they agreed, but it would still be shopping.

For some minutes they had the shop almost to themselves, as far as customers were concerned, but while they were debating the respective virtues and blemishes of two competing brands of anchovy paste they were startled by an order, given across the counter, for six pomegranates and a packet of quail seed. Neither commodity was in general demand in that neighbourhood. Equally unusual was the style and appearance of the customer; about sixteen years old, with dark olive skin, large dusky eyes, and thick, low-growing, blue-black hair, he might have made his living as an artist's model. As a matter of fact he did. The bowl of beaten brass that he produced for the reception of his purchases was distinctly the most astonishing variation on the string bag or marketing basket of suburban civilization that his fellow-shoppers had ever seen. He threw a gold piece, apparently of some exotic currency, across the counter, and did not seem disposed to wait for any change that might be forthcoming.

'The wine and figs were not paid for yesterday,' he said; 'keep what is over of the money for our future purchases.'

'A very strange-looking boy?' said Mrs Greyes interrogatively to the grocer as soon as his customer had left.

'A foreigner, I believe,' said Mr Scarrick, with a shortness that was entirely out of keeping with his usually communicative manner.

'I wish for a pound and a half of the best coffee you have,' said an authoritative voice a moment or two later. The speaker was a tall, authoritative-looking man of rather outlandish aspect, remarkable among other things for a full black beard, worn in a style more in vogue in early Assyria than in London suburb of the present day.

'Has a dark-faced boy been here buying pomegranates?' he asked suddenly, as the coffee was being weighed out to him.

The two ladies almost jumped on hearing the grocer reply with an unblushing negative.

'We have a few pomegranates in stock,' he continued, 'but there has been no demand for them.'

'My servant will fetch the coffee as usual,' said the purchaser, producing a coin from a wonderful metal-work purse. As an apparent afterthought he fired out the question: 'Have you, perhaps any quail seed?'

'No,' said the grocer, without hesitation, 'we don't stock it.'

'What will he deny next?' said Mrs Greyes under her breath. What made it seem so much worse was the fact that Mr Scarrick had quite recently presided at a lecture on Savonarola.

Turning up the deep astrachan collar of his long coat, the stranger swept out of the shop, with the air, as Miss Fritten afterwards described it, of a Satrap proroguing a Sanhedrim. Whether such a pleasant function ever fell to a Satrap's lot she was not quite certain, but the simile faithfully conveyed her meaning to a large circle of acquaintances.

'Don't let's bother about the 3.12,' said Mrs Greyes; 'let's go and talk this over at Laura Lipping's. It's her day.'

When the dark-faced boy arrived at the shop next day with his brass marketing bowl there was quite a fair gathering of customers, most of whom seemed to be spinning out their purchasing operations with the air of people who had very little to do with their time. In a voice that was heard all over the shop, perhaps because everybody was intently listening, he asked for a pound of honey and a packet of quail seed.

'More quail seed!' said Miss Fritten. 'Those quails must be voracious, or else it isn't quail seed at all.'

'I believe it's opium, and the bearded man is a detective,' said Mrs Greyes brilliantly.

'I don't,' said Laura Lipping; 'I'm sure it's something to do with the Portuguese Throne.'

'More likely to be a Persian intrigue on behalf of the ex-Shah,' said Miss Fritten; 'the bearded man belongs to the Government Party. The quail seed is a countersign, of course; Persia is almost next door to Palestine, and quails come into the Old Testament, you know.'

'Only as a miracle,' said her well-informed younger sister; 'I've thought all along it was part of a love intrigue.'

The boy who had so much interest and speculation centred on him was on the point of departing with his purchases when he was waylaid by Jimmy, the nephew-apprentice, who, from his post at the cheese and bacon counter, commanded a good view of the street.

'We have some very fine Jaffa oranges,' he said hurriedly, pointing to a corner where they were stored, behind a high rampart of biscuit tins. There was evidently more in the remark than met the ear. The boy flew at the oranges with the enthusiasm of a ferret finding a rabbit family at home after a long day of fruitless subterranean research. Almost at the same moment the bearded stranger stalked into the shop, and flung an order for a pound of dates and a tin of the best Smyrna halva across the counter. The most adventurous housewife in the locality had never heard of halva, but Mr Scarrick was apparently able to produce the best Smyrna variety of it without a moment's hesitation.

'We might be living in the Arabian Nights,' said Miss Fritten excitedly.

'Hush! Listen,' beseeched Mrs Greyes.

'Has the dark-faced boy, of whom I spoke yesterday, been here today?' asked the stranger.

'We've had rather more people than usual in the shop today,' said Mr Scarrick, 'but I can't recall a boy such as you describe.'

Mrs Greyes and Miss Fritten looked round triumphantly at their friends. It was, of course, deplorable that any one should treat the truth as an article temporarily and excusably out of stock, but they felt gratified that the vivid accounts they had given of Mr Scarrick's traffic in falsehoods should receive confirmation at first hand.

'I shall never again be able to believe what he tells me about the absence of colouring matter in the jam,' whispered an aunt of Mrs Greyes tragically.

The mysterious stranger took his departure; Laura Lipping distinctly saw a snarl of baffled rage reveal itself behind his heavy moustache and upturned astrachan collar. After a cautious interval the seeker after oranges emerged from behind the biscuit tins, having apparently failed to find any individual orange that satisfied his requirements. He, too, took his departure, and the shop was slowly emptied of its parcel and gossip-laden customers. It was Emily Yorling's 'day,' and most of the shoppers made their way to her drawing-room. To go direct from a shopping expedition to a tea-party was what was known locally as 'living in a whirl.'

Two extra assistants had been engaged for the following afternoon, and their services were in brisk demand; the shop was crowded. People bought and bought, and never seemed to get to the end of their lists. Mr Scarrick had never had so little difficulty in persuading customers to embark on new experiences in grocery wares. Even those women whose purchases were of modest proportions dawdled over them as though they had brutal drunken husbands to go home to. The afternoon had dragged uneventfully on, and there was a distinct buzz of unpent excitement when a dark-eyed boy carrying a brass bowl entered the shop. The excitement seemed to have communicated itself to Mr Scarrick; abruptly, deserting a lady who was making insincere inquiries about the home life of the Bombay duck, he intercepted the newcomer on his way to the accustomed counter and informed him, amid a death-like hush, that he had run out of quail seed.

The boy looked nervously round the shop, and turned hesitatingly to go. He was again intercepted, this time by the nephew, who darted out from behind his counter and said something about a better line of oranges. The boy's hesitation vanished; he almost scuttled into the obscurity of the orange corner. There was an expectant turn of public attention towards the door, and the tall bearded stranger made a really effective entrance. The aunt of Mrs Greyes declared afterwards that she found herself subconsciously repeating 'The Assyrian came down like a wolf on the fold' under her breath, and she was generally believed.

The newcomer, too, was stopped before he reached the counter, but not by Mr Scarrick or his assistant. A heavily veiled lady, whom no one had hitherto noticed, rose languidly from a seat and greeted him in a clear, penetrating voice.

'Your Excellency does his shopping himself?' she said.

'I order the things myself,' he explained; 'I find it difficult to make my servants understand.'

In a lower, but still perfectly audible, voice the veiled lady gave him a piece of casual information.

'They have some excellent Jaffa oranges here.' Then with a tinkling laugh she passed out of the shop.

The man glared all round the shop, and then, fixing his eyes instinctively on the barrier of biscuit tins, demanded loudly of the grocer: 'You have, perhaps some good Jaffa oranges?'

Every one expected an instant denial on the part of Mr Scarrick of any such possession. Before he could answer, however, the boy had broken forth from his sanctuary. Holding his empty brass bowl before him he passed out into the street. His face was variously described afterwards as masked with studied indifference, overspread with ghastly pallor, and blazing with defiance. Some said that his teeth chattered, others that he went out whistling the Persian National Hymn. There was no mistaking, however, the effect produced by the encounter on the man who had seemed to force it. If a rabid dog or a rattlesnake had suddenly thrust its companionship on him he could scarcely have displayed a greater access of terror. His air of authority and assertiveness had gone, his masterful stride had given way to a furtive pacing to and fro, as of an animal seeking an outlet for escape. In a dazed perfunctory manner, always with his eyes turning to watch the shop entrance, he gave a few random orders, which the grocer made a show of entering in his book. Now and then he walked out into the street, looked anxiously in all directions, and hurried back to keep up his pretence of shopping. From one of these sorties he did not return; he had dashed away into the dusk, and neither he nor the dark-faced boy nor the veiled lady were seen again by the expectant crowds that continued to throng the Scarrick establishment for days to come.

'I can never thank you and your sister sufficiently,' said the grocer.

'We enjoyed the fun of it,' said the artist modestly, 'and as for the model, it was a welcome variation on posing for hours for "The Lost Hylas".'

'At any rate,' said the grocer, 'I insist on paying for the hire of the black beard.'

THE OPEN WINDOW

'My aunt will be down presently, Mr Nuttel,' said a very self-possessed young lady of fifteen; 'in the meantime you must try and put up with me.'

Framton Nuttel endeavoured to say the correct something which should duly flatter the niece of the moment without unduly discounting the aunt that was to come. Privately he doubted more than ever whether these formal visits on a succession of total strangers would do much towards helping the nerve cure which he was supposed to be undergoing.

'I know how it will be,' his sister had said when he was preparing to migrate to this rural retreat; 'you will bury yourself down there and not speak to a living soul, and your nerves will be worse than ever from moping. I shall just give you letters of introduction to all the people I know there. Some of them, as far as I can remember, were quite nice.'

Framton wondered whether Mrs Sappleton, the lady to whom he was presenting one of the letters of introduction, came into the nice division.

'Do you know many of the people round here?' asked the niece, when she judged that they had had sufficient silent communion.

'Hardly a soul,' said Framton. 'My sister was staying here, at the rectory, you know, some four years ago, and she gave me letters of introduction to some of the people here.'

He made the last statement in a tone of distinct regret.

'Then you know practically nothing about my aunt?' pursued the self-possessed young lady.

'Only her name and address,' admitted the caller. He was wondering whether Mrs Sappleton was in the married or widowed state. An undefinable something about the room seemed to suggest masculine habitation.

'Her great tragedy happened just three years ago,' said the child; 'that would be since your sister's time.'

'Her tragedy?' asked Framton; somehow in this restful country spot tragedies seemed out of place.

'You may wonder why we keep that window wide open on an October afternoon,' said the niece, indicating a large french window that opened on to a lawn.

'It is quite warm for the time of the year,' said Framton; 'but has that window got anything to do with the tragedy?'

'Out through that window, three years ago to a day, her husband and her two young brothers went off for their day's shooting. They never came back. In crossing the moor to their favourite snipe-shooting ground they were all three engulfed in a treacherous piece of bog. It had been that dreadful wet summer, you know, and places that were safe in other years gave way suddenly without warning. Their bodies were never recovered. That was the dreadful part of it.' Here the child's voice lost its self-possessed note and became falteringly human. 'Poor aunt always thinks that they will come back some day, they and the little brown spaniel that was lost with them, and walk in at that window just as they used to do. That is why the window is kept open every evening till it is quite dusk. Poor dear aunt, she has often told me how they went out, her husband with his white waterproof coat over his arm, and Ronnie, her youngest brother, singing, "Bertie, why do you bound?" as he always did to tease her, because she said it got on her nerves. Do you know, sometimes on still, quiet evenings like this, I almost get a creepy feeling that they will all walk in through that window –'

She broke off with a little shudder. It was a relief to Framton when the aunt bustled into the room with a whirl of apologies for being late in making her appearance.

'I hope Vera has been amusing you?' she said.

'She has been very interesting,' said Framton.

'I hope you don't mind the open window,' said Mrs Sappleton briskly; 'my husband and brothers will be home directly from shooting, and they always come in this way. They've been out for snipe in the marshes today, so they'll make a fine mess over my poor carpets. So like you men-folk, isn't it?'

She rattled on cheerfully about the shooting and the scarcity of birds, and the prospects for duck in the winter. To Framton it was all purely horrible. He made a desperate but only partially successful effort to turn the talk on to a less ghastly topic; he was conscious that his hostess was giving him only a fragment of her attention, and her eyes were constantly straying past him to the open window and the lawn beyond. It was certainly an unfortunate coincidence that he should have paid his visit on this tragic anniversary.

'The doctors agree in ordering me complete rest, an absence of mental excitement, and avoidance of anything in the nature of violent physical exercise,' announced Framton, who laboured under the tolerably wide-spread delusion that total strangers and chance acquaintances are hungry for the least detail of one's ailments and infirmities, their cause and cure. 'On the matter of diet they are not much in agreement,' he continued.

'No?' said Mrs Sappleton, in a voice which only replaced a yawn at the last moment. Then she suddenly brightened into alert attention—but not to what Framton was saying.

'Here they are at last!' she cried. 'Just in time for tea, and don't they look as if they were muddy up to the eyes!'

Framton shivered slightly and turned towards the niece with a look intended to convey sympathetic comprehension. The child was staring out through the open window with dazed horror in her eyes. In a chill shock of nameless fear Framton swung round in his seat and looked in the same direction.

In the deepening twilight three figures were walking across the lawn towards the window; they all carried guns under their arms, and one of them was additionally burdened with a white coat hung over his shoulders. A tired brown spaniel kept close at their heels. Noiselessly they neared the house, and then a hoarse young voice chanted out of the dusk: 'I said, Bertie, why do you bound?'

Framton grabbed wildly at his stick and hat; the hall-door, the gravel-drive, and the front gate were dimly noted stages in his headlong retreat. A cyclist coming along the road had to run into the hedge to avoid imminent collision.

'Here we are, my dear,' said the bearer of the white mackintosh, coming in through the window; 'fairly muddy, but most of it's dry. Who was that who bolted out as we came up?'

'A most extraordinary man, a Mr Nuttel,' said Mrs Sappleton; 'could only talk about his illnesses, and dashed off without a word of good-bye or apology when you arrived. One would think he had seen a ghost.'

'I expect it was the spaniel,' said the niece calmly; 'he told me he had a horror of dogs. He was once hunted into a cemetery somewhere on the banks of the Ganges by a pack of pariah dogs, and had to spend the night in a newly dug grave with the creatures snarling and grinning and foaming just above him. Enough to make anyone lose their nerve.'

Romance at short notice was her speciality.

LOUISE

'The tea will be quite cold, you'd better ring for some more,' said the Dowager Lady Beanford.

Susan Lady Beanford was a vigorous old woman who had coquetted with imaginary ill-health for the greater part of a lifetime; Clovis Sangrail irreverently declared that she had caught a chill at the Coronation of Queen Victoria and had never let it go again. Her sister, Jane Thropplestance, who was some years her junior, was chiefly remarkable for being the most absent-minded woman in Middlesex.

'I've really been unusually clever this afternoon,' she remarked gaily, as she rang for the tea. 'I've called on all the people I meant to call on, and I've done all the shopping that I set out to do. I even remembered to try and match that silk for you at Harrod's but I'd forgotten to bring the pattern with me, so it was no use. I really think that was the only important thing I forgot during the whole afternoon. Quite wonderful for me, isn't it?'

'What have you done with Louise?' asked her sister. 'Didn't you take her out with you? You said you were going to.'

'Good gracious,' exclaimed Jane, 'what *have* I done with Louise? I must have left her somewhere.'

'But where?'

'That's just it. Where have I left her? I can't remember if the Carrywoods were at home or if I just left cards. If they were at home I may have left Louise there to play bridge. I'll go and telephone to Lord Carrywood and find out.'

'Is that you, Lord Carrywod?' she queried over the telephone; 'it's me, Jane Thropplestance. I want to know, have you seen Louise?'

' "Louise," ' came the answer, 'it's been my fate to see it three times. At first, I must admit, I wasn't impressed by it, but the music grows on one after a bit. Still, I don't think I want to see it again just at present. Were you going to offer me a seat in your box?'

'Not the opera "Louise"—my niece, Louise Thropplestance. I thought I might have left her at your house.'

'You left cards on us this afternoon, I understand, but I don't think you left a niece. The footman would have been sure to have mentioned it if you had. Is it going to be a fashion to leave nieces on people as well as cards? I hope not; some of these houses in Berkeley Square have practically no accommodation for that sort of thing.'

'She's not at the Carrywoods', announced Jane, returning to her tea; 'now I come to think of it, perhaps I left her at the silk counter at Selfridge's. I may have told her to wait there a moment while I went to look at the silks in a better light, and I may easily have forgotten about her when I found I hadn't your pattern with me. In that case she's still sitting there. She wouldn't move unless she was told to; Louise has no initiative.'

'You said you tried to match the silk at Harrod's,' interjected the dowager.

'Did I? Perhaps it was Harrod's. I really don't remember. It was one of those places where every one is so kind and sympathetic and devoted that one almost hates to take even a reel of cotton away from such pleasant surroundings.'

'I think you might have taken Louise away. I don't like the idea of her being there among a lot of strangers. Supposing some unprincipled person was to get into conversation with her.'

'Impossible. Louise has no conversation. I've never discovered a single topic on which she'd anything to say beyond "Do you think so? I dare say you're right." I really thought her reticence about the fall of the Ribot Ministry was ridiculous, considering how much her dear mother used to visit Paris. This bread and butter is cut far too thin; it crumbles away long before you can get it to your mouth. One feels so absurd, snapping at one's food in mid-air, like a trout leaping at may-fly.'

'I am rather surprised,' said the dowager, 'that you can sit there making a hearty tea when you've just lost a favourite niece.'

'You talk as if I'd lost her in a churchyard sense, instead of having temporarily mislaid her. I'm sure to remember presently where I left her.'

'You didn't visit any place of devotion, did you? If you've left her mooning about Westminster Abbey or St Peter's, Eaton Square, without being able to give any satisfactory reason why she's there, she'll be seized under the Cat and Mouse Act and sent to Reginald McKenna.'

'That would be extremely awkward,' said Jane, meeting an irresolute piece of bread and butter halfway; 'we hardly know the McKennas, and it would be very tiresome having to telephone to some unsympathetic private secretary, describing Louise to him and asking to have her sent back in time for dinner. Fortunately, I didn't go to any place of devotion, though I did get mixed up with a Salvation Army procession. It was quite interesting to be at close quarters with them, they're so absolutely different to what they used to be when I first remember them in the 'eighties. They used to go about then unkempt and dishevelled, in a sort of smiling rage with the world, and now they're spruce and jaunty and flamboyantly decorative, like a geranium bed with religious convictions. Laura Kettleway was going on about them in the lift of the Dover Street Tube the other day, saying what a lot of good work they did, and what a loss it would have been if they'd never existed. "If they had never existed," I said, "Granville Barker would have been certain to have invented something that looked exactly like them." If you say things like that, quite loud, in a Tube lift, they always sound like epigrams.'

'I think you ought to do something about Louise,' said the dowager.

'I'm trying to think whether she was with me when I called on Ada Spelvexit. I rather enjoyed myself there. Ada was trying, as usual, to ram that odious Koriatoffski woman down my throat, knowing perfectly well that I detest her, and in an unguarded moment she said: "She's leaving her present house and going to Lower Seymour Street." "I dare say she will, if she stays there long enough," I said. Ada didn't see it for about three minutes, and then she was positively uncivil. No, I am certain I didn't leave Louise there.'

'If you could manage to remember where you *did* leave her, it would be more to the point than these negative assurances,' said Lady Beanford; 'so far, all that we know is that she is not at the Carrywoods', or Ada Spelvexit's, or Westminster Abbey.'

'That narrows the search down a bit,' said Jane hopefully; 'I rather fancy she must have been with me when I went to Mornay's. I know I went to Mornay's, because I remember meeting that delightful Malcolm What's-his-name there—you know whom I mean. That's the great advantage of people having unusual first names, you needn't try and remember what their other name is. Of course I know one or two other Malcolms, but none that could possibly be described as delightful. He gave me two tickets for the Happy Sunday Evenings in Sloane Square. I've probably left them at Mornay's, but still it was awfully kind of him to give them to me.'

'Do you think you left Louise there?'

'I might telephone and ask. Oh, Robert, before you clear the tea-things away I wish you'd ring up Mornay's, in Regent Street, and ask if I left two theatre tickets and one niece in their shop this afternoon.'

'A niece, ma'am?' asked the footman.

'Yes, Miss Louise didn't come home with me, and I'm not sure where I left her.'

'Miss Louise has been upstairs all the afternoon, ma'am, reading to the second kitchenmaid, who has the neuralgia. I took up tea to Miss Louise at a quarter to five o'clock, ma'am.

'Of course, how silly of me. I remember now, I asked her to read the *Faërie Queene* to poor Emma, to try to send her to sleep. I always get some one to read the *Faërie Queene* to me when I have neuralgia, and it usually sends me to sleep. Louise doesn't seem to have been successful, but one can't say she hasn't tried. I expect after the first hour or so the kitchenmaid would rather have been left alone with her neuralgia, but of course Louise wouldn't leave off till someone told her to. Anyhow, you can ring up Mornay's, Robert, and ask whether I left two theatre tickets there. Except for your silk, Susan those seem to be the only things I've forgotten this afternoon. Quite wonderful for me.'

THE DREAMER

It was the season of sales. The august establishment of Walpurgis and Nettlepink had lowered its prices for an entire week as a concession to trade observances, much as an Archduchess might protestingly contract an attack of influenza for the unsatisfactory reason that influenza was locally prevalent. Adela Chemping, who considered herself in some measure superior to the allurements of an ordinary bargain sale, made a point of attending the reduction week at Walpurgis and Nettlepink's.

'I'm not a bargain hunter,' she said, 'but I like to go where bargains are.'

Which showed that beneath her surface strength of character there flowed a gracious undercurrent of human weakness.

With a view to providing herself with a male escort Mrs Chemping had invited her youngest nephew to accompany her on the first day of the shopping expedition, throwing in the additional allurement of a cinematograph theatre and the prospect of light refreshment. As Cyprian was not yet eighteen, she hoped he might not have reached that stage in masculine development when parcel-carrying is looked on as a thing abhorrent.

'Meet me just outside the floral department,' she wrote to him, 'and don't be a moment later than eleven.'

Cyprian was a boy who carried with him through early life the wondering look of a dreamer, the eyes of one who sees things that are not visible to ordinary mortals, and invests the commonplace things of this world with qualities unsuspected by plainer folk – the eyes of a poet or a house agent. He was quietly dressed – that sartorial quietude which frequently accompanies early adolescence, and is usually attributed by novel-writers to the influence of a widowed mother. His hair was brushed back in a smoothness as of ribbon seaweed and seamed with a narrow furrow that scarcely aimed at being a parting. His aunt particularly noted this item of his toilet when they met at the appointed rendezvous, because he was standing waiting for her barehead.

'Where is your hat?' she asked.

'I didn't bring one with me,' he replied.

Adela Chemping was slightly scandalized.

'You are not going to be what they call a Nut, are you?' she inquired with some anxiety, partly with the idea that a Nut would be an extravagance which her sister's small household would scarcely be justified in incurring, partly, perhaps, with the instinctive apprehension that a Nut, even in its embryo stage, would refuse to carry parcels.

Cyprian looked at her with his wondering, dreamy eyes.

'I didn't bring a hat,' he said, 'because it is such a nuisance when one is shopping; I mean it is so awkward if one meets anyone one knows and has to take one's hat off when one's hands are full of parcels. If one hasn't got a hat on one can't take it off.'

Mrs Chemping sighed with great relief; her worst fear had been laid at rest.

'It is more orthodox to wear a hat,' she observed, and then turned her attention briskly to the business in hand.

'We will go first to the table-linen counter,' she said, leading the way in that direction; 'I should like to look at some napkins.'

The wondering look deepened in Cyprian's eyes as he followed his aunt; he belonged to a generation that is supposed to be over-fond of the rôle of mere spectator, but looking at napkins that one did not mean to buy was a pleasure beyond his comprehension. Mrs Chemping held one or two napkins up to the light and stared fixedly at them, as though she half expected to find some revolutionary cypher written on them in scarcely visible ink; then she suddenly broke away in the direction of the glassware department.

'Millicent asked me to get her a couple of decanters if there were any going really cheap,' she explained on the way, 'and I really do want a salad bowl. I can come back to the napkins later on.'

She handled and scrutinized a large number of decanters and a long series of salad bowls, and finally bought seven chrysanthemum vases.

'No one uses that kind of vase nowadays,' she informed Cyprian, 'but they will do for presents next Christmas.'

Two sunshades that were marked down to a price that Mrs Chemping considered absurdly cheap were added to her purchases.

'One of them will do for Ruth Colson; she is going out to the Malay States, and a sunshade will always be useful there. And I must get her some thin writing paper. It takes up no room in one's baggage.'

Mrs Chemping bought stacks of writing paper; it was so cheap, and it went so flat in a trunk or portmanteau. She also bought a few envelopes – envelopes somehow seemed rather an extravagance compared with notepaper.

'Do you think Ruth will like blue or grey paper?' she asked Cyprian.

'Grey,' said Cyprian, who had never met the lady in question.

'Have you any mauve notepaper of this quality?' Adela asked the assistant.

'We haven't any mauve,' said the assistant, 'but we've two shades of green and a darker shade of grey.'

Mrs Chemping inspected the greens and the darker grey, and chose the blue.

'Now we can have some lunch,' she said.

Cyprian behaved in an exemplary fashion in the refreshment department, and cheerfully accepted a fish cake and a mince pie

and a small cup of coffee as adequate restoratives after two hours
of concentrated shopping. He was adamant, however, in resisting
his aunt's suggestion that a hat should be bought for him at the
counter where men's head-wear was being disposed of at temptingly reduced prices.

'I've got as many hats as I want at home,' he said, 'and besides,
it rumples one's hair so, trying them on.'

Perhaps he was going to develop into a Nut after all. It was
a disquieting sympton that he left all the parcels in charge of
the cloak-room attendant.

'We shall be getting more parcels presently,' he said, 'so we need
not collect these till we have finished our shopping.'

His aunt was doubtfully appeased; some of the pleasure and
excitement of a shopping expedition seemed to evaporate when
one was deprived of immediate personal contact with one's
purchases.

'I'm going to look at those napkins again,' she said, as they
descended the stairs to the ground floor. 'You need not come,'
she added, as the dreaming look in the boy's eyes changed for
a moment into one of mute protest, 'you can meet me afterwards
in the cutlery department; I've just remembered that I haven't
a corkscrew in the house that can be depended on.'

Cyprian was not to be found in the cutlery department when
his aunt in due course arrived there, but in the crush and bustle
of anxious shoppers and busy attendants it was an easy matter to
miss any one. It was in the leather goods department some quarter
of an hour later that Adela Chemping caught sight of her nephew,
separated from her by a rampart of suitcases and portmanteaux
and hemmed in by the jostling crush of human beings that now
invaded every corner of the great shopping emporium. She was
just in time to witness a pardonable but rather embarrassing mistake on the part of a lady who had wriggled her way with unstay-
able determination towards the bareheaded Cyprian, and was now
breathlessly demanding the sale price of a handbag which had
taken her fancy.

'There now,' exclaimed Adela to herself, 'she takes him for one
of the shop assistants because he hasn't got a hat on. I wonder it
hasn't happened before.'

Perhaps it had. Cyprian, at any rate, seemed neither startled nor
embarrassed by the error into which the good lady had fallen.
Examining the ticket on the bag, he announced in a clear, dispas-
sionate voice:

'Black seal, thirty-four shillings marked down to twenty-eight. As a matter of fact, we are clearing them out at a special reduction price of twenty-six shillings. They are going off rather fast.'

'I'll take it,' said the lady, eagerly digging some coins out of her purse.

'Will you take it as it is?' asked Cyprian; 'it will be a matter of a few minutes to get it wrapped up, there is such a crush.'

'Never mind, I'll take it as it is,' said the purchaser, clutching her treasure and counting the money into Cyprian's palm.

Several kind strangers helped Adela into the open air.

'It's the crush and the heat,' said one sympathizer to another; 'it's enough to turn any one giddy.'

When she next came across Cyprian he was standing in the crowd that pushed and jostled around the counters of the book department. The dream look was deeper than ever in his eyes. He had just sold two books of devotion to an elderly Canon.

DUSK

Norman Gortsby sat on a bench in the Park, with his back to a strip of bush-planted sward, fenced by the park railings, and the Row fronting him across a wide stretch of carriage drive. Hyde Park Corner, with its rattle and hoot of traffic, lay immediately to his right. It was some thirty minutes past six on an early March evening, and dusk had fallen heavily over the scene, dusk, mitigated by some faint moonlight and many street lamps. There was a wide emptiness over road and sidewalk, and yet there were many unconsidered figures moving silently through the half-light or dotted unobtrusively on bench and chair, scarcely to be distinguished from the shadowed gloom in which they sat.

The scene pleased Gortsby and harmonized with his present mood. Dusk, to his mind, was the hour of the defeated. Men and women who had fought and lost, who hid their fallen fortunes and dead hopes as far as possible from the scrutiny of the curious, came forth in this hour of gloaming, when their shabby clothes and bowed shoulders and unhappy eyes might pass unnoticed, or, at any rate, unrecognized.

> A king that is conquered must see strange looks,
> So bitter a thing is the heart of man.

The wanderers in the dusk did not choose to have strange looks fasten on them, therefore they came out in this bat-fashion, taking their pleasure sadly in a pleasure-ground that had emptied of its rightful occupants. Beyond the sheltering screen of bushes and palings came a realm of brilliant lights and noisy, rushing traffic. A blazing, many-tiered stretch of windows shone through the dusk and almost dispersed it, marking the haunts of those other people, who held their own life's struggle, or at any rate had not to admit failure. So Gortsby's imagination pictured things as he sat on his bench in the almost deserted walk. He was in the mood to count himself among the defeated. Money troubles did not press on him; had he so wished he could have strolled into the thoroughfares of light and noise, and taken his place among the jostling ranks of those who enjoyed prosperity or struggled for it. He had failed in a more subtle ambition, and for the moment he was heart sore and disillusionized, and not disinclined to take a certain cynical pleasure in observing and labelling his fellow wanderers as they went their ways in the dark stretches between the lamp-lights.

On the bench by his side sat an elderly gentlemen with a drooping air of defiance that was probably the remaining vestige of self-respect in an individual who had ceased to defy successfully anybody or anything. His clothes could scarcely be called shabby, at least they passed muster in the half-light, but one's imagination could not have pictured the wearer embarking on the purchase of a half-crown box of chocolates or laying out ninepence on a carnation buttonhole. He belonged unmistakably to that forlorn orchestra to whose piping no one dances; he was one of the world's lamenters who induces no responsive weeping. As he rose to go Gortsby imagined him returning to a home circle where he was snubbed and of no account, or to some bleak lodging where his ability to pay a weekly bill was the beginning and end of the interest he inspired. His retreating figure vanished slowly into the shadows, and his place on the bench was taken almost immediately by a young man, fairly well dressed but scarcely more cheerful of mien than his predecessor. As if to emphasize the fact that the world went badly with him the new-comer unburdened himself of an angry and very audible expletive as he flung himself into the seat.

'You don't seem in a very good temper,' said Gortsby, judging that he was expected to take due notice of the demonstration.

The young man turned to him with a look of disarming frankness which put him instantly on his guard.

'You wouldn't be in a good temper if you were in the fix I'm in,' he said; 'I've done the silliest thing I've ever done in my life.'

'Yes?' said Gortsby dispassionately.

'Came up this afternoon, meaning to stay at the Patagonian Hotel in Berkshire Square,' continued the young man; 'when I got there I found it had been pulled down some weeks ago and a cinema theatre run up on the site. The taxi driver recommended me to another hotel some way off and I went there. I just sent a letter to my people, giving them the address, and then I went out to buy some soap – I'd forgotten to pack any and I hate using hotel soap. Then I strolled about a bit, had a drink at a bar and looked at the shops, and when I came to turn my steps back to the hotel I suddenly realized that I didn't remember its name or even what street it was in. There's a nice predicament for a fellow who hasn't any friends or connections in London! Of course I can wire to my people for the address, but they won't have got my letter till tomorrow; meantime I'm without any money, came out with about a shilling on me, which went buying the soap and getting the drink, and here I am, wandering about with twopence in my pocket and nowhere to go for the night.'

There was an eloquent pause after the story had been told. 'I suppose you think I've spun you rather an impossible yarn,' said the young man presently, with a suggestion of resentment in his voice.

'Not at all impossible,' said Gortsby judicially; 'I remember doing exactly the same thing once in a foreign capital, and on that occasion there were two of us, which made it more remarkable. Luckily we remembered that the hotel was on a sort of canal, and when we struck the canal we were able to find our way back to the hotel.'

The youth brightened at the reminiscence. 'In a foreign city I wouldn't mind so much,' he said; 'one could go to one's Consul and get the requisite help from him. Here in one's own land one is far more derelict if one gets into a fix. Unless I can find some decent chap to swallow my story and lend me some money I seem likely to spend the night on the Embankment. I'm glad, anyhow, that you don't think the story outrageously improbable.'

He threw a good deal of warmth into the last remark, as though perhaps to indicate his hope that Gortsby did not fall far short of the requisite decency.

'Of course,' said Gortsby slowly, 'the weak point of your story is that you can't produce the soap.'

The young man sat forward hurriedly, felt rapidly in the pockets of his overcoat, and then jumped to his feet.

'I must have lost it,' he muttered angrily.

'To lose an hotel and a cake of soap on one afternoon suggests wilful carelessness,' said Gortsby, but the young man scarcely waited to hear the end of the remark. He flitted away down the path, his head held high, with an air of somewhat jaded jauntiness.

'It was a pity,' mused Gortsby; 'the going out to get one's own soap was the one convincing touch in the whole story, and yet it was just that little detail that brought him to grief. If he had had the brilliant forethought to provide himself with a cake of soap, wrapped and sealed with all the solicitude of the chemist's counter, he would have been a genius in his particular line. In his particular line genius certainly consists of an infinite capacity for taking precautions.'

With that reflection Gortsby rose to go; as he did so an exclamation of concern escaped him. Lying on the ground by the side of the bench was a small oval packet, wrapped and sealed with the solicitude of a chemist's counter. It could be nothing else but a cake of soap, and it had evidently fallen out of the youth's overcoat pocket when he flung himself down on the seat. In another moment Gortsby was scudding along the dusk-shrouded path in anxious quest for a youthful figure in a light overcoat. He had nearly given up the search when he caught sight of the object of his pursuit standing irresolutely on the border of the carriage drive, evidently uncertain whether to strike across the Park or make for the bustling pavements of Knightsbridge. He turned round sharply with an air of defensive hostility when he found Gortsby hailing him.

'The important witness to the geniuneness of your story has turned up,' said Gortsby, holding out the cake of soap; 'it must have slid out of your overcoat pocket when you sat down on the seat. I saw it on the ground after you left. You must excuse my disbelief, but appearances were really rather against you, and now, as I appealed to the testimony of the soap I think I ought to abide by its verdict. If the loan of a sovereign is any good to you –'

The young man hastily removed all doubt on the subject by pocketing the coin.

'Here is my card with my address,' continued Gortsby; 'any day this week will do for returning the money, and here is the soap – don't lose it again ; it's been a good friend to you.'

'Lucky thing your finding it,' said the youth, and then, with a catch in his voice, he blurted out a word or two of thanks and fled headlong in the direction of Knightsbridge.

'Poor boy, he as nearly as possible broke down,' said Gortsby to himself. 'I don't wonder either; the relief from his quandary must have been acute. It's a lesson to me not to be too clever in judging by circumstances.'

As Gortsby retraced his steps past the seat where the little drama had taken place he saw an elderly gentleman poking and peering beneath it and on all sides of it, and recognized his earlier fellow occupant.

'Have you lost anything, sir?' he asked.

'Yes, sir, a cake of soap.'

THE HEDGEHOG

A 'mixed double' of young people were contesting a game of lawn tennis at the Rectory garden party; for the past five-and-twenty years at least mixed doubles of young people had done exactly the same thing on exactly the same spot at about the same time of year. The young people changed and made way for others in the course of time, but very little else seemed to alter.

The present players were sufficiently conscious of the social nature of the occasion to be concerned about their clothes and appearance, and sufficiently sport-loving to be keen on the game. Both their efforts and their appearance came under the four-fold scrutiny of a quartet of ladies sitting as official spectators on a bench immediately commanding the court. It was one of the accepted conditions of the Rectory garden party that four ladies, who usually knew very little about tennis and a great deal about the players, should sit at that particular spot and watch the game. It had also come to be almost a tradition that two ladies should be amiable, and that the other two should be Mrs Dole and Mrs Hatch-Mallard.

'What a singularly unbecoming way Eva Jonelet has taken to doing her hair in,' said Mrs Hatch-Mallard; 'it's ugly hair at the best of times, but she needn't make it look ridiculous as well. Some one ought to tell her.'

Eva Jonelet's hair might have escaped Mrs Hatch-Mallard's condemnation if she could have forgotten the more glaring fact that Eva was Mrs Dole's favourite niece. It would, perhaps, have been a more comfortable arrangement if Mrs Hatch-Mallard and

Mrs Dole could have been asked to the Rectory on separate occasions but there was only one garden party in the course of the year, and neither lady could have been omitted from the list of invitations without hopelessly wrecking the social peace of the parish.

'How pretty the yew trees look at this time of year,' interposed a lady with a soft, silvery voice that suggested a chinchilla muff painted by Whistler.

'What do you mean by this time of year?' demanded Mrs Hatch-Mallard. 'Yew trees look beautiful at all times of the year. That is their great charm.'

'Yew trees never look anything but hideous under any circumstances or at any time of year,' said Mrs Dole, with the slow, emphatic relish of one who contradicts for the pleasure of the thing. 'They are only fit for graveyards and cemeteries.'

Mrs Hatch-Mallard gave a sardonic snort, which, being translated, meant that there were some people who were better fitted for cemeteries than for garden parties.

'What is the score, please?' asked the lady with the chinchilla voice.

The desired information was given her by a young gentleman in spotless white flannels, whose general toilet effect suggested solicitude rather than anxiety.

'What an odious young cub Bertie Dykson has become!' pronounced Mrs Dole, remembering suddenly that Bertie was rather a favourite with Mrs Hatch-Mallard. 'The young men of today are not what they used to be twenty years ago.'

'Of course not,' said Mrs Hatch-Mallard; twenty years ago Bertie Dykson was just two years old, and you must expect some difference in appearance and manner and conversation between those two periods.'

'Do you know,' said Mrs Dole confidentially, 'I shouldn't be surprised if that was intended to be clever.'

'Have you any one interesting to stay with you, Mrs Norbury?' asked the chinchilla voice hastily; 'you generally have a house-party at this time of year.'

'I've got a most interesting woman coming,' said Mrs Norbury, who had been mutely struggling for some chance to turn the conversation into a safe channel; 'an old acquaintance of mine, Ada Bleek –'

'What an ugly name,' said Mrs Hatch-Mallard.

'She's descended from the de la Bliques, an old Hugenot family of Touraine, you know.'

'There weren't any Hugenots in Touraine,' said Mrs Hatch-Mallard, who thought she might safely dispute any fact that was three hundred years old.

'Well, anyhow, she's coming to stay with me,' continued Mrs Norbury, bringing her story down to the present day; 'she arrives this evening and she's highly clairvoyante, a seventh daughter of a seventh daughter, you know, and all that sort of thing.'

'How very interesting,' said the chinchilla voice; 'Exwood is just the right place for her to come to, isn't it? There are supposed to be several ghosts there.'

'That is why she was so anxious to come,' said Mrs Norbury; 'she put off another engagement in order to accept my invitation. She's had visions and dreams, and all those sort of things, that have come true in a most marvellous manner, but she's never actually seen a ghost, and she's longing to have that experience. She belongs to that Research Society, you know.'

'I expect she'll see the unhappy Lady Cullumpton, the most famous of all the Exwood ghosts,' said Mrs Dole; 'my ancestor, you know, Sir Gervase Cullumpton, murdered his young bride in a fit of jealousy while they were on a visit to Exwood. He strangled her in the stables with a stirrup leather, just after they had come from riding, and she is seen sometimes at dusk going about the lawns and the stable yard, in a long green habit, moaning and trying to get the thong from round her throat. I shall be most interested to hear if your friend sees –'

'I don't know why she should be expected to see a trashy, traditional apparition like the so-called Cullumpton ghost, that is only vouched for by house-maids and tipsy stable-boys, when my uncle, who was the owner of Exwood, committed suicide there under the most tragical circumstances, and most certainly haunts the place.'

'Mrs Hatch-Mallard has evidently never read *Popple's County History*,' said Mrs Dole icily, 'or she would know that the Cullumpton ghost has a wealth of evidence behind it –'

'Oh, Popple!' exclaimed Mrs Hatch-Mallard scornfully; 'any rubbishy old story is good enough for him. Popple, indeed! Now my uncle's ghost was seen by a Rural Dean, who was also a Justice of the Peace. I should think that would be good enough testimony for any one. Mrs Norbury, I shall take it as a deliberate personal affront if your clairvoyante friend sees any other ghost except that of my uncle.'

'I dare say she won't see anything at all; she never has yet, you know,' said Mrs Norbury hopefully.

'It was a most unfortunate topic for me to have broached,' she lamented afterwards to the owner of the chinchilla voice; 'Exwood belongs to Mrs Hatch-Mallard, and we've only got it on short lease. A nephew of hers has been wanting to live there for some time, and if we offend her in any way she'll refuse to renew the lease. I sometimes think these garden parties are a mistake.'

The Norburys played bridge for the next three nights till nearly one o'clock; they did not care for the game, but it reduced the time at their guest's disposal for undesirable ghostly visitations.

'Miss Bleek is not likely to be in a frame of mind to see ghosts,' said Hugo Norbury, 'if she goes to bed with her brain awhirl with royal spades and no trumps and grand-slams.'

'I've talked to her for hours about Mrs Hatch-Mallard's uncle,' said his wife, 'and pointed out the exact spot where he killed himself, and invented all sorts of impressive details, and I've found an old portrait of Lord John Russell and put it in her room, and told her that it's supposed to be a picture of the uncle in middle age. If Ada does see a ghost at all it certainly ought to be old Hatch-Mallard's. At any rate, we've done our best.'

The precautions were in vain. On the third morning of her stay Ada Bleek came down late to breakfast, her eyes looking very tired, but ablaze with excitement, her hair done anyhow, and a large brown volume hugged under her arm.

'At last I've seen something supernatural!' she exclaimed, and gave Mrs Norbury a fervent kiss, as though in gratitude for the opportunity afforded her.

'A ghost!' cried Mrs Norbury, 'not really!'

'Really and unmistakably!'

'Was it an oldish man in the dress of about fifty years ago?' asked Mrs Norbury hopefully.

'Nothing of the sort,' said Ada; 'it was a white hedgehog.'

'A white hedgehog!' exclaimed both the Norburys, in tones of disconcerted astonishment.

'A huge white hedgehog with baleful yellow eyes,' said Ada; 'I was lying half asleep in bed when suddenly I felt a sensation as of something sinister and unaccountable passing through the room. I sat up and looked round, and there, under the window, I saw an evil, creeping thing, a sort of monstrous hedgehog, of a dirty white colour, with black, loathsome claws that clicked and scraped along the floor, and narrow, yellow eyes of indescribable evil. It slithered along for a yard or two, always looking at me with its cruel, hideous eyes, then, when it reached the second window, which was open, it clambered up the sill and vanished. I got up at once and went to the window; there wasn't a sign of it anywhere. Of course, I knew it must be something from another world, but it was not till I turned up Popple's chapter on local traditions that I realized what I had seen.

She turned eagerly to the large brown volume and read: '"Nicholas Herison, an old miser, was hung at Batchford in 1763 for the murder of a farm lad who had accidentally discovered his secret hoard. His ghost is supposed to traverse the countryside, appearing sometimes as a white owl, sometimes as a huge white hedgehog."'

'I expect you read the Popple story overnight, and that made you *think* you saw a hedgehog when you were only half awake,' said Mrs Norbury, hazarding a conjecture that probably came very near the truth.

Ada scorned the possibility of such a solution of her apparition.

'This must be hushed up,' said Mrs Norbury quickly; 'the servants—'

'Hushed up!' exclaimed Ada, indignantly; 'I'm writing a long report on it for the Research Society.'

It was then that Hugo Norbury, who is not naturally a man of brilliant resource, had one of the really useful inspirations of his life.

'It was very wicked of us, Miss Bleek,' he said, 'but it would be a shame to let it go further. That white hedgehog is an old joke of ours; stuffed albino hedgehog, you know, that my father brought home from Jamaica, where they grow to enormous size. We hide it in the room with a string on it, run one end of the string through the window, then we pull it from below and it comes scraping along the floor, just as you've described, and finally jerks out of the window. Taken in heaps of people; they all read up Popple and think it's old Harry Nicholson's ghost; we always stop them from writing to the papers about it, though. That would be carrying matters too far.'

Mrs Hatch-Mallard renewed the lease in due course, but Ada Bleek has never renewed her friendship.

THE IMAGE OF THE LOST SOUL

There were a number of carved stone figures placed at intervals along the parapets of the old Cathedral; some of them represented angels, other kings and bishops, and nearly all were in attitudes of pious exaltation and composure. But one figure, low down on the cold north side of the building, had neither crown, mitre, nor nimbus, and its face was hard and bitter and downcast; it must be a demon, declared the fat blue pigeons that roosted and sunned themselves all day on the ledges of the parapet; but the old belfry jackdaw, who was an authority on ecclesiastical architecture, said it was a lost soul. And there the matter rested.

One autumn day there fluttered on to the Cathedral roof a slender, sweet-voiced bird that had wandered away from the bare fields and thinning hedgerows in search of a winter roosting-place. It tried to rest its tired feet under the shade of a great angel-wing or to nestle in the sculptured folds of a kingly robe, but the fat pigeons hustled it away from wherever it settled, and the noisy sparrow-folk drove it off the ledges. No respectable bird sang with so much feeling, they cheeped one to another, and the wanderer had to move on.

Only the effigy of the Lost Soul offered a place of refuge. The pigeons did not consider it safe to perch on a projection that leaned so much out of the perpendicular, and was, besides, too much in the shadow. The figure did not cross its hands in the pious attitude of the other graven dignitaries, but its arms were folded as in defiance and their angle made a snug resting-place for the little bird. Every evening it crept trustfully into its corner against the stone breast of the image and the darkling eyes seemed to keep watch over its slumbers. The lonely bird grew to love its lonely protector, and during the day it would sit from time to time on some rain-shoot or other abutment and trill forth its sweetest music in grateful thanks for its nightly shelter. And, it may have been the work of wind and weather, or some other influence, but the wild drawn face seemed gradually to lose some of its hardness and unhappiness. Every day, through the long monotonous hours, the song of his little guest would come up in snatches to the lonely watcher, and at evening, when the vesper-bell was ringing and the great grey bats slid out of their hiding places in the belfry roof, the bright eyed bird would return, twitter a few sleepy notes, and nestle into the arms that were waiting for him. Those were happy days for the Dark Image. Only the great bell of the Cathedral rang out daily its mocking message, 'After joy ... sorrow.'

The folk in the verger's lodge noticed a little brown bird flitting about the Cathedral precincts, and admired its beautiful singing. 'But it is a pity,' said they, 'that all that warbling should be lost and wasted far out of hearing up on the parapet.' They were poor, but they understood the principles of political economy. So they caught the bird and put it in a little wicker cage outside the lodge door.

That night the little songster was missing from its accustomed haunt, and the Dark Image knew more than ever the bitterness of loneliness. Perhaps his little friend had been killed by a prowling cat or hurt by a stone. Perhaps ... perhaps he had flown elsewhere. But when morning came there floated up to him, through the noise and bustle of the Cathedral world, a faint heart-aching message from the prisoner in the wicker cage far below. And every day, at high noon, when the fat pigeons were stupefied into silence after their midday meal and the sparrows were washing themselves in the street-puddles, the song of the little bird came up to the parapets – a song of hunger and longing and hopelessness, a cry that could never be answered.

The pigeons remarked, between mealtimes, that the figure leaned forward more than ever out of the perpendicular.

One day no song came up from the little wicker cage. It was the coldest day of the winter, and the pigeons and sparrows on the Cathedral roof looked anxiously on all sides for the scraps of food which they were dependent on in hard weather.

'Have the lodge-folk thrown out anything on the dust-heap?' inquired one pigeon of another which was peering over the edge of the north parapet.

'Only a little dead bird,' was the answer.

There was a crackling sound in the night on the Cathedral roof and a noise as of falling masonry. The belfry jackdaw said the frost was affecting the fabric, and as he had experienced many frosts it must have been so. In the morning it was seen that the Figure of the Lost Soul had toppled from its cornice and lay now in a broken mass on the dust-heap outside the verger's lodge.

'It is just as well,' cooed the fat pigeons, after they had peered at the matter for some minutes; 'now we shall have a nice angel put up there. Certainly they will put an angel there.'

'After joy ... sorrow,' rang out the great bell.

THE THREAT

Sir Lulworth Quayne sat in the lounge of his favourite restaurant, the Galus Bankiva, discussing the weaknesses of the world with his nephew, who had lately returned from a much-enlivened exile in the wilds of Mexico. It was that blessed season of the year when the asparagus and the plover's egg are abroad in the land, and the oyster has not yet withdrawn into its summer entrenchments, and Sir Lulworth and his nephew were in that enlightened after-dinner mood when politics are seen in their right perspective, even the politics of Mexico.

'Most of the revolutions that take place in this country nowadays,' said Sir Lulworth, 'are the products of moments of legislative panic. Take, for instance, one of the most dramatic reforms that has been carried through Parliament in the lifetime of this generation. It happened, shortly after the coal strike, of unblessed memory. To you, who have been plunged up to the neck in events of a more tangled and tumbled description, the things I am going to tell you of may seem of secondary interest, but after all we had to live in the midst of them.'

Sir Lulworth interrupted himself for a moment to say a few kind words to the liqueur brandy he had just tasted, and then resumed his narrative.

'Whether one sympathizes with the agitation for female suffrage or not one has to admit that its promoters showed tireless energy and considerable enterprise in devising and putting into action new methods for accomplishing their ends. As a rule they were a nuisance and a weariness to the flesh, but there were times when they verged on the picturesque. There was the famous occasion when they enlivened and diversified the customary pageantry of the Royal progress to open Parliament by letting loose thousands of parrots, which had been carefully trained to scream "Votes for women," and which circled round his Majesty's coach in a clamorous cloud of green, and grey and scarlet. It was really rather a striking episode from the spectacular point of view; unfortunately however, for its devisers, the secret of their intentions had not been well kept, and their opponents let loose at the same moment a rival swarm of parrots, which screeched "I *don't* think" and other hostile cries, thereby robbing the demonstration of the unanimity which alone could have made it politically impressive. In the process of recapture the birds learned a quantity of additional language which unfitted them for further service in the Suffragette cause; some of the green ones were secured by ardent Home Rule propagandists and trained to disturb the serenity of Orange meetings by pessimistic reflections on Sir Edward Carson's destination in the life to come. In fact, the bird in politics is a factor that seems to have come to stay; quite recently, at a political gathering held in a dimly lighted place of worship, the congregation gave a respectful hearing for nearly ten minutes to a jackdaw from Wapping, under the impression that they were listening to the Chancellor of the Exchequer, who was late in arriving.'

'But the Suffragettes,' interrupted the nephew; 'what did they do next?'

'After the bird fiasco,' said Sir Lulworth, 'the militant section made a demonstration of a more aggressive nature; they assembled in force on the opening day of the Royal Academy Exhibition and destroyed some three or four hundred of the pictures. This proved an even worse failure than the parrot business; every one agreed that there were always far too many pictures in the Academy Exhibition, and the drastic weeding out of a few hundred canvases was regarded as a positive improvement. Moreover, from the artists' point of view it was realized that the outrage constituted a sort of compensation for those whose works were persistently "skied," since out of sight meant also out of reach. Altogether it was one of the most successful and popular exhibitions that the Academy had held for many years. Then the fair agitators fell back on some of their earlier methods; they wrote sweetly argumentative plays to prove that they ought to have the vote, they smashed windows to show that they must have the vote, and they kicked Cabinet Ministers to demonstrate that they'd better have the vote, and still the coldly reasoned or unreasoned reply was that they'd better not. Their plight might have been summed up in a perversion of Gilbert's lines—

> "Twenty voteless millions we,
>   Voteless all against our will,
> Twenty years hence we shall be
>   Twenty voteless millions still."

And of course the great idea for their master-stroke of strategy came from a masculine source. Lena Dubarri, who was the captain-general of their thinking department, met Waldo Orpington in the Mall one afternoon, just at a time when the fortunes of the Cause were at their lowest ebb. Waldo Orpington is a frivolous little fool who chirrups at drawing-room concerts and can recognize bits from different composers without referring to the programme, but all the same he occasionally has ideas. He didn't care a two-penny fiddlestring about the Cause, but he rather enjoyed the idea of having his finger in the political pie. Also it is possible, though I should think highly improbable, that he admired Lena Dubarri. Anyhow, when Lena gave a rather gloomy account of the existing state of things in the Suffragette world, Waldo was not merely sympathetic but ready with a practical suggestion. Turning his gaze westward along the Mall, towards the setting sun and Buckingham Palace, he was silent for a moment, and then said significantly, "You have expended your energies and enterprise on labours of destruction; why has it never occurred to you to attempt something far more terrific?"

'"What do you mean?" she asked him eagerly.

'"Create."

'"Do you mean create disturbances? We've been doing nothing else for months," she said.

'Waldo shook his head, and continued to look westward along the Mall. He's rather good at acting in an amateur sort of fashion. Lena followed his gaze, and then turned to him with a puzzled look of inquiry.

'"Exactly," said Waldo, in answer to her look.

' "But – how can we create ?' she asked; 'it's been done already.'

' "Do it again," said Waldo, "and again and again –"

'Before he could finish the sentence she had kissed him. She declared afterwards that he was the first man she had ever kissed, and he declared that she was the first woman who had ever kissed him in the Mall, so they both secured a record of a kind.

'Within the next day or two departure was noticeable in Suffragette tactics. They gave up worrying Ministers and Parliament and took to worrying their own sympathizers and supporters – for funds. The ballot-box was temporarily forgotten in the cult of the collecting-box. The daughters of the horseleech were not more persistent in their demands, the financiers of the tottering *ancien régime* were not more desperate in their expedients for raising money than the Suffragist workers of all sections at this juncture, and in one way and another, by fair means and normal, they really got together a very useful sum. What they were going to do with it no-one seemed to know, not even those who were most active in collecting work. The secret on this occasion had been well kept. Certain transactions that leaked out from time to time only added to the mystery of the situation.

' "Don't you long to know what we are going to do with our treasure hoard?" Lena asked the Prime Minister one day when she happened to sit next to him at a whist drive at the Chinese Embassy.

' "I was hoping you were going to try a little personal bribery," he responded banteringly, but some genuine anxiety and curiosity lay behind the lightness of his chaff; "of course I know," he added, "that you have been buying up building sites in commanding situations in and around the Metropolis. Two or three, I'm told, are on the road to Brighton, and another near Ascot. You don't mean to fortify them, do you?"

' "Something more insidious than that," she said; "you could prevent us from building forts; you can't prevent us from erecting an exact replica of the Victoria Memorial on each of those sites. They're all private property, with no building restrictions attached."

' "Which memorial?" he asked; "not the one in front of Buckingham Palace? Surely not that one?"

' "That one," she said.

' "My dear lady," he cried, "you can't be serious. It is a beautiful and imposing work of art – at any rate, one is getting accustomed to it, and even if one doesn't happen to admire it one can always look in another direction. But imagine what life would be like if one saw that erection confronting one wherever one went. Imagine the effect on people with tired, harassed nerves who saw it three times on the way to Brighton and three times again on the way back. Imagine seeing it dominate the landscape at Ascot, and trying to keep your eye off it on the Sandwich golf-links. What have your countrymen done to deserve such a thing?"

' "They have refused us the vote," said Lena bitterly.

'The Prime Minister always declared himself an opponent of anything savouring of panic legislation, but he brought a Bill into Parliament forthwith and successfully appealed to both Houses to pass it through all its stages within the week. And that is how we got one of the most glorious measures of the century.'

'A measure conferring the vote on women?' asked the nephew.

'Oh, dear, no. An act which made it a penal offence to erect commemorative statuary anywhere within three miles of a public highway.'

THE SEX THAT DOESN'T SHOP

The opening of a large new centre for West End shopping, particularly feminine shopping, suggests the reflection, Do women ever really shop? Of course, it is a well-attested fact that they go forth shopping as assiduously as a bee goes flower-visiting, but do they shop in the practical sense of the word? Granted the money, time, and energy, a resolute course of shopping transactions would naturally result in having one's ordinary domestic needs unfailingly supplied, whereas it is notorious that women servants (and housewives of all classes) make it almost a point of honour not to be supplied with everyday necessities. 'We shall be out of starch by Thursday,' they say with fatalistic foreboding, and by Thursday they are out of starch. They have predicted almost to a minute the moment when their supply would give out, and if Thursday happens to be early closing day their triumph is complete. A shop where starch is stored for retail purposes possibly stands at their very door, but the feminine mind has rejected such an obvious source for replenishing a dwindling stock. 'We don't deal there' places it at once beyond the pale of human resort. And it is noteworthy that, just as a sheep-worrying dog seldom molests the flocks in his near neighbourhood, so a woman rarely deals with shops in her immediate vicinity. The more remote the source of supply the more fixed seems to be the resolve to run short of the commodity. The Ark had probably not quitted its last moorings five minutes before some feminine voice gloatingly recorded a shortage of bird-seed. A few days ago two lady acquaintances of mine were confessing to some mental uneasiness because a friend had called just before lunch-time, and they had been unable to ask her to stop and share their meal, as (with a touch of legitimate pride) 'there was nothing in the house.' I pointed out that they lived in a street that bristled with provision shops and that it would have been easy to mobilize a very passable luncheon in less than five minutes. 'That,' they said, with quiet dignity, 'would not have occurred to us,' and I felt I had suggested something bordering on the indecent.

But it is in catering for her literary wants that a woman's shopping capacity breaks down most completely. If you have perchance produced a book which has met with some little measure of success you are certain to get a letter from some lady whom you scarcely know to bow to, asking you 'how it can be got.' She knows the name of the book, its author, and who published it, but how to get into actual contact with it is still an unsolved problem to her. You write back pointing out that to have recourse to an ironmonger or a corn-dealer will only entail delay and disappointment, and suggest an application to a bookseller as the most hopeful thing you can think of. In a day or two she writes again: 'It is all right; I have borrowed it from your aunt.' Here, of course, we have an example of the Beyond-Shopper, one has learned the Better Way, but the helplessness exists even when such bypaths of relief are closed. A lady who lives in the West End was expressing to me the other day her interest in West Highland terriers, and her desire to know more about the breed, so when, a few days later, I came across an exhaustive article on that subject in the current number of one of our best known outdoor-weeklies, I mentioned the circumstance in a letter, giving the date of that number. 'I cannot get the paper,' was her telephoned response. And she couldn't. She lived in a city where newsagents are numbered, I suppose, by the thousand, and she must have passed dozens of such shops in her daily shopping excursions, but as far as she was concerned that article on West Highland terriers might as well have been written in a missal stored away in some Buddhist monastery in Eastern Thibet.

The brutal directness of the masculine shopper arouses a certain combative derision in the feminine onlooker. A cat that spreads one shrew-mouse over the greater part of a long summer afternoon, and then possibly loses him, doubtless feels the same contempt for the terrier who compresses his rat into ten seconds of the strenuous life. I was finishing off a short list of purchases a few afternoons ago when I was discovered by a lady of my acquaintance whom, swerving aside from the lead given us by her god-parents thirty years ago, we will call Agatha.

'You're surely not buying blotting-paper *here*?' she exclaimed in an agitated whisper, and she seemed so genuinely concerned that I stayed my hand.

'Let me take you to Winks and Pinks,' she said as soon as we were out of the building: 'they've got such lovely shades of blotting-paper – pearl and heliotrope and *momie* and crushed—'

'But I want ordinary white blotting-paper,' I said.

'Never mind. They know me at Winks and Pinks,' she replied inconsequently. Agatha apparently has an idea that blotting-paper is only sold in small quantities to persons of known reputation, who may be trusted not to put it to dangerous or improper uses. After walking some two hundred yards she began to feel that her tea was of more immediate importance than my blotting-paper.

'What do you want blotting-paper for?' she asked suddenly. I explained patiently.

'I use it to dry up the ink of wet manuscript without smudging the writing. Probably a Chinese invention of the second century before Christ, but I'm not sure. The only other use for it that I can think of is to roll it into a ball for a kitten to play with.'

'But you haven't got a kitten,' said Agatha, with a feminine desire for stating the entire truth on most occasions.

'A stray one might come in at any moment,' I replied.

Anyway, I didn't get the blotting-paper.

SREDNI VASHTAR

Conradin was ten years old, and the doctor had pronounced his professional opinion that the boy would not live another five years. The doctor was silky and effete, and counted for little, but his opinion was endorsed by Mrs De Ropp, who counted for nearly everything. Mrs De Ropp was Conradin's cousin and guardian, and in his eyes she represented those three-fifths of the world that are necessary and disagreeable and real; the other two-fifths, in perpetual antagonism to the foregoing, were summed up in himself and his imagination. One of these days Conradin supposed he would succumb to the mastering pressure of wearisome necessary things – such as illnesses and coddling restrictions and drawn-out dullness. Without his imagination, which was rampant under the spur of loneliness, he would have succumbed long ago.

Mrs De Ropp would never, in her honestest moments, have confessed to herself that she disliked Conradin, though she might have been dimly aware that thwarting him 'for his good' was a duty which she did not find particularly irksome. Conradin hated her with a desperate sincerity which he was perfectly able to mask. Such few pleasures as he could contrive for himself gained an added relish from the likelihood that they would be displeasing to his guardian, and from the realm of his imagination she was locked out – an unclean thing, which should find no entrance.

In the dull, cheerless garden, overlooked by so many windows that were ready to open with a message not to do this or that, or a reminder that medicines were due, he found little attraction. The few fruit-trees that it contained were set jealously apart from his plucking, as though they were rare specimens of their kind blooming in an arid waste; it would probably have been difficult to find a market-gardener who would have offered ten shillings for the entire yearly produce. In a forgotten corner, however, almost hidden behind a dismal shrubbery, was a disused tool-shed of respectable proportions, and within its walls Conradin found a haven, something that took on the varying aspects of a playroom and a cathedral. He had peopled it with a legion of familiar phantoms, evoked partly from fragments of history and partly from his own brain, but it also boasted two inmates of flesh and blood. In one corner lived a ragged-plumaged Houdan hen, on which the boy lavished an affection that had scarcely another outlet. Further back in the gloom stood a large hutch, divided into two compartments, one of which was fronted with close iron bars. This was the abode of a large polecat-ferret, which a friendly butcher-boy had once smuggled, cage and all, into its present quarters, in exchange for a long-secreted hoard of small silver. Conradin was dreadfully afraid of the lithe, sharp-fanged beast, but it was his most treasured possession. Its very presence in the tool-shed was a secret and fearful joy, to be kept scrupulously from the knowledge of the Woman, as he privately dubbed his cousin. And one day, out of Heaven knows what material, he spun the beast a wonderful name, and from that moment it grew into a god and a religion. The Woman indulged in religion once a week at a church near by, and took Conradin with her, but to him the church service was an alien rite in the House of Rimmon. Every Thursday, in the dim and musty silence of the tool-shed, he worshipped with mystic and elaborate ceremonial before the wooden hutch where dwelt Sredni Vashtar, the great ferret. Red flowers in their season and scarlet berries in the winter-time were offered at his shrine, for he was a god who laid some special stress on the fierce impatient side of things, as opposed to the Woman's religion, which, as far as Conradin could observe, went to great lengths in the contrary direction. And on great festivals powdered nutmeg was strewn in front of his hutch, an important feature of the offering being that the nutmeg had to be stolen. These festivals were of irregular occurrence, and were chiefly appointed to celebrate some passing event. On one occasion, when Mrs De Ropp suffered from acute toothache for three days, Conradin kept up the festival during the entire three days, and almost succeeded in persuading himself that Sredni Vashtar was personally responsible for the toothache. If the malady had lasted for another day the supply of nutmeg would have given out.

The Houdan hen was never drawn into the cult of Sredni Vashtar. Conradin had long ago settled that she was an Anabaptist. He did not pretend to have the remotest knowledge as to what an Anabaptist was, but he privately hoped that it was dashing and not very respectable. Mrs De Ropp was the ground plan on which he based and detested all respectability.

After a while Conradin's absorption in the tool-shed began to attract the notice of his guardian. 'It is not good for him to be pottering down there in all weathers,' she promptly decided, and at breakfast one morning she announced that the Houdan hen had been sold and taken away overnight. With her short-sighted eyes she peered at Conradin, waiting for an outbreak of rage and sorrow, which she was ready to rebuke with a flow of excellent precepts and reasoning. But Conradin said nothing: there was nothing to be said. Something perhaps in his white set face gave her a momentary qualm, for at tea that afternoon there was toast on the table, a delicacy which she usually banned on the ground that it was bad for him; also because the making of it 'gave trouble,' a deadly offence in the middle-class feminine eye.

'I thought you liked toast,' she exclaimed, with an injured air, observing that he did not touch it.

'Sometimes,' said Conradin.

In the shed that evening there was an innovation in the worship of the hutch-god. Conradin had been wont to chant his praises, tonight he asked a boon.

'Do one thing for me, Sredni Vashtar.'

The thing was not specified. As Sredni Vashtar was a god he must be supposed to know. And choking back a sob as he looked at that other empty corner, Conradin went back to the world he so hated.

And every night, in the welcome darkness of his bedroom, and every evening in the dusk of the tool-shed, Conradin's bitter litany went up: 'Do one thing for me, Sredni Vashtar.'

Mrs De Ropp noticed that the visits to the shed did not cease, and one day she made a further journey of inspection.

'What are you keeping in that locked hutch?' she asked. 'I believe it's guinea-pigs. I'll have them all cleared away.'

Conradin shut his lips tight, but the Woman ransacked his bedroom till she found the carefully hidden key, and forthwith marched down to the shed to complete her discovery. It was a cold afternoon, and Conradin had been bidden to keep to the house. From the furthest window of the dining-room the door of the shed could just be seen beyond the corner of the shrubbery, and there Conradin stationed himself. He saw the Woman enter, and then he imagined her opening the door of the sacred hutch and peering down with her short-sighted eyes into the thick straw bed where his god lay hidden. Perhaps she would prod at the straw in her clumsy impatience. And Conradin fervently breathed his prayer for the last time. But he knew as he prayed that he did not believe. He knew that the Woman would come out presently with that pursed smile he loathed so well on her face, and that in an hour or two the gardener would carry away his wonderful god, a god no longer, but a simple brown ferret in a hutch. And he knew that the Woman would triumph always as she triumphed now, and that he would grow ever more sickly under her pestering and domineering and superior wisdom, till one day nothing would matter much more with him, and the doctor would be proved right. And in the sting and misery of his defeat, he began to chant loudly and defiantly the hymn of his threatened idol:

> Sredni Vashtar went forth,
> His thoughts were red thoughts and his teeth were white.
> His enemies called for peace, but he brought them death.
> Sredni Vashtar the Beautiful.

And then of a sudden he stopped his chanting and drew closer to the window-pane. The door of the shed still stood ajar as it had been left, and the minutes were slipping by. They were long minutes, but they slipped by nevertheless. He watched the starlings running and flying in little parties across the lawn; he counted them over and over again, with one eye always on that swinging door. A sour-faced maid came in to lay the table for tea, and still Conradin stood and waited and watched. Hope had crept by inches into his heart, and now a look of triumph began to blaze in his eyes that had only known the wistful patience of defeat. Under his breath, with a furtive exultation, he began once again the paean of victory and devastation. And presently his eyes were rewarded: out through that doorway came a long, low, yellow-and-brown beast, with eyes a-blink at the waning daylight, and dark wet stains around the fur of jaw and throat. Conradin dropped on his knees. The great polecat ferret made its way down to a small brook at the foot of the garden, drank for a moment, then crossed a little plank bridge and was lost to sight in the bushes. Such was the passing of Sredni Vashtar.

'Tea is ready,' said the sour-faced maid; 'where is the mistress?'

'She went down to the shed some time ago,' said Conradin.

And while the maid went to summon her mistress to tea, Conradin fished a toasting-fork out of the sideboard drawer and proceeded to toast himself a piece of bread. And during the toasting of it and the buttering of it with much butter and the slow enjoyment of eating it, Conradin listened to the noises and silences which fell in quick spasms beyond the dining-room door. The loud foolish screaming of the maid, the answering chorus of wondering ejaculations from the kitchen region, the scuttering footsteps and hurried embassies for outside help, and then, after a lull, the scared sobbings and the shuffling tread of those who bore a heavy burden into the house.

'Whoever will break it to the poor child? I couldn't for the life of me!' exclaimed a shrill voice. And while they debated the matter among themselves, Conradin made himself another piece of toast.

THE CHAPLET

A strange stillness hung over the restaurant; it was one of those rare moments when the orchestra was not discoursing the strains of the Ice-cream Sailor waltz.

'Did I ever tell you,' asked Clovis of his friend, 'the tragedy of music at mealtimes?

'It was a gala evening at the Grand Sybaris Hotel, and a special dinner was being served in the Amethyst dining-hall. The Amethyst dining-hall had almost a European reputation, especially with that section of Europe which is historically identified with the Jordan Valley. Its cooking was beyond reproach, and its orchestra was sufficiently highly salaried to be above criticism. Thither came in shoals the intensely musical and the almost intensely musical, who are very many, and in still greater numbers the merely musical, who know how Tschaikowsky's name is pronounced and can recognize several of Chopin's nocturnes if you give them due warning; these eat in the nervous, detached manner of roebuck feeding in the open, and keep anxious ears cocked towards the orchestra for the first hint of a recognizable melody:

'"Ah, yes, Pagliacci," they murmur, as the opening strains follow hot upon the soup, and if no contradiction is forthcoming from any better-informed quarter they break forth into subdued humming by way of supplementing the efforts of the musicians. Sometimes the melody starts on level terms with the soup, in which case the banqueters contrive somehow to hum between the spoonfuls; the facial expression of enthusiasts who are punctuating potage St Germain with Pagliacci is not beautiful, but it should be seen by those who are bent on observing all sides of life. One cannot discount the unpleasant things of this world merely by looking the other way.

'In addition to the aforementioned types the restaurant was patronized by a fair sprinkling of the absolutely non-musical; their presence in the dining-hall could only be explained on the supposition that they had come there to dine.

'The earlier stages of the dinner had worn off. The wine lists had been consulted, by some with the blank embarrassment of a schoolboy suddenly called on to locate a Minor Prophet in the tangled hinterland of the Old Testament, by others with the severe scrutiny which suggests that they have visited most of the higher-priced wines in their own homes and probed their family weaknesses. The diners who chose their wine in the latter fashion always gave their orders in a penetrating voice, with a plentiful garnishing of stage directions. By insisting on having your bottle pointing to the north when the cork is being drawn, and calling the waiter Max, you may induce an impression on your guests which hours of laboured boasting might be powerless to achieve. For this purpose, however, the guests must be chosen as carefully as the wine.

'Standing aside from the revellers in the shadow of a massive pillar was an interested spectator who was assuredly of the feast, and yet not in it. Monsieur Aristide Saucourt was the *chef* of the Grand Sybaris Hotel, and if he had an equal in his profession he had never acknowledged the fact. In his own domain he was a potentate, hedged around with the cold brutality that Genius expects rather than excuses in her children; he never forgave, and those who served him were careful that there should be little to forgive. In the outer world, the world which devoured his creations, he was an influence; how profound or how shallow an influence he never attempted to guess. It is the penalty and the safe-guard of genius that it computes itself by troy weight in a world that measures by vulgar hundredweights.

'Once in a way the great man would be seized with a desire to watch the effects of his master-efforts, just as the guiding brain of Krupp's might wish at a supreme moment to intrude into the firing line of an artillery duel. And such an occasion was the present. For the first time in the history of the Grand Sybaris Hotel, he was presenting to its guests the dish which he had brought to that pitch of perfection which almost amounts to scandal. Canetons à la mode d'Amblève. In thin gilt lettering on the creamy white of the menu how little those words conveyed to the bulk of the imperfectly educated diners. And yet how much specialized effort had been lavished, how much carefully treasured lore had been ungarnered, before those six words could be written. In the Depart-ment of Deux-Sèvres ducklings had lived peculiar and beautiful lives and died in the odour of satiety to furnish the main theme of the dish; champignons, which even a purist for Saxon English would have hesitated to address as mushrooms, had contributed their languorous atrophied bodies to the garnishing, and a sauce devised in the twilight reign of the Fifteenth Louis had been summoned back from the imperishable past to take its part in the wonderful confection. Thus far had human effort laboured to achieve the desired result; the rest had been left to human genius – the genius of Aristide Saucourt.

'And now the moment had arrived for the serving of the great dish, the dish which world-weary Grand Dukes and market-obses-sed money magnates counted among their happiest memories. And at the same moment something else happened. The leader of the highly salaried orchestra placed his violin caressingly against his chin, lowered his eyelids, and floated into a sea of melody.

'"Hark!" said most of the diners, "he is playing 'The Chaplet.'"

'They knew it was "The Chaplet" because they had heard it played at luncheon and afternoon tea, and at supper the night before, and had not had time to forget.

' "Yes, he is playing 'The Chaplet, ' " they reassured one another. The general voice was unanimous on the subject. The orchestra had already played it eleven times that day, four times by desire and seven times from force of habit, but the familiar strains were greeted with the rapture due to a revelation. A murmur of much humming rose from half the tables in the room, and some of the more overwrought listeners laid down knife and fork in order to be able to burst in with loud clappings at the earliest permissible moment.

'And the Canetons à la mode d'Amblève? In stupefied, sickened wonder Aristide watched them grow cold in total neglect, or suffer the almost worse indignity of perfunctory pecking and listless munching while the banqueters lavished their approval and applause on the music-makers. Calves' liver and bacon, with parsley sauce, could hardly have figured more ignominiously in the evening's entertainment. And while the master of culinary art leaned back against the sheltering pillar, choking with a horrible brain-searing rage that could find no outlet for its agony, the orchestra leader was bowing his acknowledgments of the handclappings that rose in a storm around him. Turning to his colleagues he nodded the signal for an encore. But before the violin had been lifted anew into position there came from the shadow of the pillar an explosive negative.

' "Noh! Noh! You do not play thot again!"

'The musician turned in furious astonishment. Had he taken warning from the look in the other man's eyes he might have acted differently. But the admiring plaudits were ringing in his ears, and he snarled out sharply, "That is for me to decide."

' "Noh! You play thot never again," shouted the *chef,* and the next moment he had flung himself violently upon the loathed being who had supplanted him in the world's esteem. A large metal tureen, filled to the brim with steaming soup, had just been placed on a side table in readiness for a late party of diners; before the waiting staff or the guests had time to realize what was happening, Aristide had dragged his struggling victim up to the table and plunged his head deep down into the almost boiling contents of the tureen. At the further end of the room the diners were still spasmodically applauding in view of an encore.

'Whether the leader of the orchestra died from drowning by soup, or from the shock to his professional vanity, or was scalded to death, the doctors were never wholly able to agree. Monsieur Aristide Saucourt, who now lives in complete retirement, always inclined to the drowning theory.'

'Tell me a story,' said the Baroness, staring out despairingly at the rain; it was that light, apologetic sort of rain that looks as if it was going to leave off every minute and goes on for the greater part of the afternoon.

'What sort of story?' asked Clovis, giving his croquet mallet a valedictory shove into retirement.

'One just true enough to be interesting and not true enough to be tiresome,' said the Baroness.

Clovis rearranged several cushions to his personal solace and satisfaction; he knew that the Baroness liked her guests to be comfortable, and he thought it right to respect her wishes in that particular.

'Have I ever told you the story of St Vespaluus?' he asked.

'You've told me stories about grand-dukes and lion-tamers and financiers' widows and a postmaster in Herzegovina,' said the Baroness, 'and about an Italian jockey and an amateur governess who went to Warsaw, and several about your mother, but certainly never anything about a saint.'

'This story happened a long while ago,' he said, 'in those uncomfortable piebald times when a third of the people were Pagan, and a third Christian, and the biggest third of all just followed whichever religion the Court happened to profess. There was a certain king called Hkrikros, who had a fearful temper and no immediate successor in his own family; his married sister, however, had provided him with a large stock of nephews from which to select his heir. And the most eligible and royally-approved of all these nephews was the sixteen-year-old Vespaluus. He was the best looking, and the best horseman and javelin-thrower, and had that priceless princely gift of being able to walk past a supplicant with an air of not having seen him, but would certainly have given something if he had. My mother has that gift to a certain extent; she can go smilingly and financially unscathed through a charity bazaar, and meet the organizers next day with a solicitous "had I but known you were in need of funds" air that is really rather a triumph in audacity. Now Hkrikros was a Pagan of the first water, and kept the worship of the sacred serpents, who lived in a hallowed grove on a hill near the royal palace, up to a high pitch of enthusiasm. The common people were allowed to please themselves, within certain discreet limits, in the matter of private religion, but any official in the service of the Court who went over to the new cult was looked down on, literally as well as metaphorically, the looking down being done from the gallery that ran round the royal bear-pit. Consequently there was considerable scandal and consternation when the youthful Vespaluus appeared one day at a Court function with a rosary tucked into his belt, and announced in reply to angry questionings, that he had decided to adopt Christianity, or at any rate to give it a trial. If it had been any of the other nephews the king would possibly have ordered something drastic in the way of scourging and banishment, but in the case of the favoured Vespaluus he determined to look on the whole thing much as a modern father might regard the announced intention of his son to adopt the stage as a profession. He sent accordingly for the Royal Librarian. The royal library in those days was not a very extensive affair; and the keeper of the king's books had a great deal of leisure on his hands. Consequently he was in frequent demand for the settlement of others people's affairs when these strayed beyond normal limits and got temporarily unmanageable.

' "You must reason with Prince Vespaluus," said the king, "and impress on him the error of his ways. We cannot have the heir to the throne setting such a dangerous example."

' "But where shall I find the necessary arguments?" asked the Librarian.

' "I give you free leave to pick and choose your arguments in the royal woods and coppices," said the king; "if you cannot get together some cutting observations and stinging retorts suitable to the occasion you are a person of very poor resource."

'So the Librarian went into the woods and gathered a goodly selection of highly argumentative rods and switches, and then proceeded to reason with Vespaluus on the folly and iniquity and above all the unseemliness of his conduct. His reasoning left a deep impression on the young prince, an impression which lasted for many weeks, during which time nothing more was heard about the unfortunate lapse into Christianity. Then a further scandal of the same nature agitated the Court. At a time when he should have been engaged in audibly invoking the gracious protection and patronage of the holy serpents, Vespaluus was heard singing a chant in honour of St Odilo of Cluny. The king was furious at this new outbreak, and began to take a gloomy view of the situation; Vespaluus was evidently going to show a dangerous obstinacy in persisting in his heresy. And yet there was nothing in his appearance to justify such perverseness; he had not the pale eye of the fanatic or the mystic look of the dreamer. On the contrary, he was quite the best-looking boy at Court; he had an elegant well-knit figure, a healthy complexion, eyes the colour of very ripe mulberries, and dark hair, smooth and very well cared for.'

'It sounds like a description of what you imagine yourself to have been like at the age of sixteen,' said the Baroness.

'My mother has probably been showing you some of my early photographs,' said Clovis. Having turned the sarcasm into a compliment, he resumed his story.

'The king had Vespaluus shut up in a dark tower for three days, with nothing but bread and water to live on, the squealing and fluttering of bats to listen to, and drifting clouds to watch through one little window-slit. The anti-Pagan section of the community began to talk portentously of the boy-martyr. The martyrdom was mitigated, as far as the food was concerned, by the carelessness of the tower warden, who once or twice left a portion of his own supper of broiled meat and fruit and wine by mistake in the prince's cell. After the punishment was over, Vespaluus was closely watched for any further symptom of religious perversity, for the king was determined to stand no more opposition on so important a matter, even from a favourite nephew. If there was any more of this nonsense, he said, the succession to the throne would have to be altered.

'For a time all went well; the festival of summer sports was approaching, and the young Vespaluus was too engrossed in wrestling and foot-running and javelin-throwing competitions to bother himself with the strife of conflicting religious systems. Then, however, came the great culminating feature of the summer festival, the ceremonial dance round the grove of the sacred serpents, and Vespaluus, as we should say, "sat it out." The affront to the State religion was too public and ostentatious to be overlooked, even if the king had been so minded, and he was not in the least so minded. For a day and a half he sat apart and brooded, and every one thought he was debating within himself the question of the young prince's death or pardon; as a matter of fact he was merely thinking out the manner of the boy's death. As the thing had to be done, and was bound to attract an enormous amount of public attention in any case, it was as well to make it as spectacular and impressive as possible.

"Apart from his unfortunate taste in religions," said the

king, "and his obstinacy in adhering to it, he is a sweet and pleasant youth, therefore it is meet and fitting that he should be done to death by the winged envoys of sweetness."

' "Your Majesty means—?" said the Royal Librarian.

' "I mean ," said the king, "that he shall be stung to death by bees. By the royal bees, of course."

' "A most elegant death," said the Librarian.

' "Elegant and spectacular, and decidedly painful," said the king; "it fulfils all the conditions that could be wished for."

'The king himself thought out all the details of the execution ceremony. Vespaluus was to be stripped of his clothes, his hands were to be bound behind him, and he was then to be slung in a recumbent position immediately above three of the largest of the royal beehives, so that the least movement of his body would bring him in jarring contact with them. The rest could be safely left to the bees. The death throes, the king computed, might last anything from fifteen to forty minutes, though there was division of opinion and considerable wagering among the other nephews as to whether death might be almost instantaneous, or, on the other hand, whether it might not be deferred for a couple of hours. Anyway, they all agreed, it was vastly preferable to being thrown down into an evil-smelling bear-pit and being clawed and mauled to death by imperfect carnivorous animals.

'It so happened, however, that the keeper of the royal hives had leanings towards Christianity himself, and moreover, like most of the Court officials, he was very much attached to Vespaluus. On the eve of the execution, therefore, he busied himself with removing the stings from all the royal bees; it was a long and delicate operation, but he was an expert bee-master, and by working hard nearly all night he succeeded in disarming all, or almost all, of the hive inmates.'

'I didn't know you could take the sting from a live bee,' said the Baroness incredulously.

'Every profession has its secrets,' replied Clovis; 'if it hadn't it wouldn't be a profession. Well, the moment for the execution arrived; the king and Court took their places, and accommodation was found for as many of the populace as wished to witness the unusual spectacle. Fortunately the royal bee-yard was of considerable dimensions, and was commanded, moreover, by the terraces that ran round the royal gardens; with a little squeezing and the erection of a few platforms room was found for everybody. Vespaluus was carried into the open space in front of the hives, blushing and slightly embarrassed, but not at all displeased at the attention which was being centred on him.'

'He seems to have resembled you in more things than in appearance,' said the Baroness.

'Don't interrupt at a critical point in the story,' said Clovis. 'As soon as he had been carefully adjusted in the prescribed position over the hives, and almost before the gaolers had time to retire to a safe distance, Vespaluus gave a lusty and well-aimed kick, which sent all three hives toppling one over another. The next moment he was wrapped from head to foot in bees; each individual insect nursed the dreadful and humiliating knowledge that in this supreme hour of catastrophe it could not sting, but each felt that it ought to pretend to. Vespaluus squealed and wriggled with laughter, for he was being tickled nearly to death, and now and again he gave a furious kick and used a bad word as one of the few bees that had escaped disarmament got its protest home. But the spectators saw with amazement that he showed no signs of approaching death agony, and as the bees dropped wearily away in clusters from his body his flesh was seen to be as white and smooth as before the ordeal, with a shiny glaze from the honey-smear of innumerable bee-feet, and here and there a small red spot where one of the rare stings had left its mark. It was obvious that a miracle had been performed in his favour, and one loud murmur, of astonishment or exultation, rose from the onlooking crowd. The king gave orders for Vespaluus to be taken down to await further orders, and stalked silently back to his midday meal, at which he was careful to eat heartily and drink copiously as though nothing unusual had happened. After dinner he sent for the Royal Librarian.

' "What is the meaning of this fiasco?" he demanded.

' "Your Majesty," said the official, "either there is something radically wrong with the bees—"

' "There is nothing wrong with my bees," said the king haughtily, "they are the best bees."

' "Or else," said the Librarian, "there is something irremediably right about Prince Vespaluus."

' "If Vespaluus is right I must be wrong," said the king.

'The Librarian was silent for a moment. Hasty speech has been the downfall of many; ill-considered silence was the undoing of the luckless Court functionary.

'Forgetting the restraint due to his dignity, and the golden rule which imposes repose of mind and body after a heavy meal, the king rushed upon the keeper of the royal books and hit him repeatedly and promiscuously over the head with an ivory chess-board, a pewter wine flagon, and a brass candlestick; he knocked him violently and often against an iron torch sconce, and kicked him thrice round the banqueting chamber with rapid, energetic kicks. Finally, he dragged him down a long passage by the hair of his head and flung him out of a window into the courtyard below.'

'Was he much hurt?' asked the Baroness.

'More hurt than surprised,' said Clovis. 'You see, the king was notorious for his violent temper. However, this was the first tim he had let himself go so unrestrainedly on the top of a heavy meal. The Librarian lingered for many days—in fact, for all I know, he may have ultimately recovered, but Hkrikros died that same evening. Vespaluus had hardly finished getting the honey stains off his body before a hurried deputation came to put the coronation oil on his head. And what with the publicly witnessed miracle and the accession of a Christian sovereign, it was not surprising that there was a general scramble of converts to the new religion. A hastily consecrated bishop was overworked with a rush of baptisms in the hastily improvised Cathedral of St Odilo. And the boy-martyr-that-might-have-been was transposed in the popular imagination into a royal boy-saint, whose fame attracted throngs of curious and devout sightseers to the capital. Vespaluus, who was busily engaged in organizing the games and athletic contests that were to mark the commencement of his reign, had no time to give heed to the religious fervour which was effervescing round his personality; the first indication he had of the existing state of affairs was when the Court Chamberlain (a recent and very ardent addition to the Christian community) brought for his approval the outlines of a projected ceremonial cutting-down of the idolatrous serpent-grove.

' "Your Majesty will be graciously pleased to cut down the first tree with a specially consecrated axe," said the obsequious official.

' "I'll cut off your head first, with any axe that comes handy," said Vespaluus indignantly; "do you suppose that I'm going to begin my reign by mortally affronting the sacred serpents? It would be most unlucky."

' "But your Majesty's Christian principles?" exclaimed the bewildered Chamberlain.

'"I never had any," said Vespaluus; "I used to pretend to be a Christian convert just to annoy Hkrikros. He used to fly into such delicious tempers. And it was rather fun being whipped and scolded and shut up in a tower all for nothing. But as to turning Christian in real earnest, like you people seem to do, I couldn't think of such a thing. And the holy and esteemed serpents have always helped me when I've prayed to them for success in my running and wrestling and hunting, and it was through their distinguished intercession that the bees were not able to hurt me with their stings. It would be black ingratitude to turn against their worship at the very outset of my reign. I hate you for suggesting it."

'The Chamberlain wrung his hands despairingly.

'"But, your Majesty," he wailed, "the people are reverencing you as a saint, and the nobles are being Christianized in batches, and neighbouring potentates of that Faith are sending special envoys to welcome you as a brother. There is some talk of making you the patron saint of beehives, and a certain shade of honey-yellow has been christened Vespaluusian gold at the Emperor's Court. You can't surely go back on all this."

'"I don't mind being reverenced and greeted and honoured," said Vespaluus; "I don't even mind being sainted in moderation, as long as I'm not expected to be saintly as well. But I wish you clearly and finally to understand that I will *not* give up the worship of the august and auspicious serpents."

'There was a world of unspoken bear-pit in the way he uttered those last words, and the mulberry-dark eyes flashed dangerously.

'"A new reign," said the Chamberlain to himself, "but the same old temper."

'Finally, as a State necessity, the matter of the religions was compromised. At stated intervals the king appeared before his subjects in the national cathedral in the character of St Vespaluus, and the idolatrous grove was gradually pruned and lopped away till nothing remained of it. But the sacred and esteemed serpents were removed to a private shrubbery in the royal gardens, where Vespaluus the Pagan and certain members of his household devoutly and decently worshipped them. That possibly is the reason why the boy-king's success in sports and hunting never deserted him to the end of his days, and that is also the reason why, in spite of the popular veneration for his sanctity, he never received official canonization.'

'It has stopped raining,' said the Baroness.

THE CUPBOARD OF THE YESTERDAYS

'War is a cruelly destructive thing,' said the Wanderer, dropping his newspaper to the floor and staring reflectively into space.

'Ah, yes, indeed,' said the Merchant, responding readily to what seemed like a safe platitude; when one thinks of the loss of life and limb, the desolated homesteads, the ruined —'

'I wasn't thinking of anything of the sort,' said the Wanderer; 'I was thinking of the tendency that modern war has to destroy and banish the very elements of picturesqueness and excitement that are its chief excuse and charm. It is like a fire that flares up brilliantly for a while and then leaves everything blacker and bleaker than before. After every important war in South-East Europe in recent times there has been a shrinking of the area of chronically disturbed territory, a stiffening of frontier lines, an intrusion of civilized monotony. And imagine what may happen at the conclusion of this war if the Turk should really be driven out of Europe.'

'Well, it would be a gain to the cause of good government, I suppose,' said the Merchant.

'But have you counted the loss?' said the other. 'The Balkans have long been the last surviving shred of happy hunting-ground for the adventurous, a playground for passions that are fast becoming atrophied for want of exercise. In old bygone days we had the wars in the Low Countries always at our doors, as it were; there was no need to go far afield into malaria-stricken wilds if one wanted a life of boot and saddle and licence to kill and be killed. Those who wished to see life had a decent opportunity for seeing death at the same time.'

'It is scarcely right to talk of killing and bloodshed in that way,' said the Merchant reprovingly; 'one must remember that all men are brothers.'

'One must also remember that a large percentage of them are younger brothers; instead of going into bankruptcy, which is the usual tendency of the younger brother nowadays, they gave their families a fair chance of going into mourning. Every bullet finds a billet, according to a rather optimistic proverb, and you must

admit that nowadays it is becoming increasingly difficult to find
billets for a lot of young gentlemen who would have adorned, and
probably thoroughly enjoyed, one of the old-time happy-go-lucky
wars. But that is not exactly the burden of my complaint. The
Balkan lands are especially interesting to us in these rapidly moving days because they afford us the last remaining glimpse of a
vanishing period of European history. When I was a child one of
the earliest events of the outside world that forced itself coherently
under my notice was a war in the Balkans; I remember a sun-
burnt, soldierly man putting little pin-flags in a war-map, red
flags for the Turkish forces and yellow flags for the Russians. It
seemed a magical region, with its mountain passes and frozen
rivers and grim battlefields, its drifting snows, and prowling
wolves; there was a great stretch of water that bore the sinister but
engaging name of the Black Sea – nothing that I ever learned before or after in a geography lesson made the same impression on
me as that strange-named inland sea, and I don't think its magic
has ever faded out of my imagination. And there was a battle
called Plevna that went on and on with varying fortunes, for what
seemed like a great part of a lifetime; I remember the day of
wrath and mourning when the little red flag had to be taken away
from Plevna – like other maturer judges, I was backing the wrong
horse, at any rate the losing horse. And now today we are putting
little pin-flags again into maps of the Balkan region, and the
passions are being turned loose once more in their playground.'

'The war will be localized,' said the Merchant vaguely; 'at least
every one hopes so.'

'It couldn't wish for a better locality,' said the Wanderer; 'there
is a charm about those countries that you find nowhere else in
Europe, the charm of uncertainty and landslide, and the little
dramatic happenings that make all the difference between the
ordinary and the desirable.'

'Life is held very cheap in those parts,' said the Merchant.

'To a certain extent, yes,' said the Wanderer. 'I remember a
man at Sofia who used to teach me Bulgarian in a rather inefficient
manner, interspersed with a lot of quite wearisome gossip. I never
knew what his personal history was, but that was only because
I didn't listen; he told it to me many times. After I left Bulgaria
he used to send me Sofia newspapers from time to time. I felt that
he would be rather tiresome if I ever went there again. And then I
heard afterwards that some men came in one day from Heaven
knows where, just as things do happen in the Balkans, and mur-

dered him in the open street, and went away as quietly as they had come. You will not understand it, but to me there was something rather piquant in the idea of such a thing happening to such a man; after his dullness and his long-winded small-talk it seemed a sort of brilliant *esprit d'escalier* on his part to meet with an end of such ruthlessly planned and executed violence.'

The Merchant shook his head; the piquancy of the incident was not within striking distance of his comprehension.

'I should have been shocked at hearing such a thing about any one I had known,' he said.

'The present war,' continued his companion, without stopping to discuss two hopelessly divergent points of view, 'may be the beginning of the end of much that has hitherto survived the resistless creeping-in of civilization. If the Balkan lands are to be finally parcelled out between the competing Christian Kingdoms and the haphazard rule of the Turk banished to beyond the Sea of Marmora, the old order, or disorder if you like, will have received its death-blow. Something of its spirit will linger perhaps for a while in the old charmed regions where it bore sway; the Greek villagers will doubtless be restless and turbulent and unhappy where the Bulgars rule, and the Bulgars will certainly be restless and turbulent and unhappy under Greek administration, and the rival flocks of the Exarchate and Patriarchate will make themselves intensely disagreeable to one another wherever the opportunity offers; the habits of a lifetime, of several lifetimes, are not laid aside all at once. And the Albanians, of course, we shall have with us still, a troubled Moslem pool left by the receding wave of Islam in Europe. But the old atmosphere will have changed, the glamour will have gone; the dust of formality and bureaucratic neatness will slowly settle down over the time-honoured landmarks; the Sanjak of Novi Bazar, the Muersteg Agreement, the Komitadje bands, the Vilayet of Adrianople, all those familiar outlandish names and things and places, that we have known so long as part and parcel of the Balkan Question, will have passed away into the cupboard of yesterdays, as completely as the Hansa League and the wars of the Guises.

'They were the heritage that history handed down to us, spoiled and diminished no doubt, in comparison with yet earlier days that we never knew, but still something to thrill and enliven one little corner of our Continent, something to help us to conjure up in our imagination the day when the Turk was thundering at the gates of Vienna. And what shall we have to hand down to our children? Think of what their news from the Balkans will be in the course of another ten or fifteen years. Socialist Congress at Uskub, election riot at Monastir, great dock strike at Salonika, visit of the Y.M.C.A. to Varna. Varna—on the coast of that enchanted sea! They will drive out to some suburb for tea, and write home about it as the Bexhill of the East.

'War is a wickedly destructive thing.'

'Still, you must admit –' began the Merchant. But the Wanderer was not in the mood to admit anything. He rose impatiently and walked to where the tape-machine was busy with the news from Adrianople.

THE PHANTOM LUNCHEON

'The Smithly-Dubbs are in Town,' said Sir James. 'I wish you would show them some attention. Ask them to lunch with you at the Ritz or somewhere.'

'From the little I've seen of the Smithly-Dubbs I don't think I want to cultivate their acquaintance,' said Lady Drakmanton.

'They always work for us at election times,' said her husband; 'I don't suppose they influence very many votes, but they have an uncle who is on one of my ward committees, and another uncle speaks sometimes at some of our less important meetings. These sort of people expect some return in the shape of hospitality.'

'Expect it!' exclaimed Lady Drakmanton; 'the Misses Smithly-Dubb do more than that; they almost demand it. They belong to my club, and hang about the lobby just about lunch-time, all three of them, with their tongues hanging out of their mouths and the six-course look in their eyes. If I were to breathe the word "lunch" they would hustle me into a taxi and scream "Ritz" or "Dieudonné's" to the driver before I knew what was happening.'

'All the same, I think you ought to ask them to a meal of some sort,' persisted Sir James.

'I consider that showing hospitality to the Smithly-Dubbs is carrying Free Food principles to a regrettable extreme,' said Lady Drakmanton; 'I've entertained the Joneses and the Browns and the Snapheimers and the Lubrikoffs, and heaps of others whose names I forget, but I don't see why I should inflict the society of the Misses Smithly-Dubb on myself for a solid hour. Imagine it, sixty minutes, more or less, of unrelenting gobble and gabble.

Why can't *you* take them on, Milly?' she asked turning hopefully to her sister.

'I don't know them,' said Milly hastily.

'All the better; you can pass yourself off as me. People say that we are so alike that they can hardly tell us apart, and I've only spoken to these tiresome young women about twice in my life, at committee-rooms, and bowed to them in the club. Any of the club page-boys will point them out to you; they're always to be found lolling about the hall just before lunch-time.'

'My dear Betty, don't be absurd,' protested Milly; 'I've got some people lunching with me at the Carlton to-morrow, and I'm leaving Town the day afterwards.'

'What time is your lunch tomorrow?' asked Lady Drakmanton reflectively.

'Two o'clock,' said Milly.

'Good,' said her sister; 'the Smithly-Dubbs shall lunch with me tomorrow. It shall be rather an amusing lunch-party. At least, I shall be amused.'

The last two remarks she made to herself. Other people did not always appreciate her ideas of humour. Sir James never did.

The next day Lady Drakmanton made some marked variations in her usual toilet effects. She dressed her hair in an unaccustomed manner, and put on a hat that added to the transformation of her appearance. When she had made one or two minor alterations she was sufficiently unlike her usual smart self to produce some hesitation in the greeting which the Misses Smithly-Dubb bestowed on her in the club lobby. She responded, however, with a readiness which set their doubts at rest.

'What is the Carlton like for lunching in?' she asked breezily.

The restaurant received an enthusiastic recommendation from the three sisters.

'Let's go and lunch there, shall we?' she suggested, and in a few minutes' time the Smithly-Dubb mind was contemplating at close quarters a happy vista of baked meats and approved vintage. 'Are you going to start with caviare? I am,' confided Lady Drakmanton, and the Smithly-Dubbs started with caviare. The subsequent dishes were chosen in the same ambitious spirit, and by the time they had arrived at the wild duck course it was beginning to be a rather expensive lunch.

The conversation hardly kept pace with the brilliancy of the menu. Repeated references on the part of the guests to the local political conditions and prospects in Sir James's constituency were met with vague 'ahs' and 'indeeds' from Lady Drakmanton, who might have been expected to be specially interested.

'I think when the Insurance Act is a little better understood it will lose some of its present unpopularity,' hazarded Cecilia Smithly-Dubb.

'Will it? I dare say. I'm afraid politics don't interest me very much,' said Lady Drakmanton.

The three Miss Smithly-Dubbs put down their cups of Turkish coffee and stared. Then they broke into protesting giggles.

'Of course, you're joking,' they said.

'Not me,' was the disconcerting answer; 'I can't make head or tail of these bothering old politics. Never could, and never want to. I've quite enough to do to manage my own affairs, and that's a fact.'

'But,' exclaimed Amanda Smithly-Dubb, with a squeal of bewilderment breaking into her voice, 'I was told you spoke so informingly about the Insurance Act at one of our social evenings.'

It was Lady Drakmanton who stared now. 'Do you know,' she said, with a scared look around her, 'rather a dreadful thing is happening. I'm suffering from a complete loss of memory. I can't even think who I am. I remember meeting you somewhere, and I remember you asking me to come and lunch with you here, and that I accepted your kind invitation. Beyond that my mind is a positive blank.'

The scared look was transferred with intensified poignancy to the faces of her companions.

'*You* asked *us* to lunch,' they exclaimed hurriedly. That seemed a more immediately important point to clear up than the question of identity.

'Oh, no,' said the vanishing hostess, '*that* I do remember about. You insisted on my coming here because the feeding was so good, and I must say it comes up to all you said about it. A very nice lunch it's been. What I'm worrying about is, who on earth am I? I haven't the faintest notion.'

'You are Lady Drakmanton,' exclaimed the three sisters in chorus.

'Now, don't make fun of me,' she replied crossly. 'I happen to know her quite well by sight, and she isn't a bit like me. And it's an odd thing you should have mentioned her, for it so happens she's just come into the room. That lady in black, with the yellow plume in her hat, there over by the door.'

The Smithly-Dubbs looked in the indicated direction, and the uneasiness in their eyes deepened into horror. In outward appearance the lady who had just entered the room certainly came rather nearer to their recollection of their Member's wife than the individual who was sitting at table with them.

'Who *are* you, then, if that is Lady Drakmanton?' they asked in panic-stricken bewilderment.

'That is just what I don't know,' was the answer; 'and you don't seem to know much better than I do.'

'You came up to us in the club—'

'In what club?'

'The New Didactic, in Calais Street.'

'The New Didactic!' exclaimed Lady Drakmanton with an air of returning illumination; 'thank you so much. Of course, I remember now who I am. I'm Ellen Niggle, of the Ladies' Brass-polishing Guild. The Club employs me to come now and then and see to the polishing of the brass fittings. That's how I came to know Lady Drakmanton by sight; she's very often in the Club. And you are the ladies who so kindly asked me out to lunch. Funny how it should all have slipped my memory, all of a sudden. The unaccustomed good food and wine must have been too much for me; for the moment I really couldn't call to mind who I was. Good gracious,' she broke off suddenly, 'it's ten past two; I should be at a polishing job in Whitehall. I must scuttle off like a giddy rabbit. Thanking you ever so.'

She left the room with a scuttle sufficiently suggestive of the animal she had mentioned, but the giddiness was all on the side of her involuntary hostesses. The restaurant seemed to be spinning round them, and the bill when it appeared did nothing to restore their composure. They were as nearly in tears as it is permissible to be during the luncheon hour in a really good restaurant. Financially speaking, they were well able to afford the luxury of an elaborate lunch, but their ideas on the subject of entertaining differed very sharply, according to the circumstances of whether they were dispensing or receiving hospitality. To have fed themselves liberally at their own expense was, perhaps, an extravagance to be deplored, but at any rate, they had had something for their money; to have drawn an unknown and socially unremunerative Ellen Niggle into the net of their hospitality was a catastrophe that they could not contemplate with any degree of calmness.

The Smithly-Dubbs never quite recovered from their unnerving experience. They have given up politics and taken to doing good.

'I've asked Latimer Springfield to spend Sunday with us and stop the night,' announced Mrs Durmot at the breakfast-table.

'I thought he was in the throes of an election,' remarked her husband.

'Exactly; the poll is on Wednesday, and the poor man will have worked himself to a shadow by that time. Imagine what electioneering must be like in this awful soaking rain, going along slushy country roads and speaking to damp audiences in draughty schoolrooms, day after day for a fortnight. He'll have to put in an appearance at some place of worship on Sunday morning, and he can come to us immediately afterwards and have a thorough respite from everything connected with politics. I won't let him even think of them. I've had the picture of Cromwell dissolving the Long Parliament taken down from the staircase, and even the portrait of Lord Rosebery's "Ladas" removed from the smoking-room. And, Vera,' added Mrs Durmot, turning to her sixteen-year-old niece, 'be careful what colour ribbon you wear in your hair; not blue or yellow on any account; those are the rival party colours, and emerald green or orange would be almost as bad, with this Home Rule business to the fore.'

'On state occasions I always wear a black ribbon in my hair,' said Vera with crushing dignity.

Latimer Springfield was a rather cheerless, oldish young man, who went into politics somewhat in the spirit in which other people might go into half mourning. Without being an enthusiast, however, he was a fairly strenuous plodder, and Mrs Durmot had been reasonably near the mark in asserting that he was working at high pressure over this election. The restful lull which his hostess enforced on him was decidedly welcome, and yet the nervous excitement of the contest had too great a hold on him to be totally banished.

'I know he's going to sit up half the night working up points for his final speeches,' said Mrs Durmot regretfully; 'however, we've kept politics at arm's length all the afternoon and evening. More than that we cannot do.'

'That remains to be seen,' said Vera, but she said it to herself.

Latimer had scarcely shut his bedroom door before he was immersed in a sheaf of notes and pamphlets, while a fountain-pen and pocket-book were brought into play for the due marshalling of useful facts and discreet fictions. He had been at work for perhaps thirty-five minutes, and the house was seemingly consecrated to the healthy slumber of country life, when a stifled squealing and scuffling in the passage was followed by a loud tap at his door. Before he had time to answer, a much-encumbered Vera burst into the room with the question : 'I say, can I leave these here?'

'These' were a small black pig and a lusty specimen of black-red gamecock.

Latimer was moderately fond of animals, and particularly interested in small livestock rearing from the economic point of view; in fact one of the pamphlets on which he was at that moment engaged warmly advocated the further development of the pig and poultry industry in our rural districts; but he was pardonably unwilling to share even a commodious bedroom with samples of henroost and sty products.

'Wouldn't they be happier somewhere outside?' he asked, tactfully expressing his own preference in the matter in an apparent solicitude for theirs.

'There is no outside,' said Vera impressively, 'nothing but a waste of dark, swirling waters. The reservoir at Brinkley has burst.'

'I didn't know there was a reservoir at Brinkley,' said Latimer.

'Well, there isn't now, it's jolly well all over the place, and as we stand particularly low we're the centre of an inland sea just at present. You see the river has overflowed its banks as well.'

'Good gracious ! Have any lives been lost?'

'Heaps, I should say. The second housemaid has already identified three bodies that have floated past the billiard-room window as being the young man she's engaged to. Either she's engaged to a large assortment of the population round here or else she's very careless at identification. Of course it may be the same body coming round again and again in a swirl; I hadn't thought of that.'

'But we ought to go out and do rescue work, oughtn't we?' said Latimer, with the instinct of a Parliamentary candidate for getting into the local limelight.

'We can't,' said Vera decidedly, 'we haven't any boats and we're cut off by a raging torrent from any human habitation. My aunt particularly hoped you would keep to your room and not add to the confusion, but she thought it would be so kind of you if you would take in Hartlepool's Wonder, the gamecock, you know, for the night. You see, there are eight other gamecocks, and they fight like furies if they get together, so we're putting one in each bedroom. The fowl-houses are all flooded out, you know. And then I thought perhaps you wouldn't mind taking in this wee piggie; he's rather a little love, but he has a vile temper. He gets that from his mother—not that I like to say things against her when she's lying dead and drowned in her sty, poor thing. What he really wants is a man's firm hand to keep him in order. I'd try and grapple with him myself, only I've got my chow in my room, you know, and he goes for pigs wherever he finds them.'

'Couldn't the pig go in the bathroom?' asked Latimer faintly, wishing that he had taken up as determined a stand on the subject of bedroom swine as the chow had.

'The bathroom?' Vera laughed shrilly. 'It'll be full of Boy Scouts till morning if the hot water holds out.'

'Boy Scouts?'

'Yes, thirty of them came to rescue us while the water was only waist-high; then it rose another three feet or so and we had to rescue them. We're giving them hot boths in batches and drying their clothes in the hot-air cupboard, but, of course, drenched clothes don't dry in a minute, and the corridor and staircase are beginning to look like a bit of coast scenery by Tuke. Two of the boys are wearing your Melton overcoat; I hope you don't mind.'

'It's a new overcoat,' said Latimer, with every indication of minding dreadfully.

'You'll take every care of Hartlepool's Wonder, won't you?' said Vera. 'His mother took three firsts at Birmingham, and he was second in the cockerel class last year at Gloucester. He'll probably roost on the rail at the bottom of your bed. I wonder if he'd feel more at home if some of his wives were up here with him? The hens are all in the pantry, and I think I could pick out Hartlepool Helen; she's his favourite.'

Latimer showed a belated firmness on the subject of Hartlepool Helen, and Vera withdrew without pressing the point, having first settled the gamecock on his extemporized perch and taken an affectionate farewell of the pigling. Latimer undressed and got into bed with all due speed, judging that the pig would abate its inquisitorial restlessness once the light was turned out. As a substitute for a cozy, straw-bedded sty the room offered, at first inspection, few attractions, but the disconsolate animal suddenly discovered an appliance in which the most luxuriously contrived piggeries were notably deficient. The sharp edge of the underneath part of the bed was pitched at exactly the right elevation to permit the pigling to scrape himself ecstatically backwards and forwards, with an artistic humping of the back at the crucial moment and an accompanying gurgle of long-drawn delight. The gamecock, who may have fancied that he was being rocked in the branches of a pine-tree, bore the motion with greater fortitude than Latimer was able to command. A series of slaps directed at the pig's body were accepted more as an additional and pleasing irritant than as a criticism of conduct or a hint to desist; evidently something more than a man's firm hand was needed to deal with the case. Latimer slipped out of bed in search of a weapon of dissuasion. There was sufficient light in the room to enable the pig to detect this manoeuvre, and the vile temper, inherited from the drowned mother, found full play. Latimer bounded back into bed, and his conqueror, after a few threatening snorts and champings of its jaws, resumed its massage operations with renewed zeal. During the long wakeful hours which ensued Latimer tried to distract his mind from his own immediate troubles by dwelling with decent sympathy on the second house-maid's bereavement, but he found himself more often wondering how many Boy Scouts were sharing his Melton overcoat. The role of Saint Martin *malgré lui* was not one which appealed to him.

Towards dawn the pigling fell into a happy slumber, and Latimer might have followed its example, but at about the same time Stupor Hartlepooli gave a rousing crow, clattered down to the floor and forthwith commenced a spirited combat with his reflection in the wardrobe mirror. Remembering that the bird was more or less under his care Latimer performed Hague Tribunal offices by draping a bath-towel over the provocative mirror, but the ensuing peace was local and short-lived. The deflected energies of the gamecock found new outlet in a sudden and sustained attack on the sleeping and temporarily inoffensive pigling, and the duel which followed was desperate and embittered beyond any possibility of effective intervention. The feathered combatant had the advantage of being able, when hard pressed, to take refuge on the bed, and freely availed himself of this circumstance; the pigling never quite suceeded in hurling himself on to the same eminence, but it was not from want of trying.

Neither side could claim any decisive success, and the struggle had been practically fought to a standstill by the time that the maid appeared with the early morning tea.

'Lor, sir,' she exclaimed in undisguised astonishment, 'do you want those animals in your room?'

Want!

The pigling, as though aware that it might have outstayed its welcome, dashed out at the door, and the gamecock followed it at a more dignified pace.

'If Miss Vera's dog sees that pig—!' exclaimed the maid, and hurried off to avert such a catastrophe.

A cold suspicion was stealing over Latimer's mind; he went to the window and drew up the blind. A light, drizzling rain was falling, but there was not the faintest trace of any inundation.

Some half-hour later he met Vera on the way to the breakfast-room.

'I should not like to think of you as a deliberate liar,' he observed coldly, 'but one occasionally has to do things one does not like.'

'At any rate I kept your mind from dwelling on politics all the night,' said Vera.

Which was, of course, perfectly true.

THE STORY-TELLER

It was a hot afternoon, and the railway carriage, was correspondingly sultry and the next stop was at Templecombe, nearly an hour ahead. The occupants of the carriage were a small girl, and a smaller girl, and a small boy. An aunt belonging to the children occupied one corner seat, and the further corner seat on the opposite side was occupied by a bachelor who was a stranger to their party, but the small girls and the small boy emphatically occupied the compartment. Both the aunt and the children were conversational in a limited, persistent way, reminding one of the attentions of a housefly that refused to be discouraged Most of the aunt's remarks seemed to begin with 'Don't,' and nearly all of the children's remarks began with 'Why?' The bachelor said nothing out loud.

'Don't, Cyril, don't,' exclaimed the aunt, as the small boy began smacking the cushions of the seat, producing a cloud of dust at each blow.

'Come and look out of the window,' she added.

The child moved reluctantly to the window. 'Why are those sheep being driven out of that field?' he asked.

'I expect they are being driven to another field where there is more grass,' said the aunt weakly.

'But there is lots of grass in that field,' protested the boy; 'there's nothing else but grass there. Aunt, there's lots of grass in that field.'

'Perhaps the grass in the other field is better,' suggested the aunt fatuously.

'Why is it better?' came the swift, inevitable question.

'Oh, look at those cows!' exclaimed the aunt. Nearly every field along the line had contained cows or bullocks, but she spoke as though she were drawing attention to a rarity.

'Why is the grass in the other field better?' persisted Cyril.

The frown on the bachelor's face was deepening to a scowl. He was a hard, unsympathetic man, the aunt decided in her mind. She was utterly unable to come to any satisfactory decision about the grass in the other field.

The smaller girl created a diversion by beginning to recite 'On the Road to Mandalay.' She only knew the first line, but she put her limited knowledge to the fullest possible use. She repeated the line over and over again in a dreamy but resolute and very audible voice; it seemed to the bachelor as though some one had had a bet with her that she could not repeat the line aloud two thousand times without stopping. Whoever it was who had made the wager was likely to lose his bet.

'Come over here and listen to a story,' said the aunt, when the bachelor had looked twice at her and once at the communication cord.

The children moved listlessly towards the aunt's end of the carriage. Evidently her reputation as a story-teller did not rank high in their estimation.

In a low, confidential voice, interrupted at frequent intervals by loud, petulant questions from her listeners, she began an unenterprising, and deplorably uninteresting story about a little girl who was good, and made friends with every one on account of her goodness, and was finally saved from a mad bull by a number of rescuers who admired her moral character.

'Wouldn't they have saved her if she hadn't been good?' demanded the bigger of the small girls. It was exactly the question that the bachelor had wanted to ask.

'Well, yes,' admitted the aunt lamely, 'but I don't think they would have run quite so fast to her help if they had not liked her so much.'

'It's the stupidest story I've ever heard,' said the bigger of the small girls, with immense conviction.

'I didn't listen after the first bit, it was so stupid,' said Cyril.

The smaller girl made no actual comment on the story, but she had long ago recommenced a murmured repetition of her favourite line.

'You don't seem to be a success as a story-teller,' said the bachelor suddenly from his corner.

The aunt bristled in instant defence at this unexpected attack.

'It's a very difficult thing to tell stories that children can both understand and appreciate,' she said stiffly.

'I don't agree with you,' said the bachelor.

'Perhaps you would like to tell them a story,' was the aunt's retort.

'Tell us a story,' demanded the bigger of the small girls.

'Once upon a time,' began the bachelor, 'there was a little girl called Bertha, who was extraordinarily good.'

The children's momentarily-aroused interest began at once to flicker; all stories seemed dreadfully alike, no matter who told them.

'She did all that she was told, she was always truthful, she kept her clothes clean, ate milk puddings as though they were jam tarts, learned her lessons perfectly, and was polite in her manners.'

'Was she pretty?' asked the bigger of the small girls.

'Not as pretty as any of you,' said the bachelor, 'but she was horribly good.'

There was a wave of reaction in favour of the story; the word horrible in connection with goodness was a novelty that commended itself. It seemed to introduce a ring of truth that was absent from the aunt's tales of infant life.

'She was so good,' continued the bachelor, 'that she won several medals for goodness, which she always wore, pinned on to her dress. There was a medal for obedience, another medal for punctuality, and a third for good behaviour. They were large metal medals and they clicked against one another as she walked. No other child in the town where she lived had as many as three medals, so everybody knew that she must be an extra good child.'

'Horribly good,' quoted Cyril.

'Everybody talked about her goodness, and the Prince of the country got to hear about it, and he said that as she was so very good she might be allowed once a week to walk in his park, which was just outside the town. It was a beautiful park, and no children were ever allowed in it, so it was a great honour for Bertha to be allowed to go there.'

'Were there any sheep in the park?' demanded Cyril.

'No,' said the bachelor, 'there were no sheep.'

'Why weren't there any sheep?' came the inevitable question arising out of that answer.

The aunt permitted herself a smile, which might almost have been described as a grin.

'There were no sheep in the park,' said the bachelor, 'because the Prince's mother had once had a dream that her son would either be killed by a sheep or else by a clock falling on him. For that reason the Prince never kept a sheep in his park or a clock in his palace.'

The aunt suppressed a gasp of admiration.

'Was the Prince killed by a sheep or by a clock?' asked Cyril.

'He is still alive, so we can't tell whether the dream will come true,' said the bachelor unconcernedly; 'anyway, there were no sheep in the park, but there were lots of little pigs running all over the place.'

'What colour were they?'

'Black with white faces, white with black spots, black all over, grey with white patches, and some were white all over.'

The story-teller paused to let a full idea of the park's treasures sink into the children's imaginations; then he resumed:

'Bertha was rather sorry to find that there were no flowers in the park. She had promised her aunts, with tears in her eyes, that she would not pick any of the kind Prince's flowers, and she had meant to keep her promise, so of course it made her feel silly to find that there were no flowers to pick.'

'Why weren't there any flowers?'

'Because the pigs had eaten them all,' said the bachelor promptly. 'The gardeners had told the Prince that you couldn't have pigs and flowers, so he decided to have pigs and no flowers.'

There was a murmur of approval at the excellence of the Prince's decision; so many people would have decided the other way.

'There were lots of other delightful things in the park. There were ponds with gold and blue and green fish in them, and trees with beautiful parrots that said clever things at a moment's notice, and humming birds that hummed all the popular tunes of the day. Bertha walked up and down and enjoyed herself immensely, and thought to herself: "If I were not so extraordinarily good I should not have been allowed to come into this beautiful park and enjoy all that there is to be seen in it," and her three medals clinked against one another as she walked and helped to remind her how very good she really was. Just then an enormous wolf came prowling into the park to see if it could catch a fat little pig for its supper.'

'What colour was it?' asked the children, amid an immediate quickening of interest.

'Mud-colour all over, with a black tongue and pale grey eyes that gleamed with unspeakable ferocity. The first thing that it saw in the park was Bertha; her pinafore was so spotlessly white and clean that it could be seen from a great distance. Bertha saw the wolf and saw that it was stealing towards her, and she began to wish that she had never been allowed to come into the park. She ran as hard as she could, and the wolf came after her with huge leaps and bounds. She managed to reach a shrubbery of myrtle bushes and she hid herself in one of the thickest of the bushes. The wolf came sniffing among the branches, its black tongue lolling out of its mouth and its pale grey eyes glaring with rage. Bertha was terribly frightened, and thought to herself: "If I had not been so extraordinarily good I should have been safe in the town at this moment." However, the scent of the myrtle was so strong that the wolf could not sniff out where Bertha was hiding, and the bushes were so thick that he might have hunted about in them for a long time without catching sight of her, so he thought he might as well go off and catch a little pig instead. Bertha was trembling very much at having the wolf prowling and sniffing so near her, and as she trembled a medal for obedience clinked against the medals for good conduct and punctuality. The wolf was just moving away when he heard the sound of the medals clinking and stopped to listen; they clinked again in a bush quite near him. He dashed into the bush, his pale grey eyes gleaming with ferocity and triumph and dragged Bertha out and devoured her to the last morsel. All that was left of her were her shoes, bits of clothing, and the three medals for goodness.'

'Were any of the little pigs killed?'

'No, they all escaped.'

'The story began badly,' said the smaller of the small girls, 'but it had a beautiful ending.'

'It is the most beautiful story that I ever heard,' said the bigger of the small girls, with immense decision.

'It is the *only* beautiful story I have ever heard,' said Cyril.

A dissentient opinion came from the aunt.

'A most improper story to tell to young children! You have undermined the effect of years of careful teaching.'

'At any rate,' said the bachelor, collecting his belongings preparatory to leaving the carriage, 'I kept them quiet for ten minutes, which was more than you were able to do.'

'Unhappy woman!' he observed to himself as he walked down the platform of Templecombe station; 'for the next six months or so those children will assail her in public with demands for an improper story!'

BIRDS ON THE WESTERN FRONT

Considering the enormous economic dislocation which the war operations have caused in the regions where the campaign is raging, there seems to be very little corresponding disturbance in the bird life of the same districts. Rats and mice have mobilized and swarmed into the fighting line, and there has been a partial mobilization of owls, particularly barn owls, following in the wake of the mice, and making laudible efforts to thin out their numbers. What success attends their hunting one cannot estimate; there are always sufficient mice left over to populate one's dug-out and make a parade-ground and race-course of one's face at night. In the matter of nesting accommodation the barn owls are well provided for; most of the still intact barns in the war zone are requisitioned for billeting purposes, but there is a wealth of ruined houses, whole streets and clusters of them, such as can hardly have been available at any previous moment of the world's history since Nineveh and Babylon became humanly desolate. Without human occupation and cultivation there can have been no corn, no refuse, and consequently very few mice, and the owls of Nineveh cannot have enjoyed very good hunting; here in Northern France the owls have desolation and mice at their disposal in unlimited quantities, and as these birds breed in winter as well as in summer, there should be a goodly output of war owlets to cope with the swarming generations of war mice.

Apart from the owls one cannot notice that the campaign is making any marked difference in the bird life of the countryside. The vast flocks of crows and ravens that one expected to find in the neighbourhood of the fighting line are non-existent, which is perhaps rather a pity. The obvious explanation is that the roar and crash and fumes of high explosives have driven the crow tribe in panic from the fighting area; like many obvious explanations, it is not a correct one. The crows of the locality are not attracted to the battlefield, but they certainly are not scared away from it. The rook is normally so gun-shy and nervous where noise is concerned that the sharp banging of a barn door or the report of a toy pistol will sometimes set an entire rookery in commotion; out here I have seen him sedately busy among the refuse heaps of a battered village, with shells bursting at no great distance, and the impatient-sounding, snapping rattle of machine-guns going on all round him; for all the notice that he took he might have been in some peaceful English meadow on a sleepy Sunday afternoon. Whatever else German frightfulness may have done it has not frightened the rook of North Eastern France; it has made his nerves steadier than they have ever been before, and future generations of small boys, employed in scaring rooks away from the sown crops in this region, will have to invent something in the way of super-frightfulness to achieve their purpose. Crows and magpies are nesting well within the shell-swept area, and over a small beech-copse I once saw a pair of crows engaged in hot combat with a pair of sparrow-hawks, while considerably higher in the sky, but almost directly above them, two Allied battle-planes were engaging an equal number of enemy aircraft.

Unlike the barn owls, the magpies have had their choice of building sites considerably restricted by the ravages of war; the whole avenues of poplars, where they were accustomed to construct their nests, have been blown to bits, leaving nothing but dreary-looking rows of shattered and splintered trunks to show where once they stood. Affection for a particular tree has in one case induced a pair of magpies to build their bulky, domed nest in the battered remnants of a poplar of which so little remained standing that the nest looked almost bigger than the tree; the effect rather suggested an archiepiscopal enthronement taking place in the ruined remains of Melrose Abbey. The magpie wary and suspicious in his wild state, must be rather intrigued at the change that has come over the erst-while fearsome not-to-be-avoided human, stalking everywhere over the earth as its possessor, who now creeps about in screened and sheltered ways, as chary of showing himself in the open as the shyest of wild creatures.

The buzzard, that earnest seeker after mice, does not seem to be taking any war risks, at least I have never seen one out here, but kestrels hover about all day in the hottest parts of the line, not in the least disconcerted, apparently, when a promising mouse-area suddenly rises in the air in a cascade of black or yellow earth. Sparrow-hawks are fairly numerous, and a mile or two back from the firing line I saw a pair of hawks that I took to be red-legged falcons, circling over the top of an oak-copse. According to investigations made by Russian naturalists, the effects of the war on bird life on the Eastern front had been more marked than it has ever been over here. 'During the first year of the war rooks disappeared, larks no longer sang in the fields, the wild pigeon disappeared also.' The sky-lark in this region has stuck tenaciously to the meadows and crop-lands that have been seamed and bisected with trenches and honeycombed with shell-holes. In the chill, misty hour of gloom that precedes a rainy dawn, when nothing seemed alive except a few wary waterlogged sentries and many scuttling rats, the lark would suddenly dash skyward and pour forth a song of ecstatic jubilation that sounded horribly forced and insincere. It seemed scarcely possible that the bird could carry its insouciance to the length of attempting to rear a brood in that desolate wreckage of shattered clods and gaping shell-holes, but once, having occasion to throw myself down with some abruptness on my face, I found myself nearly on the top of a brood of young larks. Two of them had already been hit by something, and were in rather a battered condition, but the survivors seemed as tranquil and comfortable as the average nestling.

At the corner of a stricken wood (which has had a name made for it in history, but shall be nameless here), at a moment when lyddite and shrapnel and machine-gun fire swept and raked and bespattered that devoted spot as though the artillery of an entire Division had suddenly concentrated on it, a wee hen-chaffinch flitted wistfully to and fro, amid splintered and falling branches that had never a green bough left on them. The wounded lying there, if any of them noticed the small bird, may well have wondered why anything having wings and no pressing reason for remaining should have chosen to stay in such a place. There was a battered orchard alongside the stricken wood, and the probable explanation of the bird's presence was that it had a nest of young ones whom it was too scared to feed, too loyal to desert. Later on, a small flock of chaffinches blundered into the wood, which they were doubtless in the habit of using as a highway to their feeding-grounds; unlike the solitary hen-bird, they made no secret of their desire to get away as fast as their dazed wits would let them. The only other bird I ever saw there was a magpie, flying low over the wreckage of fallen tree-limbs; 'one for sorrow', says the old superstition. There was sorrow enough in that wood.

The English gamekeeper, whose knowledge of wild life usually runs on limited and perverted lines, has evolved a sort of religion as to the nervous debility of even the hardiest game birds; according to his beliefs a terrier trotting across a field in which a part-ridge is nesting, or a mouse-hawking kestrel hovering over the hedge, is sufficient cause to drive the distracted bird off its eggs and send it whirring into the next county.

The partridge of the war zone shows no signs of such sensitive nerves. The rattle and rumble of transport, the constant coming and going of bodies of troops, the incessant rattle of musketry and deafening explosions of artillery, the night-long flare and flicker of star-shells, have not sufficed to scare the local birds away from their chosen feeding grounds, and to all appearances they have not been deterred from raising their broods. Gamekeepers who are serving with the colours might seize the opportunity to indulge in a little useful nature study.

THE MAPPINED LIFE

'These Mappin Terraces at the Zoological Gardens are a great improvement on the old style of wild-beast cage,' said Mrs James Gurtleberry, putting down an illustrated paper; 'they give one the illusion of seeing the animals in their natural surroundings. I wonder how much of the illusion is passed on to the animals?'

'That would depend on the animal,' said her niece; 'a jungle-fowl, for instance, would no doubt think its lawful jungle sur-roundings were faithfully reproduced if you gave it a sufficiency of wives, a goodly variety of seed food and ants' eggs, a com-modious bank of loose earth to dust itself in, a convenient roosting tree, and a rival or two to make matters interesting. Of course there ought to be jungle-cats and birds of prey and other agencies of sudden death to add to the illusion of liberty, but the bird's own imagination is capable of inventing those – look how a domestic fowl will squawk an alarm note if a rook or a wood-pigeon passes over its run when it has chickens.'

'You think, then, they really do have a sort of illusion, if you give them space enough –'

'In a few cases only. Nothing will make me believe that an acre or so of concrete enclosure will make up to a wolf or a tiger-cat for the range of night prowling that would belong to it in a wild state. Think of the dictionary of sound and scent and recollection that unfolds before a real wild beast as it comes out from its lair every evening, with the knowledge that in a few minutes it will be hieing along to some distant hunting ground where all the joy and fury of the chase awaits it; think of the crowded sensations of the brain when every rustle, every cry, every bent twig, and every whiff across the nostrils means something, something to do with life and death and dinner. Imagine the satisfaction of stealing down to your own particular drinking spot, choosing your own particular tree to scrape your claws on, finding your own particular bed of dried grass to roll on. Then, in the place of all that, put a concrete promenade, which will be of exactly the same dimensions whether you race or crawl across it, coated with stale, unvarying scents and surrounded with cries and noises that have ceased to have the least meaning or interest. As a substitute for a narrow cage the new enclosures are excellent, but I should think they are a poor imitation of a life of liberty.'

'It's rather depressing to think that, said Mrs Gurtleberry; 'they look so spacious and so natural, but I suppose a good deal of what seems natural to us would be meaningless to a wild animal.'

'That is where our superior powers of self-deception come in,' said the niece; 'we are able to live our unreal, stupid little lives on our particular Mappin terrace, and persuade ourselves that we really are untrammelled men and women leading a reasonable existence in a reasonable sphere.'

'But good gracious,' exclaimed the aunt, bouncing into an attitude of scandalized defence, 'we are leading reasonable existences! What on earth do you mean by trammels? We are merely trammelled by the ordinary decent conventions of civilized society.'

'We are trammelled,' said the niece, calmly and pitilessly, 'by restrictions of income and opportunity, and above all by lack of initiative. To some people a restricted income doesn't matter a bit, in fact it often seems to help as a means for getting a lot of reality out of life; I am sure there are men and women who do

their shopping in little back streets of Paris, buying four carrots
and a shred of beef for their daily sustenance, who lead a perfectly
real and eventful existence. Lack of initiative is the thing that
really cripples one, and that is where you and I and Uncle James
are so hopelessly shut in. We are just so many animals stuck
down on a Mappin terrace, with this difference in our disfavour,
that the animals are there to be looked at, while nobody wants to
look at us. As a matter of fact there would be nothing to look
at. We get colds in winter and hay-fever in summer, and if a wasp
happens to sting one of us, well, that is the wasp's initiative, not
ours; all we do is to wait for the swelling to go down. Whenever
we do climb into local fame and notice, it is by indirect methods;
if it happens to be a good flowering year for magnolias the neigh-
bourhoood observes, "Have you seen the Gurtleberrys' magnolia?
It is a perfect mass of flowers," and we go about telling people
that there are fifty-seven blossoms as against thirty-nine the previous year.'

'In Coronation year there were as many as sixty,' put in the
aunt; 'your uncle has kept a record for the last eight years.'

'Doesn't it ever strike you,' continued the niece relentlessly,
'that if we moved away from here or were blotted out of existence our local claim to fame would pass on automatically to
whoever happened to take the house and garden? People would
say to one another, "Have you seen the Smith-Jenkins' magnolia?
It is a perfect mass of flowers," or else, "Smith-Jenkins tells me
there won't be a single blossom on their magnolia this year; the
east winds have turned all the buds black." Now if, when we had
gone, people still associated our names with the magnolia tree,
no matter who temporarily possessed it, if they said, "Ah, that's
the tree on which the Gurtleberry's hung their cook because she
sent up the wrong kind of sauce with the asparagus," that would
be something really due to our own initiative, apart from anything
east winds or magnolia vitality might have to say in the matter.'

'We should never do such a thing,' said the aunt. The niece gave
a reluctant sigh.

'I can't imagine it,' she admitted. 'Of course,' she continued,
'there are heaps of ways of leading a real existence without committing sensational deeds of violence. It's the dreadful little everyday acts of pretended importance that give the Mappin stamp to
our life. It would be entertaining, if it wasn't so pathetically tragic,
to hear Uncle James fuss in here in the morning and announce,
"I must just go down into the town and find out what the men

there are saying about Mexico. Matters are beginning to look serious there." Then he patters away into the town, and talks in a highly serious voice to the tobacconist, incidentally buying an ounce of tobacco; perhaps he meets one or two others of the world's thinkers and talks to them in a highly serious voice, then he patters back here and announces with increased importance, "I've just been talking to some men in the town about the condition of affairs in Mexico. They agree with the view that I have formed, that things there will have to get worse before they get better." Of course nobody in the town cared in the least little bit what his views about Mexico were or whether he had any. The tobacconist wasn't even fluttered at his buying the ounce of tobacco; he knows that he purchases the same quantity of the same sort of tobacco every week. Uncle James might just as well have lain on his back in the garden and chattered to the lilac tree about the habits of caterpillars.'

'I really will not listen to such things about your uncle,' protested Mrs James Gurtleberry angrily.

'My own case is just as bad and just as tragic,' said the niece dispassionately; 'nearly everything about me is conventional make-believe. I'm not a good dancer, and no one could honestly call me good-looking, but when I go to one of our dull little local dances I'm conventionally supposed to "have a heavenly time," to attract the ardent homage of the local cavaliers, and to go home with my head awhirl with pleasurable recollections. As a matter of fact, I've merely put in some hours of indifferent dancing, drunk some badly made claret cup, and listened to an enormous amount of laborious light conversation. A moonlight hen-stealing raid with the merry-eyed curate would be infinitely more exciting; imagine the pleasure of carrying off all those white Minorcas that the Chibfords are always bragging about. When we had disposed of them we could give the proceeds to a charity, so there would be nothing really wrong about it. But nothing of that sort lies within the Mappined limits of my life. One of these days somebody dull and decorous and undistinguishable will "make himself agreeable" to me at a tennis party, as the saying is, and all the dull old gossips of the neighbourhood will begin to ask when we are to be engaged, and at last we shall be engaged, and people will give us butter-dishes and blotting-cases and framed pictures of young women feeding swans. Hullo, Uncle, are you going out?'

'I'm just going down to the town,' announced Mr James Gurtleberry, with an air of some importance: 'I want to hear what people are saying about Albania. Affairs there are beginning to take on a serious look. It's my opinion that we haven't seen the worst of things yet.'

In this he was probably right, but there was nothing in the immediate or prospective condition of Albania to warrant Mrs Gurtleberry in bursting into tears.

A DEFENSIVE DIAMOND

Treddleford sat in an easeful arm-chair in front of a slumberous fire, with a volume of verse in his hand and the comfortable consciousness that outside the club windows the rain was dripping and pattering with persistent purpose. A chill, wet October afternoon was emerging into a black, wet October evening, and the club smoking-room seemed warmer and cozier by contrast. It was an afternoon on which to be wafted away from one's climatic surroundings, and *The Golden Journey to Samarkand* promised to bear Treddleford well and bravely into other lands and under other skies. He had already migrated from London the rain-swept to Baghdad the Beautiful, and stood by the Sun Gate 'in the olden time' when an icy breath of imminent annoyance seemed to creep between the book and himself. Amblecope, the man with the restless, prominent eyes and the mouth ready mobilized for conversational openings, had planted himself in a neighbouring arm-chair. For a twelve-month and some odd weeks Treddleford had skilfully avoided making the acquaintance of his voluble fellow-clubman; he had marvellously escaped from the infliction of his relentless record of tedious personal achievements, or alleged achievements, on golf links, turf, and gaming table, by flood and field and covert-side. Now his season of immunity was coming to an end. There was no escape; in another moment he would be numbered among those who knew Amblecope to speak to – or rather, to suffer being spoken to.

The intruder was armed with a copy of *Country Life*, not for purposes of reading, but as an aid to conversational ice-breaking.

'Rather a good portrait of Throstlewing,' he remarked explosively, turning his large challenging eyes on Treddleford; 'somehow it reminds me very much of Yellowstep, who was supposed to be such a good thing for the Grand Prix in 1903. Curious race

that was; I suppose I've seen every race for the Grand Prix for
the last –'

'Be kind enough never to mention the Grand Prix in my hearing,' said Treddleford desperately; 'it awakens acutely distressing
memories. I can't explain why without going into a long and
complicated story. '

'Oh, certainly, certainly,' said Amblecope hastily; long and
complicated stories that were not told by himself were abominable
in his eyes. He turned the pages of *Country Life* and became
spuriously interested in the picture of a Mongolian pheasant.

'Not a bad representation of the Mongolian variety,' he
exclaimed, holding it up for his neighbour's inspection. 'They
do very well in some covers. Take some stopping too once they're
fairly on the wing. I suppose the biggest bag I ever made in two
successive days –'

'My aunt, who owns the greater part of Lincolnshire,' broke in
Treddleford, with dramatic abruptness, 'possesses perhaps the
most remarkable record in the way of a pheasant bag that has
ever been achieved. She is seventy-five and can't hit a thing, but
she always goes out with the guns. When I say she can't hit a
thing, I don't mean to say that she doesn't occasionally endanger
the lives of her fellow-guns, because that wouldn't be true. In fact,
the chief Government Whip won't allow Ministerial M.P.s to go
out with her; "We don't want to incur by-elections needlessly,"
he quite reasonably observed. Well, the other day she winged a
pheasant, and brought it to earth with a feather or two knocked
out of it; it was a runner, and my aunt saw herself in danger of
being done out of about the only bird she'd hit during the present
reign. Of course she wasn't going to stand that; she followed it
through bracken and brushwood, and when it took to the open
country and started across a ploughed field she jumped on to the
shooting pony and went after it. The chase was a long one, and
when my aunt at last ran the bird to a standstill she was nearer
home than she was to the shooting party; she had left that some
five miles behind her.'

'Rather a long run for a wounded pheasant,' snapped Amblecope.

'The story rests on my aunt's authority,' said Treddleford
coldly, 'and she is local vice-president of the Young Women's
Christian Association. She trotted three miles or so to her home,
and it was not till the middle of the afternoon that it was discovered that the lunch for the entire shooting party was in a

pannier attached to the pony's saddle. Anyway, she got her bird.'

'Some birds, of course, take a lot of killing,' said Amblecope, 'so do some fish. I remember once I was fishing in the Exe, lovely trout stream, lots of fish, though they don't run to any great size –'

'One of them did,' announced Treddleford, with emphasis. 'My uncle, the Bishop of Southmolton, came across a giant trout in a pool just off the main stream of the Exe near Ugworthy; he tried it with every kind of fly and worm every day for three weeks without an atom of success, and then Fate intervened on his behalf. There was a low stone bridge just over this pool, and on the last day of his fishing holiday a motor van ran violently into the parapet and turned completely over; no one was hurt, but part of the parapet was knocked away, and the entire load that the van was carrying was pitched over and fell a little way into the pool. In a couple of minutes the giant trout was flapping and twisting on bare mud at the bottom of a waterless pool, and my uncle was able to walk down to him and fold him to his breast. The van-load consisted of blotting paper, and every drop of water in that pool had been sucked up into the mass of spilt cargo.'

There was silence for nearly half a minute in the smoking-room, and Treddleford began to let his mind steal back towards the golden road that led to Samarkand. Amblecope, however, rallied, and remarked in a rather tired and dispirited voice:

'Talking of motor accidents, the narrowest squeak I ever had was the other day, motoring with old Tommy Yarby in North Wales. Awfully good sort, old Yarby, thorough good sportsman, and the best –'

'It was in North Wales,' said Treddleford, 'that my sister met with her sensational carriage accident last year. She was on her way to a garden-party at Lady Nineveh's, about the only garden-party that ever comes to pass in those parts in the course of the year, and therefore a thing that she would have been very sorry to miss. She was driving a young horse that she'd only bought a week or two previously, warranted to be perfectly steady with motor traffic, bicycles, and other common objects of the roadside. The animal lived up to its reputation, and passed the most explosive of motor-bikes with an indifference that almost amounted to apathy. However, I suppose we all draw the line somewhere, and this particular cob drew it at travelling wild beast shows. Of course my sister didn't know that, but she knew it very distinctly when she turned a sharp corner and found herself in a mixed company of camels, piebald horses, and canary-coloured vans. The dog-cart was overturned in a ditch and kicked to splinters, and the cob went home across country. Neither my sister nor the groom was hurt, but the problem of how to get to the Nineveh garden-party, some three miles distant, seemed rather difficult to solve; once there, of course, my sister would easily find someone to drive her home. "I suppose you wouldn't care for the loan of a couple of my camels?" the showman suggested in humorous sympathy. "I would," said my sister, who had ridden camel-back in Egypt, and she overruled the objections of the groom, who hadn't. She picked out two of the most presentable-looking of the beasts and had them dusted and made as tidy as was possible at short notice, and set out for the Nineveh mansion. You may imagine the sensation that her small but imposing caravan created when she arrived at the hall door. The entire garden-party flocked up to gape. My sister was rather glad to slip down from her camel, and the groom was thankful to scramble down from his. Then young Billy Doulton, of the Dragoon Guards, who has been a lot at Aden and thinks he knows camel-language backwards, thought he would show off by making the beasts kneel down in orthodox fashion. Unfortunately camel words-of-command are not the same all the world over; these were magnificent Turkestan camels, accustomed to stride up the stony terraces of mountain passes, and when Doulton shouted at them they went side by side up the front steps, into the entrance hall, and up the grand staircase. The German governness met them just at the turn of the corridor. The Ninevehs nursed her with devoted attention for weeks, and when I last heard from them she was well enough to go about her duties again, but the doctor says she will always suffer from Hagenbeck heart.'

Amblecote got up from his chair and moved to another part of the room. Treddleford reopened his book and betook himself once more across

> The dragon-green, the luminous, the dark, the serpent-haunted sea.

For a blessed half-hour he disported himself in imagination by the 'gay Aleppo-Gate,' and listened to the bird-voiced singing-man. Then the world of today called him back; a page summoned him to speak with a friend on the telephone.

As Treddleford was about to pass out of the room he encountered Amblecope, also passing out, on his way to the billiard-room, where, perchance, some luckless wight might be secured and held fast to listen to the number of his attendances at the Grand Prix, with subsequent remarks on Newmarket and the Cambridgeshire. Amblecope made as if to pass out first, but a new-born pride was surging in Treddleford's breast and he waved him back.

'I believe I take precedence,' he said coldly; 'you are merely the club Bore; I am the club Liar.'

Everyman
A selection of titles

*indicates volumes available in paperback

Complete lists of Everyman's Library and Everyman Paperbacks
are available from the Sales Department, J.M. Dent and Sons Ltd,
Aldine House, 33 Welbeck Street, London WIM 8LX.

BIOGRAPHY

Bligh, William. *A Book of the 'Bounty'*
Boswell, James. *The Life of Samuel Johnson*
Byron, Lord. *Letters*
Cibber, Colley. *An Apology for the Life of Colley Cibber*
*De Quincey, Thomas. *Confessions of an English Opium-Eater*
Forster, John. *Life of Charles Dickens* (2 vols)
*Gaskell, Elizabeth. *The Life of Charlotte Brontë*
*Gilchrist, Alexander. *The Life of William Blake*
Houghton, Lord. *The Life and Letters of John Keats*
*Johnson, Samuel. *Lives of the English Poets: a selection*
Pepys, Samuel. *Diary* (3 vols)
Thomas, Dylan
    Adventures in the Skin Trade
    Portrait of the Artist as a Young Dog
Tolstoy. *Childhood, Boyhood and Youth*
*Vasari, Giorgio. *Lives of the Painters, Sculptors, and Architects*
    (4 vols)

ESSAYS AND CRITICISM

Arnold, Matthew. *On the Study of Celtic Literature*
*Bacon, Francis. *Essays*
Coleridge, Samuel Taylor
    Biographia Literaria
    Shakespearean Criticism (2 vols)
Dryden, John. *Of Dramatic Poesy and other critical essays*
    (2 vols)

*Lawrence, D.H. *Stories, Essays and Poems*
*Milton, John. *Prose Writings*
Montaigne, Michel Eyquem de. *Essays* (3 vols)
Paine, Thomas. *The Rights of Man*
Pater, Walter. *Essays on Literature and Art*
Spencer, Herbert. *Essays on Education and Kindred Subjects*

FICTION

*American Short Stories of the Nineteenth Century
Austen, Jane
    Emma
    Mansfield Park
    Northanger Abbey
    Persuasion
    Pride and Prejudice
    Sense and Sensibility
*Bennett, Arnold. *The Old Wives' Tale*
Boccaccio, Giovanni. *The Decameron*
Brontë, Anne
    Agnes Grey
    The Tenant of Wildfell Hall
Brontë, Charlotte
    Jane Eyre
    The Professor and *Emma* (a fragment)
    Shirley
    Villette
Brontë, Emily. *Wuthering Heights* and *Poems*
*Bunyan, John. *Pilgrim's Progress*
Butler, Samuel.
    Erewhon and *Erewhon Revisited*
    The Way of All Flesh
Collins, Wilkie
    The Moonstone
    The Woman in White
Conrad, Joseph
    *The Nigger of the 'Narcissus', Typhoon, Falk and other
        stories*
    Nostromo

　　*The Secret Agent
　　*Youth, Heart of Darkness and The End of the Tether
Dickens, Charles
　　*Bleak House
　　*A Christmas Carol and The Chimes
　　*Christmas Stories
　　*Great Expectations
　　*Hard Times
　　*Nicholas Nickleby
　　*The Pickwick Papers
　　*A Tale of Two Cities
Dostoyevsky, Fyodor
　　*Crime and Punishment
　　*Letters from the Underworld and other tales
　　*Poor Folk and the Gambler
Doyle, Arthur Conan
　　*The Adventures of Sherlock Holmes
　　*The Hound of the Baskervilles
Dumas, Alexandre
　　The Black Tulip
　　The Three Musketeers
Eliot, George
　　*Adam Bede
　　*Felix Holt
　　*The Mill on the Floss
　　*Scenes of Clerical Life
　　*Silas Marner
Fielding, Henry
　　Amelia
　　*Jonathan Wild and Journal of a Voyage to Lisbon
　　*Joseph Andrews and Shamela
Forster, E.M. A Passage to India
Gaskell, Elizabeth
　　*Cranford
　　*Mary Barton
　　*North and South
　　*Sylvia's Lovers
　　*Wives and Daughters
*Gissing, George. The Nether World

*Grossmith, George and Weedon. *Diary of a Nobody*

*Hardy, Thomas. *Stories and Poems*

  Hawthorne, Nathaniel.
     The House of the Seven Gables
     The Scarlet Letter

  James, Henry
     Selected Tales
     The Turn of the Screw

*Jefferies, Richard. *Bevis: The Story of a Boy*

*Lawrence, D.H. *Short Stories*

*Maupassant, Guy de. *Short Stories*

*Melville, Herman. *Moby Dick*

*Modern Short Stories

*Modern Short Stories 2 (1940–1980)

*Peacock, Thomas Love. *Headlong Hall* and *Nightmare Abbey*

*Poe, Edgar Allan. *Tales of Mystery and Imagination*

*Pushkin, Alexander. *The Captain's Daughter and other stories*

  Richardson, Samuel
     Clarissa (4 vols)
     Pamela (2 vols)

*Russian Short Stories

*Saki. *Short Stories*

  Scott, Walter
     The Antiquary
     The Bride of Lammermoor
     Heart of Midlothian
     Ivanhoe
     Redgauntlet
     Rob Roy
     The Talisman
     Waverley

*Shelley, Mary Wollstonecraft. *Frankenstein*

*Smollett, Tobias. *Roderick Random*

*Somerville, E. and Ross, M. *Some Experiences of an Irish R.M.*
     and *Further Experiences of an Irish R.M.*

  Stern, Lawrence
     *A Sentimental Journey through France and Italy; Journal to
        Eliza; Letters to Eliza*
     Tristram Shandy

*Stowe, Harriet Beecher. *Uncle Tom's Cabin*
Stevenson, R.L.
    Dr Jekyll and Mr Hyde, The Merry Men and other tales
    Kidnapped
    The Master of Ballantrae and *Weir of Hermiston*
    Treasure Island
Swift, Jonathan
    Gulliver's Travels
    A Tale of a Tub and other satires
Thackeray, W.M.
    Henry Esmond
    Vanity Fair
Thomas, Dylan
    Miscellany 1
    Miscellany 2
    Miscellany 3
*Tolstoy, Leo. *Master and Man and other parables and tales*
Trollope, Anthony
    The Warden
    Barchester Towers
    Dr Thorne
    Framley Parsonage
    Small House at Allington
    Last Chronicle of Barset
*Voltaire, *Candide and other tales*
*Wilde, Oscar. *The Picture of Dorian Gray*
Woolf, Virginia. *To the Lighthouse*

HISTORY

The Anglo-Saxon Chronicle
Burnet, Gilbert. *History of His Own Time*
*Crèvecoeur. *Letters from an American Farmer*
Gibbon, Edward. *The Decline and Fall of the Roman Empire*
    (6 vols)
Macaulay, T.B. *The History of England* (4 vols)
Machiavelli, Niccolò. *Florentine History*
Prescott, W.H. *History of the Conquest of Mexico*

LEGENDS AND SAGAS

*Beowulf and Its Analogues
*Chrétien de Troyes. *Arthurian Romances*
 Egils Saga
 Holinshed, Raphael. *Chronicle*
*Layamon and Wace. *Arthurian Chronicles*
*The Mabinogion
*The Saga of Gisli
*The Saga of Grettir the Strong
 Snorri Sturluson. *Heimskringla* (3 vols)
*The Story of Burnt Njal

POETRY AND DRAMA

*Anglo-Saxon Poetry
*American Verse of the Nineteenth Century
*Arnold, Matthew. *Selected Poems and Prose*
*Blake, William. *Selected Poems*
*Browning, Robert. *Men and Women and other poems*
 Chaucer, Geoffrey
     Canterbury Tales
     Troilus and Criseyde
*Clare, John. *Selected Poems*
*Coleridge, Samuel Taylor. *Poems*
*Elizabethan Sonnets
*English Moral Interludes
*Everyman and Medieval Miracle Plays
*Everyman's Book of Evergreen Verse
*Gay, John. *The Beggar's Opera and other eighteenth-century
          plays*
*The Golden Treasury of Longer Poems
 Goldsmith, Oliver. *Poems and Plays*
*Hardy, Thomas. *Selected Poems*
*Herbert, George. *The English Poems*
*Hopkins, Gerard Manley. *The Major Poems*
 Ibsen, Henrik
     A Doll's House; The Wild Dick; The Lady from the Sea
     Hedda Gabler; The Master Builder; John Gabriel Borkman

*Keats, John. *Poems*
*Langland, William. *The Vision of Piers Plowman*
  Marlowe, Christopher. *Complete Plays and Poems*
*Milton, John. *Complete Poems*
*Middleton, Thomas. *Three Plays*
*Palgrave's Golden Treasury
*Pearl, Patience, Cleanness, and Sir Gawain and the Green Knight
*Pope, Alexander. *Collected Poems*
*Restoration Plays
*The Rubáiyát of Omar Khayyám and other Persian poems
*Shelley, Percy Bysshe. *Selected Poems*
*Six Middle English Romances
*Spenser, Edmund. *The Faerie Queene: a selection*
  The Stuffed Owl
*Synge, J.M. *Plays, Poems and Prose*
*Tennyson, Alfred. *In Memoriam, Maud and other poems*
  Thomas, Dylan
      *Collected Poems, 1934–1952
      *Under Milk Wood
*Wilde, Oscar. *Plays, Prose Writings and Poems*
*Wordsworth, William. *Selected Poems*

RELIGION AND PHILOSOPHY

  Aristotle. *Metaphysics*
*Bacon, Francis. *The Advancement of Learning*
*Berkeley, George. *Philosophical Works including the works on
      vision*
*The Buddha's Philosophy of Man
*Chinese Philosophy in Classical Times
*Descartes, René. *A Discourse on Method*
*Hindu Scriptures
  Hume, David. *A Treatise of Human Nature*
*Kant, Immanuel. *A Critique of Pure Reason*
*The Koran
*Leibniz, Gottfried Wilhelm. *Philosophical Writings*
*Locke, John. *An Essay Concerning Human Understanding
      (abridgment)*
*Moore, Thomas. *Utopia*

Pascal, Blaise. *Pensées*
Plato. *The Trial and Death of Socrates*
*The Ramayana and Mahábhárata

SCIENCES: POLITICAL AND GENERAL

Aristotle. *Ethics*
*Castiglione, Baldassare. *The Book of the Courtier*
*Coleridge, Samuel Taylor. *On the Constitution of the Church and State*
*Darwin, Charles. *The Origin of Species*
George, Henry. *Progress and Poverty*
Harvey, William. *The Circulation of the Blood and other writings*
*Hobbes, Thomas. *Leviathan*
*Locke, John. *Two Treatises of Government*
*Machiavelli, Niccolò. *The Prince and other political writings*
Marx, Karl. *Capital. Volume I*
*Mill, J.S. *Utilitarianism; On Liberty; Representative Government*
Owen, Robert. *A New View of Society and other writings*
*Plato. *The Republic*
*Ricardo, David. *The Principles of Political Economy and Taxation*
Rousseau, J.-J.
   Emile
   The Social Contract and *Discourses*
Smith, Adam. *The Wealth of Nations*
*Wollstonecraft, Mary. *A Vindication of the Rights of Woman*

TRAVEL AND TOPOGRAPHY

Boswell, James. *The Journal of a Tour to the Hebrides*
*Darwin, Charles. *The Voyage of the 'Beagle'*
Giraldus Cambrensis. *Itinerary through Wales* and *Description of Wales*
Stevenson, R.L. *An Inland Voyage; Travels with a Donkey; The Silverado Squatters*
Stow, John. *The Survey of London*
*White, Gilbert. *The Natural History of Selborne*